Also by Jill Mansell

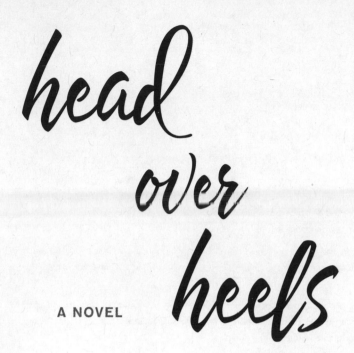

head
over
heels

A NOVEL

JILL MANSELL

sourcebooks
landmark

For my mum

Published by Sourcebooks Landmark, an imprint of Sourcebooks, Inc.
P.O. Box 4410, Naperville, Illinois 60567-4410
(630) 961-3900
Fax: (630) 961-2168
sourcebooks.com

Originally published in 1998 in the United Kingdom by Headline Publishing Group. This edition based on the paperback edition published in 2014 by Headline Review, an imprint of Headline Publishing Group, a Hachette UK Company.

Library of Congress Cataloging-in-Publication Data
Names: Mansell, Jill, author.
Title: Head over heels / Jill Mansell.
Description: Naperville, IL : Sourcebooks Landmark, [2017]
Identifiers: LCCN 2017014657 | (trade pbk. : alk. paper)
Subjects: LCSH: Triangles (Interpersonal relations)--Fiction. | Man-woman relationships--Fiction. | GSAFD: Love stories.
Classification: LCC PR6063.A395 H43 2017 | DDC 823/.914--dc23 LC record available at https://lccn.loc.gov/2017014657

Printed and bound in the United States of America.
VP 10 9 8 7 6 5 4 3 2 1

Chapter 1

"I can't decide, cider or a glass of Chablis." Jessie Roscoe leaned her elbows on the bar and chewed one arm of her paint-splattered sunglasses while she gave the matter some thought.

"I don't know if I should serve you. Are you sure you're old enough to drink?" said Oliver.

"Oh," Lili sighed. "I wish someone would say that to me."

Jessie searched energetically in the pockets of her jeans, at last unearthing a fiver. She waved it lovingly under Oliver's nose.

"Cider for your dear old mother. Better make it a shandy. Don't want to fall off my ladder. Lili, how about you?"

"Coke. Don't want to fall into a drunken stupor." Lili looked regretful. A proper drink would be lovely, but that was the drawback with small children: when they were around, you had to be so alert.

The lounge bar of the Seven Bells was cool, dark, and faintly musty, the ingrained aromas of beer and cigarette smoke mingling with beeswax polish and the smell of sizzling onions and garlic wafting through from the kitchen. When Oliver had finished serving them, they made their way through the empty pub and out into the enclosed backyard.

It was five past twelve and the sun was blazing down. Lili parked the cumbersome double stroller in the shade of a lilac tree while Jessie batted curious wasps away from their drinks and tore open a bag of chips.

"Look at them. Like a couple of pensioners on the beach at

Bournemouth." Jessie nodded at the children, both fast asleep in the stroller, facing away from each other with mouths open, chins lolling on chests, and knees apart. Two-year-old William, Lili's youngest, clutched a naked Action Man. One-year-old Freya, whom Lili looked after for another couple in the village, was managing to snore gently and simultaneously suck her thumb.

Lili prayed they'd stay asleep. If they woke up, William would bellow to be pushed on the swing and Freya would scream even louder because she wanted to go on it too. They would then yell for chips, drinks, and more drinks, and since they were both at that stage where they were driven to investigate everything—bits of broken glass, other people's drinks, the contents of ashtrays—Lili would then know she may as well give in at once and take them home.

Twenty minutes, that's all I ask, she thought without much hope of getting it. *Twenty minutes of blessed peace and adult conversation.*

"God, that's better," Jessie gasped, having gulped down half her ice-cold shandy in one go. Swiveling around on the bench, she patted both back pockets, located a tube of sunscreen, and passed it over her shoulder to Lili. "Could you put some on my back?" Her scoop-necked tank top was low-cut, front and rear, and although her skin tanned easily, there was a definite pink tinge to it. She squirmed as Lili dribbled cream onto a sunburned bit and said, "Heard from Michael?"

"He phoned last night." Lili heard the lack of enthusiasm in her own voice and was secretly appalled by it. Her husband had been away for six months, for heaven's sake, working halfway across the world in Dubai, and she couldn't even summon up the energy to miss him. Honestly, what kind of a wife was she? "He's flying back next Friday—for eight weeks. I'll have to get some marmalade in."

"And plenty of tranquilizers"—Jessie glanced over one shoulder at her—"in case you explode with overexcitement."

Lili pulled a face and screwed the top back on the sunscreen. It wasn't just her. Absence didn't appear to make Michael's heart grow fonder either.

"Do you know, when he first took the job out there, I thought it would be so romantic." She scooped a dog-paddling greenfly out of her glass and deposited it carefully on the rose bush behind her. "I imagined astronomical phone bills, not being able to sleep at night because I missed him so much, driving up to Heathrow at four in the morning to meet him off the plane, the two of us running toward each other in slow motion, him lifting me into the air and twirling me around." In Lili's fantasy, she was a sylphlike 120 pounds. "And after that," she concluded with a shrug, "well... overwhelming lust and passion, I suppose. And wall-to-wall, nonstop shagging."

"Do it next Friday." As she spoke, Jessie pulled the purple scarf out of her falling-down hair, flipped her head over, gathered together the mass of dark ringlets, and retied the scarf in a lopsided bow. "Drive up to Heathrow at four in the morning and throw yourself into his arms. See what happens."

"One, I'd look a fool because his plane doesn't get in till eleven. Two, he'd say, 'What the bloody hell are you doing here? And if that's lipstick you're wearing, don't get it on my shirt.' And three"— Lili finished counting off on her fingers—"I'd squash him."

Jessie ignored this last remark. To listen to Lili, you'd think she was the size of a tank, which she wasn't. Lili was simply well rounded, with big, hazel eyes; shiny, light-brown hair; terrific dimples; and a little mouth like a rosebud. If it weren't for the old jeans and the stripy cotton shirt, she could have been a character out of a painting by Renoir. She certainly didn't weigh enough to squash her husband.

Which was a shame, Jessie thought. Because if anyone needed a good squashing, it was Michael Ferguson.

As they sat there idly mulling over Lili's husband's deficiencies, they heard the low rumbling sound of a truck accelerating away up Water's Lane, interrupting the peaceful silence of Upper Sisley on a hot Wednesday afternoon.

"Moving van," Lili said brightly, remembering that this was the bit of news she'd meant to tell Jessie. "Two of them turned up at Sisley House this morning—huge, great things. Someone's going to be living there at last."

She sounded so much more animated. Jessie saw the spark of interest in her eyes. The prospect of new people moving into Sisley House was clearly a far more enticing prospect than that of Michael's return.

"Moving van," Oliver announced, ducking his head to avoid the honeysuckle framing the doorway as he came out to join them in the yard. "Signs of life up at the house."

"Old news," Jessie said airily. "We already know that."

Oliver looked disappointed. "Okay, but you don't know who's bought the place." Leaning across the table, he helped himself to the Twiglets. An irritating air of mystery had been engendered by Harry Norton, the local real estate agent handling the sale of the property, who had remained uncharacteristically tight-lipped about the identity of the new owner. Even Jessie, whom Harry fancied like mad, had been unable to weasel it out of him.

"Soon find out," she said, slapping Oliver's hand away as it slid back for more Twiglets. "Don't you have any work to do?"

"You're the only customers." Oliver grinned at his mother in her paint-splashed sunglasses and pinched another Twiglet anyway. "I'm clearing the table for you."

"If Harry's being this secretive, it must be someone famous," said Lili.

"We told old Cecil it was Madonna"—Oliver's grin broadened— "and he went out and bought one of her CDs."

"I heard about that." Jessie gave him a look. "Poor Cecil. He tried to play it on his wind-up gramophone."

"Might be royalty," said Lili, her hazel eyes widening.

"Might be a drug lord," said Oliver, "or an arms dealer. Or a recluse."

Freya stirred and whimpered in her sleep as Jessie's cell phone rang.

"J. R. Decorating Services. Can I help you?"

"I hope so." It was a male voice. "I need some work done and I've been given your number. I understand you're a small firm based in Upper Sisley?"

"That's right." Jessie pulled an apologetic face at Lili, who was on her knees frantically attempting to lull Freya back to sleep. Disturbed by the girl's fretful cries, William's eyes snapped open and he too began to wail.

"Oh dear, sounds like trouble." The voice at the other end of the phone seemed amused. "Look, I'll just give you my number. Maybe you could ask your husband to call me back."

Jessie watched as Oliver gamely tried to help. He flinched as Freya jabbed a finger in his eye.

"I haven't got a husband."

"Well, sorry—whoever does the work. If he rings me, we can arrange a time for him to come and look at the job."

"Actually" Jessie raised her voice to make herself heard over the bawling—"it's not a him. It's me."

"Good grief. What about the children?" He sounded appalled.

"Argh," yelled Oliver, clutching the front of his jeans as William made a furious bid for freedom. "He *kicked* me."

Jessie grinned and forced herself to concentrate. The line wasn't great. "Don't worry, hardly any of them are mine." She stood up and moved away from the noise, angling the phone this way and that in an effort to improve the reception. "Now, whereabouts are you, and when would you like me to come around?"

She still couldn't hear properly. Where was this guy phoning from, Bucharest? She hopped onto one of the rustic benches, then up again onto the table. Now she had a clear view over the high wall bordering the pub's garden, right across the village green. Another moving van was just arriving, inching around the corner and slowing as it approached the entrance gates to Sisley House.

"Sisley House," said the voice on the phone, "and you can come around as soon as you like. We're pretty chaotic here, but the work needs to be done."

The reception had abruptly improved; the crackling had cleared. Jessie felt her stomach do a slow, swooping somersault. She gazed stupidly at the gabled roof of Sisley House and at the few upstairs windows not obscured by trees. If she was speaking to who she thought she was speaking to…

Oh God, thought Jessie, *how could I not have recognized that voice before?*

Behind her, the screaming had stopped. Oliver was wearing Freya's pink-and-white sun hat and pulling fearsome faces, reducing William to fits of giggles. Lili, still on her knees, was placating Freya with a bottle of black currant juice.

"You do know where we are?" prompted the voice at the other end of the phone.

I'm in shock, that's what it is, thought Jessie. She pulled herself together. She was standing suddenly at the edge of an ice-cold river, and she could either ease herself into the water inch by inch, or close her eyes, take a deep breath, and dive.

"Yes." She took the necessary deep breath. "I know where you are. In fact, I'm in the pub just across the road from you. Why don't I come over now?"

"Mum's gone a funny color," said Oliver, looking up. "Is she going to faint? Mum, are you all right?"

"Sorry, could I have your name?" said Jessie, just to be sure. No point making a twit of herself if it wasn't him after all.

"Gillespie. Toby Gillespie."

"Come on, Mum. Get down from there." Oliver grasped her hand and helped her off the table. The line promptly went fuzzy again.

Jessie said, "Okay, I'll be with you in a minute," and switched off the phone.

Oliver gave her an odd look. "Who was that?"

"The new owner of Sisley House."

"Seriously? Who is it?"

"Toby Gillespie."

"No!" squeaked Lili, lighting up like a Christmas tree. "You mean Toby Gillespie the actor?"

If you were about to plunge headfirst into an ice-cold river, thought Jessie, *it is only sensible to take precautions.*

She looked at Lili, who never went anywhere without the contents of Boots the Chemist in her massive shoulder bag.

"That's the one. Um…got any waterproof mascara?"

Chapter 2

THE TRUCK SHE HAD just seen arriving was now parked at the top of the drive. As Jessie approached, two moving men, perspiring freely, carried a dark-blue velvet Chesterfield sofa down the ramp, across the gravel, and into the house.

The heavy, oak-paneled front door was wide open, but by the time Jessie reached it, the men had disappeared. Trying the doorbell, she discovered it had been disconnected. She hovered uncertainly in the doorway, feeling a bit of a fool. It almost came as a relief to hear a tinny crash behind the door ahead of her to the left, and a bored-sounding male voice drawl, "Oh shit."

Time to take that plunge.

Pushing the door open, Jessie found herself in the kitchen. Crates were piled everywhere, and a teenage boy with dark, shoulder-length hair was standing by the sink, staring down helplessly at an empty green tin and an explosion of sugar on the floor. A pretty blond girl wearing a white T-shirt and plenty of lilac eye shadow to match her shorts was sitting cross-legged on one of the unpacked crates, reading a magazine.

The boy looked at Jessie, his expression defensive.

"I didn't do it on purpose. It just slipped out of my hand."

The blond girl, without bothering to glance up, said, "I bet you say that to all the girls."

The boy went red. "Mum said I had to make the moving men a cup of tea. It's not fair. What am I going to do now?"

As he spoke, the kettle at his elbow came to a boil. Steam billowed out over his arm, and he let out a yell, leaping away from the sink and crunching sugar underfoot.

"Scoop it back into the tin," suggested the girl. She looked up at Jessie, eyebrows raised. "They won't notice, will they?"

Jessie hesitated. The boy's sneakers didn't look that hygienic. Not very hopefully, she said, "Do you have a dustpan and brush?"

"Somewhere. In one of the crates, probably."

The boy finished pouring boiling water into five unmatched cups and a blue-and-gold gravy boat. He threw tea bags into each of them, wiped a spoon on the leg of his jeans, then knelt down and began painstakingly piling sugar from the floor into the spoon.

"Hang on." Jessie held up her hands like a traffic cop. "Leave it. I'll be back in a second, okay?"

"Who are you, anyway?" The blond girl seemed curious rather than concerned.

"Painter and decorator. I'm here to see your father."

"Oh, right. He's around here somewhere." The girl pushed her fingers through her silky hair and smiled at Jessie. Then she resumed reading her magazine.

⁓

Next door, at Keeper's Cottage, Drew answered the door dressed in a pair of crumpled black-and-white-striped boxer shorts.

"Can I borrow a dustpan and brush?" said Jessie.

"God, I love it when you talk dirty."

"And some sugar?"

She followed him through to the kitchen, six times smaller and every bit as chaotic as the Gillespies'. Drew and Jamie, who were both veterinarians, shared the rented cottage with Doug Flynn, a resident in the emergency room at Harleston General. When they weren't working, they played rugby and cricket, and when they weren't playing rugby and cricket, they downed astonishing quantities of lager and watched rugby and cricket on TV.

All three were fast approaching thirty, but none showed any sign of settling down yet. As far as Jessie could make out, Drew and Jamie spent a lot of time talking about girls while Doug slept with an endless stream of them. She got on well with all three of them but was especially fond of Drew, with his merry eyes and boyish, self-deprecating smile.

Since domesticity wasn't high on their agenda, she was impressed when he found the dustpan and brush almost straightaway. She watched him yawn as he poured sugar into a mug.

"Sorry I woke you up. You look exhausted."

He turned and grinned at Jessie. "Not your fault. I was up all night with a cow."

"Good result?"

"Twins." He yawned again, checked his watch, and glanced out of the kitchen window at the hopelessly overgrown lawn. "I'd better get a move on. Surgery starts at two. Weird," he went on, shaking his head. "I dreamed the backyard was full of army tanks."

"You must have heard the moving vans reversing up next door's drive."

"Someone's moving in?" Drew opened the fridge, sniffed a carton of orange juice, and gulped down the contents. "Do we know who it is yet?"

"Some actor chap." Jessie felt her stomach do that thing again, that nervous loop-the-loop. "Toby Gillespie and his family."

Drew's blond eyebrows went up. "Toby Gillespie? The one with the wife?"

"Lots of people have wives, Drew." It was hard work, Jessie discovered, sounding normal.

But Drew was really grinning now, his wide mouth stretching practically from ear to ear. "Ah, but he has The Wife. Deborah. That's her name, isn't it? Now *she's* what I call a hot babe."

"She's older than I am," Jessie protested. "She must be forty, for heaven's sake. How can you call a forty-year-old a hot babe?"

Drew's shrug was good-natured. "Whatever. I'll call her anything else she likes. Well well, Deborah Gillespie, our new neighbor." He winked lasciviously at Jessie. "Could be fun."

By the time she got back, it was too late. The moving men, now somewhat unattractively stripped to the waist, had made themselves comfortable on two black suede sofas on the driveway and were stretched out in the sun, smoking and drinking their tea.

"Need any more sugar?" Jessie offered them Drew's chipped mug, but they shook their heads.

"No thanks, love, got plenty," one of them said happily. "The lad gave us some. We're fine."

There was no sign of the boy in the kitchen—just a pile of sopping tea bags on the countertop next to the kettle and more footprints in the sugar scattered across the floor.

"Hi," said the blond girl, evidently unfazed by Jessie's reappearance. "If the men keel over and die, we can blame Dizzy. He's just found something putrid stuck to the bottom of his shoe. Looks like a dead mouse." She shook her head. "Honestly, he's such a dick."

"Um…have you seen your father yet? He's expecting me."

"Don't panic. He'll come find you when he's ready. Why don't you just relax?" the girl suggested. "Feel free to make yourself a cup of tea," she added generously, reaching down from her packing case and offering Jessie the Royal Doulton gravy boat. "Here, you can use my mug."

Jessie was on her hands and knees sweeping up sugar under the kitchen table when the door burst open behind her.

"Sav, put that bloody magazine down for a minute. Why didn't you come tell me the decorator was here? According to Dizzy, she turned up ages ago and bloody went away again."

It was Toby's voice, and he sounded exasperated. Motionless under the table, Jessie swiveled her gaze to the left and saw his feet. Before she could move, the faded navy deck shoes were joined by a pair of flat bronze-and-white sandals, encasing possibly the most shapely, tanned, *glamorous* feet she had ever clapped eyes on.

"Darling, you'll have to tell those moving men to put some clothes back on. They're sweating like pigs all over the black sofas."

"She came back." Savannah Gillespie sounded bewildered. "I don't know where she's gone now. She was here just a minute ago."

"I still am," Jessie said, though she was hugely tempted to stay under the table. Coming face-to-face with Toby for the first time in over twenty years wasn't turning out quite as she had expected.

Like my life, Jessie thought as she backed gingerly out of her hiding place. Rule number one: nothing ever goes according to plan.

Deborah Gillespie, the rest of her every bit as elegant as her feet, burst out laughing.

"Good heavens! What were you doing down there, hiding from us?"

Jessie couldn't look at Toby; all she was dimly able to register was a faded denim shirt and battered jeans. She held up the half-full dustpan. "Some sugar got spilled. I was just sweeping it up."

Deborah looked mystified. "I don't understand. How did you manage to spill sugar in the first place? Don't tell me my useless children stood by and let *you* make the tea for the moving men."

"No. You see, I—"

"Jess? Jess, is that you?" Toby was staring at her.

Jessie returned his astonished gaze. Smiling slightly, she nodded. "Yes, it's me. Hello, Toby."

"Jess! This is…amazing."

He took a step forward, hesitated for a second, then moved

around the table and reached for her, clutching her forearms. Jessie wished she didn't have a loaded dustpan in one hand and a brush in the other.

She glimpsed the astonished expression in Deborah Gillespie's dark-brown eyes as Toby kissed her warmly on both cheeks. Even Savannah had by this time put down her magazine in order to watch.

"I take it you two know each other," Deborah said at last.

"From way back. Years and years ago. My God, I can't believe it." Still marveling, Toby squeezed her wrists. Delight mingled with a flicker of guilt as he studied Jessie's flushed face. "We were... Well..."

"Pretty close?" Deborah guessed.

Jessie nodded. As she moved to balance herself, more sugar crunched underfoot. She'd made a lousy job of sweeping up.

"You look just the same," said Toby. "You look great." He shook his head. "I'm still in shock."

"Weird," Savannah intoned. "Dad, lost for words."

Toby turned to Deborah. "Do you remember when the real estate agent first showed us details of this house? You asked him where Upper Sisley was and I said I knew it, that I'd come here once, years ago." He waited until Deborah had nodded, then went on. "Well, this is who I came here with. Jess and I were on a cycling vacation—"

"A cycling vacation!" Savannah rolled her eyes; this was clearly hysterical. "Dad, that is so *sad*."

"I was a drama student. We didn't have any money. We'd borrowed a tent," Toby said, remembering, "and even that was full of holes."

"Not to mention insects," said Jessie. Heavens, what was Deborah making of all this?

Clapping her hands over her mouth, Savannah gurgled, "I don't believe it. A tent."

"You can mock"—Toby grinned at his daughter—"but we had a brilliant time. When we came to Upper Sisley, there was a cricket match being played on the village green. It was a blisteringly hot summer afternoon. We lay on the grass and watched cricket. And when the players had finished their tea, we were invited to help ourselves to all the leftover cakes and sandwiches."

Savannah began playing an imaginary violin. "So the good people of the village saved you from starving to death in your sad, little wasp-infested tent. This is better than *Oliver Twist.*"

"I think it's romantic," Deborah protested.

"Actually, it wasn't," said Jessie. "The tuna sandwiches had been left in the sun too long. We spent the night rushing in and out of the tent throwing up."

"But it didn't put us off Upper Sisley," Toby went on. "I remember saying to Jess at the time how great it would be to live somewhere like this." He stopped abruptly and looked at her, and Jessie saw it again in his dark-blue eyes: that brief, unspoken flicker of guilt.

"And now you are," she said. "Living here, I mean."

He nodded, clearly desperate to say more but handicapped by the presence of his family. "And you moved here too."

"I'm starving," Savannah announced, uncrossing her brown legs and waggling her toes.

"Run over to the cricket club," said Toby. "See if they've got any leftover sandwiches."

"Ha-ha. Mum, what can I eat?"

"Don't ask me." Deborah looked alarmed. "I haven't a clue where anything is."

Savannah clutched her flat stomach and pulled a piteous face. "This is serious. I'm really, *really* hungry."

"There's the grocery store," said Jessie.

"The pub!" Toby exclaimed. "When I spoke to you on the phone, you told me you were in the pub. Does it do food?"

Jessie was gripped with panic.

Chapter 3

"Um...um...the grocery store sells great food. All kinds of stuff. Frozen too." Wildly, Jessie said, "How about pizzas?"

Deborah was looking unenthusiastic. "A pub lunch sounds far nicer. Anyway, we could all do with a break. Pub, Savvy?"

"Great! Won't be a sec." Savannah slid off her crate and out of the kitchen. "Just need to brush my hair."

"That means 'back in twenty minutes,'" said Toby with an air of long-suffering, "while she trowels on a faceful of makeup."

"Men. They just don't understand. Come on." Deborah grinned at Jessie. "While we're waiting, you can see what needs to be done."

The rooms they wanted her to decorate were upstairs. Two sunny, south-facing bedrooms and a bathroom. Taking measurements and sketching a brief plan of each room in her notebook, Jessie said, "I'm busy for the next fortnight, but I could make a start the week after that."

"That's fine," said Deborah. "Isn't it, darling?"

Toby had been miles away, gazing out of the uncurtained bedroom window. He turned to look at them both.

"Sorry?"

"Jess can start on this in a fortnight's time."

"Oh." He nodded. "Great."

Jessie wondered what he had been so lost in thought about. She felt that strange, swallow-diving sensation again in the pit of her stomach. She wondered if, when she told him what she clearly must

tell him, Toby would still think that having her working here in this
house was *oh, great.*

Jessie did her best to get out of going back to the Seven Bells with
them, but Toby wasn't having any of it.

"Don't be silly. Of course you're coming for a drink," he said as
he dragged her along the hall. "Isn't she, Sav?"

Savannah's baby-pink lipstick glistened in the sunlight.
"Definitely. You can tell us all about Dad and the things he got up
to eighty years ago, when he was young."

Leaving the moving men to it, they made their way across the
village green toward the Seven Bells. Dizzy slouched along, kicking
the heads off dandelions as he went. Deborah, effortlessly elegant
in a black off-the-shoulder jersey top and white capri pants, walked
arm in arm with Savannah. Jessie, walking behind them with Toby
alongside, realized he was holding back, attempting to slow her down.

At last he murmured, "Jess, I tried to contact you."

They were a hundred yards from the pub and less than three
yards from his wife and children. Hardly ideal.

"I know. I moved away."

"Your parents wouldn't tell me where you were. I was frantic—"

"Not now," said Jessie.

"No, I know. But we do have to talk."

"Plenty of time."

Toby glanced over his shoulder at Sisley House. "We drove
down from London the day after the real estate agent gave us the
details. As soon as I saw this place, I knew we had to live here." He
shook his head. "Is that fate?"

"No, it's coincidence."

"How long ago did you move here?"

"Fifteen years."

"And did you ever—"

"We're here," Jessie interrupted before they cannoned into Deborah and Savannah in the doorway.

"Come on, Dad. Get your wallet out." Savannah pushed open the door. "Your treat."

Lorna Blake, the bar owner, was serving behind the bar with Oliver. Lorna had run the pub for the last five years. A fortysomething divorcée with a tough, no-nonsense manner; a gin-soaked voice; an endless capacity for cigarettes; and a piercing, bright-blue gaze, she always reminded Jessie of a female Al Capone. Moll Harper, the other full-time barmaid, was carrying trays of food through from the kitchen, holding them high as she sashayed between the crowded tables. The Seven Bells, with its picturesque setting and glowing reviews in all the pub guides, attracted tourists as well as locals. The pub was far busier now than it had been at midday.

There was a brief, stunned silence as heads turned and brains registered who had just joined them. It was, thought Jessie, like walking into the OK Corral.

But the Gillespies, presumably, were used to this. If they noticed, they didn't show it. Jessie introduced them to Lorna Blake, who could be guaranteed not to gush and make an idiot of herself. Blunt, down-to-earth, chain-smoking Lorna never got excited about anything.

"Pleased to meet you." As she shook Toby's hand, she mustered a faint smile. "Welcome to the village."

"And this is Oliver," Jessie went on hurriedly. "And that's Moll over there... Now, everyone's starving, so let's get some food ordered. Then, why don't we sit outside?"

Oliver was giving her an odd look. Deeply aware of this, Jessie ignored him and grabbed a handful of menus.

Oliver leaned across the bar to attract her attention. "Lili had to take the kids home, by the way." Meaningfully, he added, "She said she'd see you later."

"Okay. The fish pie's good," Jessie announced, feeling slightly frantic. "Or the fettuccine Alfredo—that's my favorite."

"Can you believe it?" Deborah was speaking to Lorna, but her husky, actressy voice could be heard by everyone in the bar. "We move to a new house in the back of beyond and the first person we bump into"—she turned and lightly touched Jessie's arm—"turns out to be one of my husband's old flames."

Another silence of positively Hitchcockian duration.

"If you don't feel like pasta," Jessie blurted out, "there's always steak and fries."

Oliver had been pouring a pint of draft Stella. The lager, unchecked, foamed over the rim of the glass. "You didn't tell me you *knew* him," he said, his tone accusing.

Savannah, who had hopped up onto a barstool, sat with her elbows on the bar and her chin resting on one hand. "Don't panic. It's ancient history." Amused, she tilted her head at Oliver. "Why so bothered, anyway? What are you, her boyfriend?"

Outraged, Oliver said, "Don't be ridiculous. I'm her son."

"Good heavens! Are you really?" Deborah clapped her hands in delight. "A strapping, great lad like you! What are you, six two? Six three?"

"It's half past one," said Jessie, by this time close to meltdown. "Oh God, I really, really have to go... I promised the Hartwells I'd have their kitchen finished by five."

Nobody took the slightest bit of notice. Jessie watched in horror as Savannah, now perking up considerably, wriggled her bottom on the barstool, crossed her arms beneath her pert breasts, and focused all her attention on Oliver.

"So you live in the village too? Well, that's something. I was scared it'd be full of miserable old folk." She leaned closer and lowered her voice, too late to avoid offending all the miserable old folk hunched around a nearby table playing cribbage. "What's it like, then? Dead boring around here—or are there places to go?"

Oliver began to unbend. "Oh, there are places to go. You just need to know the right people. A mate of mine from college just opened a new club in Harleston—"

"So you're at college." Savannah's lilac-shadowed eyes were bright with interest. "Whereabouts?"

"Exeter. Math."

"What year?"

"I've just finished my finals."

Oliver knew the grin was spreading all over his face. He couldn't help it; every time he remembered the exams were over, it happened.

Savannah grinned back.

Deborah lit a cigarette and offered Jessie one. Jessie, who didn't smoke, wondered if this was the moment to take it up.

"The Hartwells will have my guts for garters if I don't get back to work. I'm sorry, I really must go—"

"Math. Crikey." Savannah pulled a face. "I couldn't do that. Still, must come in handy when you're working behind a bar." She sounded impressed. "You're older than I thought, then. You must be twenty-one, three years older than me."

"Which makes you eighteen. See?" Oliver said modestly. "I'm a genius."

Savannah was giggling. Jessie, feeling horribly hot and sweaty, fumbled for her car keys. They promptly slid out of her hand and clattered to the flagstone floor.

Toby reached down for them at the same time she did. Their heads met at table level. Jessie couldn't bring herself to meet his eyes.

"I must go. I really must."

"Jess…"

Toby's voice sounded strange. As well it might, Jessie had to concede. Trembling, she snatched the keys out of his hand.

But this time, he forced her to look at him.

"Oh, Jess, we definitely need to talk."

Chapter 4

Visiting her mother-in-law wasn't Lili's favorite pastime, but since William had been chanting "Gra'ma, Gra'ma" like a demented football fan for the past hour, she decided she may as well bite the bullet. Lili was terrified of Eleanor Ferguson, but William adored her, which just went to show there was no accounting for taste.

Piling an ecstatic William and a fractious Freya back into the double stroller, Lili remembered to drag a comb through her hair and squirt on some perfume before leaving the house. If she didn't, Eleanor would only remark acerbically, "Oh my, look at you. Just because your husband's away, dear, that's no reason to let yourself go."

But Lili's spirits began to lift as she set out with the children. Living in the same village as one's mother-in-law might be construed as another bit of bad luck, but at least they lived at opposite ends of it, and the walk from the Old Vicarage on the main street to Eleanor's cottage at the far end of Water's Lane was a scenic one.

It's a glorious day, thought Lili, determinedly counting her blessings. *I've finished a mountain of ironing; Jessie's bound to come around later to give me all the gossip on the new people at Sisley House—could it really be Toby Gillespie, or had that been a joke, like the Madonna one? And, best of all, Michael's not here, so I can watch* Sleepless in Seattle *tonight in peace.*

This was yet another blip on their compatibility chart. If he bothered to watch anything, Michael was a news-show type who disapproved mightily of Lili's frivolous taste in TV. *Sleepless in Seattle* wasn't his thing at all.

"Gra'ma! Gra'ma!" William yodeled, feverish with anticipation and drumming his heels on the stroller's footrest.

Lili had to smile. "That's right, going to see Grandma."

William let out a scream of delight and pointed across the road. "Raddit. *Raddit!*"

"So it is." Lili maneuvered the stroller so Freya could see it too. "Look, darling, a rabbit."

"Raddit raddit raddit!" William screeched joyfully, his flailing arm almost knocking Freya horizontal. "Mum, radd—"

The car, an old bloodred Granada belching exhaust fumes, came tearing around the corner of Compass Lane doing at least sixty. Instinctively, almost wrenching her arms out of their sockets, Lili jerked the stroller up onto the shoulder.

There were two men in the car; she saw them grinning as they swerved across the road. The rabbit didn't stand a chance. A bone-crunching thud was followed by a jubilant double thumbs-up from the driver of the car.

Lili screamed. William screamed louder. Freya stuck her thumb in her mouth and gazed wide-eyed at the dust cloud kicked up by the Granada's filthy wheels.

"You bastards!" Lili bellowed as the car disappeared up Water's Lane. She ran over to the animal, praying it was dead.

"Raddit," said William, behind her.

Oh God, oh God, it was still alive. The rabbit's eyes were open. It lay, frozen with shock, on the shoulder. Blood seeped through the brownish-gray fur and its rib cage rose and fell in rapid, panicky breaths.

"Bastards," Lili whispered, crouching over the terrified, quivering body and wondering what on earth to do. She couldn't, she *couldn't* just leave it there to die.

"Bas-tid," William said helpfully when she ran back across the road to the stroller.

Hands trembling, Lili unzipped the haversack packed with baby-changing paraphernalia. Dry-mouthed, she said croakily, "I know."

—⟡—

Farther along Compass Lane, in Keeper's Cottage, Drew finished brushing his teeth, spat into the washbasin—bull's-eye—and surveyed his reflection in the bathroom mirror without enthusiasm.

If his surname were Smith, it wouldn't have been so bad. Or Saunders or Webb or even Witherspoon. But it wasn't. His name was Andrew Darcy, and after thirty years, it still had the ability to depress him. People about to meet Mr. Darcy for the first time had certain expectations. Women particularly. And Drew, with his untamed, muddy-blond hair; big, broken nose; wide, friendly mouth; and generally unchiseled features, knew what a disappointment he must be in the flesh. He was a letdown. Okay, maybe not downright ugly. But average, certainly. Average enough to need to get by on personality where the opposite sex was concerned.

That was the trouble with girls. When they knew his name in advance, they anticipated so much more. He was supposed to look like Colin wet-shirt Firth, for Christ's sake.

It was bloody unfair—and it had happened again yesterday, when a stunning blond in a scarlet sundress had brought her Siamese kitten into the office for its inoculations.

"Oh." Her pretty face had fallen when she'd seen Drew. "Are *you* Mr. Darcy?"

Her hopes had been cruelly dashed, and so had his. Drew had found himself wishing for the millionth time that his name could be something ordinary, like Lewis, or even something ugly like Snark… At least then he could come as a nice surprise instead of a letdown.

He would have changed it legally if it weren't such a girlie thing to do. Besides, that would really give the game away. Then everyone would know how much it bothered him.

Drew, who had his pride, turned his back on his less-than-satisfactory reflection and raced downstairs, taking them three at a time. It was twenty to two; he'd better get a move on if he wasn't going to be late.

He was by the front door when someone began frantically hammering on it. Pulling it open, he found Lili Ferguson leaning against the porch in a frightful state.

"Oh, Drew, thank goodness you're in."

"What is it?" His forehead puckered. She had a stroller full of children and was clutching a plastic shopping bag in her arms. Her hair, wet with perspiration, was plastered against her temples and her shirt clung damply to her breasts.

Her eyes filled with tears as she opened the bag and showed him the rabbit. It lay there, quite still and bleeding profusely, wrapped in one of William's spare diapers.

"It's his leg."

"Poor, old thing," said Drew. "Been run over by the look of it."

"We saw it happen. They didn't stop." Lili bit her lip. "They did it on purpose. It was deliberate."

"Bas-tid," William announced, waving cheerfully at Drew.

"You can save it, can't you?" Lili knew she was overreacting—this was the countryside; wild animals died all the time—but she couldn't help it. She didn't care.

"Well…"

"It costs money, I know that. I'll pay."

"Bas-tid, bas-tid," sang William. Reaching sideways, he grabbed a fistful of dandelions and wrenched them out of the untended stone tub next to the porch. Rubbing them happily in Freya's face, he yelled, "Bas-tid Gra'ma."

Oh heavens, thought Lili. *This is all I need.*

Drew glanced at his watch. Quarter to. "Look, I'm on my way into the office now. I'll take him with me and see what I can do."

"Money's no object," said Lili recklessly, gladder than ever that Michael was thousands of miles away in Dubai. He was about as fond of rabbits as he was of *Sleepless in Seattle*.

Lili was in the kitchen slicing up tomatoes and mushrooms for a Bolognese sauce when Jessie tapped on the back door and let herself in.

"You've had your phone turned off all afternoon." Lili wagged an accusing vegetable knife. "And you haven't been home yet either. I spoke to Oliver."

Jessie went straight to the fridge, poured two enormous glasses of white wine, and plonked them on the kitchen table. It was six o'clock. Feeling guilty about the phone, she switched it back on.

"I had to finish the Hartwells' kitchen. And I needed time to think."

"I'm not surprised." Lili's eyebrows went up. "Oliver told me everything."

Jessie swallowed. "Everything?"

"About you and Toby Gillespie, and the fact that the two of you were childhood sweethearts," Lili said, "which for some reason you've never seen fit to mention to either your son or your best friend."

"Ah." *Phew.*

"Well, quite." Lili abandoned the mushrooms and folded her arms across her ample chest. "If I were in your shoes, I expect I'd want time to think about it too."

Jessie dived into her drink.

Frowning, Lili went on. "And why did you pour me one when Freya's still here? You know what Hugh and Felicity are like."

Jessie drained her glass. "I didn't pour you one. They're both for me."

"Crikey."

"Where are the kids?"

Lili poked her head around the kitchen door. In the living room Harriet, Lottie, William, and Freya—like a row of Russian dolls—sat motionless on the sofa.

"Glued to the TV."

Jessie pulled out a chair, fell onto it, dragged the purple scarf out of her hair, and began winding it around and around her knuckles like worry beads. Which was apt. "Toby Gillespie is Oliver's father."

"Oh!" Lili's hands flew to her mouth. She stared wide-eyed at Jessie, unable to speak.

"Well, quite," Jessie said.

"Jess, are you *serious*?"

Jessie examined the ends of her hair, which were encrusted with sunflower-yellow emulsion paint. "Of course I'm serious. It's hardly the kind of thing you'd make up."

"Good grief." The Bolognese sauce was well and truly forgotten now. Lili checked again through the living room door, making sure the kids hadn't overheard, then plonked herself down at the table opposite Jessie.

"Does he know?"

"Who?"

"Toby Gillespie."

"Up until today? No." Jessie tried biting one of her fingernails, but they were all spotted with paint. "Although I think he was putting two and two together as I left the pub."

"Does Oliver know?"

"Of course he doesn't."

"Are you going to tell him?"

The taste of paint was disgusting. Jessie wound the purple scarf tightly round her left wrist instead and watched her hand change color.

"Jess?"

Now her fingers were as purple as the scarf.

"I don't know, I don't know. It's up to Toby, I suppose. Blimey, today's been a big enough shock for me. God knows what it'll be like for him."

Lili was still openmouthed with shock. This was riveting stuff. Reaching behind her, she flicked the fridge open with one expert finger, tilted her chair onto its hind legs, and grabbed the bottle of wine.

"So why didn't you ever tell me the truth?"

"The first rule of deception," Jessie said with an apologetic shrug, "is keep it simple. And stick to your story. I told you the same as I told Oliver."

Lili ran through in her mind what she had been told, which was basically that, upon finding herself pregnant, Jessie and her boyfriend at the time, Tony something-or-other, had tried to make a go of things and failed dismally. They had split up before Oliver was born, and Tony had immigrated to Australia without ever seeing his son or showing the least amount of concern for either him or Jess.

It was a boring story, a story deliberately designed—Lili now realized—not to arouse interest. If anyone ever tried to question Jessie on the subject of Oliver's father, she even used a dull voice to describe him. Tony had fair hair and was quite tall. In looks and intelligence, he was average. This was about as much as she had ever been prepared to admit. No, they'd never really loved each other, and living together, let alone marriage, would have been a disaster. Tony just wasn't the settling-down type.

And no, she hadn't missed him particularly when he'd disappeared from her life. He was no loss.

As Lili put her elbows on the table, ready to listen to the real—and far more enthralling—story, Jessie's phone rang.

"Switched it back on then," Toby Gillespie remarked in laconic fashion when she answered.

"Sorry, I was…busy."

"I think *cowardly* is the word you're looking for."

"Toby, I know we have to—"

"Talk, yes. Nine o'clock at your house?"

"Um, nine—"

"I checked with Oliver. He's working tonight, so we won't be interrupted."

Jessie's hands had gone all sweaty again. "Does he... Er, has he...?"

"Nine o'clock, Jess. I'll see you then."

She opened her mouth to dither some more, but it was too late. Toby had hung up.

"Right," announced Lili, quite forcibly for her. "I think you'd better tell me the truth, the whole truth, and nothing but the—*bugger*."

Even Jessie had to smile. As Lili went to answer the door, Jessie called after her, "It's a conspiracy."

"Worse than that," Lili hissed back. "It's Hugh and Felicity."

Easygoing Lili, who liked most people, tried hard to like Hugh and Felicity Seymour, but it was hard to warm to a couple so perfect they made you feel like something stuck to the bottom of a trash can by comparison.

Felicity was superwoman in a power suit, with her geometric, ash-blond bob, flawless makeup, and Louis Vuitton briefcase. Hugh, who had sleek, chestnut-brown hair, and a year-round tan, was the belted-trench-coat type. They were both tall, both thin, both successful in business. They were wealthy, intelligent, charming, and utterly devoted to their only daughter, Freya.

Every now and again, Lili was seized with an overwhelming urge to tie them up, lead them along to Paddy Birley's dairy farm, and roll them around in a yard full of cow pies.

"Hello, how are you? How's she been today?" cried Felicity as she always did, while Hugh swung Freya up into his arms and covered her face with kisses.

"She's been great," said Lili, wondering how quickly she could get rid of them. Hugh and Felicity loved to hear every detail of Freya's day, down to the last soggy rusk. "Ate well, slept well, hasn't been sick, she and William played with the Duplo—"

"Blood," William announced, perking up at the sound of his name. "Raddit leg off." He rolled his eyes dramatically. "All blood."

"Good heavens!" Felicity looked petrified. "What's this all about?"

"Bas-tid," William said with pride.

"Sounds like I'm not the only one who's had an eventful day," Jessie observed when the Seymours had at last been dispatched.

Lili looked worried. "I meant to phone Drew to find out how the rabbit is."

"Ring him now."

Lili recognized a last feeble stab at procrastination when she heard one.

"I can't," she told Jessie, sitting back down and emptying the bottle of wine into their glasses. "I'm too busy listening to you telling me absolutely everything there is to know about you and Toby Gillespie."

Chapter 5

"WE MET AT A party in London. Toby was at the Royal Academy of Dramatic Art. I was still at school in Cheltenham. We were so happy together. It was brilliant, real first-love stuff."

"Oh my God." Lili was so excited she was biting her knuckles. "I *knew* this was going to be good."

"It couldn't have been better." Jessie dabbed her finger in a spilled drop of wine and doodled a wet spiral on the kitchen table. "We saw each other every weekend. Neither of us had any money, of course, but that didn't matter. We did all those poor-but-happy things students do, and we made a million plans for the future. But one of the things we did backfired on us," she added with a faint smile, "and a baby didn't fit in with any of those plans. I was seventeen, halfway through my exams. Toby was twenty and a drama student. The same thing had happened to one of the boys in his year. He married his girlfriend, dropped out of RADA, and got a job in a slaughterhouse."

There was an odd look in Jessie's eyes. Lili guessed what was coming next and couldn't bear it.

"You didn't tell him," she gasped. "You didn't even tell him you were pregnant!"

"Oh, I did. I told him. He said he'd marry me. But I knew it wasn't what he wanted." Fidgeting uncontrollably now, Jessie swirled the wine around in her glass, creating a mini whirlpool. "Acting was Toby's life. He was going to be the next Al Pacino. I couldn't see him working in a slaughterhouse."

"So…?"

"Everyone seemed to think the best thing all around was an abortion, not least my parents," Jessie said drily. "A penniless drama student wasn't their idea of ideal son-in-law material. So we agreed that's what would happen. It was all arranged." She took a deep breath. "Except, at the last minute, I couldn't go through with it."

"Good grief. And Toby broke up with you? The bastard." Lili bristled with indignation.

"Will you stop jumping to conclusions?" Jessie demanded. "He didn't know I didn't have it done. I decided it wasn't fair to him. He'd sold practically all his possessions to raise the money for the operation—after doing all that, how could I tell him I'd changed my mind?"

"But it was his baby!"

"I know, but he didn't really want it."

"What did your parents say?"

Jessie pulled a face. "Went mental. I was this major embarrassment to them—they could hardly bear to look at me. So I shot up to Scotland and stayed with my auntie Morag in Glasgow. I wrote to Toby and told him it was all over between us. I said I'd had the abortion and that was it—I didn't want to see him anymore. When he turned up on my parents' doorstep, they told him the same." She shrugged. "He kept on phoning them, but they weren't going to tell him where I was. Then, six months later, they moved to Oxford and that really *was* it. Toby couldn't contact them anymore. They'd disappeared."

"Oh, Jess. And now he's found you." Lili could hardly breathe. "What's he going to *say*?"

Jessie stood up, stuffed the purple scarf into the back pocket of her jeans, and reached across the table for her keys. "Haven't the foggiest. But I'd like to have a bath before I find out."

Lili jumped a mile when the doorbell rang at ten to eight. Desperately on edge on Jessie's behalf, she hadn't been able to concentrate on anything else. "Mum, you're skipping pages," an aggrieved Lottie had complained during *Postman Pat and the Mystery Thief.* "This is hopeless! You'll just have to start again from the beginning."

Having at last managed to get William and five-year-old Lottie up to bed, Lili had followed Jessie's example and wallowed in a hot bath, wriggling her toes in time with the music belting out of Harriet's room (because according to Harriet, you couldn't truly appreciate the Spice Girls unless they were causing bits of plaster to vibrate off the walls).

The doorbell ringing coincided with Lili taking her first cautious sip of just-made hot chocolate. She groaned as it slopped down the front of her white terry cloth robe, then let out a squeak as the scalding liquid seeped through to her skin.

Opening the door, she yelped, "Ooh…ow… Oh, hi! Ooh…"

Drew Darcy, on the doorstep, broke into a grin. "This is exciting. You sound like one of those sex lines—just dial 0898 something-or-other and speak to Luscious Lucy. Not," he added hastily, "that I've ever phoned one."

"It's hot chocolate," Lili gasped. "I've gone and burned my… chest." She risked a quick peek between the lapels and saw angry blotches springing up. "Ow, it still hurts."

Drew marched her through to the kitchen, held a tea towel under the cold tap, expertly wrung it out, and handed it to Lili.

"Hold this against your…er, affected area. Go on, right inside your robe. I won't look."

Heavens, what a peculiar sensation, thought Lili. Ice-cold water was dripping down her breasts, sliding over her stomach, and puddling on the floor, while the rest of her was warm and dry.

"Any blisters forming?" Drew asked.

Lili peeped again, shook her head, and peeled the top edge of the tea

towel away to reassure him. Drew was a vet after all, the next best thing
to a doctor. Anyway, what was she showing him? Just a bit of cleavage.

"You'll live." His grin broadened, revealing lots of creamy-white
teeth, many of them capped as a result of tussles on the rugby field.
"Sorry, it obviously wasn't a great time to call around."

"How's the rabbit?" Lili was still dripping. She wondered if she
looked as incontinent as she felt.

Drew stopped smiling. "I'm sorry. He died."

"Oh no. Did you operate on him?"

"He died in the car, on the way to the office," Drew said gently.
"Just closed his eyes and went. He must have had internal bleeding.
I really am sorry, Lili."

Lili wiped her eyes with her sleeve, feeling a bit stupid. You were
allowed to cry when a pet died, but this had been just a wild rabbit,
a complete stranger.

"Here." Drew passed her a handkerchief and patted her hand.

She hoped he didn't think she was crazy, a hopelessly soft case.

"This is embarrassing."

"Of course it isn't. You're upset because some idiot ran that
rabbit over for fun."

So I am, thought Lili, snuffling into his hanky and marveling at
how clean and fresh smelling it was. *Drew must keep a special supply
for weepy pet owners.* Gosh, he was kind.

"I just don't understand how anyone can do something like that.
I mean, when I'm driving, I swerve to avoid animals." Lili shook
her head, shuddering as she remembered a heart-stopping moment
last year when she'd only just managed to steer out of the way of a
bolting fox cub. "What kind of a person sees something in the road
and actually aims *for* it?"

Drew nodded. "They aren't people—they're monsters. I tell you,
some of the cases I see make me want to batter whoever did it to a pulp.
Animals starved, beaten, neglected…" His eyes hardened as he spoke.

"Like this morning, we had a puppy brought in. The owners had done a midnight run. When the landlord went to the house the place was a mess and they'd left the dog behind, locked up in one room with no food. Another couple of days and he'd have died. Sorry," Drew said, glancing up and seeing the tears rolling freely down Lili's cheeks. "I'm not doing a good job here, am I? I'm supposed to be cheering you up."

"What will happen to him?"

"Dogs' home. He's only four or five months old, just a puppy. Not what you'd call Mr. Good-Looking," Drew added with a brief smile. "Not exactly the Brad Pitt of the doggy world, but he has a lovely nature. I'm sure somebody will take him."

"And if they don't, he'll be put down," said Lili, feeling sick. "What make is he?"

"What make *isn't* he?" Drew replied. "They don't come much more mongrel than this. Terrier, greyhound, collie, maybe a dash of spaniel in there somewhere."

"I'll have him," Lili blurted out.

"You haven't seen him."

"Doesn't matter. I want him." She marveled at the certainty in her voice.

Drew, who was being more cautious, said, "Lili, this isn't dial-a-pizza. You're upset because the rabbit died. I've just made you cry—twice. You're in what we professional medical types call 'a bit of a state.'" He smiled again, to show he understood. "By all means, come into the office tomorrow and meet him, but don't make any rash promises tonight."

Lili, who had by this time stopped crying, knew she wouldn't change her mind. She wanted this dog more than anything, and as soon as he recovered, she was going to bring him home.

And I'm not even going to think about what Michael will say, Lili told herself with great firmness.

This was chiefly because she already knew what he would say. Michael had about as much time for dogs as he did for wild rabbits.

Chapter 6

HAVING BATHED AND WASHED her hair, Jessie was finding the process of deciding what to wear a complicated business. Too much effort and Toby might think she was trying to impress him. Too little, on the other hand, and he might think she was trying to make a point of deliberately not impressing him.

Or something like that.

In the end, she settled for a black cotton sundress, sleeveless and ankle-length and a bit on the tenty side, but easy to wear. On the one hand, it was a dress, so she didn't look as if she was making too little effort; on the other hand, it wasn't what you'd call smart.

She stayed barefoot but tied up her hair with a yellow bow. She put on mascara but not lipstick, deodorant but no perfume, underwear but no bra, and Bruce Springsteen but not Bryan Ferry.

Oh God, definitely not Bryan Ferry.

What a lot of fuss, thought Jessie, *and talk about pointless! Why am I so bothered about what I look like when he's already seen me covered in paint and wearing boots and my least-flattering jeans?*

<hr />

"It's not very fair, is it?" Jessie said when she opened the front door twenty minutes later. "I mean, here I am looking twenty years older than when you last saw me, but you're always in the papers or on TV, so there's no shock value, no twenty-year gap to get over."

"Twenty-one," Toby corrected, his dark-blue eyes steady. "Twenty-one and a half years, actually."

"Okay, fine. I'm just saying it must be more of a—"

"Jess, stop babbling." Toby stepped into the hall and closed the door behind him. "Don't you think we have more important things to talk about?"

Jessie's plan to be cool and calm and laid-back about it all didn't seem to be going terribly well. Things had been a lot easier, she realized, when Toby's family had been around him, serving as unwitting bodyguards. With an apologetic shake of her head, she backed into the living room.

"Sorry. Right. Well, fire away."

"*Fire* being the operative word, seeing as I've spent the whole day torn between wanting to shoot you and kiss you senseless. Dammit, Jess." Toby pushed his dark-blond hair out of his eyes just as she remembered him doing all those years ago. "I knew moving house was supposed to be a stressful experience, but I wasn't expecting this."

"Well," said Jessie, stung, "neither was I." It *had* all been a bit sudden.

"Oliver's my son," Toby said.

"Of course he's your son."

"I came face-to-face with him today. No warning, nothing."

"I didn't have time to tell you, did I?" Jessie protested.

Now Toby really looked as if he could throttle her. She watched his knuckles gleam as he gripped the back of the sofa.

Finally, he said in a low voice, "Jess, you've had twenty-one years to tell me."

There was a framed photograph on the mantelpiece of Oliver as a laughing, gap-toothed five-year-old. It embarrassed him hugely, but Jess adored it. She looked at it now. "You didn't want him," she told Toby. "You didn't want to be tied down. A baby wasn't part of the plan, was it?"

"But, *Jess—*"

"You had no money and another year to go at drama school. You said an abortion was the best thing and gave me the money to do it. When the time came…" Jessie said slowly, "I couldn't."

"You should have told me," said Toby. "You shouldn't have just disappeared."

"Except that would have been like emotional blackmail, wouldn't it?" There was pain and pride in Jessie's dark-brown eyes. "You'd have stuck by me and secretly resented me, and sooner or later, you'd have ended up hating me for forcing you into a situation you needn't have been in." She shrugged and looked again at the photograph. "I just thought it was better to go away and have the baby on my own."

"Jesus, your parents must have really hated me. They wouldn't tell me a thing," said Toby. He stuffed his hands into the pockets of his jeans. "So, where did you go?"

"Scotland. To stay with my auntie Morag. And after Oliver was born, I managed to get a place in public housing. It wasn't much of a place, but we managed." Jessie didn't elaborate. The apartment, on the seventeenth floor of a high-rise in Glasgow, had been moldy and dilapidated, with walls so thin you could hear the click of the needles as syringes full of heroin were injected into the veins of the addicts next door.

"Did it never occur to you to contact me?" Toby said carefully.

"Of course it did. I thought about it hundreds of times. But when Oliver was tiny, you were just another struggling actor. Then you landed the part in *Fast and Loose* and became a star practically overnight." Jessie lifted her eyebrows at him. "And how would it have looked if I'd contacted you then? I'd have looked like a groupie, crawling out of the woodwork, only interested in you because you'd become a success."

Toby was still gripping the back of the sofa for dear life. "I was desperate to find you," he told Jessie. "You have no idea. If you'd contacted me, I'd have been so…happy."

"Yes, well." She shrugged flippantly. "I was tempted, I can tell you. When you're eighteen and a single mother, you have your low points."

"I wish you had contacted me."

Jessie smiled to herself, deciding he might as well know everything. "Actually, I did write to you once. I addressed it to the TV company that made *Fast and Loose*. I couldn't tell you about Oliver, of course, not in a letter that was going to be opened and read by a complete stranger, but I asked you to get in touch with me and gave you my Glasgow address."

Toby was staring at her, his expression appalled, already shaking his head. "But I didn't—"

"I know you didn't see it. The letter was in my bag waiting to be posted"—Jessie's voice caught as she remembered the long-ago moment—"when it was announced on the radio that you'd just got married."

"Oh my God," sighed Toby.

"And there it was, the next day, in all the papers—your fairy-tale secret wedding to stunning actress Deborah Lane." Jessie realized she could probably still recite the articles word for word. "I saw the photographs and read all that stuff about how you'd spotted her on TV, fallen in love at first sight, and tracked her down. You were quoted as saying you were the luckiest man in the world with the most beautiful wife in the world and you couldn't wait to start a family together."

She stopped. Toby was staring at her with the oddest expression on his face.

"Well, that was pretty much that," Jessie went on when he didn't speak. To compensate, she felt herself beginning to babble again. "I felt a bit of an idiot, I can tell you. And of course I didn't post the letter. I tore it into a million pieces, actually, and flung it out of my kitchen window like confetti…"

Toby was moving toward her.

"…very melodramatic of me, I know—"

"Jess, shut up."

"Oh, Toby, please don't. You really mustn't." Unsteadily she backed away.

"Oh, Jess," he mimicked softly. "I must. I really must."

He bent his head and kissed her, gently at first, then harder, and the extraordinary thing, Jessie realized as she clung to him, was that his kiss hadn't changed at all. It was just as she remembered it, as unique as any fingerprint. And every bit as miraculous.

"Hang on," she muttered shakily, managing to pull away from the kiss at last. "This is wrong, wrong, wrong."

"How can it be?" Toby's warm hands were on either side of her face. "We should have stayed together."

Maybe. And with hindsight, Jessie thought sadly, they could have done. The drawback at the time, of course, had been that they had been too practical, too realistic. It hadn't occurred to either of them that just months after graduating from RADA, Toby would land the lead role in what was to become one of the most popular and hugely successful TV series of all time.

The odds against that happening… *Well*, Jessie mused, *you'd have more luck at Ladbrokes betting on the Loch Ness monster bursting out of the water dangling a yeti in one flipper and a winning lottery ticket in the other.*

Jessie tried hard to look as if the kiss hadn't knocked her for a loop. "You've got Deborah now," she told Toby. "And one of the happiest marriages in show business."

It was true. Everyone knew that. When any magazine ran a feature on enduring celebrity marriages, the Gillespies were always included.

"What about you?" Toby's fingers, disconcertingly, were still stroking her face. "Who have you got?"

"Oliver," Jessie replied simply. "My son."

"You've never married?"

"Don't look at me like that!" Horrified, she thought she glimpsed pity in his eyes. "I haven't spent the last twenty years celibate! I've had my moments, I can assure you."

"But you didn't find Mr. Right."

"Sometimes," Jessie replied with spirit, "you can have more fun with Mr. Wrong."

This was her excuse anyway, and she was sticking to it.

To her relief, Toby let the matter drop. "We've got so much catching up to do. I still don't know how you got from Glasgow to here."

"My parents died fifteen years ago," Jessie said matter-of-factly. "When they moved from Cheltenham, they bought a bungalow in Oxford."

"I hitchhiked down from London one weekend," Toby interrupted, "and they'd just gone." His expression changed. "How did they die?"

Jessie remained calm. In truth, her parents' what-will-the-neighbors-say attitude and total lack of interest in their grandson had reduced her relationship with them to Christmas-card level. She had no regrets. They had been ashamed of her for being an unmarried mother, and she had been ashamed of them for taking it out on Oliver.

"There was a massive gas explosion. The bungalow was destroyed. They were killed outright."

"Oh, Jess, I'm sorry."

"But they were insured to the hilt," she went on, "and with the money I was able to buy this place. I remembered Upper Sisley and drove down here to have a look at the village. After a high-rise in Glasgow, Duck Cottage was like a palace. As soon as I saw it, I knew I wanted to live here."

Toby nodded. He had felt it too.

"And I've been happy here ever since," Jessie looked up at him, "So there you go. That's me up-to-date, and I haven't even offered you a drink yet. Red wine or tea?"

They sat out in the backyard and watched the sun slide behind the trees as they drank their wine.

"Your turn now," said Jessie. She tucked her feet up on the bench and smoothed the black cotton folds of her dress over her ankles until only her red-painted toenails peeped out. "You've met Oliver. So what did you think of him?"

"Bearing in mind that I was in shock at the time, it seems to me you've done a pretty good job." Toby shook his head. "I can't believe how much I've missed. As for Oliver… I mean, has it been hard for him, growing up without a father?"

"Probably." Jessie's voice was steady. It was an awful lot easier to breathe now that Toby was sitting opposite her with a wooden table between them. "But he's never accused me of wrecking his life."

"No, of course you—"

"The thing is, what happens next?" Jessie twirled the stem of her glass between her fingers. "Do we keep this to ourselves, or do we tell him?"

Toby frowned. It hadn't occurred to him that they had a choice. "What do you think? Which would be best for you?"

"It's going to affect you more than it'll affect me," Jessie said. "There's Deborah to consider. And your children. It might not be good news for your career."

"Sod my career!" Toby retorted, sounding almost angry. Jessie wondered if he thought she was having a go at him.

"Okay, but how's Deborah going to react?"

"No idea."

Deeply curious, Jessie couldn't resist asking, "Did you tell her you were coming over to see me tonight?"

Toby nodded and helped himself to more wine.

"She didn't mind?"

He shook his head.

"Oh."

This was good in one way, Jessie told herself. Jealousy was boring and seriously overrated as an occupation, and what did it ever achieve? She was glad Deborah—who seemed so nice—didn't go in for that kind of thing.

On the other hand, it wasn't terribly flattering to be shrugged off with quite this much lack of concern. *Toby did fancy me once, after all,* Jessie thought with mild indignation. *It would be nice to be regarded as just a* bit *of a threat.*

"I want Oliver to know I'm his father." Toby nodded to show he'd made his decision.

"Right. You break it to your family first," said Jessie. "Then I'll tell Oliver."

"Do you hate me?" said Toby.

"No."

"Do you wish I hadn't bought Sisley House?"

"I don't know yet." Jessie smiled slightly. "We'll have to wait and see how all this turns out."

There were so many things to say, it was hard to know where to start. She tucked her feet right under the hem of her dress, suddenly aware of how chipped the red polish was. Toby might only be wearing a yellow polo shirt and Levi's, but the discreetly slim watch on his wrist was a Cartier and his shoes were handmade. By comparison, she couldn't help feeling a bit...well, a bit thrift shop.

"I never stopped thinking about you." His voice was low. "You broke my heart when you disappeared."

"For at least a week," Jessie riposted, alarm mingling with desire as she saw the expression in his eyes.

"Longer than that." Toby shook his head and stood up, dangling the empty wine bottle between his fingers. "Any more where this came from?"

"No," Jessie lied. "Look, why don't you go home now and tell them?"

"Are you kicking me out?" Toby laughed. "What happened? Did I miss last orders?"

Her heart was hammering away now, under the black cotton. "I'd just rather you went. I'm tired," she said. "It's been a hell of a day."

But Toby, still smiling that heartbreaking, oh-so-familiar smile, was moving toward her again.

"You aren't tired." Briefly, he touched her shoulder. "You're trembling."

"No." Jessie tried to back hastily along the wooden bench, a surefire way to get splinters. "Please, Toby, stop it. I don't want you to kiss me again. Ever," she added as firmly as she could manage.

"That's not true either." That, of course, *was* true.

"Okay, okay! You *mustn't* kiss me again. It isn't fair to Deborah, for a start." *Nor to me*, Jessie thought.

"A lot of things aren't fair. All these years," said Toby, "I've blamed myself for what happened. I'd forced you to have an abortion, and as a result, you couldn't bear to see me again. So you disappeared, and I lost you." He put the empty bottle on the table and reached for Jessie's hands, pulling her to her feet. "Now I've found you again—*both* of you—and I can't even begin to describe how that feels."

"Don't kiss me," Jessie squeaked.

"Okay, relax." He was grinning. "You can show me out instead. We'll shake hands politely over the garden gate… Will that keep the neighbors happy?"

He did too, in solemn, bank-managerish fashion.

"I can't see anybody watching."

"Well, you wouldn't." Jessie glanced briefly across the green. "They aren't amateurs, you know. We're talking SAS tactics here."

"I'll see you tomorrow."

"Right. Good luck."

Before she could stop him, Toby had lifted a stray ringlet away from her damp cheek and smoothed it behind her ear. "As beautiful as ever." He sounded almost sad. "Oh, Jess."

Oh God! I want you to kiss me, kiss me, kiss me! Jessie almost shouted aloud. But it was only a temporary lapse. She managed to control herself.

This was Upper Sisley, after all.

Beyond those motionless net curtains, a crack surveillance team lurked. The binoculars would be out in force.

Chapter 7

LILI DIDN'T HAVE LONG to wait to discover why Felicity Seymour stayed in the car the next morning.

Hugh, carrying Freya into the house, said, "Felicity was a bit concerned. She asked me to mention the bottle of wine yesterday."

"Oh, that was Jessie, not me," Lili told him cheerfully. "She'd had a bit of a shock."

"There were two glasses." Hugh smiled his charming, apologetic smile to show he wasn't about to dispense with her services on the spot. "I'm sure you think we're making a fuss about nothing—"

"They were both Jessie's!" Lili began to feel a bit sick—even to her own ears that sounded lame. She tried again. "Really, I never drink when I'm working."

She wondered whether Hugh and Felicity were planning to report her to the social services, with whom she was registered, and her cheeks flamed. Here she was, innocent and practically being accused of being drunk in charge of a baby.

Then her cheeks went even redder as she recalled grabbing one of the glasses and taking a hefty gulp of wine. Oh God, she *had* had a drink—and she hadn't even remembered doing it, a sure sign of alcoholism if ever there was one.

"Well, I just said I'd mention it." Hugh glanced at his expensive watch. "I'm sure it won't happen again. We both know how happy Freya is coming here to you."

Plus, there are no other registered childcare people in the village,

Lili thought. She watched the way Hugh's glossy, chestnut-brown hair flopped forward as he bent to kiss his daughter good-bye, then fell effortlessly back into place when he straightened up again. She wondered jealously what it must be like to have hair that did what you wanted it to do. To be perfect *and* to have perfect hair.

Lili was on her knees unloading the washing machine when she heard horribly familiar footsteps on the path leading up to the front door.

Oh God, unfair, she thought frantically. *Why can't she ring first?*

But there was nowhere to run, no place to hide—not even inside the washing machine. There was a clink of glass, a sharp rap on the door, and Eleanor Ferguson's face—alarmingly distorted—appeared pressed against the bubbled glass.

When Lili opened the door, she found her mother-in-law brandishing four slightly cloudy milk bottles.

"Morning, Lili, I'll just give these a rinse, shall I? We don't want people walking past the house thinking you don't know how to wash a milk bottle."

Lili had had sixteen years of this. She was fairly used to it by now. Instead of feeling as if a time bomb were about to go off in her chest and bursting into tears of frustration, she treasured Eleanor's crashingly insensitive remarks, collecting them like coupons, saving them up and relaying them to Jessie afterward, when they would scream with laughter and award each new insult points out of ten.

"Help yourself," Lili said with a bright smile, because this was probably a seven and a half. She picked up the top-heavy washing basket. "I've just got to shove these in the tumble dryer."

"The tumble dryer!" Eleanor looked as horrified as if Lili had suggested the shredder. "Don't be ridiculous, Lili. It's a beautiful sunny day—those clothes will dry in no time."

"I know they will," Lili replied patiently, "but they'll be creased and need ironing. This way, they don't."

"Oh, Lili." Eleanor's tone spoke volumes. She shook her head. "Those machines cost a fortune to run."

"Yes, but it saves electricity not having to iron—"

"Here, give that to me." Eleanor seized the washing basket from her. "I'll take it home, peg everything out on the line, iron it all when it's dry, and bring it back this evening."

And *happen to mention it to everyone you pass in the street until the whole village knows*, Lili thought. Still, they were as used to Eleanor as she was. And properly ironed clothes would make a nice change.

"Fine then, if you're sure." She rummaged in the freezer as she spoke, hunting for a packet of fish fingers for William's and Freya's lunches.

"I could bring a casserole as well, if you like. Something nutritious for the children's tea," said Eleanor. "It can't do them any good, growing up on all this junk food."

Lili looked at the packet of pure cod fillet fish fingers in her hand. They didn't seem to have done Captain Birdseye any harm. "Eleanor, if you'd like to make a casserole, that would be great," she said, because Eleanor was clearly dying to. It would give her the opportunity to boast—yet again—about the time she almost auditioned for *MasterChef*. "Actually, I wanted to ask another favor, but you do so much for us already."

"Some of us are just more organized than others," Eleanor preened. "What is it you need help with?"

"Could you look after the children this evening, around sixish? Just for an hour?"

"That's no problem. Why? Where are you going?" Eleanor said briskly. "The doctor's? What's the matter this time?" She did that flaring thing with her nostrils. "Not more thrush?"

Lili took a deep breath. Some months back, Eleanor had gone upstairs to the loo and returned twenty minutes later with a handful of rusty razors.

"I've sorted out your bathroom cabinet, given it a good scrub and a tidy up," she had announced, dropping the razors into the trash. "I presume the tub of antifungal cream belongs to you, Lili."

Lili, stunned, had only been able to nod.

"So you've got thrush, have you? That's not very nice, is it? Maybe if you washed your underwear properly by hand instead of throwing it all into that washing machine of yours, this kind of thing wouldn't happen."

That had been one of Jessie's favorites—she'd given it a nine.

"No, I don't have thrush," Lili said patiently now, as Freya stirred in her sleep, "and I'm not going to see the doctor. I'm going to see the vet."

"What on earth for?" Eleanor looked indignant. "You don't have any animals."

"Drew Darcy was telling me yesterday about a puppy they've taken in. It's in need of a home"—Lili braced herself—"and I said we might have it."

"But Michael doesn't like dogs!" Indignation turned to outrage. "He won't want a puppy in his house."

"It's my house too," said Lili bravely, "and I do."

On the rare occasions when Lili did stand up for herself, Eleanor never knew how to react. Consequently—as now—several seconds of stunned silence were followed by an abrupt change of subject.

"I'll put the kettle on," Eleanor announced, filling it under the tap to the two-cup level, because anything more would be wasteful. Before plugging it in, she ran a dishcloth over the base. "Anyway, I wonder what my next-door neighbor's been up to. There was a journalist knocking on her door this morning."

Lili had to bite her lip. So this was the reason for today's unscheduled visit. When Eleanor assumed her only-mildly-interested voice it meant she was about to explode with curiosity.

There was a triumphant light in Eleanor's pale-gray eyes. Bernadette Thomas kept herself frustratingly to herself. "Not that I knew it was a journalist at first, of course. I just saw the chap knocking at the door and getting no reply, so I went and told him Mrs. Thomas had gone out earlier. Then I said if he'd like to leave a message, I'd be happy to pass it on, and he gave me a card." Swelling with pride, Eleanor produced it from her cardigan pocket and waved it at Lili. "See? With his name and number printed on it. He's a freelance journalist, very interested in doing a piece on my next-door neighbor for the *Times*, no less. Now what do you suppose that could be about?"

Freya had woken up. As she lifted the baby up, Lili smelled the deliciously clean baby smell of her head and hid another smile. "Why don't you ask her?"

Eleanor was now unloading the dishwasher, peering with deep suspicion at the inside of every mug because you could only really trust something to be clean if it was scoured by hand. "Bernadette Thomas moved into this village six months ago, and I've tried to strike up numerous conversations…"

Interrogations, thought Lili.

"I've done my best to be friendly…"

Nosy, thought Lili.

"But she never tells me anything," Eleanor concluded irritably. "She's just one of those antisocial women, determined to keep herself to herself."

⸺

"Hang on, something's wrong here," said Jessie. "It's your day off, it's only one o'clock in the afternoon, and you're *up*. Dressed, even. Quick, give me a Valium."

"Ha-ha," Oliver said as she squeezed past him in the narrow kitchen, pinching a slice of toast from his plate en route. "It's the lowest form of wit."

Having slung two more slices of bread into the toaster, Jessie began spreading the stolen slice thickly with peanut butter. Oliver was wearing dark-green jeans and a T-shirt that actually looked as if it might have been ironed.

"So where are you off to?"

He shrugged. "Driving into Harleston."

"On your own?" said Jessie.

"I'm going with Savannah Gillespie."

The toast popped up.

Looking at it, Jessie said, "Oh."

"I saw her from my bedroom window this morning. She was sitting on the wall by the pond feeding the ducks," Oliver explained. "We got chatting again, and I said if she wasn't doing anything this afternoon, I could show her around the town."

Jessie could only assume that Savannah hadn't Been Told yet. "Er...were her parents happy with that?"

Oliver looked amused. "I have passed my driving test, you know. And Savannah's eighteen. She doesn't have to ask their permission."

"Yes, well, drive carefully." Jessie concentrated on scraping the last of the peanut butter out of the jar. "And be...be polite."

"Mum, are you on drugs or something?"

Jessie checked for the fiftieth time that the battery on her phone hadn't gone dead. *Oh, Toby, what's going on? Why haven't you rung yet?*

Turning to Oliver she said, "And don't be late home."

⁓

"Yoo-hoo!"

Bernadette Thomas's heart sank when she saw Eleanor Ferguson's permed, gray head bobbing over the fence that divided their properties. She wouldn't make the same mistake next time she bought a house, that was for sure. She'd hire a private detective to check out the neighbors in advance.

"Yoo-hoo-oo, Bernadette!"

The silly woman was waving at her. Bernadette, who had been peacefully clipping the edges of her lawn, stood up and made her way over to the fence.

"You had a visitor earlier, while you were out. A journalist," Eleanor announced with pride and extremely thinly disguised curiosity. "Here, he left his card, and he'd like you to contact him at your earliest convenience. I said to him, 'What's going on here? Is Bernadette a celebrity and we don't even know it?'" She laughed a bit too heartily. "'Or a bank robber, or a Russian spy?'"

"I'm not a Russian spy," said Bernadette, her palms sweating. She took the card and stepped backward, landing awkwardly on one of the stones bordering the flower bed and almost stumbling in her hurry to get away. "I don't rob banks either."

"But you are very secretive." Eleanor's tone was arch; she'd had enough of this prevarication. "The thing is, people are beginning to wonder, Bernadette. You know how some folk are about a bit of a mystery. Before long, they'll be imagining all sorts."

Bernadette's scalp began to prickle beneath her gardening hat. She knew Eleanor was right. And now a journalist was sniffing around... Oh God, it didn't bear thinking about. "Excuse me," she said hurriedly, needing time to think, to prepare. "I'm sure I can hear my phone."

———

Bernadette's phone might not have been ringing, but Jessie's was. Balanced on the top of a stepladder with a tray of pistachio-green matte emulsion paint in one hand, a roller in the other, she had to grip the roller's handle between her teeth and squeeze the phone out of a narrow pocket with one hand.

"It's me." Toby sounded relaxed. "I've spoken to Deborah, and she's fine about it. So why don't you tell Oliver this evening, and I'll tell my two, then you can both come over here for a drink and a chat."

"Is it really that simple?" said Jessie. *Heavens, how civilized.* Somehow, she'd imagined it would be a bit more dramatic than this.

But then, Jessie realized as she started up with the roller once more, *I've clearly been moving in hopelessly unsophisticated circles. Maybe when you were a member of London's glitterati, long-lost sons popping up out of the woodwork were par for the course*

The journalist, when Bernadette spoke to him, was thankfully not the pushy type. He was disappointed when she explained apologetically that she was unable to help him but assured her that he understood.

Bernadette breathed a sigh of relief as she replaced the receiver. That was one crisis averted—or postponed, at least.

Now she just had Eleanor Ferguson to deal with.

An hour later, Bernadette parked in a metered spot in the center of Harleston. She checked her reflection in the rearview mirror before getting out of the car. An anonymous woman in her midforties stared back at her, neatly made up and unobtrusively dressed in a navy blouse and gray linen skirt. She ran a comb briefly through the straight, brown hair she wore in a simple, center-parted bob. She touched her plain gold earrings—a habitual gesture of reassurance—then, satisfied that all was well, took her purse out of her bag. She needed a pound coin for the meter.

Waterstones was moderately busy but nobody bothered Bernadette, who blended in with the browsers. She spent twenty minutes searching along the fiction shelves before finding what she was looking for.

Antonia Kay was the author of four English countryside family sagas. Bernadette had never heard of her, and since the company that published her books wasn't one of the more successful ones, it stood to reason that Antonia, as a novelist, wasn't one of the publishing industry's great successes either.

Best of all, there was no author biography included in any of the four novels, nor were there any photographs to show the readers what Antonia Kay looked like. But from the style of novel, you would imagine her to be a quiet, nondescript, middle-aged woman who maybe lived, alone, in a village.

"You'll do," Bernadette murmured, piling all four paperbacks into the crook of her arm and carrying them over to the pay desk.

Chapter 8

HARRIET FERGUSON, HOME FROM school, made her traditional Thursday-afternoon trip to the grocery store to pick up her copy of *Hey Girlz!!* magazine.

"Muck. That's all it is—nothing but muck," declared Myrtle Armitage, who had run the shop for the last thirty years. "I don't know how your mother lets you read all that smutty stuff. Things aren't like they were in my day, I can tell you."

"I know," said Harriet patiently. "You tell me every week. But, Myrtle, magazines hadn't been invented in your day." God, sex probably hadn't been invented.

"Cheeky madam." Myrtle totted up the cost of the magazine and the fruit gums. "Lads—that's all you young girls think about. You'll end up in trouble."

"I won't"—Harriet flicked back her thick brown hair—"because I'm choosy."

"Oh, aye, there's plenty've said that in their time," Myrtle chuckled, "and ended up knocked up just the same."

Harriet knew Myrtle didn't believe her, but it was true—she was choosy. She didn't mean to be; she didn't even *want* to be. It was just an unfortunate side effect of reading magazines like *Hey Girlz!!* After drooling over endless photographs of all the dishiest, coolest, wickedest pop and soap stars in the country, Harriet had discovered that the real boys—the ones she went to school with—were massive letdowns.

The bell above the shop door went *ding*, but Harriet, her nose stuck in the magazine, was too engrossed in "How to Become the Kisser of the Century" to notice.

Myrtle Armitage said, "Yes, love?"

"Uh…Blu-Tack. Got any Blu-Tack?" Dizzy asked hopefully.

Myrtle shot him a suspicious look, clearly wondering if Blu-Tack was a contraceptive. "What is it?"

Dizzy began to look worried. "You use it to stick posters on your wall."

"We've got Scotch tape," said Myrtle. "That'll do the trick."

"It's for my bedroom. My parents'd go mad." Dizzy sounded resigned; he'd been down that road before. "It'll wreck the wallpaper or something. They said definitely no Scotch tape."

"Oh."

Harriet looked up from her article. ("Don't go at it like a vacuum cleaner! Give the poor guy a chance to breathe!!!") "Are you the one who's just moved into Sisley House?"

Dizzy went pink around the ears. "Yeah."

"What's your name?"

"Dizzy."

Harriet's forehead creased. "That's a bit weird, isn't it?"

He went pinker. "It's Thaddeus really. Gross. Dizzy was my dad's idea of a joke when I was a baby. Because of Dizzy Gillespie, y'know?"

Harriet didn't know, but surely anything was better than Thaddeus. And she'd thought her name was bad.

"Anyway…" Dizzy shoved his hands into his pockets and scuffed his sneakers against the counter. "It kind of stuck. Everyone calls me Dizzy now."

"Oh well, could be worse." Harriet decided to be kind. "I was sick in assembly once, and for years afterward, my nickname was Puke."

Myrtle Armitage—whose nickname at school, somewhat

predictably, had been Myrtle the Turtle—straightened a pile of *Country Life*s and registered her disapproval with a sniff.

"My sister's name is Savannah," said Dizzy, "and everyone calls her Saveloy." He looked pleased with himself. "I thought that one up."

"Anyway," said Harriet, "the thing is, I've got some Blu-Tack at home. You can have a bit of mine if you like."

"Hey, nice one!" Dizzy's face lit up. "That'd be neat. Thanks… er…Puke."

"Nobody calls me Puke anymore," Harriet said, walking with him to the door. "My name's Harriet."

———

Harriet enjoyed talking to Dizzy for all of two minutes. The other trouble with real boys, as she had already begun to discover, was that it never took them long to embarrass themselves.

And Dizzy, it soon became apparent, was no exception.

As they dawdled their way along the main street toward the Old Vicarage, they approached the Seven Bells. The pub was closed but Moll Harper, the full-time barmaid who lived above it, was stretched out on the village green, making the most of the sun before they opened again at five thirty. She was lying on a red towel. She wore a dark-green bikini, and her tortoiseshell curls were spread out Medusa-style around her head. Even when she lay flat on her back, Harriet couldn't help noticing, her astonishing boobs still pointed skyward.

Men were besotted with Moll Harper, and it mystified Harriet, who couldn't for the life of her imagine why. Moll wore peasanty, serving-wench clothes, never anything fashionable. When the magazines told you pale eye shadows and metallic lipsticks were in, Moll wore sooty, smudgy eyeliner and left her broad, red mouth bare. She had a huge bosom, curves everywhere, big hips, and had to be at least thirty pounds overweight. Anyone else sunbathing in public in a bikini, Harriet thought, would hold their stomach in. But not Moll. She had a spare tire and she wasn't afraid to show it. She simply didn't give a fig.

You couldn't imagine anyone less like a supermodel, yet the men clearly weren't bothered about that. They fell like ninepins under Moll's spell. She was famous for it; all she had to do was look at them and smile her lazy, insolent smile, and they were lost.

It'll be a test, Harriet thought as they drew closer. *If Dizzy doesn't say anything, we'll be friends forever. If he does say something…well, that'll be it. He'll just be another dork.*

Thankfully, Moll was asleep.

"Whoa," said Dizzy, veering across the road like a heat-seeking missile in order to get a better look. He ogled for a few seconds, then swerved excitedly back. "I saw her yesterday at lunchtime, working in the pub. What a body, what a bird! She's tops."

Huh. Top-heavy, certainly. "I'm surprised you didn't wolf whistle," Harriet sneered.

"Well, she's asleep. Don't want to wake her up, do I?"

Harriet contemplated telling him that Moll Harper was a slut—practically a prostitute, in fact, she slept with so many men—but guessed it would only fuel Dizzy's interest. Instead, she glanced down at her blue school shirt and vile pleated skirt and wondered if she was ever going to grow a bust.

"Is she married or anything?" Dizzy asked eagerly, still peering over his shoulder at Moll.

I'll tell him to wait in the yard and chuck the Blu-Tack out of the window, Harriet decided. *He's not coming into my house.*

Men, boys—they're all the same, she thought with scornful resignation. Dizzy Gillespie was just another sex-crazed dork.

Lili was being subversive, and it was a thrilling experience. She felt naughty and rebellious and quite unlike herself. She also felt as if she should be striding along in a leather jacket with the collar turned up and dark glasses, and maybe a pair of radically ripped 501s.

It came as something of a letdown when she glimpsed her reflection in the plate-glass double doors of the veterinary clinic and remembered that she was actually wearing a pink-and-white-flowered T-shirt and radically ironed jeans from Marks & Spencer.

Furthermore, since they had been ironed by Eleanor Ferguson, they sported creases down the front of each leg sharp enough to slice bread.

Lili consoled herself with the knowledge that though she might not look subversive, she was certainly going to *be* it. The more objections Eleanor had dredged up, the more determined she had become to bring the puppy home.

"Gosh, you look different," she told Drew when the receptionist showed her into his office.

He grinned. "It's the white coat. Makes me look intelligent. Have a seat and I'll go get him."

When he returned less than a minute later, Lili was almost knocked off her chair by a brown blur with a frantically wagging tail. He flung himself at her, whimpering with pleasure, scrambled clumsily onto her lap, and joyously licked her face.

"See? Why can't I do that when I meet a woman I like?" marveled Drew.

"Oh, he's divine!" Lili's eyes filled with tears of happiness. She held the dog's face between her hands and gazed with adoration into his chocolate-brown eyes. "Can I really take him home?"

"Looks like love at first sight." Drew was leaning back against the examination table with his arms folded across his chest, watching the pair of them. "Who am I to come between a match made in heaven?"

"Oh, Drew."

"We don't know his name, I'm afraid."

The dog was still licking Lili's wet cheeks. He was lanky and gawky, like a self-conscious teenager, and when he realized Lili was studying him again, he cocked his head to one side like a Page 3 girl posing coyly for the camera.

"I've left the kids at home with my mother-in-law," said Lili.

At once, Drew looked sympathetic: Eleanor disapproved of Drew, Jamie, and Doug almost as much as she disapproved of Lili. "I called into the shop on my way here this afternoon," he told her, "and she was in there telling Myrtle Armitage she'd just spent the last three hours doing your ironing."

"She brought it back this evening." Lili pulled a face. "She stood in the middle of the kitchen and looked around and said, 'Do you know what this place needs, Lili? This place needs a jolly good blitz.' So I think that's what we're going to have to call him," she concluded happily, rubbing the dog's lopsided ears. "Blitz."

———

Blitz peed in the car three times on the way to his new home. When they reached the Old Vicarage, he launched himself first at Harriet, then at Eleanor, his paws in all directions like Bambi's as he shot from one end of the kitchen to the other.

He peed twice more on the quarry-tiled floor, leaped up onto the window seats to admire the view, let out a series of ecstatic howls, and hurdled the kitchen table in one go, sending Eleanor's basket of faultlessly ironed clothes flying.

"He's not even house-trained!" shouted Eleanor, purple in the face with outrage.

"He is," Lili assured her, keeping her fingers crossed behind her back. "He's just pleased to see us."

"I don't know what Michael's going to say about this, I really don't."

Feeling amazingly brave, Lili said, "Oh, I thought you did." She looked innocent. "You said he'd be furious."

"Well, he'll certainly be that." Eleanor's lips were welded

together. She knew Lili had visited the shop earlier this afternoon. Six cans of Pedigree Chum and a bag of dog biscuits, that's what she'd bought. She'd had no intention of coming back from Harleston without that blasted dog.

"Mum, he's *cool*," Harriet exclaimed, her eyes shining. "What's he called? Can we wake up Lottie and show her?"

"No you cannot." Eleanor was horrified by the suggestion. "Children need their routine. I put her to bed twenty minutes ago."

"But it is a special occasion," said Lili. Golly, *more* subversion. "And Lottie would so love to meet him. Go on—run upstairs and get her," she told Harriet. "And he's called Blitz."

"I might have known," said Eleanor disparagingly. Her nostrils flared like tents. "It's a ridiculous name for a dog."

Chapter 9

BLITZ WASN'T THE ONLY one being introduced to his new family that evening.

"Are you sure you're okay?" said Jessie for the twentieth time as she and Oliver made their way along Compass Lane toward Sisley House.

"Mum, don't fuss. Why wouldn't I be okay?"

She had sat Oliver down and told him everything, just as she had told Lili yesterday. Except it had been altogether easier telling Lili.

"I don't know." Jessie hated not knowing the answers to questions; she was just trying to help. "I suppose I'm saying don't worry if you feel a bit funny about it. I know how much of a shock it must be."

"But some shocks are nicer than others. I mean, if you'd told me my father was a mass murderer, that would be one of the nastier ones," Oliver pointed out reasonably. "This is Toby Gillespie we're talking about. I've met him. I've met his family. They're all great. Okay, it's a shock," he went on, "but when you think about it, it's a pretty nice shock. It could be a hell of a lot worse."

"Oh, darling." Jessie longed to throw her arms around him but she wasn't allowed to, not in public. Oliver had put a stop to that at the age of eight.

"The weird thing is"—Oliver sounded thoughtful—"when I was little, I used to fantasize that my dad was rich and famous." He smiled briefly. "And it was true—he was."

They were approaching the gates of Sisley House. Jessie slowed down. "Should I have told you before now?" She looked worried. "Did I do the wrong thing?" She felt terrible. Oliver had never mentioned this before. It broke her heart to imagine him fantasizing about his absent father.

Oliver guessed at once what was on her mind. "Look, nearly everyone does it. We talked about it at college; it's just something kids like to do. Even the ones who knew their parents were their biological parents. They still daydreamed about discovering they were adopted. Then they could fantasize that their real father was George Clooney or Rod Stewart or someone, and that their real mother was…God, I don't know…Meryl Streep."

Toby answered the front door. To Jessie's relief, he didn't try anything embarrassing, like putting his arms around Oliver. He just winked and smiled and ushered Jessie past him into the hall.

"Let me have a quiet word with Oliver. Jess, go on through to the sitting room, would you? Oliver can come into the kitchen and help me with the drinks."

The sitting room, with its yellow-gold walls and impractical, pale-yellow carpet, was flooded with early evening sunlight. Jessie felt her heart begin to break into a canter. She felt as if she were on a stage, in a play, and nobody had let her see a copy of the script.

Deborah was standing by the french windows, her black hair gleaming, her flawless body wrapped in a plain gray silk tank top and narrow, gray trousers. The only splashes of color were her red lipstick and strappy red leather sandals.

She was smoking a menthol cigarette and her eyes narrowed as she caught sight of Jessie in the doorway.

If this were a play, Jessie hardly needed a script to know that here was the female villain of the piece, the ultimate baddie.

Except it wasn't a play.

"Bloody cigarettes." Deborah stubbed it out in a nearby ashtray, blinking and dabbing a forefinger under each eye in turn to check her mascara hadn't run. "God, I'm useless at smoking. It always gets in my eyes." And then, in a rush, "Oh, Jess, can you believe it? We're practically related to one another! Living here is going to be so much *fun*."

"You don't mind?" said Jessie, hugely relieved. "About Oliver?"

Deborah looked amazed. "Why would I? That all happened before Toby and I even met. Heavens, it's not as if he's suddenly produced a bawling baby out of nowhere." She raised her dark eyebrows and said, straight-faced, "If he tried that I might be a bit miffed."

"I'm glad you're okay about it." Jessie perched on the arm of one of the sofas and gazed admiringly around the sitting room. "You've settled in fast. You must have put in some hours to get this much done."

"The men did most of it. I just supervised the unpacking and told them where to put everything." Deborah broke into a grin. "Bossed them about, made them cry, threatened to make them drink another cup of Dizzy's tea, that kind of thing."

I like you, thought Jessie. *You're brilliant. I really like you. I wish I didn't, but I do.* Her stomach lurched with shock as the implications of this last thought struck home. This last *rogue* thought.

"Drinks," Toby announced, pushing the door open and coming through with Oliver.

"Most people take their gap year before college, but I couldn't wait to get there," Oliver was saying, "so I'm taking mine now. That's why I'm working in the Seven Bells, to get some money together. As soon as I've saved enough, I'm going to travel around Europe."

"Jess tells me you got an excellent grade," Toby said. "I'm impressed."

"Come on. Let's have a proper look at the two of you," Deborah urged. She studied them in silence for several seconds, then turned to Jessie. "It's definitely there, isn't it? I mean, you wouldn't catch sight of Oliver and say straightaway, 'God, that boy's the spitting image of Toby Gillespie.' But when they're side by side, you can see the likeness in the eyes, the cheekbones are there... They even stand in the same way."

"Same blond hair," said Jessie, nodding.

"Like Savannah." Toby looked amused. "Except she has more of it."

"Speaking of Savannah," said Oliver, "where is she?"

The door creaked and opened wider.

"I'm here."

Savannah seemed to be clutching the door handle for support as she surveyed the assembled company. She had changed into a midriff-baring black top and an orange denim skirt, and Jessie wondered if she had been crying.

Turning to her, holding his breath, Oliver mouthed, *Okay?* And for a long, terrifying moment, Savannah didn't react.

Then, breaking into a huge grin, she rushed over and threw her arms around him. "Of *course* I'm okay. You're my new big brother. And you know what that means?"

Oliver shook his head. "What?"

"Somebody else buying me fantastic presents at Christmas."

Phew. Jessie relaxed, thankful to have been wrong. For several appalling seconds, she'd thought Savannah was genuinely upset. She watched her kiss Oliver noisily on both cheeks.

"We were just looking at the similarities between us," said Toby.

"Do we look like brother and sister?" Savannah sounded delighted. "There's the hair, of course. Are we really alike? What else is the same?"

She was gaily standing next to Oliver, ready for inspection, when Dizzy slouched in almost unnoticed.

"Bet you Oliver doesn't have a tattoo on his bum," he remarked, almost to himself. "At least not one that says 'I love Jez.'"

"You little *sneak*!" Savannah squealed, going bright red. She seized Oliver's arm. "Here, this is a job for big brother. Just beat him to a pulp, will you? No—better make it a puree."

Toby, sounding appalled, said, "Savannah, for God's sake, tell me you don't have a tattoo."

Jessie and Deborah, exchanging glances, tried not to laugh.

"Darling, I can't keep track of all these boys." Deborah frowned as she struggled to remember. "Which one was Jez?"

———

"Look at the state of you two."

Home from the hospital, Doug Flynn good-naturedly surveyed the living room of Keeper's Cottage. Cricket from Australia was on the TV. Drew and Jamie, in shorts and T-shirts bearing the respective slogans "I'm a *Baywatch* Babe" and "Look Out—Here Come the Rugger Buggers," were sprawled in armchairs, clutching cans of lager. More cans littered the coffee table. Empty bags of cheese-and-onion chips, crumpled up and hurled at the TV set whenever the Aussies hit a six, dotted the carpet. Drew wore a hat with corks bobbing around the brim. Jamie was wearing a pair of red-and-white-striped briefs on his head.

"Join us." Drew waved his half-full can enticingly under Doug's nose. "Plenty more in the fridge. Australia is 208 for 6. Actually, it's a bloody good match."

"Can't. I'm going out." Doug was already pulling off his shirt and heading upstairs for a shower.

"Alison?" Jamie's eyes were fixed on the screen, but he was interested enough to ask. He liked Alison; she had colossal boobs.

"Melissa."

Ten minutes later, Doug clattered down the stairs again, showered, changed, and clearly ready for anything. For someone who had just finished a twenty-four-hour shift in the ER, he looked unfairly good. Drew never knew how he did it. Even his shirt was ironed.

"Busy today?"

Doug grinned. "A chap came in complaining of lower abdominal pain. Real bank-manager type. We x-rayed him, and he had a Marmite jar up his bum."

Drew snorted into his lager. "Full of Marmite?"

"No, peanuts."

This was par for the course in the ER. You could think of the weirdest things and put them in the most unlikely orifices, and somebody somewhere would have thought of it before you.

"Did he say why?" Jamie marveled.

"No. Just cried and begged us not to tell his wife."

"When did you iron that shirt anyway?" Drew was mystified.

"I didn't. Alison volunteered. She did a whole stack of stuff."

"Didn't do any of mine," Jamie said gloomily.

Doug laughed. "Ah, but you have to earn it."

First, Drew wondered how Alison would feel if she knew Doug was wearing one of the shirts she had so lovingly ironed out on a date with someone else. Then, he wondered how it would feel to go out with one girl actually wearing a shirt that had been lovingly ironed for you by another. Finally, he wondered what it must be like to be Doug Flynn, to be *so* good-looking and apparently irresistible that wherever you went, there were girls—gorgeous girls at that—falling over themselves to go out with you. And to iron your shirts.

"Look at that, look at that!" howled Jamie, leaping out of his seat. "Catch it, you idiot! Catch it, catch it! YES! OUT!"

"Me too." Doug glanced out of the window as a car pulled up on the shoulder outside the cottage.

"You're kidding," Drew exclaimed. "You mean she's actually come to pick *you* up?"

How did the lucky sod do it?

"She offered. What could I say?" Shrugging, Doug slung a cream linen jacket over his shoulder and headed for the door.

"Don't go straight out. Bring her in and introduce her," Jamie begged. "I haven't seen Melissa yet." He was on his knees in front of the TV, the briefs falling over one eye.

"The thing is," said Doug, "would she want to see you?"

By ten o'clock, the Australians were 270 for 8 and Drew was beginning to wish he hadn't eaten five bags of cheese-and-onion chips. The taste in his mouth was diabolical. He took another swig of lager and tried swilling it, mouthwash style, around his teeth. No good. He balanced the half-empty can on his knee, and that was no good either; it promptly toppled over, tipping its contents over his shorts.

Still, it was a hot night. At least the lager was cool. And, Drew thought contentedly, there were plenty left in the fridge.

"You get it," he told Jamie when the doorbell rang.

"No, you."

Drew indicated the sodden front of his shorts. "What, in this state?"

"Look," said Jamie, who was lying on the floor, "I'd love to answer the door, but I think I'm too drunk to stand."

"Good grief," Drew said when he saw who was on the doorstep. "I mean…hello."

When he swallowed, there was an audible gulping sound, just like in a cartoon.

Embarrassing or what?

Chapter 10

Deborah Gillespie understandably looked entertained.

"Hi. I'm your new neighbor." She held up the dustpan and brush Jessie Roscoe had borrowed the day before. "Just returning these."

Numb with shock, Drew took them. He knew, of course, that the Gillespies had moved into Sisley House, but it was still something of a first, opening the front door and coming unexpectedly face-to-face with someone you'd only ever seen before on TV or in the papers.

"Oh, right, great…thanks." Instinctively, he held the dustpan in front of his groin, attempting to cover the stain. Oh God, that looked even worse. He saw Deborah Gillespie's gaze drop to his shorts.

"I spilled some lager. It isn't… I mean, I haven't—"

"Wet yourself?" said Deborah, straight-faced. "Well, good."

Hell, he felt like a fourteen-year-old. What on earth was he supposed to say next?

Mercifully, Deborah did it for him. "So, are you the doctor or one of the vets? You see"—she smiled a disarming smile—"I've been hearing all about you."

What? What have you heard? Was it all *bad?* wondered Drew, mesmerized by her dark eyes and dazzling beauty. Hell, she'd asked him a question—he was supposed to be coming up with a sensible answer.

"Um, vet."

"On your own tonight?"

Drew cringed as Deborah peered past him. If she'd been any normal visitor, he would have invited her in without a second thought.

"Who is it?" yelled Jamie from the living room.

Oh God, oh God…

"Doctor?" Deborah inquired brightly.

"Another vet."

"Oh, right." She nodded. "Actually, I dropped by to ask if I could borrow some milk. And if you can spare a bit of dish soap, even better."

This was ridiculous, Drew realized. How long could he reasonably stand here like this—like a prison warder, for heaven's sake—barring her way?

"Look," he blurted out in desperation, "you can come in but the place is a dump. And I mean a *real* dump."

"Are you worried I might be shocked?" Deborah sounded cheerful.

"Well, it's not a pretty sight."

"You're three single males sharing a house," she consoled him. "If it were immaculate, I'd just assume you were gay."

"Who's gay?" Jamie demanded indignantly from the floor as Drew led her through to the living room. "Not me, that's for bloody sure." Having started on the lager earlier than Drew, he peered up from beneath the drooping pair of underwear on his head at Deborah. "Drew, are you sure this is the pizza delivery boy? His hair isn't greasy enough."

Drew flushed, embarrassed already, and gave Jamie's bare foot a hefty warning kick. "It's our new neighbor, you moron—Deborah Gillespie. I'm really sorry about Jamie," he added, glancing at Deborah. "He's drunk."

"At least I haven't pissed myself," cackled Jamie, pointing to the front of Drew's shorts.

"Right. What was it you wanted—milk and dish soap?" Drew made for the kitchen; the quicker he got her out of here, the better.

"Only if you can spare them."

"Milk and dish soap?" Jamie sounded bemused. "What is that, some kind of cocktail? Okay, I'll try one," he called through the open doorway, "but stick a vodka in mine."

"Coming from London, we're used to shops that stay open all night," Deborah explained. "It's going to take some getting used to, remembering not to run out of things after six o'clock in the evening."

"Well, you can always borrow from us." Drew's hands trembled slightly as he poured most of their own remaining milk into a chipped Independence Day cup. When he had squeezed a decent amount of dish soap into the only other clean container—it had to be, didn't it, the mug featuring the over-endowed girl whose bikini disappeared when it heated up—he handed them to Deborah. "There you go."

"You're an angel." Smiling, she put them down on the crowded worktop. "The thing is, I don't have to dash straight back. You wouldn't by any chance have a lager going begging?"

"Our lagers don't beg," Jamie yelled. "We're the ones who beg—for lager!"

"I'm sorry he's *so* bloody rude." Drew grabbed another can from the fridge and gazed around frantically, wondering what to pour it into.

"Come on, calm down." Taking the icy can, Deborah patted his arm. "Don't panic, and stop trying to treat me like the Queen Mother. I have seen a man a little the worse for drink before," she added with an innocent smile. "I've mixed with actors for the last twenty years."

"Okay. Right." Drew tried to smile back, but he still felt like rolling Jamie up in the dirty carpet and chucking him, stupid briefs on his head and all, into the village pond.

He was still hunting without success for a glass that wasn't a pint mug. Deborah grinned and tackled the ring pull. "Don't bother. I'm fine like this."

As they headed back to the living room, she clinked her can, first against Drew's, then—leaning down—Jamie's. "New neighbors and happy times ahead. Cheers."

Drew found he'd gone weak at the knees—an alarmingly sissy thing to happen to a grown man. He wondered if Deborah Gillespie was the most hypnotically beautiful, charming, and totally amazing woman he'd ever met in his life, decided almost at once that of course she was, and murmured, "Cheers."

What was he getting so het up about anyway? That was the thing about hypnotically beautiful, charming, and amazing women: they were way, way, *way* out of his league.

———

"Where have you been?" Toby protested when Deborah finally reappeared. "You said you were going to make coffee." He looked at his watch. "That was almost an hour ago."

"We'd run out of milk." Deborah balanced the tray on the table. "I borrowed some from the boys next door. Stayed to chat. You were right," she told Jessie cheerfully. "They're sweet."

Sweet? Jessie hid a smile. She hadn't gone quite that far. She'd said they were good fun.

"Was Doug there?" she asked. She especially couldn't imagine anyone calling Doug Flynn "sweet."

"The doctor? Oh, he was out. I just met the vets. Jamie and the big freckly one… What's his name? Drew, is it?"

Oliver was on the sofa comparing exam results with Savannah. He looked up.

"Drew Darcy."

Deborah started to laugh. "Really, that's his surname? Was that who I met, the dashing Mr. Darcy? Oh dear, poor lamb. How dreadful to be a big, freckly rugby player and saddled with a name like that."

———

Jamie was snoring on the carpet, but Drew couldn't sleep. He was still thinking about the events of the evening when Doug came in with his arm around Melissa. He glanced at the hideous state of the living room and at Jamie's inert form and led Melissa promptly toward the stairs.

"What happened?" he said over his shoulder to Drew, meaning the match.

"Oh, nothing much. Deborah Gillespie dropped by…that's all." Drew yawned and stretched as if this was the kind of thing that went on in his life all the time. "We chatted, drank a few lagers—quite a few lagers, actually. Got on pretty well together."

"Yeah, yeah." Grinning, Doug patted Melissa's perky bottom. "Hear that, sweetheart? The sad fantasies of the lonely, sex-starved, single bloke. Promise you'll never let that happen to me."

———

"Just one thing before you go," Toby said as they all made their way into the hall. It was past midnight, and Jessie had to make an early start in the morning. "Any weirdos in the village that you know of?"

"Why?" Jessie winked at Deborah. "Are you dying to meet some?"

But Toby wasn't smiling. He pulled a folded envelope from his back pocket and handed it to her with a shrug. "It's probably nothing, a one-off. I just wondered if anyone sprung to mind."

Jessie unfolded the envelope, which had been hand delivered, and drew out a single sheet of paper. On it were the words *Mr. Gillespie, you are not wanted here.*

That was all, written in shaky capitals in the center of the page.

"Someone right-handed, writing with their left hand," said Jessie. She looked up, feeling like Miss Marple.

Toby raised an eyebrow. "Any ideas?"

"I can't imagine who'd do something like this."

"It's probably kids," said Deborah, unconcerned.

"When did you get it?" said Jessie.

"Shoved through the letter box sometime last night. When we came downstairs this morning, it was on the mat."

"Are you going to show it to the police?"

Toby shook his head. "It's hardly a threatening letter. I only asked because you might have said straightaway, 'Oh, that'll be old so-and-so, he's always doing stuff like that.'"

"Well…no, there's no one obvious." Jessie looked doubtful. Toby and Deborah didn't seem alarmed, but weren't anonymous letters the tiniest bit worrying?

Deborah, reading her thoughts, said, "This kind of thing happens when you're in the public eye. Toby's had his share of weird letters and obsessed fans over the years. One woman even thought she was married to him." She shrugged. "It's boring but harmless. You get used to it after a while."

"The only difference being, they usually wish you *would* move into their village." With a faint smile, Toby pushed the letter back into its envelope and shoved it into one of the drawers in the dresser. "Whereas this one seems to want me out."

Chapter 11

ANOTHER SIZZLING HOT DAY. By eleven o'clock, the sky was a cloudless peacock blue. Since the earth was cracked and dry, and her poor, parched plants were screaming out for water, Bernadette Thomas began filling her watering can at the kitchen sink. It would take at least an hour and a great deal of toing and froing, but the hosepipe ban had been put into force—and with a neighbor like Eleanor Ferguson, you didn't flout bans lightly. She'd have the hosepipe police on to you in a flash.

As it was, Eleanor's head soon popped up over the fence dividing their yards. Bernadette made a private bet with herself that the word *journalist* would feature in the third sentence Eleanor uttered.

"Morning," sang Eleanor. "Goodness, that looks like hard work!"

Bernadette smiled and nodded. *One.*

"Well, seems a shame to waste a nice sunny drying day like this: I think I'll wash my curtains."

"Good idea," said Bernadette, carefully watering her petunias. *Two—just.*

"Oh, by the way." Eleanor's tone was elaborately casual. "Did you manage to get ahold of that journalist chappie?"

Three. Bingo.

Without being aware of it—for they had only exchanged smiles and brief pleasantries in passing—Bernadette and Lili Ferguson had hit on precisely the same method of staying sane. Turning Eleanor's incurable nosiness into a form of entertainment made all the difference in the world—it really did the trick.

Bernadette shook her almost-empty watering can at the sweet peas and straightened up. "Yes, thank you. I did."

"Oh."

If Eleanor had had whiskers, they would have been aquiver. (Actually she *was* prone to whiskers, but she religiously plucked them out, using the excellent tweezers in her Swiss Army knife.)

"And…um, was it about something to do with the…the village?"

Bernadette took a deep breath. "As a matter of fact, he wanted to interview me about my work. But, as you know, I'm a private person. I really do prefer to keep myself to myself."

"Your work?"

Never mind aquiver—aquiver was old hat. Eleanor was, by this time, agog.

"I don't give interviews. I told him that and he understood," Bernadette concluded innocently, turning back toward the house with the empty watering can in her hand. "So thank you for taking an interest, but I'm afraid speaking to journalists isn't my idea of fun."

"But…" Eleanor's mouth was gaping, guppy fashion. "But…I don't… You've never told me what kind of work you do!"

Bernadette paused on her doorstep, as if giving the matter some thought. She exhaled slowly. "I'm sorry. Some people welcome publicity and some don't. I write books, that's all. Novels."

"You're a writer? But how *exciting*!" Eleanor's expression was avid. "I had no idea! What kind of novels do you write?"

Another pause, then Bernadette inclined her head toward her house.

"Come over if you like, and I'll show you."

Inside, the cottage was sparingly furnished but—Eleanor noted with approval—scrupulously clean.

As Bernadette reached up to the shelf above one of the recessed alcoves, her white lace petticoat showed beneath the hem of her pale-green shirtwaist dress. Eleanor approved of this too. In her opinion, far too many women these days went without petticoats.

"Here we are." Bernadette passed over a small handful of books. She looked embarrassed. "They don't exactly sell in their millions, but I scrape a living."

Eleanor was enthralled. Her next-door neighbor was a published author! Fancy that!

"Antonia Kay—that's your pen name, then? Your... what-d'you-call-it?"

"Pseudonym." Bernadette nodded. "Again, I prefer the privacy."

"Well, to think you actually wrote these yourself," Eleanor marveled. "I've always meant to write a book, but where would I find the time? Three and a half hours I was, yesterday, doing my daughter-in-law's ironing for her. Always busy, that's me. No time to *read* a book, let alone write one."

"Well, yes. Of course. I understand—"

"But I'll read yours," Eleanor exclaimed as Bernadette made a move to take the books back. "If you'd lend me one."

Bernadette retrieved the books anyway. She shuffled through them in search of the one she had stayed up reading until three o'clock this morning—not because it was unputdownable, but because if she was going to be lending it to Eleanor Ferguson, she needed at least some idea of what it was about.

"Here we are. This is the first one I wrote. And don't worry, I won't be offended if you hate it."

Greedily Eleanor clasped the book in both hands. Weren't first novels always autobiographical? This was the perfect way to get to know her odd, reclusive neighbor. "I'm sure it's wonderful," she declared with an air of grandeur. "I can't wait."

"And I'd be grateful if you'd keep this to yourself." Bernadette's tone was delicate. "I know I don't even need to ask; I can rely on your discretion. It's just that…well, the rest of the village…"

"Say no more. My lips are sealed." Regally, Eleanor leaned closer. "And I was thinking earlier: humping that heavy watering can up and down the garden can't be doing your back any good. You could always use your hosepipe, you know. I think under the circumstances, I can turn a blind eye." On her way out, still clutching the book triumphantly to her chest, she spotted a smallish framed photograph on a highly polished occasional table. Intrigued, since there were no other photos in sight, Eleanor stopped and picked it up.

"She looks pleasant."

The photograph was of a thin, shyly smiling woman in her early thirties. "Who's this then?" Eleanor waggled the frame at Bernadette. "Younger sister?"

"Er…just a friend."

Oh dear. When she saw the brief flush of color in Bernadette's cheeks, Eleanor understood at once. Her mouth instantly narrowed with disgust and disapproval. She regretted being so friendly now.

No wonder husbandless, childless Bernadette Thomas kept herself to herself.

Eleanor knew perfectly well what "Er…just a friend" meant.

———

Home from school, Harriet changed out of her uniform and into a T-shirt and shorts. When she looked at herself in the wardrobe mirror, her heart sank. Plain brown hair, plain gray eyes, and a totally useless, straight-up-and-down figure like a frankfurter. Hell's bells, when was she going to start going in and out?

At this rate I'll end up in an old folk's home, eighty years old, pushing a walker and still wearing a training bra, she thought, glancing out of her bedroom window and recognizing Dizzy Gillespie's lazy, loping walk as he made his way along Compass Lane, no doubt heading for the grocery store.

Huh, he's a dick anyway. Just like all the rest of them—obsessed with boobs.

And why? Why? Harriet wondered frustratedly. *What is the point?*

She dragged her sneakers out from under the bed, yanked open her sock drawer, and pulled out a pair of last winter's thick, gray hockey socks. Then, carefully rolling up each one in turn, she pulled up her T-shirt, tucking it under her chin, and stuffed them into her astonished—but luckily quite stretchy—bra.

———

"Oh, hi!" Dizzy was careful to look elaborately surprised when he saw Harriet. He would rather have died than admit he'd been hanging around hoping to bump into her ever since he'd seen her jump off the school bus.

"Hi." Harriet clung on to Blitz's leash as the dog hurled himself, yapping joyfully, at Dizzy. With great pride, she said, "His name's Blitz. He's our new dog. We got him yesterday."

"That's nothing," said Dizzy. "We got a new brother."

"What? You mean your mother actually gave birth?" Harriet's jaw dropped. "Crikey!"

"Nah—it's Oliver Roscoe."

"Oliver? *Crikey.*"

"Seems his old lady had a thing with our old man, years ago." Bending down, Dizzy nonchalantly ruffled Blitz's ears.

"Is that weird?" Harriet looked doubtful. She thought it must feel extremely weird to have a full-grown half brother suddenly pop out of nowhere.

Dizzy shrugged. "Dunno. I don't know him properly yet. You can't get a word in edgewise with Saveloy around. Still, he seems okay."

"Down, Blitz!" Harriet yanked the straining leash as the dog tried to scramble into the garbage can outside the shop. "He's after that ice-cream wrapper, I was about to take him for a walk in Compass Hill wood, give him a bit of a guided tour seeing as he's new to the area."

When she glanced up, Harriet saw Dizzy staring at her chest. For a split second, she panicked—but no, it was okay. It wasn't a you've-got-socks-stuffed-in-your-bra kind of stare. It was an admiring one. *For the first time in my life, I'm being eyed-up,* she thought delightedly. *Now I know how Moll Harper feels. Blimey, no wonder she always looks so pleased with herself.*

Yesterday's disgust with Dizzy, when he had—*yuck*—so grossly ogled Moll, had evaporated like morning mist. Now he was ogling *her*, and Harriet experienced a heady rush of power.

She no longer felt plain. She felt like…oh, like an enchantress.

"I'm new to the area," said Dizzy. "Can I come on your guided tour too?"

Harriet, flushed with triumph, was too busy being an enchantress to notice that Blitz was inching closer to the tantalizing ice-cream wrapper. Nor did she know that already occupying the wrapper was a contented wasp. Blitz launched himself, seizing the paper in his jaws. The wasp, outraged, buzzed furiously and stung the dog on the nose. Howling, Blitz leaped out of the garbage can and tried to hide behind Harriet. As his leash wrapped itself around her knees, he did another frantic circuit and Harriet, effectively lassoed, toppled to the ground.

"It's okay!" Dizzy shouted, grabbing Blitz by the collar and unraveling the leash from Harriet's bound legs. "I've got him! Poor, old boy, what did that wasp do to you, eh? That'll teach you to stick your nose in garbage cans." He crouched down and soothed the dog's wounded pride. When Harriet didn't move, he glanced at her. "You can get up now. What's the matter? Are you hurt?"

Harriet kept her arms clamped across her chest. It may not have been a violent toppling-over, but it had been enough to jolt one of the hockey socks out of her overstuffed bra.

Dizzy's concern turned to alarm when he saw which part of herself she was clutching. "Is it your heart?"

Oh yes, brilliant, thought Harriet, flinching as Blitz lunged forward with enthusiasm to lick her forehead. *Dial 999 and call an ambulance, why don't you? Tell them I need sock massage. Humiliate me completely...*

But since Dizzy looked as if he really might, she said stoically, "I'm fine. It's not my heart."

Just my sock.

Dizzy frowned. "You don't look fine to me."

"I feel a bit sick." Harriet pulled a nauseated face and massaged her chest a bit, wondering if she could somehow manage to slide the sock unobtrusively back into place. But it was hopeless. She had more chance of getting a jellyfish into a Coke bottle.

"Maybe if we start walking you'll feel better." Dizzy was unable to tear his eyes away. He'd give anything for the chance to massage her chest like that.

Harriet levered herself cautiously to her knees. "I don't think so. Actually, I think I'll just go home."

"Oh."

The sock began to slip. Harriet caught it just before it fell out from under her T-shirt. "I'll take Blitz." She grabbed the dog's leash with her free hand. *Bloody stupid animal.* Her cheeks burned as she turned hurriedly away, heading for the Old Vicarage. "Bye."

Something was definitely up. She wasn't ill. *Now* what had he said to upset her?

Feeling totally rejected, Dizzy stuffed his hands into the pockets of his baggy, holey jeans and said in a casual, I'm-not-bothered voice, "Okay, see ya."

Chapter 12

JESSIE CALLED IN ON Lili when she finished work at six. Harriet was entertaining Lottie and William in the sandbox at the far end of the yard, so they had the sunbaked patio to themselves. Better still, since Freya had already been picked up (by a beady-eyed Felicity), Lili could actually relax and pour herself a glass of wine.

Or even two.

"So what did Oliver call him? Dad?"

"Just Toby."

"God, imagine." Lili, who couldn't begin to, stretched out her pale legs and wished she could get them as brown as Jessie's. "Was it awkward?"

Jessie was feeding chips under the table to Blitz, who had come to cool off in the shade and dribble affectionate ribbons of saliva over her bare feet. "Not at all. I thought it might be, but it wasn't. Mainly thanks to Deborah, because she could have made it awkward. She didn't though. She was great."

"And you said she disappeared for an hour—so she isn't bothered about leaving you and Toby alone together. It doesn't worry her," Lili probed. "The fact that you two used to be…well, you know."

Jessie was busy polishing her sunglasses on the sleeve of her white shirt. "No, she's not jealous."

"Oh." Lili felt miffed on her friend's behalf. "Well, I suppose that's good in one way…"

"And not terribly flattering in the other," Jessie finished drily.

"Well, she could at least be a bit concerned." Lili was indignant. "How does she know you and Toby won't fall in love with each other all over again? You could be a huge threat to her marriage!"

"You mean, how dare she be so friendly?" Jessie teased, loving the way Lili's eyes grew bright as she sprang to her defense. "How dare she trust me not to snatch her husband from under her nose?"

"Oh, now you're making fun of me. But how does she know you wouldn't?"

"Come on. Deborah Gillespie is stunning. No best dressed list is complete without her name on it. She's glamorous and charming and about as nice as it's possible to get without actually making people physically sick. What's more," Jessie went on, counting the reasons on paint-stained fingers, "you only have to read the gossip columns to know they're the happiest married couple on the planet. And I should know," she added with a brief, rueful smile, "because I've been reading them for the last twenty years. Nobody, I promise you, has paid more attention to those articles than me."

Lili opened her mouth, then abruptly shut it again. This was an admission and a half coming from proud, fiercely independent Jess.

A diversion was created by William, at the bottom of the yard, emptying a bucket of sand over Lottie's head. Lottie screamed and gave him a resounding slap. William, grabbing handfuls of sand, flung them furiously in Lottie's face. Lili went to help Harriet separate them, thankful only that Hugh and Felicity weren't here to witness the fracas.

Order was eventually restored.

"So how do you feel about him? I mean, all that old stuff between you?" Lili ventured on her return. "Is the attraction still there?"

Jessie, prevaricating, said, "Things are a bit different now."

"And that's no answer. What I'm saying is, if Toby weren't married and he came around to your place tonight…" Lili's hazel eyes widened. "And he swept you into his arms and said, 'Oh, Jess, I've never been able to forget you,' *what would you do?*"

"Oh, he's already done all that."

"You are kidding!"

"Yes, I'm kidding."

Jessie was bursting to tell Lili everything. She knew she mustn't.

"God, I hate you," Lili groaned. Her heart had begun to gallop. She flopped back in her chair, patting her ample chest. "Don't *do* this to me."

Jessie, smiling faintly and twiddling the stem of her glass between her fingers, thought, *I wish Toby hadn't done it to me.*

Except that wasn't quite true. She was glad he had. Dammit, she had loved every blissful second.

She just wished he weren't married.

"What's this?" To change the subject, Jessie reached for the book lying facedown on the table. "Didn't know you were keen on this kind of thing."

"Eleanor brought it around this afternoon. You know that woman living next door to her? She wrote it."

"Really? Bernadette Thomas?"

Lili nodded and grinned. "It's been driving Eleanor mad for months, not being able to find out anything about her new neighbor. But she twisted those thumbscrews a few extra notches and finally wore Bernadette down. She cracked and admitted she was a novelist."

Interested, Jessie looked at the cover, which featured a rocking chair, a sleeping cat, and a grandfather clock. A John Grisham thriller it clearly wasn't. "So Eleanor's read this, has she? Did she enjoy it?"

"Ah, well, this is where it becomes interesting," said Lili. "She insisted I read it first. She put on her prune face and told me she had no intention of reading a book with marauding lesbians in it."

"*Marauding* lesbians? Good grief!" Jessie glanced again at the cover. "Not terribly likely, is it? Gentle, cake-baking lesbians maybe."

"Whatever. I'm the official censor, anyway. And Eleanor's torn between being thrilled to be living next door to a writer—even an unfamous one—and horrified by the discovery that she's gay."

"Poor woman," sighed Jessie, feeling deeply sorry for Bernadette. She'd feel sorry for anyone who had to live next door to Eleanor Ferguson.

"No wonder she keeps herself to herself." Lili was thinking along much the same lines. "I used to wonder if she was a bit odd—you know, one of those weird, reclusive types—but I bet that's *why* she's like it. She's probably afraid the rest of the village is as narrow-minded as Eleanor, and that once her secret gets out, we'll drown her in the duck pond."

Odd. Weird. Remembering Toby's words of the night before, Jessie tried to imagine Bernadette Thomas slipping an anonymous note through the letter box of Sisley House. Bernadette: the quiet lady novelist with the lovingly tended garden, the old-fashioned dresses, and the neatly bobbed brown-with-a-hint-of-auburn hair.

"Oh my God!" Lili gasped when Jessie told her about the anonymous note. "But how horrible! How could anyone do it? Nothing like that's ever happened here before."

It hadn't. And Bernadette Thomas had only moved to Upper Sisley a few months ago.

"Maybe it was someone's idea of a joke." Jessie bent down and rubbed Blitz's big, comforting, silky ears. The fact that Bernadette was a relative newcomer to the village was hardly rock-solid evidence. "Perhaps it won't happen again."

⌁

"It's who? Oh, hi, Melissa! Hang on. He's in the shower. DOUG!"

"What?"

"MELISSA ON THE PHONE!"

"Tell her I'm out."

"I CAN'T TELL HER YOU'RE OUT, YOU IDIOT. I JUST SAID YOU WERE IN THE SHOWER!"

Upstairs, Doug laughed to himself and carried on soaping his chest.

Downstairs, Jamie lowered his voice from a bellow to normal volume. "Melissa, hi. Listen, I *thought* he was in the shower, but—What?"

Even Drew, who was in the kitchen making himself an french-fry sandwich, could hear the furious squawking at the other end of the phone. The next minute, Jamie was staring at a silent receiver.

"She hung up. She called *me* a bastard," he said, aggrieved, "and just hung up. I don't get it. Doug's the one who's dumped her. How come I'm the bastard?"

Doug, coming down the stairs with a dark-green towel slung around his waist, said, "Anything to eat?"

"Why did you dump her anyway?" Jamie was fretful. He'd never dump someone like Melissa.

"She snored."

Hmm. Jamie wondered if—when she'd had a chance to cool down a bit—Melissa might be interested in going out with a vet instead. Snoring wouldn't bother him; he could always wear earplugs.

Drew watched Jamie resume his ironing. It was fascinating to see a man, a qualified vet capable of operating on a canary, make such a pig's ear of a shirt.

But Jamie was intent on his task. It was Friday night, he hadn't gotten laid in ages, and he was going to the Rattles Club in Harleston. What's more, he wasn't going to come home again until he *had* gotten laid.

"Sure you don't want to come along?" he said to Drew when he'd finished the shirt—after a fashion. A cab shared, after all, is a cab fare halved. "Come on, it's Friday night," he added persuasively. "The place'll be crawling with crumpet."

"Most of it underage," said Drew. God, he was twenty-nine,

almost thirty. He was too old to trawl the nightclubs in search of girls who would only bore him rigid within minutes. "What do you find to *talk* to them about, once you've asked them which school they go to?"

Astonished, Jamie said, "Who wants to talk?"

"Anyway, you can't call them crumpet. That's at least twenty years out of date. It's almost as bad as wearing a toupee and flares and calling girls 'chicks.'"

Jamie looked superior. "Flares are back in, so there."

"Wrong," said Drew. "Flares are back in for teenage girls. If you tried wearing them, I promise you, you'd be laughed out of the club."

"So you're not coming tonight?"

The phone rang again. Doug answered it.

"No." Finishing his french-fry sandwich, Drew licked his fingers. "You can keep your jailbait, your pounding music, and your overpriced drinks. I'm going to the Bells with Doug."

"God, you sound ancient," Jamie scoffed. "And I'm telling you now, you'll never meet any decent women in the Bells."

Doug, still on the phone, said, "Okay, great. Meet you in the Bells at eight thirty."

"Not Melissa," Jamie and Drew chorused when he had hung up.

"Not Melissa." Doug grinned as he reemerged from the kitchen, swigging from a can of Coke. "Patsy."

"Patsy." Jamie tried to remember. "Is she new?"

"Met her this morning. She brought her mother into the ER with a fractured femur."

Drew's heart sank. He didn't want to spend the evening watching Doug work his all-too-familiar magic while the besotted Patsy fell helplessly under his spell. He sighed.

"What?" said Doug.

Drew looked doubtful. "Am I going to be the third wheel?"

"Oh, come on," Doug protested, combing his wet hair into place and raising his eyebrows at Drew in the mirror. "Of course not."

Chapter 13

By EIGHT THIRTY, THE Seven Bells was filling up nicely. Drew's spirits lifted no end when Moll—looking luscious in a dark-red velvet bodice-type thing and a calf-length, swirly, black skirt—winked at him and ignored Doug completely.

"You two boys out on your own tonight?" asked Lorna Blake as she served them their drinks. Lorna always spoke her mind, wasn't afraid of anyone, looked as if she'd know how to handle a gun, and laughed uproariously at all the dirtiest jokes. Yet beneath the armor plating, she was as vulnerable as anyone. Devoted to her beloved cats, she freely admitted they were her surrogate children. When one of them had developed a malignant growth in the esophagus last year, she had been as distraught as any mother. Yet even this grief she had kept almost entirely to herself. Drew, who had finally been forced to put the cat down, was the only person in Upper Sisley ever to have seen her cry.

"Out on our own and looking for the women of our dreams." Doug rested his elbows on the bar, doing an unconvincing imitation of forlorn. "What I'm really after is someone with straight, shoulder-length hair; green eyes; a dazzling smile; and a white, sleeveless dress with yellow buttons all the way down the front."

"Oh, *you*!" Patsy cried delightedly over his shoulder. "I *crept* up behind you! How on earth did you know I was here?"

Drew and Lorna exchanged glances. That was it, done. Patsy was smitten already.

Is that really all it takes? Drew silently marveled. *The ability to out-blarney the Blarney Stone and a mirror behind the bar?*

"So tell me how it happened," he said to Patsy when Doug had performed the introductions and bought her a vodka and diet tonic. "Your mother broke her leg, you went along with her to the hospital, and the next thing you know, you're being asked out by this smooth-talking doctor."

Patsy smiled and glanced up at Doug from beneath her lashes. She carried on lovingly stroking his denim sleeve.

"Not quite," Doug said. "Actually, she asked me out."

Oliver flushed with pleasure twenty minutes later when the door swung open and Savannah, wearing a Manics tour T-shirt and frayed khaki shorts, sauntered up to the bar.

"Hi. You're late."

"Mum and Dad decided to come too." As she wriggled onto a barstool, Savannah surveyed the drinks. "They'll be here in a sec. I think I'll have a glass of red."

"How about white? We've got a terrific new Chardonnay." Oliver rummaged in the ice bucket, found the bottle he was looking for, and showed her the label.

Savannah giggled as droplets of icy water splashed on to her bare legs. "Okay, big brother, if that's what you recommend."

"Here they come," said Oliver as Toby and Deborah appeared.

"Blimey," Lorna Blake murmured as another brief hush descended on the bar, "it's like being visited by bloody royalty." She looked amused. "Why do people have to gawp? They'll be curtseying next."

"It'll be okay when the novelty wears off." Oliver, instinctively defending his new family, nodded toward Toby and Deborah. "Anyway, it's not their fault."

A ladybug had landed on Savannah's foot. Seeing that she was temporarily distracted, Lorna gave Oliver a nudge and said archly, "You're getting on well with the daughter, aren't you? Very cozy. Pretty girl, too. Although I'm not sure the big-brother image is quite what you're after. It's hardly—"

"But he is." Savannah, having flicked the ladybug off her ankle, was paying attention again. "He is my brother."

Oliver stared at her.

Stunned, Lorna stared at Oliver.

Savannah looked from one to the other and said, "Wasn't I supposed to say that? Is it meant to be a secret?" Her eyes widened in self-defense. "Nobody said anything about having to keep it a secret."

This was true—nobody had. But only because the subject hadn't come up yet. Feeling uneasy, Oliver poured the chilled wine and wondered how Toby was likely to react.

He didn't have long to wait.

"Are you serious?" Lorna said to Savannah.

"Serious about what?" Reaching the bar, Toby prodded his daughter in the ribs. "What's she done, asked for a gin and Baileys? Sav, I've told you before: you can't order a drink that looks like something the cat puked up."

"Oliver?" said Lorna.

"Don't look at me," Oliver replied hurriedly. "I didn't say anything."

Deborah said, "What's going on?"

Lorna, never afraid to speak out, turned her attention to Toby Gillespie. "Is Oliver your son?"

"Yes, he is." Toby, in turn, smiled at Oliver.

"So…so you and Jess…"

"Yes, we did."

"There," said Savannah, hugely relieved. "I told you it wasn't a secret."

Lorna Blake looked stunned. "But...we never knew that. You never told us." She turned to Oliver.

Oliver said simply, "I never knew."

—⁓—

Recognizing Drew at one of the tables at the far end of the bar, Deborah made her way over.

"Hello! I haven't forgotten I owe you a cup of milk."

Drew said, "And some dish soap."

"Not to mention several cans of lager." Clutching her forehead, Deborah mimed a hangover. "Maybe I should buy you a drink."

Flushed with pride and pleasure, Drew introduced her to Doug and Patsy.

"So you're the doctor," said Deborah. "I missed you last night."

"I knew I should have stayed in."

"And you work in the emergency room, Drew tells me. Is it as exciting as it looks in *ER*?"

"Oh well." Doug grinned. "*ER*'s pretty slow and dreary compared with Harleston General."

"So what's it like?" Deborah turned to Patsy. "Being a doctor's girlfriend?"

Patsy was overwhelmed—she was having quite a day. First her mother's leg, then Doug, and now here she was having an actual conversation with Deborah Gillespie. "I don't know yet. I only met him this morning." She giggled and squeezed Doug's arm. "But I don't care if he has to work long hours," she went on joyfully. "I'm sure it's going to be great."

Drew saw the look exchanged between Doug and Deborah.

"Lucky you," said Deborah. "There's something about a man in a white coat," she added with a complicit smile. "Don't you think?"

"I could always introduce you to Ernie Alpass," Drew offered. "He's the baker in the next village."

"Okay, a white coat and a stethoscope. But I'm right, aren't I?" Deborah went on. "Millions of women just go weak at the knees at the sight of a doctor. Why *is* that?"

If anyone knows the answer, it's Doug, Drew thought drily. Over the years he's certainly carried out enough research.

"The thing is, you can be the most respectable woman in the world," said Doug, "happily married and utterly faithful. But if a male doctor asks you to take your clothes off and lie down on the cot because he needs to examine you...well, you do it. Doctors are the only men in the world apart from your husband who get to see you naked."

"Unless you pose for *Playboy,*" Drew pointed out.

"So it's a power thing," Deborah mused, nodding. Leaning closer to Doug, she added, "Ah, but what about all you young, male doctors? Is it ever a turn-on, or does it just get boring in the end—seeing women's naked bodies day in, day out?"

"Are you kidding?" Doug's mouth twitched. "Why do you suppose we wear those long, white coats?"

After that, it started to get embarrassing. Drew saw what was happening and wished to God he'd stayed at home. He wished he could bring himself to get up and leave, but he couldn't, because then Patsy really wouldn't have had anyone to talk to.

Most of all, though, he wished Doug would leave Deborah Gillespie alone.

It wasn't Deborah's fault, he thought with growing irritation; she was treating Doug just as she treated everyone, with natural friendliness and effortless charm. Drew, having experienced this himself for the first time last night, had—okay, he admitted it—been utterly bowled over. Maybe even a bit smitten. But with a woman as stunning as Deborah Gillespie, that was only natural. Being smitten was par for the course. Anyone not smitten had to be pretty weird.

But the difference between us, Drew thought, *is I don't automatically assume Deborah Gillespie fancies me in return. And Doug clearly does.*

Doug couldn't take his eyes off her. He couldn't stop talking to her and he couldn't talk to her without touching her. He was firing on all cylinders, flirting as Drew had never seen him flirt before.

Poor Patsy wasn't getting a word in. Admittedly, she hadn't helped her cause, butting in excitedly at first with such gems as "I've seen all your husband's films" and "Fancy famous people like you coming out to a pub," but it was still cruel.

Drew spent an unhappy hour trying to make polite conversation—so that maybe Patsy wouldn't notice the way Doug was ignoring her—and buying hundreds of rounds of drinks. By ten o'clock, Patsy had had enough. Tears glittered on her eyelashes as she scraped her chair back and stood up. Drew wondered if she was about to tip Doug's untouched pint over his head—which would have been good—but it didn't happen. All Patsy flung at him was a look of anger, which was wasted, frankly, since Doug was too busy flirting with Deborah to notice.

Chapter 14

DREW CAUGHT UP WITH Patsy in the corridor leading to the loos. She slumped against the whitewashed wall, clutching her white leather handbag like a security blanket, her mouth wobbling and her face blotchy with the effort it was taking not to cry.

"What a bastard. Is he always like this?"

"Well, yes."

"It's so humiliating. I thought he really liked me."

"I'm sorry," said Drew. *God, talk about pathetic. Doug does this to her and I'm the one saying sorry.*

"I was so excited when he asked me out." Patsy's voice began to break. "I told all my roommates how dishy he was and they were really j-j-jealous."

"Here." The mascara was beginning to slide. As Drew passed her a handkerchief, he realized he was doing it again. The world, it seemed, was divided into two kinds of men: the good-looking ones who make girls cry, and the rest, who supply the mopping-up equipment.

"What am I going to do?" Patsy trumpeted into the hanky, blowing her nose in front of Drew as she would never have dreamed of blowing her nose in front of Doug. "I told them not to expect me home tonight. I can't drive back now. They'll laugh at me."

Drew made the supreme sacrifice.

"Look, I'll phone for a cab. We'll go into Harleston." He didn't want to, but she was so desperate. "I'll take you to Rattles. How about that?"

"Not likely. That's where my roommates'll be. I've told them I'm going out with a drop-dead-gorgeous doctor." Patsy was distraught, beyond caring. "They're hardly going to be impressed, are they," she sobbed, "when I turn up with you instead?"

———

"Where's…?" said Doug when Drew reappeared.

"Patsy. She's gone."

"What, to buy a drink?"

"She's left. Gone home." Drew spoke evenly. "I'm amazed you noticed she was missing. Even if you couldn't remember her name."

Deborah looked horrified. "You're not serious! Oh Lord, this is all my fault. I just know it is. I only popped over to say hello and I've been here for"—she peered at her watch—"good grief, an *hour*. That poor girl! No wonder she got fed up. Once I start yakking, no one else can get a word in edgewise."

"Please," said Doug, "relax. She wasn't important."

Drew's fingers closed over the slip of paper in the palm of his hand. Even with the tears rolling down her cheeks, as she'd climbed into the taxi, Patsy hadn't been able to stop herself burrowing frantically in her bag and scribbling her phone number on the back of an old Sainsbury's receipt. "Just in case he wants to ring me," she had said, embarrassment mingling with desperation as she pressed it into Drew's hand. "I know. Don't say it. But he might change his mind."

Drew crumpled up the receipt and dropped it on the floor.

"Litter bug," said Moll, clearing glasses at the next table.

"But you were important to her," Deborah exclaimed, shaking her head. "This is awful. I feel *terrible*."

Moll was humming to herself as she gave the empty table an energetic wipe down. Glad of the distraction, Drew watched the way her amazing breasts danced a little dance together in absolutely perfect time. They were, he decided, the Astaire and Rogers of breasts.

When Moll glanced across and gave him one of her smiles, Drew said in a low voice, "Can I take you out to dinner one night?"

He had drunk enough to enable the words to slip out with ease.

"Sounds great," said Moll. "I'm not sure yet which evenings I'm working, but I can always ask Lorna."

"How about coming back to the cottage with me tonight?" Drew realized he didn't want to sleep with Moll sometime next week; he wanted to sleep with her now.

The great thing about Moll was, she was never offended.

The bad thing about her was she sometimes said no.

Moll, who was fond of Drew, smiled again and shook her head. "I don't think so, not tonight. I'm pretty exhausted."

He didn't even have a chance to try to change her mind. With a last swish of her cloth and a clink of glass, Moll was gone.

Drew downed his pint and ruminated on the fact that tonight clearly wasn't going to be his night for getting laid.

At least neither Doug nor Deborah had heard him being turned down.

"It's been great seeing you again," Deborah told him, standing up. She turned from Drew to Doug. "Lovely meeting you, as well. I'd better head back to my group. They're going to wonder where I've got to." She winked at Drew. "Again."

Drew watched Doug smile at her and squeeze her hand.

"See you again soon."

They both watched Deborah make her way back to the far end of the bar, slip her arm around Toby Gillespie's waist, and say something that made Lorna Blake throw back her head and laugh.

"She is stunning," Doug breathed out slowly.

Drew said, "Her husband thinks so too."

Amused, Doug changed the subject. "Shame about Patsy going off in a huff. That's the trouble with girls like her. They're like policemen, never around when you need them."

"She was crying."

"She'll live."

"You are such a shit." Drew pushed his chair back and drained his glass.

"It's my round," Doug protested as he rose to his feet. "I'll get these."

"Not for me." Drew couldn't be bothered to stay. He couldn't be bothered to drink any more, even if Doug was buying. "I'm going home."

––––––

Drew woke up with a start, midway through a dream about Lili Ferguson. For a split second, he was able to recall the dream with utter clarity: Lili was running across the village green stark naked, being chased by her mother-in-law clutching a pile of white lab coats. Eleanor Ferguson was shouting, "It took me three hours to iron these. For pity's sake, put one on, girl! Cover yourself up before anyone sees you. You're a disgrace!"

And I was standing outside the pub watching them, thought Drew, *and I yelled out to Lili… Dammit, I yelled something out to Lili. What did I yell?*

But it was useless. The dream had gone, slithering away like mercury. Drew gave up trying to remember and rolled onto his back. It was a hot night and he had developed a raging thirst. Peering at the luminous hands on his watch, he discovered he hadn't been asleep for hours after all. It was still only twenty past midnight.

Then he heard a creaking door downstairs, followed by the sound of footsteps, and he realized that this was what had woken him up.

God, he was thirsty! That was what fifteen lagers did for you. Rolling onto his side again, he felt around on the floor next to the bed until he found an empty pint glass. Okay, he'd called Doug a shit earlier, but he wouldn't have taken offense, would he? If he asked him now to fill up the glass from the bathroom tap, Doug would do it. Save having to get out of bed.

About to call out, Drew heard whispering. He closed his mouth again and listened harder.

There were two sets of footsteps on the stairs.

Doug murmured, "It's okay. He's asleep."

This was followed moments later by a burst of laughter and a muffled shriek.

"Doug, get off! Not on the staircase!"

Drew closed his eyes. It was Moll's voice.

As his thirst raged on, he clutched the dusty glass to his chest, not even noticing as a hugely grateful hairy-legged spider scuttled out.

Chapter 15

THE JOURNALIST FROM THE *Daily Mail* arrived the following Tuesday, promptly at eleven thirty.

"Is this going to be awful?" said Jessie, watching the car pull up the drive. She was apprehensive, never having had to deal with the press before.

"Don't worry. It'll be fine." Toby put down the script he'd been reading and came to stand behind her at the window. "This woman's one of the best. Anyway, far better to do it like this, all over in one go." He gave Jessie's shoulder a reassuring squeeze. "As soon as they've got what they want, they leave you alone. Start slamming doors in their faces and yelling 'no comment,' and you'll have them pestering you for months, digging for dirt and making up all kinds of rubbish."

The journalist was climbing out of her car, lowering her dark glasses in order to study the front of the house. Jessie, damp with sweat, wished she could be back upstairs in her overalls, getting on with the marbling she'd started yesterday in the master bathroom. The walls had already been primed and undercoated. She had given them two coats of eggshell. This morning, she had begun applying the glaze, made up from equal parts of raw linseed oil, white spirit, and white undercoat. Now, with a fine, hog's-hair brush, a dust brush with tapered bristles, a goose feather, and a soft cloth, she was ready to create the marbling effect.

Except I'm not, thought Jessie as the doorbell rang. *I'm down here instead, about to be interviewed by one of the shrewdest journalists in the business.*

And if that on its own wasn't scary enough, Jessie had another worry. The journalist wasn't only going to go over all that old stuff, was she? She was bound to ask how Jessie and Toby felt about each other now.

Fibbing to Lili was one thing, but lying convincingly to an eagle-eyed journalist was quite another.

Jessie just prayed she'd be able to pull it off without going puce.

———

She didn't blush, thank God. When the subject came up, Toby laughed and said easily, "Wouldn't it have been great? Like a Hollywood film. Except I wouldn't have married and had a family. I'd have to have been a lonely old bachelor, bitter and miserable for twenty years before finally rediscovering my lost love."

The journalist laughed too, and Deborah knocked on the door, poking her head around.

"Lunch is ready. We're eating out on the terrace. Jess, are you really allergic to lobster, or is Oliver having me on?"

Jessie smiled and said, "He's joking. It's my absolute favorite."

"How about you, Jessie?" the journalist asked as they made their way through the house. "After all, you never did marry, did you?"

"I haven't spent the last twenty years being bitter and miserable either." Jessie concentrated on a white wall, which was supposed to help. *Oh please, don't let me blush, mustn't blush...*

"Look at him, though. Toby Gillespie, hugely successful, stunningly attractive." The older woman lowered her voice. "You must still have some feelings for him."

"It's water under the bridge now." Jessie could feel the perspiration prickling along her spine. "We've both grown up. We get on well together." She shrugged damply. "That's as far as it goes."

"But you *loved* each other."

"Look, did you ever eat a reheated baked potato?"

"Well—"

"It still looks like a baked potato. It even tastes like a baked potato," Jessie improvised wildly as they stepped out on to the terrace, "but it's been reheated, so it just isn't the same."

Oliver, Savannah, and Dizzy were already sitting around the table. The journalist was charmed by Oliver, and he, in turn, answered her questions with cheerful enthusiasm.

"God no, I've never wanted to be an actor. I was pressed into being a donkey once in the school nativity play and that put me off for life."

"He told me about that." Savannah giggled. "He said one of the shepherds spent the entire performance trying to shove a raw carrot up his nose."

"I did that once," Dizzy joined in eagerly. "Well, it was a broad bean, but I got it stuck up my nose. Didn't I, Mum? Remember—you had to take me to the ER?"

"Speaking of the emergency room." Deborah was mopping up salad dressing from her plate with a piece of olive bread. "I forgot to tell you, Jess. We met Doug Flynn on Friday night. He was in the pub with Drew."

The lobster was heavenly; Jessie had to force herself not to lick the plate. She confined herself to licking her fingers instead and glanced across the table at Deborah. "So, what's the verdict?"

Deborah rolled her dark eyes. "Well, *doesn't* he think he's gorgeous?"

"Absolutely. The bee's knees." Jessie was grinning. "Trouble is, he's not the only one."

"Um, so I gathered."

"That chap you were talking to for ages?" Savannah looked indignant. "Why are you both laughing like that? He *was* gorgeous. I thought he was completely—"

"Don't even think it," Jessie protested. "Yogurts have a longer shelf life than Doug Flynn's girlfriends."

Deborah gave her daughter's arm a consoling pat. "There you are, darling. You wouldn't want a use-by date stamped on your bottom."

"He disappeared with Moll on Friday," put in Oliver.

"Ah well, that's allowed," Jessie said easily. "He won't break her heart, will he? He knows he's safe with Moll; they're two of a kind."

"God, sorry," Dizzy exclaimed, accidentally knocking over the journalist's glass of red at the thought of Moll's breasts.

The photographer arrived as they were finishing lunch. For the next hour and a half, he took endless assorted group photos.

Jessie and Deborah were sitting together on the lawn watching him use up another reel of film on Oliver, Savannah, and Dizzy when the journalist rejoined them.

"Oliver, move closer to Dizzy," the photographer instructed. "And, Savannah, pull your skirt down, darling—we don't want to see your underwear."

"*He* doesn't, certainly," Deborah murmured to Jessie. "He's gay."

The journalist smiled. "You really do get along together well, don't you? I'm going to enjoy writing this piece. Our readers love a story with a happy ending."

"Come back and see us in a year," said Deborah. "It could all be different then. Just think," she went on playfully, "Toby could leave me for Lorna, the pub's owner."

"Dizzy could have a torrid affair with Moll, the man-eating trollop," said Jessie, joining in.

"Oliver can be his rival in love. They can fight a duel on the village green." Deborah's eyes were alight with laughter. "And Savvy could get hopelessly entangled with devilish doctor Doug. He'd dump her, of course."

"I was going to have an affair with him," Jessie protested.

"Go on, then," Deborah said generously. "You can tame him. He can fall in love with you and that'll make Savvy madly jealous."

Jessie, who had been trying to make a daisy chain, pulled a face. "I'm going off this idea already. You can have Doug if you want."

"Thanks, but no thanks." Deborah looked cheerful. "I've rather got my eye on dashing Mr. Darcy."

The journalist, who had always hankered after a cottage in the country but had worried that village life might be boring, looked enthralled. "Heavens, is he as handsome and arrogant as he sounds?"

Deborah burst out laughing. "Drew Darcy, bless his heart, is about as arrogant and handsome as a battered, old sofa. Savvy, push your hair away from your face. And stop swinging your legs!"

Shielding her eyes from the midafternoon sun, the journalist watched her photographer attempt to organize a shot of Oliver and Savannah sitting together on the wall. "Look at them, both so blond and tanned. They certainly make a striking pair." She smiled at Jessie and Deborah. "You must be proud of them."

"I'd be a lot prouder," said Deborah, "if my daughter wasn't still flashing her underpants. *Savvy!*" She raised her voice again. "Knees together, skirt *down*!"

"She's a stunning girl though."

"Oh, she's the one with the looks," Deborah agreed, rolling onto her front and propping herself up on her elbows. "Poor, old Dizz... Well, fingers crossed, he'll improve as he gets older."

Dizzy, lying unnoticed in a hammock some fifteen feet behind them, already knew why the photographer was taking so many more shots of Savannah than he had of him. She was the photogenic one, and he was the lank-haired adolescent. He was used to the lack of attention and he didn't need to overhear his mother's tactless remarks to know he was no Brad Pitt.

It still hurt though.

"Wonderful, great, terrific," chirruped the photographer, snapping away ecstatically across the lawn. "Ollie, move your head closer to your sister's. That's it, that's it, you're a *star*."

The photographer probably fancied Oliver too, Dizzy decided, closing his eyes and making the hammock sway from side to side. He pulled his baseball cap lower over his face and gave himself up to the far more pleasurable fantasy he had overheard earlier, the thrilling one suggested by Jess.

The one about me, Dizzy thought happily, *having a torrid affair with man-eating Moll.*

⁓

When the journalist and the photographer had left for London, Jessie went back upstairs to her marbling. After visiting her briefly, Toby came back down and found Oliver eating leftover salad in the kitchen. Dizzy was still in his hammock, Savannah was chattering on the phone to a school friend, and Deborah was in the sitting room, catching up with tennis on television.

"I've had a word with Jess and she's agreed." Toby plunged straight in. "Look, this Europe trip of yours. When were you planning to go?"

Oliver was taken aback. What was this about? Surely they weren't suggesting he call it off?

"As soon as I've got enough money," he said defensively. "I'm saving as hard as I can. The idea is to work here for three months, go off for three months, come back and work in the pub for another three months, then take off again. That's the theory anyway," he concluded worriedly. "Cash flow permitting."

"Well, I can help you there." Toby held out a folded check.

Oliver took it and stared at the figures. "I don't believe it. Five thousand pounds!"

"I've got some catching up to do," said Toby. "Please, just take it."

Oliver was still gazing at the check in wonder. "This is amazing. I could go to Europe straightaway. I could go *tomorrow*."

"You don't have to rush off quite that fast. And don't think I'm trying to get rid of you," Toby went on hurriedly, "because that's the last thing I want. I just know it's what you want to do. And I'd like to help out."

Overwhelmed, Oliver shoved the check into his jeans pocket.

"Thanks. I don't know what else to say." *Paris, Tuscany, Rome, Vienna...I can do it all...*

"Nothing. You don't need to thank me."

"Is it okay to tell the others? I mean, can I tell Sav?"

As he said it, the sound of Savannah screeching with laughter drifted through the hall. Toby, who was waiting for a call to come through from his agent, lifted his eyebrows in resignation.

"Of course. That is, if you ever manage to get her off the damn phone."

Chapter 16

Oliver and Savannah were banished to Savannah's bedroom.

"It's Dad's idea of hell, having to watch himself on TV." Savannah put the DVD into the machine, then threw herself onto the bed and rummaged under the crumpled duvet for the remote control. "If we ever want to watch anything of his, we have to do it well out of earshot. This film's one of my favorites actually. I can't believe you've never seen it." Pressing fast-forward, whizzing through the opening titles, Savannah jabbered on. "Four BAFTA nominations, an Oscar for best supporting actress, and the theme song went to number one in seven countries, *including* Belgium, so if you visit Belgium on your grand tour—"

"Shh," said Oliver, taking the remote control from her and pressing play. He slid down into a sitting position on the floor and turned the volume up, wondering why Savannah was so rattled. Something was up. He really hoped it wasn't what he thought it was. "Let's just watch the film."

He tried, but it was hard to get into a psychological thriller when the person noisily filing their nails behind you kept telling you what was about to happen next.

"As soon as he's fallen asleep, she sneaks out to meet the lawyer. She thinks he's on her side but he isn't."

"Thanks."

They watched Toby kissing the actress.

"Weird, isn't it? Seeing your own father kiss another woman.

Everyone thinks she's so perfect," Savannah went on, "but Dad says she had diabolical bad breath. It was like kissing King Kong."

"I can't hear this." Oliver turned up the volume again.

"They go to Venice next, to see the lawyer's cousin. I expect you'll visit Venice, won't you? Do all those dorky touristy things."

"Right," said Oliver, switching off the video and swiveling round to face her. "That's it. You win. Now why don't you tell me what this is all about?" His jaw was tense. "Or can I guess?"

Savannah avoided his eyes. She carried on filing her nails, faster and faster. "I don't know what you mean."

"Don't you? I think I do."

"Go on then." File, file. "You tell me."

"It's the money, isn't it?" Oliver reached over and took the emery board away from her; it was a miracle she had any nails left. "The check for five thousand pounds. You don't think he should have given it to me."

This time Savannah looked straight at him. "I *wish* he bloody hadn't given it to you, that's for sure."

"Because you think it's unfair." Oliver was lacerated with guilt. "He's given me all that money, and he hasn't given you the same amount—"

"Oh, come on, don't be such an idiot!" Savannah howled suddenly. "I'm not jealous! I'm...I'm..."

Bemused, Oliver said, "You're what?"

"I'm *miserable*." She promptly burst into tears. "I don't want you to go."

What was going on? Helplessly, Oliver said, "You've lost me."

"I know. That's just it," Savannah sobbed, wiping her eyes with a handful of duvet. "I don't *want* to lose you. We've only just found you and the last week's been so brilliant...and now you're going away for months and months...and I'm going to h-hate it so m-m-much."

Touched beyond belief, Oliver ruffled her curtain of blond hair. There was even a lump in his own throat.

"Please, please don't cry. I'll miss you too, but it won't be forever. I'll send postcards," he said soothingly.

"Oh, brilliant." Savannah sniffed. "That'll make all the difference."

"We can talk to each other on the phone."

"It won't be the same!" she wailed.

"I know." Oliver looked unhappy. Hell, now she was making him feel terrible. "But if you knew how long I've dreamed of going to Europe. We've never had any money. I've never even been abroad, you see. The most Mum could manage was an RV vacation in Totnes."

Savannah reached for her nightie—actually an extra-large Oasis T-shirt—and blew her nose on it. Liam's face got off worst. "And we've been everywhere. God, I'm a selfish cow! It's just such rotten timing, that's all." She dredged up a watery smile. "It's your fault. Why couldn't you take your gap year at the same time as everyone else?"

"You really want to know?" Oliver grinned, hugely relieved she'd stopped crying at last. "I was seeing this girl. We were mad about each other. When she said she was applying for a place at Exeter, I couldn't bear the thought of her meeting someone else. So that was it. I applied too. And we both got in."

"What was her name?"

"Claire."

"Pretty?"

He looked offended. "Of course she was pretty. I don't go out with dogs."

"So what happened?" Savannah said.

"It lasted about three months." Oliver's shrug was philosophical; this had all happened three long years ago. "Then the novelty wore off."

"But who finished with who?"

"We just gradually drifted apart. I was into sports, and she liked singing madrigals."

Savannah nodded, envisaging a pretty girl warbling churchy-type songs. Was she tall or short, thin or fat, blond or dark?

Oh my God, thought Savannah, *I'm jealous of Claire.*

"When will you go?" she asked Oliver bravely. "Did you mean it about setting off next week?"

Quite suddenly, next week seemed awfully soon. Oliver thought of the brand-new passport he had acquired in April, sitting in his sock drawer at home. It would be short notice, anyway, for Lorna to replace him in the pub. He couldn't leave her in the lurch, could he?

"No hurry," he told Savannah, his tone reassuring. "These trips take time to plan properly. Maybe in a couple of months."

Savannah was relieved. Two months, that was eight weeks. Eight weeks was ages away.

She nodded. "Okay."

"Now," said Oliver, waving the remote control, "maybe we could watch the rest of this film."

The doorbell rang at eight o'clock that evening just as Toby was coming down the stairs. When he saw the outline of a motorcyclist's helmet through the stained glass he assumed his agent had arranged for the script he'd been waiting for to be delivered by courier.

Instead, when he opened the door, he was knocked sideways by a great waft of garlic.

"Pizza delivery," announced a muffled voice, thrusting a pile of eight boxes at Toby. Pulling a bill from his pocket, he added, "That'll be seventy-three pounds eighty."

"Sorry, wrong address."

"Gillespie, Sisley House, Upper Sisley," recited the delivery boy.

Now that his own hands were free he flipped up his visor. "Hey, you're that film star, Can I have your autograph?"

"We haven't ordered any pizzas."

"Come on," the boy protested. "I've come all the way from Harleston. We don't even come this far out normally, but you promised to pay an extra twenty quid for delivery. See?" He pointed to the bill.

"I didn't promise anything," said Toby, "because I didn't phone you."

"What is it?" Dizzy, appearing behind Toby, peered over his shoulders and sniffed. "Pizzas? Hey, Dad, great! I'm starving."

"But I haven't—"

"Mr. Gillespie, I've come all this way. It's my first week on the job." The boy began to look scared. "Do you have any idea what my boss'll do to me if I go back with eight cold pizzas and no money?"

Toby heaved a sigh and reached for his wallet. Dizzy joyfully seized the pizzas and disappeared into the kitchen.

"You might want to stick them in the oven," said the delivery boy as he shoved the bundle of notes into his pocket. "I had a flat tire on the way over."

"Right." Wearily Toby began to close the door.

The boy put his foot over the step to stop him. "Aren't you forgetting something, Mr. Gillespie? Autograph?"

"Ugh!" Savannah surveyed the pizzas in disgust. "They've all got extra anchovies. What did you do that for, Dad? You know none of us can stand anchovies."

"I didn't order the bloody pizzas," said Toby, exasperated, "let alone the anchovies."

"Don't be so fussy." Dizzy gave his sister a look of scorn. "You can peel them off."

Savannah looked mystified. "So who did order them?"

"I don't know." The same person, Toby presumed, who had delivered the anonymous note. "Just someone's idea of a joke."

"Well, we can't eat all eight," said Deborah. "Why don't I take a few next door? Maybe Drew or Doug would be glad of them."

She took three of the pizzas around to Keeper's Cottage, but both Doug and Drew were out at work.

Jamie, unable to believe his luck, thanked Deborah and offered her a can of Guinness, which, regretfully, she declined.

Then he sat down to watch yet more cricket, showered the pizzas with chili sauce, and happily ate all three.

Chapter 17

LILI WAS ON HER hands and knees in the kitchen performing a mass diaper change when Michael arrived home on Friday afternoon.

William, as agile as an eel, squirmed off the changing mat and out of reach the moment Lili had cleaned him up. Rather than hare around trying to catch him, she armed herself with more baby wipes and decided to tackle Freya's diaper. The stench was horrendous. William, screeching with delight, yelled, "Pooh, yuck!" and raced around the kitchen table, weeing at intervals on the floor.

"I'm back," Michael announced, opening the door. "God, what a smell! William, Daddy's home. Come and give me a hug."

"Nooo!" howled William, alarmed by the sudden appearance of the father he hadn't seen for three months and going briskly into reverse. He cannoned into the dog basket, tipped over backward, and landed on Blitz. Yelping, Blitz shot out of the basket, skidded in a puddle of wee, and ricocheted off Michael's legs.

"Hello, darling." Lili scrambled to her feet before Michael, who was standing behind her with a grandstand view of her track-suited bottom, could tell her she'd put on weight. "You're early. William, stop hiding. It's Daddy. Hang on, I need to get rid of these and wash my hands."

Michael flinched as she headed past him with the offending diapers. William peered at him over the rim of the dog basket.

"You're a pushover, that's your trouble," Michael told Lili. He looked without enthusiasm at Blitz, who was tentatively wagging his tail. "Let me guess. The owners are away on vacation, and they asked you to look after it for a couple of weeks, save them forking out on kennel fees—"

"Actually he's ours." Lili, scrubbing her hands at the sink, gave him a bright, over-the-shoulder smile.

"This is a joke," said Michael slowly.

"He's adorable. Brilliant with the children—they love him to bits."

"I don't like dogs."

"And company for me." Having dried her hands, Lili crossed the kitchen and dutifully gave her travel-weary husband a peck on the cheek. His suit was crumpled, and he smelled of all the different aftershaves he'd tried out in the duty-free shops. "He's got a lovely temperament, wouldn't hurt a fly. Anyway, it makes sense to have a guard dog—"

"Oh, perfect sense. Especially one that wouldn't hurt a fly."

Eagerly, Lili said, "But he can bark. He's terrific at barking! That'll be enough to scare any burglars away."

"In other words it's a fait accompli." Michael's jaw tightened. "You know I can't stand dogs, but you went ahead and got one anyway." He slung his jacket over his shoulder and headed for the kitchen door. "I mean, why should I have a say in anything? I'm only the one who slogs his guts out to pay the bills and support you all."

"Where are you going?" Lili said, feeling a bit sick. This wasn't the best of starts.

"Upstairs, to take a shower. After all," Michael added, "I want to be smart for the occasion."

Freya poked William in the eye. William let out a roar and gave her a thump back.

"What occasion?" Lili had to raise her voice to be heard over the cacophony of wails.

"The massive surprise party you've organized to celebrate my happy homecoming."

Sarcasm. Oh help.

"Your mother's coming over at seven,"

"That's all I need."

"It's steak and fries for dinner," Lili said hopefully. "I got some really nice sirloin yesterday. Your favorite." She was patting Blitz, stroking his silky ears as she spoke.

"Well, it's easy to see who's the most popular around here," Michael said. "You may as well just open a can of Pedigree Chum for me and give the steak to the dog."

As he stood under the shower, Michael acknowledged that he had overreacted downstairs. The dog was only partly to blame for his short temper; for the first time since leaving school, he had suffered the indignity this morning of actually being dumped.

His fling with Sandra had begun three months earlier. When you both worked for the same company in Dubai and socialized with the same crowd, it seemed a natural progression—sooner or later—to end up in the same bed. And Michael had been more than happy with the situation. As with most of his extracurricular relationships, Sandra was the opposite of Lili. Thin, with short, dark hair, she wore business suits and worked as hard as she played. He needed a mistress who knew her own mind, one who didn't make a fuss over nothing, and Sandra fitted the bill.

Annoyingly, she hadn't made a fuss about this morning either, when Michael had dropped in to say good-bye. "It's been fun, Mike, but now it's over," she had told him breezily, quite out of the blue.

His stomach still lurched at the recent memory. Okay, theirs wasn't the romance of the century, but why on earth would she want to end it?

"But...but..." he had spluttered, standing in the middle of her apartment while she sat back and efficiently lit a cigarette.

"I've been seeing quite a bit of Ned Armstrong," Sandra announced. "Oh, come on. Cheer up. You're going home to little wifey and the kids, aren't you? You'll be gone for eight weeks. What did you expect me to do, put myself on ice until you get back?"

And that had been that. Done and dusted. Sandra had given him a brisk kiss good-bye and he had driven in a daze to the airport, maybe not heartbroken but definitely put out.

Hence the filthy mood.

Michael sighed and switched off the shower. It wasn't Lili's fault; he mustn't take it out on her.

Lili was chopping mushrooms to go with the steak when he returned downstairs. Moving up behind her, he slid his arms around her waist and nuzzled her soft neck.

"Rough journey. I'm sorry."

"Me too." His chin was bristly. Lili resisted the urge to duck away. *Once upon a time,* she thought guiltily, *I loved having my neck nuzzled by Michael.*

He peered out of the window. The dog was in the garden, joyously digging up Lili's prized herbaceous border. Pushing open the door to the sitting room, Michael saw William and Freya fast asleep together on the sofa.

"Where's Lottie?"

"Birthday party." Lili was deeply envious of Lottie's social life, which was as hectic as any debutante's.

"And Harriet?"

"Swimming." *Oh dear,* thought Lili, *no wonder he's miffed. He must feel horribly left out.* She said apologetically, "We weren't expecting you back till six."

Michael wasn't the least bit miffed; this was fine by him. When you hadn't seen your wife for three months, the sex was always more fun; it was like riding a new bike.

"Argh!" Lili screeched as a warm hand snaked beneath the elasticized waistband of her tracksuit bottoms. The chopping knife slipped from her grasp as Michael's other hand deftly unfastened her bra.

This was his party trick and he was immensely proud of it, but Lili could have done with some warning. Mushrooms went flying and the knife pirouetted to the floor, bouncing off her ankle en route.

"Mike...not now!"

"*Yes*, now."

"But the children—"

"Are asleep." He began enthusiastically to drag her tracksuit trousers down over her hips.

Lili, trying hard to tug them back up again, gasped, "They might wake up!"

"Any more excuses," Michael murmured, maneuvering her toward the kitchen table, "and I just might take offense."

"Oh my God!" Lili yelped as a movement at the kitchen window caught her eye. "Get off me. Felicity's here!"

It was close, but as she stumbled to the door Lili consoled herself with the knowledge that it could have been a hundred times worse. If Felicity had turned up just five minutes later...

Except then, she thought, *it would have been over and done with, and I'd have been back to chopping mushrooms.*

"You're early," she exclaimed brightly, smoothing her T-shirt over her hips and thanking her lucky stars Michael hadn't managed to tug her tracksuit bottoms right off.

Felicity's jaw was rigid. "Where's Freya?"

"She's fine—fast asleep in the other room," Lili babbled. "Oh, she's been as good as gold."

"Can I see her?"

"And here's Michael, home again after three months!"

"So I see," Felicity said, pink-cheeked with disapproval. "By the way, there's a knife on the floor behind you."

Lili was consumed with guilt. She pushed open the sitting-room door and watched Felicity scoop the sleeping Freya into her arms, murmuring, "It's all right, darling, Mummy's here now."

"I'm so sorry. Michael's just glad to be back." As she spoke, Lili wondered if this was it, whether this time she really was about to get the sack. She couldn't for the life of her imagine Hugh and Felicity being overcome with lust and doing it on the kitchen table. She couldn't even imagine them doing it on less-than-perfectly ironed sheets.

To Lili's amazement, it was Michael who came to her rescue.

"I'm entirely to blame," he announced, appearing in the doorway and smiling broadly at Felicity. "Please don't be cross with Lili. I ambushed her. The reason I wasn't getting anywhere," he explained ruefully, "was because she kept yelling that she couldn't leave the children."

"I understand." Felicity's expression softened. She stroked Freya's rosebud mouth adoringly as a ribbon of dribble draped itself across her lime-green Jasper Conran jacket. "Anyway, we'll be off." With a flicker of a smile, she said to Michael, "Have a nice evening."

"You *charmed* her," Lili exclaimed when Felicity and Freya had left. "I don't believe it. How did you *do* that? You actually made the Ice Queen smile!"

Michael wondered for a brief moment if a fling with Felicity Seymour would be playing it a bit too close to home. Reluctantly he decided it would. That was the trouble with small villages—you couldn't get away with a damn thing.

Happily, William was still sprawled across the sofa, fast asleep and lovingly clutching a naked Barbie to his chest.

Moving toward Lili with a familiar sparkle in his eyes, Michael said, "Like father, like son. I think he has the right idea, don't you?"

"Did Lili tell you about that new next-door neighbor of mine?" asked Eleanor that evening, over coffee and slices of the fruit cake she had brought around in a tin because "I guessed you wouldn't have had time to make him one, dear."

Lili had fought back the urge to reply innocently, "No, we were too busy having sex."

Michael looked bemused. "No."

"Writes books," Eleanor began triumphantly.

"Ahem," said Lili. "Didn't she want to keep it quiet?"

"Ha! That's not all she wants kept quiet! Being a writer wasn't the only thing I found out about her," Eleanor declared with satisfaction.

Michael tried to sound interested. "Oh yes?"

Eleanor mouthed the word *lesbian* across the table at him.

Michael had never mastered lipreading. "What?"

"You know. One of them."

"One of what?"

Harriet, who had been doing her best to pick out all the sultanas and leave the cake, watched her grandmother mouth the terrible word again. "You can say it out loud," she told Eleanor. "I do know what 'lesbian' means."

"Well, really." Eleanor looked shocked.

Harriet shrugged and ate another sultana. What was the big deal? "Everyone knows."

"Well, you shouldn't." Eleanor turned to Lili, who had already guessed this would be her fault. "This is what happens when you let children read those dreadful magazines. Myrtle Armitage showed me one the other day in the shop. Disgusting," she pronounced heatedly. "What do fourteen-year-olds need to know about those matters?"

"One of our teachers at school is a lesbian," said Harriet, unperturbed. "Miss Hegarty. She lives with her girlfriend."

"Then she should be reported," Eleanor snapped.

"But she's our favorite teacher," Harriet protested. "She's great."

Eleanor's eyes narrowed. "The next thing you know, she'll be making improper advances."

"Huh, if you want improper advances, try Mr. Florian, our

chemistry teacher," Harriet declared. "Or Fingers Florian as we call him. Disgusting, old letch."

"Can we change the subject?" Lili pleaded before Eleanor's blood pressure reached eruption level.

"How are the Gillespies settling into the village?" Michael said to be helpful.

"That Jessie Roscoe." Eleanor tutted and shot a disapproving glance—yet another one—in Lili's direction. "That friend of yours. I always said she was a shameless trollop. Sleeping around with film stars…"

Patiently, Lili said, "He wasn't a film star when she slept with him."

"Hmm." Eleanor sniffed and raised her eyebrows meaningfully at Michael. Trust Lili to defend her friend.

"The children seem nice, anyway," said Lili.

The urge to boast was too much for Eleanor Ferguson to resist.

"I was chatting to the boy yesterday outside the shop. Thaddeus, his name is, though everyone calls him Dizzy. We had a most pleasant conversation about the weather."

In reality, Eleanor had been the one carrying on the pleasant conversation while Thaddeus had examined his shoes and mumbled the odd reply—but he'd seemed a nice enough lad.

Eleanor prepared to make amends with Harriet, who was now kneading her picked-to-pieces cake into pellets. "I saw you talking to him the other afternoon, didn't I, dear? What with school and exams coming up, the two of you must have lots in common."

"You must be joking," said Harriet disparagingly. "The only thing Dizzy Gillespie's interested in is massive breasts."

Chapter 18

THE PHONE IN BERNADETTE'S tiny cottage was out in the hallway. Every time she answered it, she glanced at the framed photograph of April on the hall table as she spoke. Once a week, usually on a Saturday morning, the caller would be April. They would chat for several minutes, talk about their respective careers, catch up on any news, tell each other how they were getting on, and generally pass the time of day.

Which was what they were doing now.

"My nosy neighbor asked me yesterday when my next book was coming out." As she spoke, Bernadette gazed at the photograph. With her big Bambi eyes and the familiar shy tilt of her head, April looked far younger than thirty-six. Then again, the photograph had been taken last year, when her hair was short. It could have grown; she might look different now.

They hadn't seen each other since Christmas. Realizing how upsetting April found their meetings, Bernadette had suggested they should leave it for a while. But the regular phone calls, which they both looked forward to, had continued. They could still speak to each other; they could still be friends.

Bernadette was truly grateful for that.

"The dreaded Eleanor, you mean?" April hadn't met Eleanor, but she'd heard plenty about her. "What did you say?"

"I told her I wasn't sure because my editor was juggling publishing schedules. Afterward, I rang up the publishers and asked them when the new Antonia Kay novel would be out. Keeping my fingers crossed," she went on drily, "that they wouldn't say, 'Oh, I'm sorry, Antonia Kay's dead.'"

April giggled. "And is she?"

"No, thank God. Her next novel hits the bookshelves on August 10, and it's called *A Frond of Honeysuckle*. Poor old Antonia," Bernadette mused. "I can't help thinking she might sell a few more copies if she could come up with snappier titles."

"At least you can tell Eleanor. Just pray she doesn't ask to see an advance copy. Damn, is that the time?" April sounded distracted. "I'm going to be late. I'm meeting someone for lunch at one."

Meeting someone.

Her tone deceptively casual, Bernadette said, "A man?"

"No, not a man. Just one of the girls from work. We're having lunch at Webster's, then going for a bit of a shop. There's this gorgeous dress in Principles I've had my eye on for weeks. You'd love it."

"Off you go, then." Bernadette stepped firmly into the breach, filling the awkward silence. "Have a great afternoon and make sure you buy that dress. I'll speak to you next week."

For a moment April sounded almost tearful. "I will, Bernie. You look after yourself. Bye."

―――

Bernadette knew she was being weak, but she couldn't help herself. Anyway, where was the harm? She wanted to see April, that was all. And if April wasn't to be upset, she had to do it this way—without April seeing her.

Bernadette hovered inside the entrance to Habitat, across the road from Webster's. It was ten to one, which meant that April—who was far too courteous to keep a friend waiting—would be arriving any minute now.

"Can I help you, madam?" asked a friendly salesgirl.

"No thanks," Bernadette shook her head. "I'm just waiting for someone."

And there, moments later, was April. Safely tucked out of sight, Bernadette watched her make her way along the street. Her shiny, light-brown hair was still short, she was wearing a pale-blue shirt and a white skirt, and her beautiful eyes were revealed as she approached the entrance to Webster's and took off her dark glasses.

In less than ten seconds, it was all over. April had disappeared from sight. *This was what I drove into Harleston for*, thought Bernadette, *and it was worth it.*

She pulled a lace-edged handkerchief from her handbag and dabbed carefully at her brimming eyes.

The kind salesgirl, watching from the other side of the shop, came back over and said, "Are you sure you're okay?"

"Yes, thank you." Bernadette took a deep breath before putting the mascara-stained handkerchief away again. She mustered a faint smile. "I'm fine."

Dizzy was bored. There was nothing to do in this dump, and since it was still only the end of June, he had weeks and weeks more of nothingness to endure before going back to school in September.

He wondered gloomily why villages had to be so dull. God, no amusement arcades, nothing. You couldn't even drink because everyone in the pub knew you were underage.

When the telephone rang for the seventh time that morning, he answered it without getting his hopes up. This was just as well, since not one of his mates in London had bothered to get in touch, despite breezily assuring him they would. Dizzy hadn't rung them either, but that wasn't the point.

He picked up the receiver. "No, she's out," he said with a sigh.

Even the receiver reeked of his sister's revolting perfume. "Okay, yeah, I'll tell her."

He hung up, feeling more depressed than ever. Yet another call for Savannah. *How come*, Dizzy thought resentfully, *her friends hadn't forgotten her?*

—~~—

Jessie was upstairs putting the finishing touches to the spare bedroom when the door was nudged open and Dizzy appeared carrying two mugs.

"Brought you some tea," he announced, slopping a fair amount on to the floorboards as he approached.

"Great."

"Only because I'm bored."

"Oh, right." Jessie, who had been ragging bronze glaze over a matte bottle-green base coat, flexed her fingers and stepped back to survey the results.

Dizzy handed her the mug, and she flinched as droplets of hot tea spattered her bare feet. She flinched again when she drank the tea, which was too sweet, too milky, and tasted of tomato ketchup.

Dizzy slumped down in the window seat and looked at the green-and-gold walls. "It's not bad," he said, sounding surprised. This was huge praise coming from him. "Looks like crushed velvet. How'd you do that?"

Jessie held up the linen rag she'd been using. "You just scrunch this up and press it into the wet glaze. Pretty, isn't it?"

"Yeah. Can I have a go?"

"Um…" Jessie hesitated. Ragging was like handwriting; it was personal. If Dizzy did a bit, the difference would show.

"Doesn't matter." Dizzy lost interest as soon as he saw the look on Jessie's face. He was used to that look—it was the same one his chemistry teacher used when he offered to light the Bunsen burners in the lab.

"I'm almost finished." Jessie wiped her bronze-glazed fingers on her jeans. "This is the last room. I'm starting at Lorna's next week." She looked regretful. Lorna wasn't interested in marbling and scumble glaze. "Magnolia paint everywhere. Nothing like the stuff I've been doing here."

"You're decorating the pub?"

"Not downstairs, just the living quarters."

Dizzy perked right up. Moll lived over the pub. That meant Jessie would be decorating Moll's room, the one she actually slept in. "I could give you a hand if you like," he blurted out. Upstairs would mean the bathroom too, wouldn't it? Imagine decorating the room where Moll took her baths. Better still, imagine decorating the room while she was in it…

Taken aback by this astonishing show of enthusiasm, Jessie said, "Well, I would speak to your dad. I had no idea you were interested in decorating, Dizzy."

Dizzy, who wasn't, shrugged and said, "It's okay." He paused, then realized he should pretend to be. "I mean, it's great." He put on his interested face, like the one his dad used when he was being introduced to royalty. "Uh…what made you go into this line of work?"

Jessie took another slurp of ketchupy tea and shuddered. "It was an accident. I'd done all sorts of jobs, anything that fit in with bringing up Oliver. Then I moved to Upper Sisley. Our cottage was a tip; it hadn't been decorated for fifty years, so to save money, I did everything myself. One of the neighbors saw what I'd done and asked if I'd paint a couple of rooms in her house. After that, word got around. Not that I was particularly brilliant," Jessie admitted, "not then, anyway. It was just that the nearest painter and decorator lived miles away and people trusted me not to rip them off."

"Right," murmured Dizzy, his thoughts elsewhere. Maybe Moll preferred showers to baths.

"Well, I'd better get on." This evidently wasn't interesting enough for Dizzy; she'd lost him. Jessie picked up her crumpled rag. "Thanks for the tea."

Still slumped in the window seat, Dizzy nodded vaguely. The next second, a flash of scarlet in the distance caught his eye and his head whipped around so fast he almost knocked himself out on the glass.

It was Moll, in an amazing red dress, sauntering along the main street with a bag slung over one shoulder and her hair tumbling down her back. Dizzy watched, hypnotized, as she approached the bus shelter and slowed down. He saw her take a pair of sunglasses and a red-and-white scarf out of her bag. She put on the glasses first, then dabbed at her perspiring breasts and began fanning herself with the scarf.

Only two buses a day passed through Upper Sisley; Dizzy knew that. This one, heading into town, and the one that brought you back again several hours later.

"Think I'll go into Harleston," he muttered, scrambling down from the window seat and sending Jessie's cans of paint flying. Luckily the lids were on.

"Catching the bus?" Jessie glanced at her watch. "It takes ages. I'm driving in myself later. I could give you a lift if you like."

Dizzy didn't care if the journey by bus took ages. He *wanted* it to take ages. Sounding oddly breathless, he said, "It's okay. I'd rather go now," and raced out of the room.

Chapter 19

STANDING LESS THAN SIX feet away from Moll, actually being able to see at close range the sheen of perspiration on her awesome chest, was a mind-blowing experience. Dizzy tried to look as if he wasn't looking, but it wasn't easy.

When he managed to smile at Moll, she smiled back. When he cleared his throat and said, "Are you waiting for the bus too?" she smiled again.

Dizzy could have kicked himself. Not only a totally dumb question, but his voice had come out all weird and squeaky. God, what must Moll think of him now?

He looked away, embarrassed, and tried to comb his hair with his fingers, but basically it needed more than that.

Like him, it was badly in need of help.

"Know any good hairdressers?" Dizzy blurted out, inspired. "That's why I'm going into Harleston, to get it cut."

"There's a place in Church Street," she said at last. "Rococo. They're good."

"Oh, right."

"You could get it cheered up a bit while you're there. Have some highlights."

She was still smiling at him. There were dimples in her cheeks. Dizzy wondered if she was serious or if it was a windup. He cleared his throat again and said, "You reckon?" The squeak had gone, thank God. "Uh…what color?"

Moll studied him, her head still tilted sideways, one hand idly rubbing her throat. Dizzy Gillespie had a teenage crush on her, that much was obvious, but would he really change his hair that drastically on her say-so?

Oh well, thought Moll. *Only one way to find out.*

Her mouth twitched. Finally, she said, "I think blonds have more fun, don't you?"

That wasn't cruel, Moll reassured herself. Blond was okay.

She could have said purple.

Dizzy still didn't know if she was teasing him, but that was okay—he had plenty of time yet. They could sit together on the bus and talk about hair all the way to Harleston.

Oh, what wouldn't he give to stroke her throat like that…

"Here it comes," said Moll as the bus rounded the corner of Water's Lane and trundled toward them.

Dizzy said, "It's tiny. Not like the double-deckers we have in London."

"Ah, well, size isn't always everything." Moll waved at the driver as the bus approached. Grinning back at her, he began to brake. Moments later, a dark-blue MG with its roof down screeched to a halt behind the bus and Doug Flynn, in the driver's seat, shouted, "Hey, Moll! I'm on my way into work. I'll give you a lift."

Dizzy almost yelled "Don't you *dare*" at Doug Flynn. Mercifully, the words died in his throat. He watched, dry-mouthed, as Moll lifted up her full skirt and leaped joyfully into the passenger seat of the MG.

Why does stuff like this always happen to me? Dizzy thought miserably.

"Getting on?" sighed the bus driver, who was disappointed too.

"I don't know."

"Son, do I look like a personal chauffeur? This is a bus, not an executive limo."

In desperation, Dizzy glanced at Moll.

"Sorry, it's only a two-seater," Doug said, not sounding sorry at all.

"Can't wait to see the new hairdo," Moll shouted, waving her fingers at him as Doug reversed rapidly, then accelerated away in a cloud of dust.

"Look, are you catching this bus or what?" the bus driver demanded.

With Moll's last words echoing in his brain, Dizzy climbed aboard.

He was halfway to Harleston before he discovered he only had two pounds fifty in his pocket. Not even enough for a trim.

———

Toby, who had spent the last two hours sitting with his feet up in the conservatory reading scripts, watched, unnoticed, from the bedroom doorway as Jess, the tip of her pink tongue just visible between her teeth, eased the scrunched-up linen rag into the corner where the wall met the fireplace. He waited until she had finished before pushing the door shut behind him, the squeaking hinge letting her know he was there.

Jessie sat back on her heels, arched her shoulders, and stretched. "I'm getting old. Backache."

Toby helped her up. "It's looking great."

"Thanks. And you look harassed." Jessie gestured with amusement toward his ruffled blond hair.

Toby, who habitually ran his fingers through his hair when he had a decision to make, heaved a sigh. "I've just read through two scripts. Which one do I go with—the low-budget British comedy drama or the big-bucks American thriller?"

"Which one did you like most?"

"The thriller."

"Which one pays best?"

"Are you serious?" Toby grinned. "Moneywise, we're talking

about the difference between a mile-long buffet on the QE2 and a french-fry sandwich at an all-night cafeteria."

"So why can't you decide?" said Jessie, who was rather fond of fry sandwiches.

"The American film will be shot on location in L.A. and Acapulco. Six weeks minimum."

"Oh, you poor thing. It's a hard life."

Toby held up his hands. "Okay, I know. But six weeks is a long time to be away."

"And you'll miss Deborah and the kids." Jessie stopped teasing him. She nodded, realizing what he was getting at. "But couldn't they come out and visit you, stay for a couple of weeks? Or Deborah could fly out on her own. I could easily keep an eye on Dizzy and Savannah—it wouldn't be any trouble."

Was it her imagination, or was this suggestion followed by a bit of a pregnant pause?

And why was Toby looking at her in that funny way?

He spoke at last. "The trouble is, Deborah wouldn't be the one I'd miss." Toby chose his words with care. "The one I'd miss would be you."

There, he'd said it.

Oh shit, thought Jessie. Her stomach lurched. *He said it.* "Don't be stupid."

"I'm not being stupid."

"Look, you managed perfectly well for twenty-one years. Another six weeks is hardly going to make a difference."

"I might have *managed* without you for twenty-one years"— Toby shook his head at her willful stupidity—"but I missed you too. All the time. And now we've—"

"Don't say it," Jessie pleaded. "Don't say any more."

"It isn't easy, you know, feeling like this. I want to kiss you," Toby said slowly, "all the time. Every time I see you. It's driving me mad, Jess. This whole just-good-friends bit is doing my head in. And what I really can't figure out is if you feel the same way about me."

Oh God, oh God. Jessie closed her eyes for a second and went to lean against the still-wet wall. With a yelp of horror, she jerked herself away just in time.

Toby's gaze was still on her, unwavering.

"I'm doing my best not to," Jessie told him, her voice unsteady.

"So you *do*—"

"Toby, it doesn't matter how we feel about each other. It just can't happen. You've got Deborah and the children. You have a fantastically happy marr—*mmmfph!*"

Toby's mouth came down on hers. His hands held each side of her face, and as his tongue slid into her mouth, she felt the frantic hammering of his heart against her chest.

It was blissful, totally blissful.

And utterly, utterly wrong.

"Now you've got paint all over you," Jessie mumbled when she finally pulled away, clutching his arms for support. She gazed at the smudges of green and gold on the front of his white shirt, perfectly mirroring the ones on her T-shirt. Talk about a dead giveaway.

"Don't change the subject."

"Oh, Toby, for God's sake, we *have* to change the subject."

"Okay. I love you."

"That isn't changing—"

"Look, either you listen to me, hear what I have to say, or I kiss you again." Toby's mouth twitched. "So it's up to you. I'm easy."

"You're married. And don't you dare try to make me laugh," said Jessie. "Because this isn't a laughing matter."

"It's still there though, isn't it? You do feel the same way about me."

"Toby! You have to listen to me." Jessie was beginning to feel like a student teacher struggling to keep an unruly class in check.

"Deborah is one of the nicest women I've ever met. I really like her. Even if I did want to—"

"Ah, but you *do* want to."

He was grinning now. Jessie could have thumped him. "But don't you *see*?" It came out as a wail. "It only makes it *more* impossible."

Toby held her hands and stroked her balled-up fists. He shook his head. "What if I were to tell you my fantastically happy marriage isn't quite as fantastically happy as it looks?" The moment the words were out, he regretted them. The look on Jessie's face said it all. He felt her withdraw. He could have kicked himself. The timing was all wrong. If he'd told her some other day, told her when everything that had just happened hadn't just happened…well, it would have sounded more valid. She might even have believed him. Saying it now just made it sound like some desperate excuse, along the well-worn lines of *My wife doesn't understand me*, *Since the baby she's not interested in me anymore*, and *We haven't had sex for years*. The kind of persuasive patter used by casually unfaithful husbands the world over when the women they pick up protest feebly that they don't sleep with married men.

"Well, yes," Jessie drawled. "I had noticed, of course. You two can't stand the sight of each other. It's blindingly obvious."

This time the mockery was humorless. Toby knew he had blown it. Anything he said now would only make the situation worse.

Even if it was true.

Jessie stared hard out of the window. She felt sickened and horribly cheap. Until now, she'd believed Toby when he'd told her he had never been unfaithful to Deborah. Now she realized how naive she had been.

That famous line of Mandy Rice-Davies's came to mind: "Well, he would say that, wouldn't he?"

And Toby's an actor too. He can say anything—from "The aliens have landed!" to "And now I'm going to shoot you"—and make it sound totally believable. That's what he's good at. It's his job. He probably sleeps with all his costars, Jessie thought. *He could have notched up dozens of affairs behind Deborah's back. God, how could I have been so* stupid?

"Jess, I'm sorry, I can't—"

"Time I got back to work." Without looking at him, she reached for the linen cloth and carefully re-crumpled it into the palm of her hand. "I want to be finished by tomorrow."

What a complete and utter foul-up.

Since there was nothing more he could say, Toby quietly left the room.

Chapter 20

THE NEXT MORNING, TOBY—thank God— had driven up to London to meet with a producer friend of his. Deborah and Savannah had gone into Harleston. When Jessie heard a bloodcurdling howl coming from the bathroom, her paintbrush flew out of her hand and clattered against the windowsill. For the last hour the house had been silent; she hadn't realized Dizzy was still here.

The bathroom door was shut.

"Dizzy? Are you all right?"

No reply.

Jessie knocked. "Dizzy, it's me, Jessie. Say something."

Nothing.

"Look, I know you're in there. If you don't answer me, I'm opening the door."

"Don't." Dizzy sounded anguished. "Just don't, okay?"

Jessie leaned against the wall, relieved that at least Dizzy wasn't lying unconscious in the bath. But something was definitely still up.

"What's the matter?" she called out. "Are you ill?"

"No."

"What then?"

She heard a sigh, followed by a clunk as something fell over.

"Dizzy, have you fainted?"

"God, you're nosy!" Dizzy sounded exasperated and dangerously close to tears. "Can't you just leave me alone?"

"Not until you tell me what's wrong."

Moments later, the door abruptly swung open.

"I thought you were dead," said Jessie. "You frightened the life out of me. When I heard that yell, I thought you'd electrocuted yourself in the bath."

"I wish I had," Dizzy groaned, his voice muffled by the dark-blue towel draped over his head.

Glancing behind him, Jessie saw what had made the hefty clunk just now. A bottle of toilet-cleaning bleach with its top off had toppled into the bath. The contents were quietly dissolving the bath mat. The plughole was clogged with what looked like yellow teddy bear fur.

"Oh, Dizzy, come here." Gently she pulled the towel away to reveal the matted, orangey-yellow tufts of hair sticking out all over his head.

"I wish I were dead." Furiously, Dizzy blinked back tears of shame.

"No you don't." Jessie touched the still-damp hair, which had the texture of coconut matting. She wanted to hug him. "We'll sort it out."

"Nothing's going to sort this out." His shoulders slumped. "Christ, what a mess! I just… All I wanted was to be a bit blond."

Jessie screwed the top back on the bleach and ran the water into the bath. The rubber mat was like chewing gum where the bleach had eaten into it.

"You're lucky it didn't burn your scalp. Straight bleach can take your skin off."

"I didn't use straight bleach. I diluted it." Dizzy was defensive. "I'm not stupid, you know."

"No, of course not."

Jessie's tone was soothing, but he didn't even hear her. The mirror had claimed his attention once more.

"Oh hell. Oh bloody *bloody* hell!"

"I'll drive you into Harleston," Jessie offered for the second time in two days. "We'll find a brilliant hairdresser—"

"They'll laugh at me," Dizzy wailed, on the verge of hysteria. "I can't bear it. I won't go!" Knowing his luck, he'd be bound to bump into his mother and sister. Or worse still, Moll.

"Okay. Hang on." Jessie ran downstairs. When she reappeared two minutes later, Dizzy was hunched, looking more suicidal than ever, on the side of the bath.

"All arranged." She grabbed his arm and yanked him toward the door. "Lili's doing it."

"Lili who?"

"My friend Lili, Harriet's mother. Don't panic—Harriet won't be there," Jessie pointed out before Dizzy could open his mouth to protest.

"Is her mother a proper hairdresser?" He looked terrified.

"Well, she's a qualified hedge trimmer, but it's all pretty much the same thing, isn't it?" said Jessie. She broke into a grin and pushed Dizzy in the direction of the stairs. "Joke."

"This is great," Jessie announced, driving out through the gates of Sisley House, turning right along Compass Lane, and waving cheerily as she passed old Cecil Barker walking his dogs. "I feel like the SAS. Keep your head down and don't move a muscle until I tell you."

"This blanket stinks of turpentine," Dizzy grumbled.

"Stay under it. Here's Lili's nightmare of a mother-in-law coming out of the shop. Morning, Eleanor!" Jessie shouted, beaming through the open window as she rounded the left-hand bend and headed up the main street.

"Are we there?" said Dizzy moments later when the car stopped.

"Just opening the gate so I can park on the drive," Jessie explained. "Then you'll be able to sneak in the back door. Oh look, there's Moll. Hi, Moll! Gorgeous day!"

"Right, Jess said it was an emergency," said Lili, "so take off your hood and let's have a look. Will, leave those dog biscuits alone."

"I'll look after Will and Freya, keep them occupied." Jessie scooped both children into her arms and whisked them outside before they could laugh.

Miserably, without much hope that anything could be done, Dizzy removed his hood.

Lili examined the evidence. "The hair's breaking off. We'll have to cut it short."

"I know. I don't care about that." He did, but even he could see he didn't have much choice. "It's just the color."

"What I can do," said Lili, thoughtfully investigating the tangled mess, "is restore the natural pigments. Get it back, more or less, to your own color. It isn't easy, and it'll take a while—"

"When will Harriet be back?"

"Not for ages. She's gone to a tennis tournament."

For the first time, the muscles in Dizzy's shoulders unclenched. He even managed a brief smile. "Okay. Thanks."

"Any danger of anything to eat?" said Michael, coming into the kitchen two hours later.

"Sorry, darling, I've been a bit tied up. There's some cold chicken in the fridge." Lili gestured vaguely with plastic-gloved hands stained red like a surgeon's. "This is Dizzy, by the way. Dizzy, this is my husband, Michael."

"He won't tell anyone, will he?" Dizzy turned to her in anguish when Michael had gone.

Lili, patting his skinny shoulder, said, "Don't worry. I'll make sure he doesn't."

When Hugh and Felicity arrived at five o'clock on the dot, they found the back door open and Lili carefully cutting the hair of a nervous-looking teenage boy.

"Goodness, aren't you busy?" Felicity announced. "Doing two jobs at once." Her perfectly made-up eyes darted around the kitchen. "Although I can't actually see Freya anywhere…"

"Sorry, I usually keep the hairdressing to the evenings." Lili felt herself going red. "But this was such an emergency—"

"Thanks a lot," Dizzy muttered, going even redder.

"—and Freya's fine, really she is. She's playing outside with Will and Jess—"

"Of course. There she is," Felicity cut in as the three of them burst out of the playhouse. "I didn't realize your friend Jessie was a qualified child caregiver too."

"She disapproves of me so much," Lili fretted over dinner later that evening. "She picks up on every tiny thing. Honestly, she's worse than your mother."

Michael's mouth tightened. He didn't mind criticizing his own mother, but he wasn't amused when someone else tried it, particularly when that person was Lili. "My mother does a great deal for you," he announced coolly. He knew this because Eleanor had told him so only yesterday. "You should be grateful for her help."

"Dad, I need new sneakers," said Harriet. "My old ones are too small."

"Now who did I see wearing a pair of sneakers with lights in the soles?" Michael looked thoughtful. "Every time he tapped his foot, the lights flashed. Oh, right, got it now—the lad who was here this afternoon."

Lili stared at him and slowly shook her head.

Harriet frowned. There was only one person in the village with those kind of sneakers. "Dizzy Gillespie? Is that who you mean, Dad?" Her eyes widened in astonishment. "What was *he* doing here?"

Lili was still giving him one of her iciest looks—which, being Lili, wasn't actually that icy. Michael, who hadn't forgiven her yet for the anti-Eleanor remark, decided he didn't much care for the silent threat, however feeble.

"Dizzy. That's it, that was his name. Your mother was doing something drastic to his hair."

Harriet swiveled round to Lili. "Mum?"

"Michael," Lili warned, "I told you not to—"

"Tipped a bottle of toilet-cleaning bleach over his head, apparently." Michael smiled, taking great pleasure in watching the dismay on Lili's face. *That*, he thought with satisfaction, *will teach her to have a dig at Mother.*

"Toilet bleach!" Harriet squealed, almost falling off her chair. "What color did his hair go?"

"According to your mother, something pretty similar to Colman's mustard. The bits that were left, that is. Most of it," Michael concluded with malicious relish, "shriveled up and dropped off."

Dizzy had to dawdle casually past the Seven Bells half a dozen times before Moll emerged to clear up the accumulation of empty glasses littering the tables outside the pub.

She was wearing an almost transparent emerald-green shirt over a red tube top. A lacy black bra strap was sliding off one shoulder. Dizzy watched longingly as she leaned across one of the tables, her heavenly breasts—one slightly lower than the other—almost brushing the weather-beaten surface. *Oh lucky, lucky table...*

"Hi," he said, when Moll had straightened up again.

She turned, her arms full of stacked-up glasses clutched to her chest.

"Well well, look at you." Moll smiled her slow, appraising, come-to-bed smile. "Decided to give the highlights a miss then? Went for the snip instead."

"The snip" was what Dizzy's mother called vasectomies. Thinking of vasectomies made Dizzy think of sex even more than he was thinking of it already. His ears, long hidden from public view but now hopelessly exposed, grew hot. He prayed they weren't glowing as neon red as he thought they were.

"Thought it was time for a change." Bravely, he ignored his flaming ears.

"Very smart. Can't beat a nice short-back-and-sides." Still smiling to herself, Moll began to move toward the pub.

Desperate to keep the conversational ball rolling, Dizzy blurted out, "That's a nice top. Is it new? Did you buy it this afternoon in Harleston?"

Moll glanced down at the gauzy, green shirt, frayed at the neckline and damp where the dregs from one of the beer mugs had spilled over. "This old thing? God no, it's ancient." She hauled the lacy black bra strap back onto her shoulder and proudly gave it a twang. "New bra, though."

Dizzy couldn't speak. His tongue had glued itself to the roof of his mouth.

"Well, I'd better get back inside," said Moll, "or Lorna'll think I've done a runner with one of her precious customers."

"Is that doctor bloke…the one who gave you the lift into town…is he your boyfriend?" Dizzy rushed the words out before his courage failed.

"What, Doug?" Dimpling, Moll shook her head. "He's a good friend, that's all. The kind who'll stop and give you a lift when you need one. That's what having friends is all about, isn't it, sweet pea?"

What was she implying? Was there some hidden agenda here? Assuming his man-of-the-world stance, pretending he knew exactly what she meant, Dizzy peeled his tongue unstuck again and stammered, "I s-suppose so."

"No suppose about it." Moll's catlike eyes glittered with amusement. "I make sure I look after my friends." As she disappeared through the doorway, she added lightly over her shoulder, "That way, everybody's happy. I do favors for them; they do favors for me."

Chapter 21

THE EMERGENCY WARD AT Harleston General had been frantically busy all day. Doug Flynn, who was due off at six, had dealt with a constant stream of patients ranging from a severed leg to a lost-behind-the-eye contact lens. Fifteen cases of heatstroke, two dog bites, and a functional hemiparesis later—not to mention a paralytic fourteen-year-old who had thrown up in truly spectacular fashion in the waiting room—he was ready for a drink of his own. Unlike the teenager, however, he wouldn't be downing eighteen Budweisers.

At four o'clock Doug stuck his head around the door of the coffee room. "Who's for a session at the Antelope later? Susie? James? Esther, you'll definitely come."

"Promises, promises." Esther, one of the nurses, giggled.

James, who was a senior charge nurse, looked regretful. "I've got to pick the kids up."

"April," said Doug, clasping the receptionist's arm as she tried to slip past him. "How about you?"

April blushed. Doug Flynn had never invited her along before; in fact, he seldom paid her much attention at all. She knew he was only asking her now to make up the numbers. "Well, thanks...but I don't think I—"

"No excuses." Dimly aware that she was divorced and not having much of a time of it, Doug flashed her a reassuring grin. April was totally not his type, but even he was capable of the occasional altruistic gesture. "Do you good to get out for a bit. And don't worry about transport," he added casually. "I'll give you a lift."

By six o'clock Doug had managed to rustle up several more willing contenders. In the end, there were eight of them, in three cars, traveling in convoy to the Antelope, a pretty riverside pub on the outskirts of Harleston.

The top was down on Doug's dark-blue MG. April, touched that he hadn't forgotten her, was nevertheless thankful the journey was a short one. She'd always wanted to be driven in an open-topped sports car with the wind blowing through her hair. The trouble was, now that it was actually happening, she was terrified to open her mouth in case she swallowed a wasp.

The Antelope heaved with after-work drinkers. As they made their way up to the bar, April's courage began to falter. She knew she should be making an effort to get out more, but staying at home was so much easier, so much less hassle. Going out, on the other hand, forcing herself to socialize, attempting to rebuild her life… Heavens, just the thought of it was enough to bring on a panic attack.

"What would you like?" said Doug, effortlessly attracting the attention of the prettiest barmaid.

"Oh, um, an orange juice? Hang on, let me—"

"Boring," said Doug. "Have a glass of wine. Don't worry," he added, gently pushing April's purse away. "I'm getting these."

April was under no illusions; she knew he was just being kind. With his dauntingly glamorous good looks, Doug Flynn could have any woman he wanted and, from what she could gather, frequently did. The last person he would be interested in was someone as mousy as her.

Still, he had bought her a drink, and horribly out of practice though she might be, even April knew this meant she now had to engage in a spot of polite conversation in return.

"Did Esther tell you, the chap who fell off his ladder yesterday sent us a basket of fruit this afternoon?" Oh, *well done*, April.

Riveting stuff. Battling on in desperation, she said, "He owns a chain of greengrocers, apparently. I don't know how he'll manage to run them with both arms in casts."

"Let's not talk about work," said Doug.

"Oh, right."

"Why don't you tell me about you?"

"N-nothing to tell," April stammered, hopelessly unprepared for all this attention.

"Did I hear Susie mention you were divorced?"

"Well...yes."

"Kids?"

"No."

"Met anyone else yet?"

"No."

"Sorry, I know this sounds like an interrogation." Doug's smile was the one he used when he was putting a nervous patient at ease. "It really isn't meant to. I'm just curious. You don't have to answer if you don't want to."

"That's okay." April took a reassuring gulp of icy white wine. If she was ever going to rejoin the rest of the world, she'd have to get used to questions like these. "I don't mind. My husband and I separated three years ago. Now we're divorced. I live in a one-bedroom apartment on the other side of Harleston. I'm afraid I've become a bit of a hermit."

Doug's dark eyes, trained on hers, were mesmerizing. "Why did you split up?"

Not that mesmerizing.

"Just didn't work out," said April, her fingers tightening around the stem of the glass.

Doug nodded and wisely didn't press her for details. "These things happen," he observed lightly. "Sitting at home on your own isn't going to help much though."

"I know, I know. It's just hard to make the—"

"Hello there," said a male voice inches from April's right ear, and she jerked around in astonishment only to feel a complete idiot when she realized the owner of the voice hadn't been saying hello to her.

"Hi," Doug replied easily, recognizing Michael Ferguson, husband of pretty, overweight Lili from the village. Michael wasn't around much—he worked abroad for months on end, something to do with computers—but they saw each other from time to time, chiefly in the bar of the Seven Bells.

"Busy here," Michael commented, taking his change from the barmaid and easing his pint of lager through the crush of bodies. He smiled briefly at April as he began to move away. "Sorry, didn't mean to make you jump just now."

April went pink, only thankful she hadn't made an even greater fool of herself and said hello back.

"Who's he, a friend of yours?" she asked Doug when the man was out of earshot, but Doug was busy peering over heads, searching for the rest of their party.

"Not a friend, just someone I vaguely know to say hello to." Without bothering to elaborate, he added with some relief, "There are the others, outside on the terrace. Let's join them."

‒‒‒‒

April left the Antelope at eight thirty, having assured Doug—who clearly didn't want to leave yet—that she was fine, she could catch the bus home; there was one that ran past the Antelope practically all the way to her front door.

Exhilarated by the success of her first proper social outing in over a year, she half smiled at the man who had earlier spoken to Doug as she made her way toward the exit. Then, because three glasses of wine and a rattling bus journey could be uncomfortable, she veered left and nipped into the ladies' loo.

Above the mirror in the cloakroom someone had stuck a poster advertising "Singles Nite at the Antelope." It was held each Wednesday, April read, admission was free, and everyone who arrived before nine o'clock received a complimentary drink.

A plump girl emerged from one of the cubicles tucking her shirt into her jeans. She saw April looking at the poster. "You should come along," she announced. "Everyone's dead friendly and there's always loads of blokes."

Taken aback by the girl's up-front approach, April said, "Oh, I don't know…"

"Go on, live a little!" The girl washed her hands, dried them on her jeans, and began redoing her lipstick. "No need to feel awkward. We're all in the same boat." She shrugged cheerfully at April's reflection in the mirror. "What have you got to lose anyway? It's just a laugh."

Chapter 22

THE FOLLOWING AFTERNOON, AS soon as Hugh and Felicity had picked up Freya, Lili spruced up Will and Lottie and took them to stay with Eleanor for a couple of hours.

Bernadette Thomas was tending the hollyhocks in her front garden. She waved at Will, who had been bawling "HELLO! HELLO!" at her all the way along Water's Lane and clearly had no intention of stopping until he got a reply.

"Hello." Bernadette turned to Lottie. "That's a pretty dress. Have you come to visit Grandma?"

"Mum, that's the lady who smells."

"*Nice*, Lottie. That's the lady who smells *nice*." Lili pulled an apologetic face at Bernadette, who wore Arpège and always smelled wonderful.

"Anyway," Lottie told Bernadette with an air of lofty disdain, "she isn't your grandma. She's *our* grandma."

"Kids," Lili sighed, shaking her head. "Couldn't you just chuck them in a soundproof closet and leave them there for a fortnight?"

"Don't worry about it." Bernadette smiled reassuringly and pushed a loose strand of hair behind one ear. In the sunlight, a pretty opal-and-sapphire ring glinted on her right hand.

"I'm dropping them off for a couple of hours," Lili explained. "Our dog's got a sore paw so I'm taking him into Harleston. Drew Darcy's going to have a look at him. Lottie, don't take your shoes off. Your feet will get filthy."

Lottie looked mutinous. "Don't want to wear shoes."

"Yes, well, Grandma likes you to wear them." Lili exchanged a glance with Bernadette. "She says only tinkers' children run around barefoot."

"Better keep them on." Bernadette nodded kindly at Lottie. "Don't want to upset your grandma."

As their eyes met again, Lili and Bernadette silently sympathized with each other, acknowledging the respective difficulties of being Eleanor Ferguson's daughter-in-law and next door neighbor.

"Do you do Postman Pat?" Lottie demanded suddenly.

Confused, Bernadette said, "Excuse me?"

"Grandma said you write books. Do you write Postman Pat stories?"

"Er...no. Sorry."

"That's all right. I just wondered. Anyway," Lottie announced, "you only have to say excuse me if you do a burp or a—"

"I read the novel you lent Eleanor." Lili dived in hastily before she could finish; bodily functions were currently Lottie's big interest. "I know you don't want the whole village knowing about your work, but she just happened to mention to us that you wrote novels."

Bernadette sounded faintly amused. "You mean the whole village doesn't know?"

"Oh, I'm sure she wouldn't tell anyone else." Mentally Lili crossed her fingers. "But I really enjoyed your book." Damn—she couldn't remember the title. "I thought it was brilliant."

This was another fib; she'd found the book soporific, genteel, and extremely average, but at least it hadn't had any lesbians in it. Anyway, Lili reasoned, when you were telling an author you'd read one of their books, you could hardly say you'd found it average, could you?

Unless, of course, you were Eleanor.

Bernadette smiled, but rather embarrassingly looked as if she didn't believe her. "Thank you."

"When's the next one out?" Lili was floundering, but she knew it was a good question to ask.

"August. It's called…um, *A Frond of Honeysuckle*."

Good grief.

"Well, I'll definitely buy it."

"There's Grandma!" Lottie yelled as the front door opened. Running up the path, she hurled herself into Eleanor's outstretched arms.

Lili scooped Will up onto her hip and smiled at Bernadette as she followed Lottie into the house.

"Bye. See you again."

"I've been watching from the bedroom window." Eleanor's tone was frosty. "You were very friendly, chatting away like that, laughing together."

Puzzled by her evident disapproval, Lili said, "She seems nice."

"I daresay she does. But you should be careful, Lili. Too much fraternizing…well, it could be construed as encouragement."

"Encouragement?" A couple of seconds later, Lili figured out what Eleanor was getting at. "Oh! You mean she might think I'm a—"

"You know perfectly well what I mean. No need to spell it out." Eleanor's mouth looked like a purse with the drawstring pulled tight. She shepherded Lottie through to the kitchen. "And how you can let this child run around without shoes on is beyond me, Lili. She looks like a tinker's child. The next thing you know she'll step on a piece of glass and get blood poisoning." She shook her head in sorrowful, told-you-so fashion. "Mark my words, they'll end up having to amputate her leg."

***

"Lili, come on in. How nice to see you."

Drew was touched that Lili had made an appointment and taken the trouble to drive over to the clinic. Just as Doug was plagued by people accosting him at parties with, "You're a doctor, aren't you?

What d'you think could be wrong with my shoulder?" so he and Jamie were used to people in the village bringing their pets along to Keeper's Cottage and explaining that they were sure it wasn't serious, but could Drew or Jamie just take a quick look?

Ironically, Lili Ferguson was one of the very few people he wouldn't have minded seeing on his doorstep. Entertained by her efforts to persuade Blitz to sit on the examination table, Drew was so pleased to see her, he forgot he was supposed to be keeping his feet out of sight.

"I heard him give a yelp in the yard this morning, as if he'd hurt himself," Lili explained. "And now he's limping. Something's wrong but I can't see what. Did you know you're wearing odd shoes?"

She flipped her shaggy, light-brown hair away from her face and held Blitz still while Drew examined the sore paw.

"I was in a hurry, had to take my car to the garage. I only found out at lunchtime why everyone was smirking at me." He sounded resigned. "Our receptionist ran a sweepstake all morning, taking bets on when I'd catch on."

"Poor you." Lili giggled. "Is the car all right, at least?"

Drew searched in a drawer for a magnifying glass. "The mechanical equivalent of going to the doctor with a dizzy spell and finding out you've got a brain tumor the size of a turnip. I only took the damn thing in for a service." He looked rueful. "From what I could make out when I rang the garage just now, they're about to give it the last rites."

"Oh dear, poor you *and* poor car," said Lili. She watched him study Blitz's paw through the magnifying glass. "How will you manage?"

Drew had located the problem, a deeply embedded thorn. He reached for the fine tweezers.

"They're lending me a replacement car, but not until tomorrow. I told our receptionist she can have the pleasure of driving me home, to make up for making fun of me all morning."

"Does she live near us?"

"Nope, it's miles out of her way," Drew announced with relish.

"Well, that's silly. I can give you a lift home," said Lili.

With a deft movement, Drew tweezered the thorn out of Blitz's paw. "There, done."

"Drew, tell her she doesn't have to do it."

"Now where's the fun in that?" His grin was unrepentant. "Anyway, I won't finish before seven."

"It's okay, darling, all over now." Lili gave Blitz a reassuring hug. "I mean it, Drew. Look, it's six fifteen already. I'll take Blitz for a run in Canford Park. By the time I get back, you'll be ready to go."

Blitz, evidently having forgiven Drew for attacking him with a pair of tweezers, was now vigorously licking his hand.

"Go on then. I always was a sucker for a wet tongue. Oh God," Drew groaned, clapping his hand to his forehead and going hot and cold all over. "I can't believe I just said that."

"I'm glad you did." Lili smiled her dimpliest smile at poor, perspiring Drew. "It's so lovely to know that accidentally coming out with something daft happens to other people too."

"It must be great having your husband home." Drew held Blitz on his lap in the passenger seat as Lili tried hard not to crunch gears. She never did as a rule, but the minute any man climbed into her car, she became hopelessly self-conscious. Probably because Michael had spent the last twenty years moaning in long-suffering fashion, "And for God's sake, don't crunch the gears."

"I don't know about great. It takes a bit of getting used to," she admitted. "You get yourself into a routine, then, all of a sudden, there's this huge disruption. Of course it isn't easy for Michael either," Lili went on hastily, in case she sounded disloyal. "After a week or two the novelty of being home wears off. He gets bored, he feels in the way, and we both start getting irritable... Ah, well, thank goodness for snooker." Lili sounded rueful. "That's where he is this evening, at the Take a Cue club in Harleston." She accelerated violently through a yellow light because Michael always bawled "GO GO GO!" at her like a demented steersman. "At least it keeps him out of mischief."

"Oh dear. And there was me thinking you were one of the blissfully married brigade."

Lili couldn't imagine what was happening to her. She didn't normally go around blurting out details of her private life to strange men.

Except Drew wasn't strange. Well, not if you didn't count the odd shoes. And he'd been in a rush, Lili thought with a surge of protectiveness. They weren't really his fault.

"I wouldn't call us blissful." She thought back to this afternoon's argument, triggered by Blitz shredding her entire stock of Pampers. This had prompted a furious "that bloody dog" reaction from Michael, swiftly compounded when Lili had asked him to pick up a couple more packs of diapers before disappearing off to the snooker club. "Oh, we muddle along, but we're no Hugo and Felicity." She glanced sideways at Drew. "If it's blissful you're after, they're your couple."

Drew laughed. "We call them the Thunderbirds—perfect cars, perfect clothes, perfect hair. I wonder if they have perfect sex?"

"Oh, definitely. Orgasms on tap, multiple *and* simultaneous."

They reached Upper Sisley. As she approached the brow of Compass Hill, Lili braked and nodded toward Treetops, the Seymours' splendid house, ahead of them on the right. Their yard was immaculate, the gravel freshly raked, and even their cars were parked with geometric precision on the driveway.

"I'm only saying it because I'm jealous," she admitted. "Hugh and Felicity are devoted to each other. It must be wonderful to feel like that. I mean, how many couples are truly happy these days? One in a hundred? One in a thousand?"

"Now I'm depressed," said Drew. "If things are that bad, I may as well give up now." He gave Blitz's arched neck an affectionate rub. "Settle for a dog instead."

Lili pulled up outside Keeper's Cottage, whose yard was in no danger whatsoever of being described as immaculate. Through the wide-open sitting room window came the sound of Jamie bawling tunelessly along to Blur.

Blitz, recognizing the song from Harriet's CD, pricked up his ears and began to whimper with excitement.

"Just so long as it's a faithful dog," said Lili.

"Come in for a drink?" Drew offered casually.

"Better not." She checked her watch with regret. "Eleanor's expecting me."

"Maybe some other time then." Something about the way Lili's cheeks dimpled when she smiled was getting to Drew. Without stopping to think, he leaned across and landed a brief kiss on the nearest dimple. "Thanks for the lift."

"I could drive you in tomorrow morning," said Lili. *Good grief, what's going on here? Is this how it feels to be possessed—when you open your mouth and words you never meant to say come tumbling out?*

"That's really kind, but I couldn't let you. It's too far." Drew felt himself go hot again. There was definitely something happening and he wasn't sure he liked it. Or rather he liked the feelings but he wasn't at all sure Lili Ferguson was the right person to be causing them.

"It's no trouble, honestly." Lili's eyes were wide, her expression earnest. "I need to go to the supermarket anyway for diapers."

Diapers.

The dreaded d-word. *As if I needed reminding*, thought Drew, exasperated because this wasn't supposed to be happening to him. Let's face it, he was youngish, free, and single, and—in his own way—a reasonably eligible bloke. What was more, he had a picture fixed in his mind of his ideal woman—the one he would one day meet and fall in love with—and she was young, blond, and busty, the kind of girl who wouldn't look out of place on Page 3 of the *Sun*.

"What time do you have to be at the clinic?"

"Eight thirty."

"That's fine. I don't have Freya tomorrow anyway." Lili smiled across at him. "Michael can look after the kids and I'll pick you up at eight."

"Well, if you're sure." Drew felt his insides beginning to churn. God, how ridiculous! He was getting butterflies already. Twenty-nine years old and acting like a teenager on a first date.

This was wrong, all wrong. It didn't fit in with his plans at all.

The woman of his dreams definitely wasn't supposed to be seven years older than him with floppy, light-brown hair, a rounded figure, three noisy children, and an irritable husband to boot.

Chapter 23

"FOR YOU," SAID OLIVER, handing Jessie the phone. He spent the next five minutes listening to her chattering happily to Jonathan, a divorced sculptor from Cheltenham, of whom she had seen a fair bit last year. But chatting, it seemed, was as far as it went nowadays. Before long, Oliver heard Jessie making her usual feeble excuses.

Sometimes he despaired of his mother; at this rate, she was never going to settle down with a man.

"He was asking you out, wasn't he?" he said when she had hung up. "You like him; you get on well together...so why don't you go?"

Jessie ruffled his blond hair as she wandered through to the kitchen in search of food. "Can't be bothered." She shrugged; it was the truth. "Fancied a night in, just me and a video and a condensed milk sandwich." Taking the tin out of the fridge she waved it enticingly at Oliver. "Want one?"

"You are gross."

This was a term he had picked up from Savannah. Having got by without it for so many years, it had recently begun to feature heavily in Oliver's conversation. Everything from Dutch eggnog to zebra-print wallpaper was gross.

Smiling to herself, Jessie grabbed a knife and began energetically slicing bread. "Anyway, you turn girls down. I've heard you do it a million times."

"That's different. I'm not a middle-aged spinster," said Oliver.

Jessie was only briefly tempted to pour condensed milk over his head; that would be a waste.

"What about the girl from Bath, the pretty redhead?" she persisted. "I thought you were keen on her. Now you won't even return her calls."

It was Oliver's turn to shrug and gaze out of the window. Across the village green, Drew Darcy was climbing out of Lili Ferguson's filthy red Volvo. "I got bored."

As she was putting the tin back in the fridge, Jessie spotted a bottle of already-opened wine, rough but just about drinkable. She sloshed some into a glass and carried her sandwich back through to the living room.

"What are you looking at?"

"Your friend Lili, trying to pull away in third gear. Ha, now she's stalled." He shook his head in amusement. "She's a terrible driver."

"Don't you have to be at work by seven thirty?" said Jessie.

"Yes."

"It's seven thirty."

"Hell, my watch must've stopped." Oliver raced upstairs to shower and change.

Jessie was licking her fingers, watching *EastEnders*, and making the discovery that cheap white wine and condensed milk sandwiches didn't go, when the doorbell rang.

Toby stood on the doorstep, looking dauntingly handsome in a dark-blue shirt and white jeans. His blond hair lifted in the breeze as he took off his dark glasses, fixing Jessie with those famous—and even more daunting—navy-blue eyes.

"I've brought the rest of your money. I thought you'd prefer cash."

He was holding a manila envelope but not offering it to her.

"Cash or check, either's fine. I do pay tax on my earnings." Meaningfully, Jessie added, "I'm not a cheat."

"Look, are you going to invite me in?" Toby lowered his voice. "Jess, we need to talk."

At that moment, Oliver clattered down the stairs, combing his wet hair with one hand and carrying his shoes in the other. He panted, "Oh, hi—I'm late for work."

"I'm in a hurry too," Jessie told Toby. "I'm going out."

Oliver was in the middle of pulling his shoes on. He stopped and stared up at her. "Who with?"

"Jonathan."

"You turned him down!"

"He rang back while you were in the shower," Jessie lied. "He's picking me up at eight o'clock." She whisked the envelope from Toby's grasp, tore it open, and flipped briefly through the wad of twenty-pound notes. "That's fine. Thanks very much. Now if you'll excuse me, I have to change."

From upstairs, she heard Toby and Oliver leaving together. Oliver was saying, "Don't take any notice of Mum. She's been in a funny mood for the last couple of days."

Huh, thought Jessie, *I wonder why.*

"Who's this chap then?" said Toby. "This Jonathan?"

"Oh, he's okay. Mad about Mum." Oliver sounded amused. "Just goes to show there's no accounting for taste. Coming over for a drink later?"

"Could do," said Toby.

Jessie had forgotten Jonathan's number. She had to look it up. Absence makes the heart forgetful...

"It's me. I'm sorry, can I change my mind?"

"About what?"

"I'd really like to see you tonight."

"Call that groveling?" said Jonathan.

"I'd really, really, *really* like to see you tonight."

"What a shame, you're too late," Jonathan sighed. "I've made other plans."

"You haven't!"

"Okay, I haven't. What time do you want me to pick you up?"

This wasn't as wholly unselfish as it sounded. Jonathan, a classic car enthusiast, couldn't bear to be driven anywhere in anything remotely ordinary. If he wasn't behind the wheel of his beloved yellow Lagonda, he didn't see the point in going out.

"Eight o'clock?" said Jessie.

"It's ten to eight now," Jonathan protested. "Give me a break."

"Okay, half past."

———

This was definitely what she needed, Jessie realized later that evening in the Seven Bells. A partner. An other half. Someone whose name people could link with hers so that whenever they were thinking of having a party, they could happily invite not just Jessie-on-her-own, but Jessie and Thing.

And the next time some philandering married man made a pass at her, he wouldn't be able to insinuate that she should be grateful for the attention, what with her being so...well, so embarrassingly *single*.

It was just a shame there wasn't some magic switch she could flick that would make her suddenly fancy Jonathan.

"Why does Oliver think I phoned you twice this evening and *begged* you to come out with me?"

"Probably because I told him you had."

Jonathan was nothing if not easygoing. He merely raised a quizzical eyebrow. "Am I allowed to ask why?"

"It's complicated," Jessie said with a sigh.

"Could it have anything to do with that piece in the *Daily Mail* last week?"

Jessie, her eyes bright, rattled the ice cubes around her empty glass like dice. "Why should it be anything to do with that?"

"Oh, no reason. I just wondered why we were sitting over *here* and Toby Gillespie was standing at the bar over *there*," Jonathan remarked mildly. "I also can't help noticing the way he keeps looking at me. As if he'd quite like to hit me over the head with a shovel."

Jessie trusted Jonathan, but she wasn't sure she trusted him one hundred percent. "Don't be daft. He's happily married."

Jonathan shrugged. "I'm just telling you what I see."

"Shall we go?" said Jessie. It was nine o'clock, she was starving, and she had made her point.

Jonathan smiled slightly. So he was right. Poor Jess. What kind of a mess had she gotten herself into now?

"Would you like me to put my arm around you as we leave?" he offered, since she had clearly dragged him along for a reason.

Jessie shot him a look of gratitude. "Yes, please."

"So Jess and Jonathan are back together," Lorna Blake observed, wiping the bar with such vigor she almost sent Toby's tumbler of Glenfiddich flying.

"Looks like it." Oliver listened to the throaty roar of Jonathan's Lagonda as it pulled out of the parking lot. "That could be the sound of my future stepfather." He grinned at Savannah. "Except he'd never let me borrow his precious car."

"I'll have another Scotch," said Toby.

Lorna gave him a pointed look. "Please."

"Sorry." He exaggerated the word. "*Please.*"

"You've had loads, Dad," Savannah said with a frown.

A middle-aged couple who had been murmuring encouragement to each other now approached the bar.

"Toby Gillespie? We're great fans of yours," gushed the woman, thrusting a beer coaster under his nose. "Could we have your autograph?"

"Please," prompted Toby.

The woman blushed all the way to her frizzy gray roots.

Toby shook his head. "No."

"Dad!" exclaimed Savannah.

"I don't want to."

"I'm really sorry." Savannah turned to the couple. "He's had a bit of a bad day."

"One of his friends has died," Oliver joined in. "A dear old actor friend—"

"Oh, you poor thing." The woman touched Toby's arm. "How horrid for you. Who was it? Anyone we'd know?"

"He wasn't famous." Oliver's tone was somber. "They were just very close." Glimpsing the look of astonishment in the woman's eye, he hastily added, "Not that kind of close."

Toby still wasn't saying anything.

"We're sorry to have disturbed you," Crestfallen, the woman and her husband backed away. The next minute, their drinks still unfinished, they had left the pub.

"Well, that was bloody rude," snapped Lorna.

"Look, people have been coming up to me asking for my autograph for the last twenty years." Toby wasn't in the mood to defend himself. "This is the first time I've ever said no."

"It is, it is," said Savannah loyally.

"Once in twenty years. That's not a bad record, is it?"

"I don't know," said Lorna Blake, nodding in the direction of the door. "Ask the couple who just left."

Guilt began to kick in. Defensively, Toby said, "They'll survive."

"Of course they will. Don't you worry about them," Lorna said coldly. "They're not important, are they? You're the one that matters." As she turned away to serve another customer, she added, "So long as you feel good about yourself, that's what counts."

"Oh shit," sighed Toby, finishing his drink and sliding off his stool. "Good night."

———

"Did you see Dad go home?" Savannah asked when Moll came back in weighed down with empties.

"He's still outside. Breathe in." As Moll squeezed past Oliver, she wiggled her hips teasingly against his jean-clad bottom. She winked at Savannah. "I can't resist this boy's body. Couldn't you just see him taking his clothes off in one of those Levi's ads?"

"What's he doing outside?" Oliver looked worried.

"Sitting at one of the tables talking to some middle-aged couple."

"Saying what to them?"

"What is this—twenty questions?" Wondering why Oliver should be so concerned, Moll gave him a playful dig in the ribs. "The usual stuff, that's all. I had to lend him my pen so he could give them an autograph. Now are you going to stack these glasses in the dishwasher?" She aimed another teasing prod at Oliver's flat stomach. "Or am I going to have to tickle you until you beg for mer—"

"I'll do it!" gasped Oliver, who was hopelessly ticklish. He tried to back away. "Moll! I'll do it, just stop!"

"Has anything ever happened between you two?" said Savannah when Moll had disappeared for a five-minute cigarette break.

"What, me and Moll?" Oliver looked amused. "No."

"Why not?"

"What do you mean?"

Savannah shrugged and fiddled with the thin straps of her striped cotton top. "Just that she seems to have slept with pretty much everyone else around here. And it's obvious she's keen on you."

"She's just friendly," Oliver protested, laughing.

But Savannah had been watching Moll Harper; she'd figured out her method. Any man Moll wasn't interested in got the saucy, flirty, you-should-be-so-lucky smile. The ones who did interest her, meanwhile, were treated to the slow, sultry, think-of-the-fun-*we*-could-have variety.

And while the banter she exchanged with Oliver might be saucy, the smile certainly wasn't.

Savannah, not fooled for a second, gave him a long look. "Bullshit. She fancies you rotten."

He shrugged. "Okay, maybe she's not my type."

"Well, good." Savannah was torn between relief and confusion that it should have mattered so much to her in the first place. The compulsion to protect Oliver from the attentions of other girls was as strong as ever.

She just wished she knew why.

Chapter 24

Now this is what I call stupid, Lili thought at seven thirty the next morning as she stood in her bra and panties in front of the wardrobe, wondering what to wear.

Pink shirt or orange top?

White skirt held together at the waist with a safety pin or black trousers?

Green sandals or purple flip-flops?

Hair up in a ponytail or—

"Decisions, decisions." Harriet, wearing the Spice Girls T-shirt she used as a nightie and clutching a bowl of Cheerios, appeared in the bedroom doorway. "You must be going somewhere brilliant."

"Sainsbury's, actually." It was too hot for black trousers and the orange top had gone weird around the neckline. Lili seized the pale-pink shirt and safety-pinned skirt and tried to look as if she always gave such careful thought to what clothes she put on each morning, rather than rummaging in the heap on the chair for yesterday's T-shirt and leggings.

"Oh wow, Mum! You've got lipstick on!"

Um, um… "It's a very smart Sainsbury's."

"But you never—"

"Lili, *quick*! Get down here and sort out this son of yours," Michael bawled up the stairs.

"He's done something hideous in his diaper," Lottie screeched, determined to sound as outraged as her father, "and it's all shot up his back."

As she made her way downstairs, grateful for the diversion, it occurred to Lili that Michael had never actually changed a diaper in his life.

———

Doug Flynn was rushing out of Keeper's Cottage as she arrived.

"I'm giving Drew a lift into work," Lili explained.

"Are you?" Doug looked surprised but held the front door open for her. "He isn't up yet."

When Doug's car had roared away up Compass Hill, Lili realized how utterly silent it was in the cottage.

The place was messy—certainly messy enough to send a shiver down Eleanor's fastidious, germ-free spine—but it wasn't as awful as it could have been. There was just the kind of general clutter you'd expect in a cottage shared by three single blokes. It actually had quite a relaxed atmosphere, Lili decided, feeling like Goldilocks as she wandered about.

Except one of the three bears, presumably, was still in the house.

"Uh...hello?" Lili aimed the words tentatively up the stairs.

No reply.

"Drew, are you there?"

Still nothing. This was getting silly. What if Drew had gone out last night, with his girlfriend for example, and stayed over at her place? What if he'd simply forgotten about her offer of a lift?

But Lili was fairly sure Drew didn't have a girlfriend. And although the sensible thing would be to go home and see if he phoned her, she couldn't do it without just checking first...

"Hello? Drew?" Ridiculously, she realized she was creeping up the stairs, trying not to make the floorboards creak. Lili cleared her throat as she reached the landing and called out again. "Drew? It's me—Lili."

The bathroom door was wide open, as was the door to Doug's

bedroom. Lili could tell it was his by the reek in the air of recently applied Eau Sauvage and the upturned copy of *Grey's Anatomy* lying on the unmade bed.

She knocked on the first of the two closed doors, peered inside, and saw a heap of Jamie's sweatshirts kicked into a corner. Lili wrinkled her nose. *No sign of any aftershave in here, more's the pity.*

The last door had to be Drew's. Lili tapped and pushed it open, convinced by now that he wouldn't be here.

The room was in almost total darkness, the curtains drawn. She let out a squeak of alarm when the bedclothes shifted and Drew's head poked out from under the duvet.

"Lili?"

"Oh, good grief. I'm sorry!" She scuttled backward, clinging to the door handle for support. "I thought you were… I mean, I didn't think you'd be—"

"What time is it?" Drew groaned, cutting across her babble.

"Five past eight. Um, shall I open the curtains?"

"Five past eight! Hell."

He sounded terrible. Lili wondered if he was horribly hungover.

She switched the light on, then cautiously approached the bed. "Don't you have to be at the clinic by half past—"

"Mind the bucket," Drew mumbled, not quite fast enough.

There was a resounding clunk as Lili stumbled against the aluminum bucket. At least it was empty.

"God, how much did you have to drink last night? Are you going to be sick?"

Now that the gloom had dissipated, she could see Drew's face. He was the color of dishwater and looked every bit as terrible as he sounded.

"I didn't have anything to drink," he croaked. "It's that bloody bug. I've been throwing up all night."

"Oh, Drew, you poor thing!" The stomach bug had been

doing the rounds of the village, knocking its sufferers for a loop in dramatic fashion. Lottie and Will had both gone down with it the week before. Happily, they hadn't been ill for long; it was only a twenty-four-hour virus.

Lili pressed a cool hand to Drew's forehead and felt how hot he was.

"You might catch it," he protested feebly.

"I won't. I'm never ill."

"Neither am I."

"I'll get you a drink. Mineral water's good," said Lili. "And that sheet's all twisted. Let me sort your bed out for you. Then you'll be more comfortable."

"You shouldn't be here. What if I'm sick again?" Drew miserably shook his head from side to side on the pillow. He'd never felt this terrible before.

"I'm a mother. I'm terrific at clearing up vomit. Now, what about work?"

"I'll need to ring Jamie on his cell. He was called out to help with a difficult foaling last night. He'll have to cover my shift... Where are you going?"

"I'll get that water for you and bring up the phone."

He gave her a soulful look. "I could be dead by the time you get back."

Lili smiled. "Try to keep breathing for the next couple of minutes."

By half past eight, Drew was sitting up in a freshly made bed, sipping mineral water, and actually feeling a bit better.

"You're an angel. You know that, don't you? I'm pathetically grateful," he told Lili. "Not to mention ravenous. I think I could manage some toast."

She shook her head. "It's too soon."

"No, really, I'll be okay."

Lili made him some toast.

At nine o'clock, Drew threw up again into his bucket.

"Why don't you try to get some more sleep?" Lili sponged his burning forehead with a blissfully cold cloth.

"You haven't even said I told you so," Drew marveled, closing his eyes.

She sounded amused. "I hate it when anyone says it to me."

"Is your car outside?"

"Yes."

He raised an eyebrow. "People will talk."

Glad that his eyes were still closed, Lili said lightly, "Shows how thick they are, then. If we were having a mad passionate affair I'd hardly park my car right outside your front door, would I?"

Slowly, Drew opened his eyes. "Unless it was a double bluff."

"Anyway, I'm sure people are talking already. When I pulled your curtains earlier, Myrtle Armitage was walking past. She looked pretty scandalized," said Lili.

Drew mustered a faint smile. "She'll tell everyone. If you switch on the TV, it'll probably be on there."

"Or she's working her way through every newspaper in the shop," Lili giggled, "sticking Post-it notes onto the bottom of all the gossip column pages: 'News just in from Upper Sisley. Frumpy mother of three flaunts fling with dashing Darcy.'"

"You aren't frumpy and I'm not dashing. Well, only to the loo," said Drew. His eyelids were closing again. He sounded as if he was having to struggle to stay awake.

"I'll leave you in peace." Lili put the phone on the bedside table next to his glass of water. "Give me a ring if you need anything. I'll pop back later anyway, shall I? Make sure you're all right."

She half expected Drew to protest that there was no need, he'd be fine. But he didn't.

"Thanks. There's a spare front door key on the mantelpiece."

Sounding resigned, he went on, "If I'm not breathing when you get here, just give me mouth-to-mouth resuscitation."

"Don't worry. Jamie said on the phone he'd be home by three," Lili consoled him. "If you're not breathing, I'll ask him to do it."

Chapter 25

Lɪʟɪ ᴡᴀs ᴏɴ ʜᴇʀ hands and knees in the garden, digging up Beachcomber Barbie, when a shadow fell over the flower bed.

"What's going on?" said Jessie.

"Oh, Lottie buried her yesterday. Ken's down here somewhere too—under that rosebush, I think. She said they were just too old." Lili imitated her younger daughter's dramatic manner. "It was time for them to die."

"I'm not talking about Barbie and Ken. I'm more interested in you and Drew Darcy," said Jessie. "I came home for lunch and Oliver told me."

"Oliver?"

"He heard it from Lorna."

"Who told Lorna?"

"Who d'you think? Myrtle."

"Ah." Lili nodded and smiled and shook a lump of earth out of Barbie's hair.

"Shameless, that's what you are. Pulling open Drew's bedroom curtains and not caring who sees you." Jessie mimicked the shopkeeper's outraged tone. She might only have heard the gossip thirdhand, but it wasn't hard to imagine how Myrtle would have put it. "Bold as brass, pleased as Punch, happy as Larry," she began to improvise freely, "whoever Larry might be."

"Did she really say that?"

"Well, maybe not. But apparently there was some mention of a midlife crisis."

"Cheek!" exclaimed Lili. "I'm only thirty-six."

Jessie grinned. "So what was he like in bed?"

"Sick."

"What, like perverted?"

"Like in a bucket." Lili jacked Barbie into a bent-over position and mimed her throwing up into the flower bed. "Poor thing, he's got that bug."

"And you were just doing your Florence Nightingale bit?" Jessie looked disappointed. "Mopping up puke? This is such a letdown."

Lili sat back on her heels and dusted the earth off her hands. She knew when she was being teased. She was the least likely person in the village to carry on an affair. Well—one of the least likely, she corrected herself as a mental picture of her mother-in-law in a negligee flitted through her mind.

She wondered what Jessie would say if she told her how long she'd spent in front of the mirror this morning, dithering over what to wear. "Anyway," she said to divert attention from herself, "why aren't you working?"

"I wanted to talk to you."

Lili could guess what this was about. The village grapevine traveled in both directions. Last night, while Harriet had been walking Blitz around the green, she had reported seeing Jess being driven away from the pub in a bright-yellow sports car.

"You're seeing Jonathan again."

Jessie sank down on the grass next to her and nodded. "Kind of."

"Why? I mean, he's really nice," Lili amended hastily, "but… well, I thought you'd got bored with all that tinkering-under-the-hood business. You told me if he spent as much time on foreplay as he spent polishing his spark plugs he'd be able to give Bradley Cooper a run for his money."

"I'm not sleeping with him this time. Just seeing him. It isn't a romantic thing." Jessie was fiddling with the orange scarf in her hair. Since it didn't need fiddling with, this was a sure sign that she was plucking up the courage to say something else.

"Come on," pressed Lili. "What?"

"Oh God. I just want people to *think* we're a couple."

"Why?"

Here goes, thought Jessie. She stopped twiddling the ends of the orange scarf, took a deep breath, and told her what had been going on with Toby.

"What a toad," Lili gasped when she had finished. Then "Oh, poor *you*" as Jessie's eyes filled up with tears. Jessie never cried, not even at *Little House on the Prairie*.

"Isn't it stupid?" Jessie found a use for the scarf at last, furiously wiping her eyes with one end. "I can't believe I actually fell for it, all that stuff about how he'd never stopped loving me, never felt like this about anyone else…and all the time it was just a stinking *line*."

Wondering if she'd missed something, Lili said cautiously, "You didn't go to bed with him though?"

Jessie shook her head. "But I wanted to."

"Oh, Jess…"

"I wouldn't, because of Deborah." Jessie struggled to make herself understood. "But if he weren't married, I would have." Sadly, she added, "Like a shot."

Lili was still trying to think of something consoling to say when Michael appeared outside.

"Haven't you been to Sainsbury's yet?" he grumbled. "We've run out of coffee."

"I've been busy." Lili pushed her shaggy fringe out of her eyes and gazed up at him, determined not to apologize.

"Looks like it. Gossiping with your friends on the lawn." He smiled slightly at Jess to soften the accusation. "Nice work if you can get it."

"If you're desperate for coffee, walk up to Myrtle's," said Lili.

"She doesn't sell the kind I like."

This was what drove Lili mad. Not long after returning home, Michael grew as dull and fractious as any teenager, and—quite unfairly—she felt obliged to keep him occupied. She found herself saying things like "Well, the lawn needs mowing" or "Why don't you have a nice game of golf?"

"You could go to Sainsbury's if you like," she suggested now, keen to get him out of the house so she and Jess could carry on uninterrupted. "The list's on the kitchen table."

Michael looked underwhelmed. He'd seen the list; it was a mile long and full of riveting stuff like toilet bleach, potatoes, and dishcloths.

"Or you could fix those shelves in the bathroom," Lili went on brightly.

Shelves. Steady on there, too much excitement wasn't good for a man.

He hated fixing bloody shelves anyway.

"I'll get the shopping."

"Oh, and while I think of it, can you look after the kids on Wednesday evening? Myrtle wants me to perm her hair, and it's easier if I do it at her house."

Irritation welled up. Trawl around Sainsbury's, babysit the kids… What was he, the sodding hired help?

"I'll get the shopping," Michael repeated tightly, "but you'll have to manage without me on Wednesday. I'm playing snooker. There's a competition on at the club."

He had no intention of going to the snooker club. He was sick to death of snooker. He would pay another visit to the Antelope, he decided, and check out Singles Nite instead.

—∞—

Oliver and Savannah were going swimming as soon as Oliver finished his lunchtime shift at the pub.

"We're rushed off our feet," he told her when she wandered into the bar at two thirty with a rolled-up towel under her arm.

Savannah, who was wearing a pale-gray crop top and frayed white shorts, wasn't concerned. "I'll have a drink and wait outside." She patted her brown midriff and grinned. "Work on my tan."

Plenty of people had chosen to eat their lunch in the backyard. When Oliver emerged into the blazing sunshine twenty minutes later carrying two plates of vegetarian cannelloni, all the tables were occupied and he couldn't immediately pick out Savannah.

Then he saw her at the far end of the yard, squashed onto a bench between two men he didn't know. Three more sat opposite her, and they were all howling with laughter. When Oliver moved to one side to get a better view, he saw why. One of the men was wearing Savannah's pink-and-black-striped bikini top over his shirt.

"Um…excuse me, are those our cannelloni?"

Savannah was laughing so much she choked on her orange juice. The chap next to her began patting her on the back. The man in the bikini top pretended to choke as well and got the strap across his back vigorously twanged.

Feeling increasingly uneasy, Oliver watched Savannah murmur something to the one who'd been patting her on the back. The man leaned across, lifted the curtain of blond hair away from her ear, and whispered something that made her burst out laughing again.

Moments later, she looked up and spotted Oliver. Still giggling, she beckoned him over, clearly eager to introduce him to her new friends.

Oliver had no intention of going over to be introduced. Why would he want to meet that bunch of idiots?

"Are they for us?" said the same slightly irritated voice behind Oliver as he stood there with the cannelloni going cold.

"Sorry? Oh, right." He put the plates down on the table, bits of glistening red leaf lettuce and tomato spilling to the ground.

The man on the other side of Savannah had progressed to rubbing his thigh against her bare leg. Now he was checking out the amount of fray on her shorts. Oliver quashed a terrifying urge to rush across and deck him.

"Hang on. This is vegetarian. We aren't vegetarians," complained the customer, who was overweight and perspiring freely in the heat. "We ordered ordinary."

The pink-and-black-striped bikini top was coming off now, striptease style. Its wearer swung it around his head and gyrated his hips suggestively. The next minute it sailed through the air, landing in one of the apple trees and catching on a low branch.

"Are you listening to me? I *said*, we don't want this vegetarian rubbish."

"It might do you some good," Oliver couldn't stop himself snapping back. "Just stop moaning and eat it."

—⁓—

It was her job to unpack and put away, Lili realized when she opened the door to the kitchen and saw the dozen or so plastic bags groaning with groceries. Michael had already disappeared upstairs to have a shower. *Oh well, he deserves a rest,* she thought drily, discovering three tubs of rapidly melting Crunchy Nut Toffee Explosion ice cream in the first bag she peered into. *He's only a man, after all. He can't be expected to do everything.*

"Can you keep an eye on the children for ten minutes?" she asked an hour later. Michael, evidently still suffering from shop-lag, was stretched out on one of the chaise longues listening to cricket on the radio. This, to Lili's mind, was about as riveting as listening to knitting on the radio.

He deigned to raise his dark glasses. "What?"

"Just for ten minutes. I promised Drew I'd pop back and make sure he's okay."

Michael squinted up at her. "Are you wearing lipstick?"

"No!" Lili felt the back of her neck prickle with belated guilt; after this morning, she hadn't had the nerve to risk it again. Instead, purely to combat lip dryness, she had grabbed one of the million tubes of lip balm Harriet was addicted to and had applied a quick layer as she was running downstairs.

Michael shrugged. "Okay. Don't be long. I'm starving."

As she made her way across the sun-bleached village green, Lili felt like Gary Cooper in *High Noon*. Myrtle Armitage was bound to be watching avidly, informing anyone else who happened to be in the shop that there she was, as bold as brass and old enough to know better, off again to visit her fancy man.

Lili wondered if the fact that Jamie's car was now parked on the shoulder outside Keeper's Cottage would defeat the gossips or add to the intrigue. Myrtle might start spreading even wilder rumors about threesomes.

"Hi!" Jamie said cheerfully, opening the front door. "He must be ill—I offered him a beer and he turned it down."

Jamie wasn't helping much by wearing only a pair of beige shorts. If Myrtle had her Hubble-strength binoculars trained on Keeper's Cottage, she might just think he was naked.

"I brought him another bottle of mineral water," said Lili.

Jamie looked appalled. "He'll never get drunk on that. Still, come on in. At least he's stopped throwing up."

Drew was lying in bed, watching cricket—God, what *was* it with men and that stupid game?—on a grainy, black-and-white portable TV. He was still looking white and drawn but smiled and sat up when Lili came into the room.

"Am I glad to see you."

"Why?"

"I need sympathy." He rumpled his hair and looked sorry for himself. "No danger of that Philistine downstairs being sympathetic."

"You poor, wounded soldier." Lili grinned.

"He came home with Indian takeout," Drew protested. "Asked me if I fancied some of his chicken vindaloo."

"Ah well, men are beasts."

"I'm not a beast. I'm just thirsty."

She held up the family-size bottle of mineral water. "Ta-da!"

"Brilliant."

Drew heaved a sigh of relief and watched her unscrew the top. Sadly, Lili's hurried progress across the green had given the bottle a thorough shaking up. The next moment, icy, carbonated water fountained everywhere, drenching them both.

"Are you trying to tell me I need a shower?" said Drew.

There was a box of man-size tissues half-hidden under the bed. Hooking it out with her foot, Lili went pink as she realized she had dragged out a packet of condoms along with the Kleenex. Hurriedly, before Drew saw what she'd done, she tried to kick them back.

"Owww!"

"What's happened?" Drew leaned over the side of the bed.

Lili, who had missed the condoms completely, collapsed to the floor clutching her big toe.

"Ow ow ow," she moaned, rocking to and fro and feeling quite sick. The pain was excruciating.

"Here, let me have a look." Drew threw back the covers, hopped out, and lifted her onto the bed.

"I'm so clumsy," Lili wailed. Last time it had been her scalded chest. "I'm such an idiot. Oh yuck, and this pillow's soaking wet."

Having pulled off her dusty sandal, Drew sat on the edge of the mattress and examined her foot. Lili prayed it wasn't dirty. Then she prayed even harder that it didn't smell.

"Not broken. You'll have a bit of a bruise."

The pain was beginning to wear off, Lili, wondering why her mouth felt so weird, licked her lips. "You're the one who's supposed to be in bed, not me."

Drew grinned at her. He was wearing nothing but a pair of red boxer shorts, and his face and chest were still damp. The boxer shorts were covered with mini *Baywatch* babes, Lili couldn't help noticing. She wondered if he was holding his stomach in.

"Jamie's idea of a witty Christmas present," Drew said, holding his stomach in so hard he was in danger of getting cramp. "Sophisticated or what?"

Lili's mouth still felt really odd. She licked her lips again, then wondered if Drew would think she was doing it for his benefit, trying to be provocative.

"Anyone fancy a coffee? Lili, how about you?"

Jamie, appearing in the doorway, stopped dead as he took in the scene: Lili on the bed licking her lips, Drew—looking decidedly damp—sitting next to her in his *Baywatch* boxers. On the floor, the condoms had shot out of their packet.

"Blimey." Jamie gazed at Drew and let out a low whistle of admiration. "That's what I call fast work."

———

"What's the matter with your mouth?" said Michael when Lili arrived back at the house.

"I don't know."

Mystified, she rummaged in the drawer of the Welsh dresser where she had thrown Harriet's lip salve after using it.

"And why are you limping?"

"I stubbed my toe."

"You're all wet too. What have you been doing, giving the poor sod a sponge bath?"

"Oh, for pity's sake!" Lili exclaimed, half laughing as she found the black-and-white tube and read the words printed on the side. "It isn't lip salve at all. It's a glue stick."

Chapter 26

Doug Flynn hadn't spoken much to April since their outing last week to the Antelope, but she was flattered on Wednesday morning when he noticed her hair.

"Had it cut," he said with a nod of approval as he leaned against the desk in reception and flipped idly through a set of notes. "I like it."

"Thanks." April touched the new, feathery tendrils around the nape of her neck, her confidence boosted. She wondered how Doug would react if he knew she was going back to the Antelope tonight. Find it hugely amusing, no doubt. When you were as outrageously good-looking as Doug Flynn, wondering how you were ever going to meet a potential partner simply wasn't an issue. Women swarmed out of the woodwork wherever you went.

"Hmm, can't wait," Doug murmured, turning a page. The set of case notes, as thick as a telephone directory, belonged to one of their regulars, a homeless alcoholic in his twenties with a reputation for peeing in the trash can next to the coffee machine and roaring that all doctors in this dump were murderers. He smelled outrageous and, to amuse himself, liked to scrawl four-letter words across the tattered copies of *People's Friend* and *Reader's Digest* peppering the waiting room.

He had deigned to visit them today because his latest tattoo had gone violently septic.

"He's just visiting the loo," said April when Doug heaved the notes under one arm without much enthusiasm and turned to scan the rows of seats.

"Lucky loo." Glancing at his watch, Doug dumped the notes back on the desk. "In that case he can wait another five minutes. I don't know if I can face this on an empty stomach. I'm going to grab a sandwich."

April was busily tapping details into the computer when the bell on the desk went *ding* to attract her attention. Hoping it wasn't Doug's patient come back to tell her she was a whore and a bloody murderer just like the rest of them, she glanced cautiously over her shoulder and said, "Won't be a sec."

It took her a couple of seconds to recognize the woman standing there, simply because her presence was so out of context. Just as you didn't expect to find Oprah Winfrey waiting in line behind you in the post office, you didn't expect to look up and see Deborah Gillespie smiling at you across the desk in the emergency room of Harleston General.

It was weird, coming face-to-face with someone you'd only ever seen before in the papers or on television.

"Sorry." Realizing how moronic she must look, April stopped staring and pulled herself together. "Can I help you?"

"I'm such an idiot," said Deborah Gillespie, gripping her stomach and wincing. "We just moved down here and I haven't got around yet to registering with the local GP. The thing is, I think I've got appendicitis."

Although clearly in pain, she managed a rueful smile. April was dazzled. She couldn't imagine how anyone could look so effortlessly chic in just a pale-gray cardigan and faded jeans.

Neither could Doug's next patient, back from the loo and eyeing Deborah's rear view with interest.

"If you give me your details, I'll make up a file," April told her. "Don't worry. We'll get someone to take a look at you."

"I'll take a look at you." Doug's patient leered, breathing hideous alcohol fumes over Deborah's shoulder, patently under the impression that he had a chance here. "C'mon, c'mon…" Clumsily he tried to grab her wrist, "Let's go and find an empty cubicle. You're my kind of woman, y'know that?"

The security guard was on his break. Mortified, April looked around for Doug. The sooner he cleaned up this awful man's septic tattoo and sent him back out into the real world, the better. *Heavens, what must poor Deborah Gillespie be making of this?*

Deborah leaned across the desk and said in a low voice, "It's okay. I'm married to an actor. I'm used to drunks."

"Yeah? This is your lucky day, sweetheart," Doug's patient crooned happily. "Just be careful with my back, all right? No getting carried away and digging your nails in." He twisted around, showing her which shoulder blade to avoid. "This tattoo's giving me trouble."

"Hang on a sec," April said to Deborah. "I'll just go and find this gentleman's doctor, then—"

"Before you go, is Doug Flynn on duty?" Deborah interrupted. "Sorry, it's an awful cheek—but I know him, you see. If he isn't here, it doesn't matter," she went on, skillfully ignoring the alcoholic's grubby fingers pawing her arm, "but if he is, I'd prefer to be dealt with by Doug."

Septic Tattoo was swiftly delegated to Rosie, the resident on duty. "Oh great," she grumbled. "You get Deborah Gillespie, and I get *him*. Just how fair is that?"

Doug gave her shoulder a reassuring squeeze. "When Will Smith walks in, he's all yours. Promise."

Walking carefully, holding her stomach, Deborah followed him along the corridor to the examination cubicle.

"Lie down on the cot," said Doug, "and I'll have a look at you. Why don't you tell me how this started?"

"I think it's appendicitis." She half unzipped her jeans and lifted the pale-gray angora cardigan out of the way. "It started this morning."

Gently Doug began to palpate her abdomen. "Tell me if it hurts."

"Ouch," said Deborah as his cool fingers pressed beneath her ribs. "Ouch," as they moved down to the left. "Ouch, ouch," she murmured when he slid them to the right.

"That was McBurney's point," Doug told her, having elicited an "ouch" much the same as all the others upon investigating the area on the right side, two thirds of the way from navel to jutting hip bone. "You don't have appendicitis."

"I don't?"

"If you did, you'd hit the ceiling when I did this." He pressed again.

Deborah, trying to keep a straight face, said, "Ouch."

"Pulse normal," Doug remarked, dropping her wrist and scribbling a figure in the notes. "How did you get here? Did your husband bring you?"

"He's in London. I drove."

"Is that sensible, when you're in this much pain?"

"I knew you were on duty today. I heard your car going up the road at half past nine."

"Respiration's normal. Blood pressure normal." Carefully, playing for time, Doug wrote down the results. Something was going on here. Deborah was smiling up at him now, not paying the least bit of attention to the findings of his examination.

"Appetite okay?" As he spoke, Doug heard one of the nurses talking to another patient as she pushed him along in a wheelchair. The flimsy curtain separating the cubicle from the corridor fluttered as they moved past.

"Fine," said Deborah.

Doug couldn't look at her. He didn't want to say this, but it was a question that had to be asked: "How are your bowels?"

"Very well, thank you. How are yours?" Still smiling up at

him, Deborah watched the curtain billow again as an EKG cart was wheeled past. She put a finger to her lips and beckoned Doug closer.

Doug wondered if the fact that they could be overheard so easily was embarrassing her. Maybe she wanted to tell him something incredibly intimate about her bowels. He leaned down, breathing in her soapy scent, trying to keep his eyes averted from her cleavage.

Deborah lifted her head and kissed him, slowly and very thoroughly, full on the mouth.

Jesus, thought Doug, stunned by the unexpectedness of the kiss, and both appalled and hopelessly aroused by the fear of being caught.

Jesus...

"Guess what, Doctor?" Deborah breathed in his ear. "My stomachache's all gone. Almost as if it were never there in the first place. It's a miracle."

Unable to speak—not daring to utter a word—Doug nodded his head. His heart was kicking against his chest like a demented donkey. This was unbelievable. How could it be happening? What did it *mean*?

Deborah smiled and kissed him again, sliding her tongue into his mouth and arching her back as she pulled him closer still.

"Have any of your patients ever done this to you before?" she murmured.

Thankfully, the words were barely audible. Doug shook his head. If someone came into the cubicle now, he would face instant dismissal. He'd lose his license. All those grueling years of training would have been for nothing.

"No."

"Good." Deborah winked. "I'd hate to be unoriginal."

With some difficulty, Doug pulled himself upright. He reached for the notes on the cart.

"I have to write something down. I can't just leave it—"

"Anything you like," Deborah murmured back, handing him the pen, which had rolled under her leg. She surveyed Doug with evident pleasure. "So long as it isn't the truth. What time do you finish work?"

More voices outside. Doug, so used to being in control of every situation, knew he wasn't the one in control now.

He mouthed *Six o'clock*, and Deborah nodded.

"That's fine. Come to my house." Glimpsing the expression on Doug's face, she added, "Toby won't be back before midnight."

"And the rest of your family?"

Deborah looked amused. "All under control, Doctor. I'm not a complete novice, you know."

Dear God…

—◆—

"So how was the glorious Mrs. Gillespie?" said Rosie an hour later, launching herself into the coffee room for what was laughingly known as a lunch break. This meant ten minutes on a good day. More often than not it meant no break at all.

Doug frowned, pretending to be engrossed in an article on Marfan syndrome in this month's *BMJ*. Without even glancing up, he said, "Who? Oh, she was okay."

"Wow, such enthusiasm." Rosie threw herself into a chair and tore the wrapper off a half-melted Mars bar. "What was the problem in the end? I noticed you didn't admit her."

"Didn't need admitting. All she had was trapped wind," Doug said shortly. "I prescribed charcoal tablets, sent her home, and told her to get herself registered with a GP."

Rosie pulled a face. "What a letdown. That's not very glamorous, is it? You don't expect women like her to suffer from gas."

Doug let her babble on between mouthfuls of Mars bar. If she dragged the *BMJ* out of his hands and announced that she was going to test him on it, he would fail abysmally. The game would be well and truly up.

She didn't, thank goodness.

As he turned a page for appearance's sake, he checked his watch. Four and a half hours to go before six o'clock.

"Still…" Rosie swallowed the last bit of Mars, licked her fingers, and wiped her hands happily on the inside of her white coat. "Look on the bright side. At least your patient didn't pee in the sink like mine did."

Chapter 27

THE BACKYARD OF KEEPER'S COTTAGE was a dandelion-infested no-go area. Hardly able to believe he was doing this, Doug made his way through the chest-high Queen Anne's lace to the stone wall separating their untamed jungle from the landscaped grounds of Sisley House.

As he hopped over the wall, he saw Deborah waiting for him on the terrace.

"Handy, having adjoining yards," she announced cheerfully when he reached her. "This way nobody can start asking awkward questions."

Doug's mouth was dry. Deborah was leading him over to the french windows.

"Asking awkward questions about what?"

"About why, every time the rest of the family is away, you turn up at my house."

Every time? My God, Doug thought. *This is Deborah Gillespie speaking*. This is unreal. "The rest of your family…" he croaked as she unfastened his shirt with deft fingers and pushed him gently backward on to a crimson velvet-upholstered sofa.

"Are all in London." Deborah undid the last button with a flourish. "Toby's doing a talk show and the other guests are the Spice Girls." She shrugged. "That was it. Sav and Dizzy were out of here. I didn't see them for dust."

Doug had a million questions, but he didn't get a chance to ask them. Deborah slid the straps of her black dress off her shoulders and stood naked before him, lithe and golden, every red-blooded male's fantasy come true.

Her dark eyes sparkled as she unbuckled the belt on his jeans and said, "Well, Doctor, my turn to examine you now. I think this is going to be fun."

—⁓—

Afterward, Doug had to put his jeans and shirt back on straightaway. It felt too weird, lying there on the sofa naked. Imagine if Toby came back early.

"Ready for the quick getaway?" Teasing, Deborah reached over for the remote control and flipped the television on. "Relax, you're quite safe. It's a live show."

Doug turned, and there was Toby on the screen, making an appearance in order to plug the release on video of last year's film.

"So…you and Deborah, still happily married after all these years," marveled the interviewer, who was divorced four times himself. "How *do* you do it?"

It was a run-of-the-mill question, one that Toby had been asked a thousand times before.

"We're great friends, I suppose." His smile was self-deprecating. "We talk, we trust each other, we don't—"

The screen abruptly went blank.

Doug, who had grabbed the remote control from Deborah's hand, said, "Aren't you taking a bit of a risk here? How do you know I won't go to the papers? I could sell a story like this for thousands."

"You could." Deborah nodded, unperturbed. "But you'd lose your license. I was your patient."

"This afternoon, when you said you weren't a complete novice…" Doug hesitated, searching for the right words. "Do you… I mean, is it a regular thing?"

Laughing, Deborah pulled him back down next to her. "Look,

you aren't the first. But you aren't the hundredth either. I'm very fussy, extremely discreet, and I only get involved with men who have as much to lose as I do." She stroked Doug's tanned chest. "I have a nice life, and I don't want to put my marriage at risk. But some opportunities are just too good to pass up." With a grin, Deborah went on. "We moved into this house and there you were, our new next-door neighbor. Not only dishy but something of an expert when it comes to covering your tracks with women." She waved a teasing index finger at him and added, "Plus, you have a career you wouldn't want to put at risk."

"Does Toby do this as well?" Doug was stunned by her matter-of-factness.

"God no!"

"Never?"

"Never."

"Does he know *you* do it?"

Patiently Deborah shook her head. "I told you, I'm very discreet."

"What would happen if he found out?"

"About you and me?" Sweeping back her dark hair, Deborah wriggled down on the sofa, her words becoming muffled as she trailed kisses across his flat stomach. "He won't find out about us. I trust you," she added, glancing up briefly and breaking into a bewitching smile. "You're a doctor."

When Doug could speak again, he asked, "Don't you even love him?"

"Of course I do." Deborah sounded amused.

"So why do this?"

She shrugged carelessly. "Adventure, I suppose. Fun. Why not, if no one gets hurt?"

"I still can't believe this is happening." Doug shook his head. "You're Deborah Gillespie. You're married to Toby Gil—"

"And you have no idea how bloody *boring* it is, being constantly described as Mr. and Mrs. Happy-Show-Business-Couple," Deborah blurted out. "You have no idea how humiliating it is when the only reason people know you is because you're Toby Gillespie's wife."

The phone rang and Deborah answered it, still naked. Doug, watching her, recalled that she had once been a bit-part actress, the highlight of her career an appearance in a TV commercial for shampoo. That was when Toby had, famously, spotted her and tracked her down. Soon afterward they had married, the children had come along in smart succession, and as far as Deborah's fledgling career was concerned, that had been that.

"How do you spell Spielberg?" Deborah sighed, hanging up the phone and frowning at what she'd written. Doug reached across and corrected it. The message was for Toby to ring Steven Spielberg's office first thing tomorrow.

He tried to imagine how that made Deborah feel. Was she envious of Toby's success? Did she wonder if it could have been her, being rung up by Steven Spielberg, desperate for her to star in his next movie?

Doug followed Deborah through to the kitchen and watched her bottom wiggle as she pinned the note up on the message board behind the door.

"What are those? Fan mail?" He pointed to a cluster of envelopes bulldog-clipped together and addressed to Toby in oddly childish writing.

"Hate mail." Deborah unpinned them and held them out to him. "Someone in the village isn't overjoyed to have us here."

"Have you told the police?" Doug skimmed through the contents. "They could check for fingerprints."

"The letters aren't threatening. The police have more important things to worry about. What are they going to do—fingerprint the whole village?"

"But—"

"Don't let it bother you," Deborah said lightly. Drawing him against her, she wound her arms around his neck. "We've got far more interesting things to think about," she murmured in his ear, "like when and where we're going to meet next."

—~~—

April knew she looked hopelessly out of place. She'd been so determined not to appear tarty, she'd ended up resembling an off-duty nun instead. The white, high-necked blouse felt as if it would choke her; the navy skirt was too long and too dark; sixty opaque tights had been a huge mistake. If the temperature outside was Mediterranean, the heat inside the Antelope Inn was positively tropical. *I might not look tarty but I definitely look stupid*, she thought, leaning against a wall and feeling the sweat crawling down the backs of her legs.

Singles Nite was more popular than she had imagined—but nobody else had come dressed as a nun.

She checked her watch. Her new way of coping was to set herself small challenges and see them through. Coming along here tonight had been the first challenge. Sticking it out for an hour, no matter how awful it turned out to be, was another. According to the magazine someone had left behind in the waiting room, this was a surefire method of getting your life back on track. Before you knew it, you'd find yourself brimming over with bucketloads of confidence and fabulous men would be falling over themselves to whisk you off on a paragliding adventure in Peru.

"Test Your Mettle!" the article had urged. "Take Risks! Seize the Moment *and* the Man of Your Dreams!"

April wasn't sure about the paragliding in Peru bit, but she wouldn't say no to a cottage in Cornwall. The man of her dreams wouldn't even need to be fabulous, she had decided wistfully. Just caring and decent and...well, nice.

But she couldn't help wondering if maybe she'd been meant to read this advice. If Doug Flynn's patient—the one with the septic tattoo—hadn't scrawled "FUCK" and "BOLLOCKS" all over the front cover of the glossy magazine, she wouldn't have had to take it out of the waiting room, the article would have passed her by, and she might well have given in to the temptation to stay in tonight and sob her way through *Ghost* on television.

Oh well, so much for fate. It was eight forty-five. Fifteen more minutes, then she could go home. Nobody had spoken to her yet, and it was looking increasingly unlikely that anyone would.

Serves me right for getting my hopes up, thought April, sipping her lukewarm grapefruit juice to make it last.

The bad news was that being whisked away by Mr. Fabulous clearly wasn't going to happen. The good news, though, was that at least she'd set herself a goal and stuck to it. The even better news was she'd recorded *Ghost*.

At two minutes to nine, someone did actually speak to her.

"Oh, hi, it's you!"

It was the girl April had met in the loo last week, the friendly one who had urged her to come along to Singles Nite.

"Hello." Clutching her empty glass, April attempted to shrink away from a noisy group of women swarming past. She managed to smile at the girl, who was wearing a fluorescent-pink blouse tied under her breasts and a microscopic pair of orange shorts. But the clothes didn't matter; she was just glad to be having a conversation.

"Told you it was a laugh here, didn't I?" The girl in turn beamed at April and accidentally sloshed red wine down the leg of a tall man's cream trousers. "Oops, sorry!" She gave his arm an apologetic pat. "Let me buy you a drink, love. See you around," she added over her shoulder to April, winking as she led the man toward the bar. "Don't do anything I wouldn't do, eh?"

"No," said April, chastened. "Bye."

Chapter 28

"MUST BE NICE FOR the kiddies," said Myrtle, "having their Dad back."

"Mmm." Lili gave Myrtle's freshly permed, just-washed, gray-with-a-hint-of-lilac curls a brisk rub with the towel.

"Nice for you too."

"Well, yes." Lili ran a comb through Myrtle's hair and picked up her scissors. "Just a trim, is that what you want? A general tidy up?"

"Your Michael doesn't mind you visiting other men, then?" Myrtle inquired archly. "I mean, he's not bothered about you spending time over at Keeper's Cottage?"

The scissors, nice and sharp, could snip out Myrtle's tongue with no trouble at all. Resisting the urge, Lili smiled into the mirror and began cutting her hair instead. "Drew was ill. He caught that rotten bug. I was making sure he was okay, Myrtle, that's all."

"Hmm."

"It's called being neighborly. What did you imagine?" Lili went on brightly. "That Drew and I are having a torrid affair?"

"Of course not." Myrtle pursed her lips as the scissors snip-snipped around the nape of her bulbous neck. "But you know what some folk around here are like for gossip."

"Anyway, Drew's years younger than me. He's a young man and I'm almost forty. Heavens," Lili said cheerfully. "I've even got cellulite!"

"I'm just saying some women go a bit funny when they reach that age." Myrtle was partial to a bit of doom and gloom. "I'm talking about the change, dear. Their hormones start going up the creek and that's it, they're off, having hot flashes all over the place and chasing after anything in trousers."

Was this what had happened when Myrtle had hit menopause? Stifling a grin, Lili said, "I didn't know that."

Myrtle, who spent much of her free time in the shop, propped against the counter idly leafing through magazines, regarded herself as something of an expert. She frequently got her facts wrong but always pronounced them with authority. "Mark my words, there's a lot of it about these days," she told Lili sternly. "These women have to have tablets to keep them under control. Maybe that's what you need."

Amazed, Lili said, "What kind of tablets?"

"You go along to your GP, dear, and tell him you're nearing the change." Myrtle turned to make sure Lili was paying attention and almost got her ear sliced off. "He'll put you on some of that HRT."

The parking lot at the Antelope was full. Michael, forced to leave the car on the opposite side of the road, only realized who the girl in the high-necked white shirt and unflattering blue skirt was when he walked past her at the bus stop.

"Hello there." His eyes crinkled in friendly recognition. "We met briefly last week, didn't we? You're Doug's friend."

"Well, kind of. We just work together." Flustered, April realized how foolish she must sound. As if anyone would assume she was one of Doug Flynn's girlfriends. "I mean…only vaguely, in the same department," she stumbled on. "He's a doctor… Of course you know that. And I'm just one of the receptionists."

"No 'just' about it. Where would a hospital be without receptionists to keep everything running smoothly?"

The road was clear now but Michael didn't attempt to cross it. Instead, he nodded in the direction of the pub. "I saw you coming out while I was trying to find somewhere to park. Is Doug inside?"

The prospect didn't alarm him. Doug Flynn wasn't the type to whisper a word of friendly warning to Lili along the lines of "Guess where I bumped into your husband the other night."

But April shook her head. "No, he's not there."

"And you've given up already, at"—Michael consulted his watch—"ten past nine. That's a bad sign. What's it like inside?"

"Hot," said April. "The air conditioning's broken down."

"And busy, by the look of the parking lot."

"I...I was meant to be meeting a friend there, but she didn't turn up," April fibbed. This was the excuse she had prepared in case she bumped into anyone she knew.

"Some friend." Not believing her for a minute, Michael was touched by her air of vulnerability. "Well, I'm here now. Why don't we go in and have a drink together?"

He was really quite good-looking. And he seemed kind. If only she hadn't worn these stupid clothes. "Actually, I thought I'd just go home." April gestured apologetically at her skirt and tights. "I feel a bit overdressed."

He looked sympathetic. "Is that your receptionist's uniform?"

"No, I just wore the wrong thing." In a burst of honesty, she admitted, "I didn't want to look like a tart."

She wasn't Michael's usual type at all, but there was something about her that attracted him—definitely. He glanced across once more at the Antelope. "Well, you've put me off the idea of that place."

"I'm sorry," April said humbly.

"Don't be sorry. You've done me a favor. No air conditioning and a heaving bar isn't my idea of fun. Look," he went on, as if on impulse, "I don't even know your name."

"April."

"And I'm Michael." He grinned at her. "Why don't we both give this a miss and find somewhere quieter? Do you live far from here?"

"Um...a couple of miles."

"I could drive you to your house, you could dash in and change into something more...summery, and then we can go wherever we like."

April was lost for words. She wanted to, more than anything—but how could she? Hopping into a car with a virtual stranger was dangerous. Testing Your Mettle and Seizing the Moment was all very well, but what about those dreadful stories you saw in the papers?

"I know, I know," Michael said when she hesitated. "I could be a murderer, a raving psychopath. I'm not," he told her with a smile, "but you don't know that. So look, how about this for a plan? You catch the bus home. Change your clothes. Name a nice pub or restaurant, and I'll see you there in an hour. That way I won't even know where you live."

April shifted from foot to foot, hotter than ever with embarrassment and racked with indecision. She imagined Bernadette's reaction if she told her she'd climbed into the car of a strange man she'd met at a bus stop.

"Okay," she said finally.

"Okay." Michael's smile broadened. He took his car keys from his pocket. "Where shall we meet?"

He had nice eyes. They crinkled at the corners.

And there was still no sign of the bus.

April was beginning to wonder if she had missed it.

Oh, what the hell. Who said she needed to tell Bernadette anyway?

Blinking rapidly, she looked at Michael and took the plunge. "It's okay. I'll come with you."

Chapter 29

"THAT'S US IN SARDINIA. We spent a month there after Dad finished filming *The Weekenders*." Savannah pointed to a photo of Dizzy and herself on a beach, wearing shorts and floppy sun hats and waving Frisbees.

"How old were you then?" said Oliver.

"Eight. And Dizzy was six." She shook her head. "God, he was a real pain when he was six."

"I was not," Dizzy retorted from the depths of the hammock.

"You were. You still are." Savannah lobbed a peach stone at him. "Go back to sleep."

Oliver flipped over to the next page of the album. Savannah had found the photographs in an old suitcase and stuck them in willy-nilly, paying no attention to chronological order. The next picture, far more recent, was of Toby, Deborah, Savannah, and a good-looking boy he didn't recognize. They were all sitting around a restaurant table studded with bottles. Savannah, wearing a sequined white dress, was deeply tanned and showing miles of leg.

"That was in Cannes," she told Oliver, "at the film festival. After that meal we went on to Bruce Willis's party. I drank three tequila slammers and fell into the pool."

"Who's he?" Oliver pointed to the good-looking boy.

"Henri. Wasn't he gorgeous? He had a part in one of the French films nominated for the Palme d'Or." Savannah sighed happily.

"He was brilliant. We were mad about each other. That was one of the best vacations of my life."

Oliver looked at her, lying on her front on the lawn, a dreamy expression on her face. "How long were you seeing each other?"

"Oh, it was hopeless. He had to fly off to do a film in Toronto. Then he went on location with Dad to Switzerland. We wrote to each other for a few weeks, but it was never the same."

She was still gazing at the photograph.

Oliver felt a knot tighten in the pit of his stomach. "Do you still like him?"

"Of course she still likes him." Dizzy's scornful voice drifted across from the hammock. "She keeps a photo of him in her diary."

"You little sneak!" Savannah said furiously. "How *dare* you read my diary."

"And saying you wrote to each other's a bit of an exaggeration." Dizzy, slotting a Blur CD into his CD player, sounded triumphant. "You wrote him about fifty letters and he sent you one postcard of a Canadian Mountie. It's hardly the same, is it? Ouch, get off!"

Savannah, on her feet and across the lawn in a flash, tipped Dizzy out of the hammock. She wrenched the CD player off him, snapped his precious *Parklife* CD in two, and threw it in his face. "You're a beastly little shit and I hate you!"

"You smell of garlic," Dizzy retaliated. "It's probably the only reason Henri liked you in the first place. He always stank of garlic too."

Oliver, who was getting used to their fights by now, turned to the next page in the album. At least this one was Henri free.

He studied a photograph of Savannah and Deborah in Rome, throwing coins into the Trevi Fountain. The Gillespies had been everywhere. He'd been nowhere. And the money Toby had given him was just sitting, gathering dust in his savings account.

"That's where I'm going," he said when Savannah had finished beating up Dizzy and thrown herself back down on the grass next to him.

"Not yet though."

Oliver didn't look at her. He couldn't carry on like this, feeling jealous whenever he thought of Savannah with past boyfriends. He had to get away.

"You promised you wouldn't go yet," said Savannah when he didn't reply.

"I know, but I've changed my mind."

"What did I tell you?" Dizzy jeered from a safe distance. "It's your garlic breath."

Savannah sat up, her heart racing. As she moved, her long, blond hair brushed against Oliver's bare arm and she saw him flinch away. Actually *flinch*.

"Why?" she demanded, beginning to panic.

Oliver shrugged, feeling sick and unable to meet her wounded gaze. "I'm bored here. I just want to go."

———

Dizzy had disappeared on one of his aimless meanderings around the village, Toby was on the phone to his agent, and Deborah was in the bath when the doorbell rang.

Up in her bedroom, Savannah stuck her fingers in her ears but the ringing didn't stop. She was in no mood to answer the door. Her life was a disaster, she didn't know what the hell to do about it, and worst of all, there was no one she could tell.

"Would somebody *please* answer that bloody door?" Toby yelled from his study, and Savannah heaved herself off the bed. Only the faint hope that it could be Oliver, come back to forgive her for screaming at him, propelled her down the stairs.

But it wasn't Oliver; it was a taxi driver.

"Cab for Mr. Gillespie," he announced, stubbing his cigarette out on the doorstep.

Savannah frowned. Her father wasn't due to go anywhere. "I don't think we ordered one."

"Toby Gillespie, Sisley House. A cab was ordered to take him to London."

"Dad?" Savannah poked her head around the door of the study. "There's a taxi here to take you to London."

"Oh, for God's sake." Toby sighed into the phone. "Hal, can I ring you back in five minutes?"

Savannah, chewing one of her thumbnails in the hall, listened to her father explain to the taxi driver that the call had been a prank.

"It's the third time it's happened this week," he said wearily. "I'm sorry. It's a pain for you, and it's a pain for me."

"So there's no fare to London?"

London, Savannah thought, wincing as she chewed her nail down to the quick. Maybe that was what she needed to do—escape for a while and sort herself out.

But how?

And who could she stay with?

For the third time in a week, Toby gave twenty quid to a taxi driver to console him for missing out on a lucrative fare. The driver left and Toby, unamused, disappeared back into his study.

And Savannah, taken with the idea of disappearing for a few days, suddenly had an idea.

Of course! There was someone she could stay with *and* confide in. How silly not to have thought of it before!

Savannah raced after Toby, snatched the receiver out of his hand before he could begin dialing, and said breathlessly, "Dad, before you ring Hal, could I just call Aunt Phoebe, pleeease?"

"You mean you're off to London *now?*" said Dizzy the next morning, watching Savannah lug a suitcase down the stairs. He'd give anything to get out of this boring, crappy village for a few days, see a bit of action, visit a few amusement arcades.

"I am. And here—this is for you." Savannah, who was feeling unusually magnanimous, slid a ten-pound note out of the back pocket of her jeans. "Buy yourself another CD."

Dizzy beamed. He had two more copies of *Parklife* anyway.

"And you're staying with Aunt Phoebe?"

"Yup." Bending down, Savannah tightened the strap on the case. She didn't want all her underwear bursting out on the train.

"Can I come too?" said Dizzy hopefully, seeing as they were friends again.

Straightening up, Savannah wondered if ringing a local taxi company would work. They'd probably think it was another prank and tell her to bugger off. She looked at Dizzy, who was still standing there with an eager expression on his face.

"No you bloody well can't."

⸺⸺

Bernadette knew at once what had happened—she could tell by the sound of April's voice—and her heart began to race. Clutching her chest, glancing instinctively at the photograph on the table next to the phone, she experienced a peculiar mix of emotions. She would do anything—anything in the world for April. All she wanted was for her to be happy again. But at the same time, it was odd, hearing her breathless words as she spoke about the wonderful new man in her life.

"Of course it's early days yet, I know that"—April couldn't conceal her joy—"but he really seems to like me. I haven't felt this way since...well..."

"I'm so glad," Bernadette said gently. "Now, tell me all about him. What does he do?"

His name was Michael, she learned. He was something in computers. They'd met on Wednesday night and gone to an Italian restaurant and…oh, just talked and talked for hours, about *everything*.

"Everything?" Bernadette asked.

"Well, no—not that, of course. I just told him I was divorced. But I couldn't believe how quickly the time went," April babbled on. "One minute the restaurant was full; the next minute we looked around and all the chairs were up on the tables. This sweet, old Italian woman was vacuuming the carpet and winking at us. Oh, it was *so* romantic." She sighed. "Like something out of a film."

Since Bernadette could hardly ask how the evening had ended, she said instead, "How old is he?"

"Early forties."

"Single? Divorced?"

"Almost divorced. Separated."

Bernadette frowned. "How long?"

"I don't know. Quite a long time, I think. He isn't—"

"Why did they split up?"

"He didn't go into detail." April sounded edgy, almost irritated. "Just something to do with him locking her in the cellar for a week with nothing to eat or drink. Bernie, what are you trying to do—spoil everything for me?"

Bernadette watched a bluebottle fly launch itself dementedly around the narrow hallway, buzzing and bouncing off walls. She opened the front door and let it out. "Of course not. I just don't want you to get hurt, that's all. You know what I'm talking about. There are some men out there who—"

"My God, you have a nerve," April whispered and hung up.

Chapter 30

FREYA HAD BEEN ASLEEP when Hugh and Felicity had picked her up from the Old Vicarage. Lili, tidying the sitting room an hour later, found Colin the Crocodile stuffed behind the cushions on the sofa and realized that Freya couldn't have woken up yet. If she had, she'd be yelling her head off by now.

"I'll be five minutes," she told Michael, waggling Colin's chewed tail at him in silent explanation. Will was asleep, and Lottie was in the yard teaching Blitz how to dance on his hind legs. ("No, no, not like that—try to be like a Spice Girl.")

"Fine." Michael glanced up at Lili as she made her way past him. "I could make a start on dinner if you like. What shall I do, peel some potatoes?"

Startled, Lili saw that he was actually smiling at her. Actually smiling and offering to peel potatoes.

Spooky.

"Potatoes…that'll be great." She said it casually, as if this were the kind of offer he made every week.

Michael, who had been sprawled across the sofa reading the *Radio Times*, yawned and stood up.

"Nothing much on television tonight. I was going to stay in, but Harry rang earlier to see if I fancied a game of snooker."

"Oh well, if there isn't anything on the telly…" Lili was relieved; too busy with Myrtle Armitage's hair on Wednesday night to watch *Ghost*, she'd recorded it instead. If Michael went out, she and Harriet would be able to sit down and enjoy it in peace. "If I were you, I'd go down to the club."

~m~

Freya had woken up. Lili heard her indignant wails the moment she stepped out of the car. Indeed, Freya was yelling so loudly she drowned out the doorbell.

"Oh, thank heavens," Felicity sighed when Lili, having made her way around to the side of the house, tapped on the kitchen window. "Come in. Brilliant. I tried ringing just now but you were engaged. There, there, darling. It's all right. Look, Colin's here…"

Freya stopped wailing in an instant. She clasped the battered velvet reptile to her chest, gave Lili a dazzling smile, and wriggled to be put down. The transformation was so sudden it was comical.

"If only all our problems could be solved so easily," said Lili with a grin. She gazed around the showroom of a kitchen and admired a white ceramic bowl overflowing with pink and yellow roses.

"Are those from your garden? They're amazing."

Felicity was watching Freya's wriggling, diaper-clad bottom disappear under the kitchen table. She nodded absently.

"Has Hugh gone out?" Lili had noticed his car wasn't there. When Felicity nodded again she added cheerfully, "Got rid of him for the evening, have you? Me too. Michael's playing snooker in Harleston."

Felicity was wearing only one earring, Lili realized—a smooth, beaten-gold oval the size of a sparrow's egg. Opening her mouth to tell her, Lili promptly shut it again, remembering that Felicity had just tried to ring her. Unclipping an earring before speaking on the phone was one of those things high-flying female executives did.

But Felicity still seemed distracted. Lili took a step toward the door.

"Well, Freya's happy now. I'll be going."

"Yes. Right. Well, thanks."

"Bye, sweetheart." Bending down, Lili waved at Freya as she tottered out from beneath the table. "Goodness, what's happened to you?"

Freya was walking, but her eyes were half-closed. She looked odd.

"Freya? You can't still be sleepy," Felicity exclaimed. "You've only just woken up."

Lili saw the blue-gray tinge around the child's lips and picked her up. "She's swallowed something. She's choking."

"No she isn't." Felicity's eyes widened in astonishment. "How can she be choking? She hasn't made a sound!"

Lili sat down, opened Freya's mouth, gently felt inside, and flipped her over onto her stomach. A gurgling noise began to escape from Freya's throat.

"Omigod!" Felicity shrieked, losing it in an instant and trying to snatch her daughter off Lili's lap. "She's going to die. She's going to die! What do we do? Shall I phone 999?"

"Not yet." Lili held Freya facedown on her lap, keeping her head tilted below her trunk. She banged the heel of her hand sharply between the child's shoulder blades. If this didn't work, she would have to perform chest thrusts. If that failed, it was on to the Heimlich maneuver.

The fourth bang between the shoulder blades did the trick. The smooth gold earring shot out of Freya's throat and bounced off Lili's dusty sandal. Freya took a great gulp of air and Lili gave her a quick hug before handing her over to her mother.

"There you go. She's fine."

Felicity burst into noisy tears. "She could have died! You saved her life. Oh, to think what might have happened—"

"Babies swallow anything that looks interesting. Lottie choked on a pickled onion once. When Harriet was tiny, she had a thing about pebbles," said Lili. "Nightmare on the beach."

The shuddering sobs finally subsided. Felicity, still clutching an indignant Freya, shook her head. "You were so calm."

"I've got three children." Lili shrugged and smiled. "Like I said, I'm used to it."

"Well, thank you." Wiping her eyes, Felicity handed Freya back to her. She crossed the kitchen, opened a cupboard, and took out an old newspaper. "The least I can do," she told Lili as she lifted the glorious mass of yellow and pink roses from the bowl and laid them, dripping, onto the newspaper, "is give you these."

———

When Lili got home, Michael was watching the news. Next to a saucepan of cold water on top of the stove was a bag of potatoes and a potato peeler.

"It says on the bag you don't have to peel them."

Ah well, it's the thought that counts, Lili decided.

Carefully, she laid the roses on the table and began to unwrap the wet stems, peeling back layers of sodden newspaper and wincing when a thorn speared the base of her thumb.

Blood dripped as she carried on unwrapping. Lili used the dry outer pages to blot up the blood. When she unfolded another sheet of the paper and saw more red, she wondered if a thorn had got the better of Felicity too, but this was a less muddy, altogether more vibrant shade.

Although Lili wouldn't put it past Felicity to have more attractive blood than her.

Except it wasn't blood; it was felt pen. As she smoothed out the damp page and inspected the three circled ads more closely, Lili's heart sank.

Helping Hands Nannies. Our quality of service is second to none.

Au Pairs a La Carte

The Happy Mother Agency: Qualified and experienced staff available.

———

Well, that puts me in my place, thought Lili, crumpling up the soggy papers and biting her lip as she squashed them into the trash.

———

It hadn't taken Jessie long to freshen up the living quarters of the Seven Bells. True to form, all Lorna had wanted was a couple of coats of white-with-a-hint-of-apricot splashed on throughout.

"It's dry," she told Moll, who was peering into her room. It was seven o'clock on Friday evening, but Jessie was determined to get the job finished. As she carried on rolling matte emulsion paint onto the landing wall, she added, "You can take the dust sheets off if you like."

Moll pulled off the sheets, straightened her bedspread, and pushed the small amount of furniture in the room back into place. From a wooden chest in the living room, she lifted all the framed paintings and photographs that had been placed there for safekeeping.

"That's better," she said with satisfaction when she'd finished, and Jessie climbed off her stepladder to admire the transformation.

It was bizarre. Moll's fringed and tasseled silks and velvets clashed violently with the sterile walls.

"Hmm," said Jessie.

"I know." Moll grinned, unconcerned. "Gypsy Rose Lee meets Martha Stewart."

"Wouldn't Lorna have let you choose your own color scheme?"

"I'm not bothered." Picking up a purple satin scarf, Moll tied it around the waist of her black cotton dress. "It's only a bedroom. Anyway, who knows when I might move on?"

The pictures on the walls were an eclectic assortment of prints, but Jessie's attention was drawn to a photograph in a plain wooden frame propped up on the bedside table. Whoever would have thought that Moll, of all people, would sleep with a photo of a good-looking young man next to her bed? Jessie couldn't resist taking a closer look. She glanced over her shoulder at Moll.

"I know." Moll's eyes sparkled. "Bit gorgeous."

"Who is he, an ex?"

"His name's Stevie," Moll said with pride. "He's my little brother."

Moll made them both a cup of tea. In the living room, repainted and already returned to normality, Jessie's gaze fell on another photograph left on the mantelpiece.

"That's one of Lorna's," Moll explained. "It's her twin sister."

Jessie knew about this already; Lorna had mentioned it once or twice in passing. But in response to the question everyone automatically asked, all she ever said was, "No, we weren't identical."

"How long ago did she die?" Jessie asked now, studying the photograph of the young woman in a wheelchair.

"Ten years ago, something like that." Moll blew on her hot tea. "Before Lorna took over the pub here. They were close though. She still gets upset when she talks about her."

Jessie put the photograph carefully back on the mantelpiece and wondered why Lorna Blake had never mentioned the fact that her twin sister was disabled.

"So, what's up with Oliver?" Moll asked easily, changing the subject. "Girlfriend trouble or what?"

"I don't think so." Jessie shrugged. Oliver definitely hadn't been himself for the last couple of days. "I tried asking, but I'm only his mother," she added with a brief smile. "He won't tell me."

Chapter 31

COMING TO STAY WITH Aunt Phoebe had been a brilliant idea, Savannah thought happily. The moment she had rung the bell and Phoebe had flung open the front door, Savannah had known she'd done exactly the right thing.

"Oh, Aunt Phoebe, I'm sooo glad to see you!"

Phoebe gave her a mock clip around the ear. "Don't call me aunt! We're going out to lunch and I want everyone to think we're sisters."

Savannah gave her a bear hug. Phoebe wasn't a real aunt anyway; she was one of her mother's oldest and dearest friends, christened "aunt" by Toby and Deborah because it irritated her so much.

But even if she wasn't family, she had made a terrific pretend aunt over the years, buying Savannah all manner of wildly unsuitable gifts, treating her to memorable days out, and carting her along to glamorous parties.

Savannah loved to hear Phoebe's tales of the old days, when she and Deborah had shared an apartment off the King's Road. This had been back in the day while they were still single and doing their actressy-modelly stuff, and by all accounts, their social life had been a riot.

"Then Deborah went and spoiled it all, of course," Phoebe would drawl, exhaling a plume of Marlboro Light, "and fell in love with this incredibly ugly, failed actor."

"You mean Daddy." Savannah grinned. She never tired of hearing these stories. "And you got married too, don't forget. To Baz."

This was where Phoebe shuddered theatrically. Baz, the lead

singer with Whinegum, had been the first of four useless husbands. The marriage had been over within seven months. The alimony, thankfully, had lasted a lot longer.

"Right," Phoebe announced now, taking Savannah's heavy case from her and dumping it in the hall. "No time to lose. I've booked us a table at The Ivy for one o'clock. After that, we shop. Okay with you, sweetheart?" She took Savannah's chin between tanned fingers, turning her face up to the light. "You look peaky. And you sounded desperate on the phone. Am I going to hear about this, hmm? Is that why you're here?"

"Yeah." Savannah nodded and pressed her lips together, desperate not to cry. If you looked a mess, you'd never get into The Ivy.

Phoebe seemed dubious. "I could cancel the table."

"God no!" Savannah shook her head. "I want to go. I won't embarrass you, I promise. Let's just have some fun first," she begged. "Then I'll tell you all the horrid stuff later."

"Come on, then." As Phoebe led the way down the steps of the ultra-smart Islington town house, she tucked her arm through Savannah's and gave it a reassuring squeeze. "Fun's what I do best."

———

Fun, it transpired, also involved a fair amount to drink. Between them they put away three bottles of wine over lunch, and Phoebe soon had Savannah in fits of giggles, regaling her with wicked details of her latest affair with a high-profile cartoonist. By unspoken common consent, they talked only about Phoebe, and when lunch was over, they launched into a frenzy of shopping.

Cushioned by the wine, they tried on a dozen different outfits in Harvey Nichols. Phoebe would flash her platinum American Express card and glossy shopping bags would appear as if by magic. Hazily, Savannah realized she was having an absolute fortune spent on her and she couldn't even remember if she liked any of the stuff she'd tried on.

"You can't buy me all these," she protested, waving the bags in feeble fashion as Phoebe steered her toward Donna Karan.

"I already have." Phoebe looked pleased with herself. "Anyway, I can do anything I like. You're the daughter I never had." She waved an index finger at Savannah's chest. "I'm your doting aunt and it's my job to spoil you rotten." She studied the girl's face intently. "Is it working? Are you cheering up?"

"Oh yes." Savannah nodded because—let's face it—what else could you say when someone had just spent eight hundred pounds on you? "Definitely much better now."

It didn't last. By six o'clock they were back home and the post-lunch hangover had begun to kick in. Phoebe sent Savannah upstairs for a bath, poured herself a reviving gin and tonic, and switched on the television. If they were going to have that heart-to-heart, she preferred the murmur of voices on television as background noise, rather than music.

"After the news, tonight's feature film," purred the announcer, "*The Battle of the Sandersons*." And even after all these years, something in Phoebe's chest—behind the silicone bosoms—went *ziiing.*

It was so silly. Simon Colman wasn't the star of the film—he'd never starred in any film—but she knew she'd have to watch it again anyway, just to see him in his feeble supporting role.

A friend of a friend who had bumped into Simon last summer had reported joyfully back to Phoebe that he was overweight and losing his hair. The looks that had made her heart skip more than its fair share of beats over the years had faded as spectacularly as his career. According to the informant, he was out of the business now, working as a driving instructor and living with his frump of a wife and four children in Hounslow.

Phoebe stirred the ice in her glass with her finger and pondered the vagaries of fate. She had been married four times and had notched up no children. Each of her husbands had been a millionaire—heavens, Asil had practically been a trillionaire—yet she had loved none of them as much as she had loved Simon.

It was impossible not to wonder how her life might have turned out if they'd never split up. Would she be happier now, living in Middlesex, the wife of a balding, flabby driving instructor, surrounded by kids?

The sitting room door opened and Savannah trailed in. She was wearing a pink-and-white *Love Is...* nightshirt, and her blond hair hung damply over her shoulders. She looked about fourteen and heartbreakingly in need of comfort.

It was time to talk.

Phoebe adored her surrogate daughter. She patted the sofa cushion next to her and let Savannah snuggle up.

"I like your slippers."

"Mum calls them my Oasis slippers." Savannah wiggled each furry monster in turn. "That one's Liam and this is Noel."

Shifting herself for maximum comfort, Phoebe kissed the top of Savannah's head. This was what mothering was all about. *I should have had children. I really should have*, she thought emotionally. *I'd have made a great mother.*

Phoebe wondered if Simon ever thought back to the old days and regretted giving her the heave-ho.

They could have had such beautiful children together. Even in a semidetached in Hounslow...

But that wasn't why they were here now.

"So, what's up?"

Savannah leaned across, took a sip of Phoebe's drink, and said, "Can I have one as well?"

"It's gin. It'll make you depressed."

"I'm there already."

"In that case it'll make you suicidal. And nothing's that bad," Phoebe said. She uncurled herself and headed for the kitchen.

"I haven't told you yet." Savannah's bottom lip began to tremble.

"Wait there. I've got a bottle of Moët in the fridge."

Chapter 32

Too late, Phoebe remembered that champagne only cheered you up if you were cheerful in the first place. Savannah, gulping it down at a rate of knots, was in a flood of tears in no time flat.

Phoebe listened, appalled, as the whole story came tumbling out.

"I just don't know how I'm going to cope with it," Savannah sobbed, reaching for another tissue. "That's why I had to get away... and then he's going away...but the problem's still there, isn't it? In six months or a year, whenever Oliver gets back, he's still going to be my brother and I'll still feel the same about him. I *know* I will...and I'm s-s-sooo ashamed!"

Her fragile body shook and Phoebe rocked her in her arms, lost for words. Over Savannah's heaving shoulder, she saw that the film was about to start. In less than five minutes, she would catch her first glimpse of Simon. It hadn't been a large part—he was the dishy, young neighbor of the battling Sanderson family—but he reappeared several times as the story unfolded.

Simon was my love, thought Phoebe, the Moët going to her head. *My one and only true love, and I lost him. And to this day I don't even know why.*

"It's so unfair," Savannah stormed, letting it all out now. "If we'd met on vacation, if I'd been lying on a beach somewhere and he'd come up and started chatting to me...we wouldn't even have known we were related. I mean, when you meet someone gorgeous and you fancy each other rotten, you don't say, 'Hang on a sec. We'd better not kiss each other, just in case your mum once had a fling with my dad…'"

"Oh, Savvy."

Savannah lifted her head from Phoebe's shoulder. Her eyes were red-rimmed, her expression desolate. "You see? There's nothing you can do to help. There's nothing anyone can do to make me feel better. There are some problems," she concluded mournfully, "you just can't solve."

Phoebe emptied the bottle into their glasses, a lump the size of a golf ball in her throat. "You'll get over this."

"I won't." Savannah closed her eyes and shook her head, hot tears trickling down her cheeks. "I know I won't. I love him, Aunt Phoebe. Like I've never loved anyone before."

"Does…does Oliver feel the same way?"

"He hasn't said he does. But I'm pretty sure—yes. And it explains why he's been acting weird."

Phoebe was desperate for another drink but she knew she mustn't have one. Any more and she risked blurting out things she absolutely mustn't blurt out. Exerting heroic self-control, she said brightly, "Strong coffee, that's what we need. I'll put the machine on."

When emotions and alcohol levels were running high, it was so easy to let your tongue run away with you. *And I can't let that happen*, Phoebe thought, carefully levering herself up from the sofa. *I just can't.*

The next moment, her heart did its familiar skip-and-a-jolt as Simon, behind her, said, "Morning, Mr. Sanderson. How's Mrs. Sanderson feeling today? Hey, that was some party last night!"

Oh, that corny dated dialogue.

And that *voice*…

Phoebe turned and looked at Simon: young and beautiful then, plump and balding now.

But so what?

Savannah was right. There were some men you just never stopped loving.

Only by the time I realized it, thought Phoebe, *it was too late.*

"Coffee?"

"Please." Savannah gave her nose a last honking blow, collected up the scattered tissues, and dumped them in the nearby wastepaper basket. "End of round one," she said with a watery smile, and glanced at the television screen. "What's this film?"

"*The Battle of the Sandersons.*"

Savannah nodded. "That's it."

Phoebe watched her unfold her legs, slowly, like an invalid. "Where are you going?"

"Just to the loo."

⸻

Phoebe was engrossed in the film when Savannah came back. She kicked off her hairy monster slippers and curled her feet beneath her on the sofa, her eyes dry now but her face still pinched and pale.

"I've seen this before."

Nobly, Phoebe said, "Would you rather watch something else?"

Well, she could always record it.

But Savannah shook her head. "It's okay. I like it. I love the bit at the barbecue when he throws his wife and all the food in next door's swimming pool."

Simon's swimming pool. With Simon diving in to fish his neighbor out, emerging from the water with his dark hair slicked back and his white shirt clinging to his body.

Phoebe smiled and said, "That's my favorite bit too."

They didn't have long to wait. Savannah actually laughed when the wife was launched, screaming, into the pool.

"Mum had a bit of a fling once with that chap there."

She was pointing at the screen. Phoebe frowned. *What chap where?*

"Him," Savannah said as the camera zoomed in on Simon lifting the woman, kicking and yelling, over his shoulder.

Phoebe opened her mouth to say no, she'd got it wrong; *she* was the one who'd had a bit of a fling with Simon. But Savannah was chattering on.

"Before she met Dad, of course. She told me about it once when we were watching this film together. His name's Simon something, isn't it?"

Numbly, Phoebe nodded.

"He was supposed to be seeing one of Mum's friends, but he kept pestering her to go out with him. In the end, he whisked her off to Paris. The next thing Mum knew he was going down on one knee at the top of the Eiffel Tower." Savannah giggled. "He produced this whacking great emerald ring and asked Mum to marry him, but she wasn't interested. She said she went off him when she found out he wore purple briefs in bed."

Until this moment, Phoebe had been praying that this was all a silly mistake, that Savannah had confused Simon with someone else.

But Simon had always worn briefs in bed.

And his favorite pair had been purple.

"So...so what happened?"

"Mum said thanks but no thanks and dumped him, smartish." Savannah shrugged. "Told him to go back to his girlfriend. But he took it badly, apparently. Said if he couldn't have Mum, he didn't want second best. He dumped the girlfriend and went off to make his name in Hollywood. Except he didn't," she concluded, "because I've never seen him in anything else since." Savannah turned her head and grinned. "Just as well Mum turned him down and married Dad instead."

Second best...

There was a pain in Phoebe's chest, like a serrated knife being twisted beneath her ribs. She could hardly breathe. Fury and grief rose up like bile. Simon and Deborah, her lover and her best friend, had both cheated on her

It was the ultimate double betrayal.

So much for her long-cherished fantasies. Simon—the bastard—had never loved her. She'd been second best.

Phoebe felt the blade of the knife jab a little deeper.

And as for Deborah... Well, what did she owe her oldest friend now? Nothing at all.

"Listen to me," said Phoebe. All of a sudden, she felt eerily calm. She had kept Deborah's secret for eighteen years and had vowed to take it with her to the grave.

But that had been then, when she had been blissfully unaware of the secret Deborah had in turn been keeping from her. She had no compunction about breaking that vow of silence now. Especially when it could make all the difference in the world to Savannah.

"What?" Savannah looked bemused as Phoebe reached out with a trembling hand and switched off the television.

The room abruptly fell silent. All Phoebe could hear was the sound of her own blood thrumming in her ears. "This problem of yours," she said slowly, taking Savannah's thin fingers between her own, "this thing with Oliver."

Tears sprang instantly to Savannah's eyes once more. She managed a hopeless little nod. "Yes?"

"How would you feel," said Phoebe, "if I told you that Toby Gillespie might not be your father?"

Chapter 33

"It's me," said Savannah. "Are you working today?"

Oliver hesitated, twiddling the phone cord around his index finger. "Not until five."

"Will you meet me? I'm catching the eleven thirty train from—"

"Look, I'm pretty busy," Oliver cut in. "I have to see a friend of mine; he's helping me work out an itinerary." He paused. Savannah had sounded excited. "Where are you going?"

"I'm not going anywhere. I'm coming home," she explained impatiently. "I'm at Paddington now. The train gets into Harleston at twelve fifty-five. Please, Oliver. Say you'll meet me."

"Well…"

"It's important," said Savannah, and hung up.

"More flowers?" Lili gasped. "Oh, really, you shouldn't have. This is far too—"

"You saved Freya's life," Felicity insisted, thrusting the glossy, cellophane-wrapped bouquet into Lili's arms and holding out an even glossier box of chocolates. Charbonnel et Walker, no less. "It's the least, the *very* least we can do to thank you. If you hadn't been there when it happened… Well, it gives me nightmares to think about it." She shook her head, looking as if she were about to cry. "I wouldn't have had a clue what to do."

Overcome, Lili tried to bury her nose in the roses to admire their scent. She felt a twit when she remembered, too late, that they were sealed in cellophane.

"Well, thanks."

"And I have to apologize"—Felicity went pink—"for something else."

"Oh?"

"The newspaper I wrapped those roses in yesterday. Heavens, this is embarrassing. Um…the thing is, I don't even know if you… if you saw…"

"The ads," Lili said, to put her out of her misery. "Yes, I did see them. But it's okay, I understand."

"No—that's what I needed to tell you. We *want* you to keep on looking after Freya. The nanny thing… Well, it was just a silly idea." Felicity was getting redder by the second, but she stumbled on toward the finishing line. "Anyway, just to let you know, we won't be pursuing it. We're more than happy for her to stay with you."

Hanging out of the train's open window, Savannah saw Oliver waiting for her on the dusty station platform. He was wearing a red shirt and his oldest Levi's, and—typically impatient—he was jangling his car keys with one hand and twiddling his sunglasses in the other.

Her heart did a little leap of joy. Oliver had never looked more gorgeous. She wished she could race along the platform and just throw herself into his arms.

Except if I did that, she thought, *someone would be bound to steal my suitcase.*

Anyway, she couldn't.

Yet.

"Here, give that to me." Wasting no time, Oliver seized her case and began to head for the exit.

Savannah hurried after him. She had been playing this scene in her mind all the way from Paddington.

"Can we have a coffee?" She jerked her head in the direction of the station café. It didn't bear much relation to the one in *Brief Encounter*, but the film had made a lasting impression on Savannah. In her mind, station cafés seethed with dramatic possibilities. Besides, she wanted the comfort of other people around her.

Oliver wasn't slowing down. "I've parked on double yellows."

"Please. Just five minutes."

"I thought you had something important to sort out."

"I do." Savannah stopped at the entrance to the café and gave him a long look. Even her expression, she felt, seethed with dramatic possibilities. "We both do."

"If I get a ticket, you can pay the fine," warned Oliver.

She grinned back at him, so happy she could burst. "Okay."

Biting her lip with excitement, Savannah waited until they had sat down with their coffees at a red Formica-topped table. She tore open a sachet of sugar and spilled most of it over her orange Lycra skirt.

"So what's this about?" asked Oliver.

"I know why you've been avoiding me. I know why you're going away," said Savannah.

He looked uncomfortable. "I haven't been avoiding you."

"Oh yes you have." She couldn't stop the smile spreading across her face. "But I may have the answer."

Oliver tore the edge off a sachet and poured salt into his tea. His hand shook as he stirred it in. "The answer to what?"

Savannah couldn't contain herself a minute longer. "I might not be Dad's daughter."

"What?"

"Mum had an affair with someone else. Dad might not be my real dad. Which would mean," Savannah said simply, "you and I aren't related."

"Don't be ridiculous!" Oliver was scandalized. "Your mum? Someone's been teasing you. Deborah would never have an affair."

"Oliver, trust me. This is on the level."

"But this is your mother we're talking about."

"I know, I know. She's so wonderful. Everyone loves her. She's the perfect wife." Laughing at the expression on his face, Savannah said, "Think about it—it's the perfect cover. She's the last person in the world people would suspect of ever having an affair. Her very niceness is her alibi."

"You don't seem too stunned," said Oliver.

Savannah shrugged. "I never knew for sure, but I've had my suspicions."

"You mean about Toby not being—"

"Oh no! The dad thing came as a surprise. But over the years, I have wondered if she sees other men."

The dad thing. Oliver was too dumbstruck to absorb all the implications. He couldn't get over how calmly Savannah appeared to be taking the news.

He looked across the Formica table, deep into her eyes. Blue eyes, a lighter shade of blue than Toby's. And silky, white-blond hair. "Are you upset?"

"What, about Dad? Nooo, he's still my dad. Just not biologically," Savannah added with remarkable sangfroid. "Which, basically, is the answer to all our prayers."

"But you don't know for certain." Still dazed, Oliver took a mouthful of tea. As he spat it back into the cup, an elderly woman at a nearby table shook her head in disgust and ostentatiously buried herself behind the *Daily Telegraph*.

"I know, but I'm pretty sure."

"How did you find all this out anyway?"

"My aunt Phoebe. She told me everything—about Dad working abroad for weeks on end and Mum meeting this chap. He was married too, so they had to be really careful. That's how Phoebe got involved," Savannah explained patiently. "She used to let them meet at her place."

"What makes you so sure this other man's your father?"

Another shrug. "As soon as Phoebe told me who he was, I just thought, *of course.*"

Oliver took a deep breath. This was getting weirder by the minute. "You mean he's someone you already *know*?"

"Only by sight," said Savannah. "Not to say hello to."

"Who is it?" Oliver knocked his cup with his elbow, sending it clattering across the table. The elderly woman behind Savannah glared and rattled her paper.

Following Oliver's gaze, Savannah looked over her shoulder. "Well, that's handy." She started to laugh. "See that photograph on the front page?"

Oliver frowned and nodded. "So what?"

Her blue eyes sparkled. "So that's him."

"Oh Jesus!" exclaimed Oliver. "Not a politician."

. . .

Savannah, in dazzling form, managed to persuade the traffic cop to put his pen and ticket pad away.

As they drove toward Harleston, she filled Oliver in with the rest of the details. "He wasn't a member of the cabinet then, of course. He'd only just been elected as a member of Parliament. But he was in London all week and his wife and kids were hundreds of miles away in his constituency. You can see how these things happen."

Oliver was in deep shock. This was too much to take in. David Mansfield's entire political career had been built around a staunch commitment to honesty, loyalty, and family values. If it got out that he was an adulterer, he would be finished, forced to resign, out on his ear—

Hell's bells, this was *serious*.

"Sav, what are you going to do?"

"Hmm?" On their way out of the station she had stopped at the newspaper stand and bought a copy of the *Telegraph*. Now, her blond head bent over the front-page photograph, she was scrutinizing David Mansfield's facial features. Short, blond hair, cobalt-blue eyes, the trademark lopsided smile that had won the hearts and votes of women all over the country.

The implications could be catastrophic.

"What are you going to do?" Oliver repeated.

Savannah looked surprised. "Find out if he's my father, of course."

Shit. "How?"

She shrugged. "Blood tests. DNA, that kind of thing."

"And then what?"

"Come on, Oliver! What planet are you on? What do you *think* I'm going to do?"

Wreck a few lives? Create wholesale political turmoil? With Savannah, who knew?

He heaved a sigh. "I don't know. Tell me."

"If I'm his daughter"—Savannah jabbed happily at the photograph on her lap—"it means we aren't related." Her grin was jaunty, no-holds-barred. "It means we can be together!"

Chapter 34

DEBORAH AND DOUG WERE in bed when they heard the crunch of tires on gravel outside.

"Christ, who's that?" Doug was out of bed in a flash. He peered around the edge of the curtain. "It's Oliver's car… Bloody hell, he's got Savannah with him!"

"He can't have. She's in London."

"She isn't. She's getting her suitcase out of the trunk."

Doug, thankfully, had had plenty of practice at getting dressed at the speed of light. Deborah stayed where she was.

"Down the back staircase and out through the french windows." Amused, she lifted her face for a fleeting kiss. "Never mind, maybe we can catch up later. When the coast's clear, I'll give you a ring."

Only moments after Doug's escape, the bedroom door swung open. "Mum, what are you doing in bed?"

"Oh, darling, I've got the most stinking headache. A real killer." Deborah rolled onto her side and held her hand an inch above her forehead. "I've taken heaps of painkillers, but it won't go away."

"Have you seen a doctor?"

"Oh, I don't want to be a nuisance. Anyway, what are you doing back?"

Savannah plonked herself down on the bed. "Mum, Aunt Phoebe told me something and I have to find out if it's true."

"Heavens," said Deborah, "what kind of something? That

Rotterdam is the capital of Belgium? That horizontal stripes make your hips look bigger? That you can't get pregnant standing up?"

"Actually she told me that this chap might be my father." Savannah produced the folded-up front page of the newspaper from her shirt pocket. "Is he?"

Deborah sat bolt upright. "No."

"Don't say no, just like that. And mind your head. Here, let me put a pillow behind you—that's better. Now come on, Mum. Is he?"

"Sweetheart, what an extraordinary thing to—"

"Mum, Phoebe told me all about it. The whole thing. You had an affair with David Mansfield, you used her house, you met him at a charity fund-raising dinner, and he phoned you the next day to ask if you'd like to—"

"Oh, good grief, that's enough," said Deborah faintly, closing her eyes. The fictitious headache threatened to become real. "Yes, yes—that's all true."

"And when you found out you were pregnant, you didn't know if I was his or Daddy's," Savannah persisted.

"Darling, I'm *sure* you're Daddy's."

"Well, we need a blood test."

This was too much. This was a nightmare.

Deborah clutched at Savannah's hand. "We *don't* need a blood test. You're Toby's daughter. I don't know why Phoebe told you all this, but it really is best forgotten. Think of the trouble it would cause. Sweetheart, Toby *loves* you. He's your father—"

"I know he's my father, but he might not be my *biological* father." Savannah was implacable, her blue eyes bright. "And I don't want him to be, either, because he's Oliver's father too. And I love Oliver," she said.

"Why?" Deborah demanded when Phoebe picked up the phone. "Why did you tell her?"

It was still only three o'clock in the afternoon. Phoebe had to hand it to Savannah; she didn't hang around. When she had a job to do, she got on and did it.

"I thought she had a right to know. She's in love with that boy."

"She is *not* in love with him!" Deborah was ready to explode with frustration. "She's got a stupid crush on him. She's had them before and she'll have them again. She's eighteen, for God's sake! Getting crushes on boys is what eighteen-year-olds *do*."

"Didn't sound like a crush me." In London, Phoebe poured herself a hefty vodka and tonic.

"You promised, Phoebe. You're my oldest friend and you promised *never* to tell anyone."

"So?"

"*So?*" Deborah almost screamed. "I can't believe you've done this to me!"

"Well, now we're even." Phoebe spat out the words with grim satisfaction.

"What?" Deborah closed her eyes. "What are you talking about now?"

"I think you mean *who* am I talking about now. Let me put this simply." Phoebe's tumbler clinked against the receiver as she took an icy gulp. "Simon Colman—that's who."

"Where are you going?" Oliver asked when Jessie came downstairs carrying a small overnight case.

"Cornwall. With Jonathan. He'll be here by five."

"It's going to rain." Oliver nodded at the TV, where a manically cheerful weathergirl was gleefully pointing at thunder and lightning symbols on a map.

"Never mind." Jessie checked her watch; she wasn't planning to lie on a beach. "Are you okay?"

Oliver nodded again. He wasn't okay; he was sick with worry. Savannah was on a mission, she was unstoppable, and there was nothing he could do to dissuade her.

God knows what was going on over at Sisley House right now.

Oliver was just glad Toby was in New York. Maybe Deborah would be able to make her willful daughter see sense.

"I'll be back tomorrow evening." In the distance came the roar of Jonathan's car approaching the crest of Compass Hill. Jessie picked up her case, sunglasses, and emergency supply of Rolos. She looked at Oliver, who seemed distracted. "Sure you're all right?"

"I'm fine. You and Jonathan have a good time." He smiled up at Jessie to reassure her. They got on well; they had always been close. But this time Oliver couldn't bring himself to tell her what was going on.

It was just easier if she didn't know.

"Are you sure you want to do this?" Jonathan had to raise his voice to be heard above the noise of the car.

"What, eat four packets of Rolos all at once?"

"No thanks." He shook his head as Jessie offered him one. "I'm talking about Cornwall. I don't want you to do something you might regret afterward."

"This is what I want," Jessie said. "Of course I won't regret it afterward." She unwrapped another Rolo. "I never regret anything I do."

"Would that be a double room?" asked the receptionist at the hotel overlooking Saint Austell Bay.

Jonathan cast a hopeful sidelong glance in Jessie's direction.

"No thanks. Two singles." Jessie wasn't looking, but she knew his face had fallen. Jonathan lived in hope of resuming their old relationship.

The receptionist handed them their keys. "Well, enjoy your stay."

"I'll do my best," Jonathan told her mournfully.

"Come on." Jessie tapped his arm. "Before the restaurant closes. I'll buy you dinner to make up for the lack of sex."

———

They ate on the terrace, admiring the view of the bay and sifting through the dozens of real estate agents' details Jessie had had sent to her during the last couple of days. There were eight properties she particularly wanted to inspect.

"Couldn't you just rent one for the summer?" Jonathan frowned, shaking his head at the short list. "Selling Duck Cottage, buying something down here... It's pretty final. You might hate it."

The terrace was bordered by palm trees. Far below them, an inky sea glittered in the moonlight. The lights from the cottages dotted along the curve of the bay illuminated the waves lapping the shoreline.

"How could I hate living here?" Jessie waved an airy hand at the view. "It's beautiful."

Besides, the whole point of selling her home and buying another was to *make* it final.

"No friends," Jonathan pointed out. "You could be lonely."

"I'll make new ones."

"Oliver won't approve."

"Oliver's twenty-one—he doesn't need to approve. He can live where he likes."

"You'll have to build up your business again from scratch."

"Jonathan, if I wanted to be depressed I'd read Anita Brookner novels. It was your idea to come down here with me," Jessie reminded him, "The least you can do is be on my side."

"You're running away." His tone was blunt.

"I'm not running away." Jessie sighed and watched him signal the waiter for more wine. "I just can't stay there anymore. I thought I could cope with Toby being there, but I can't."

Jonathan was incredibly fond of Jessie, but he was glad he no longer loved her. If he'd been sitting here now, pining for her to come to her senses and love him back... Well, thank goodness he wasn't was all he could say. Otherwise, the look on her face when she talked about Toby Gillespie would be breaking his heart.

"I don't want you making a huge mistake." He reached across the table, covering her hand with his long, thin fingers.

"I won't be," said Jessie, inwardly touched by his concern. She plastered on a bright smile. "I told you before, I never regret anything I do."

But her flippant manner was no longer fooling Jonathan. And it wasn't the first time Jessie had run away.

"Really?" He gave her a shrewd look. "Not even jumping on a train to Scotland all those years ago and not letting Toby Gillespie know he was about to become a father?"

Chapter 35

DEBORAH HAD DONE HER best, but she was getting nowhere. It was like trying to persuade a spoiled six-year-old that she didn't want an ice cream, that she'd be much happier with a plate of steamed vegetables instead.

"It's no good, Mum. This is the most important thing in the world to me and I'm not going to let you fob me off." It was midnight, and Savannah, frustratingly, was showing no signs of caving in. "One way or another, we're going to find out the truth. Either Dad has the blood test—"

"Not your father. No, *no!*" Deborah had always taken such care not to be found out. If there was a way around this, any way at all that meant Toby wouldn't know about her infidelity, she would take it.

After all, Savannah could still be his.

"Okay." Savannah flicked the newspaper photograph of David Mansfield with her finger. "So we get it from him."

"For goodness sake, have you any idea—?"

"Mum, chill out. It's not that big a deal. We can be discreet."

Discreet. Deborah buried her face in her hands and shook her head. "I don't know how you think—"

"Right, that's enough," Savannah announced briskly. "We're going around in circles here. All you have to do is phone him up and explain the situation. He seems a decent enough chap. I'm sure he'll understand."

Deborah wished she could press Rewind, just go back a couple of days and start from scratch

"But, darling—"

"I mean it, Mum." Pushing back her blond hair, Savannah spoke with an air of horrible finality. "If you don't do it, I will."

———

Leaving the message was ridiculously simple. Directory Assistance gave Deborah the number of the House of Commons. Dialing, she expected an answering machine, but a cheerful man replied, explaining that the switchboard was manned twenty-four hours a day.

Feeling sick, Deborah gave him a brief message to pass on to David Mansfield. Just her name and number and that it was urgent. She had to add this last bit because Savannah was sitting directly opposite her, cross-legged on the sofa, saying, "Tell him it's urgent. Make sure he knows he has to call you back. Say it's a matter of life and death."

"He'll be given the message tomorrow." Deborah hung up and massaged her aching temples. "Now, can we please go to bed?"

Not that she'd be able to sleep a wink. So this was how it felt to be emotionally drained.

Savannah flung her arms around her.

"Isn't this just *fantastic*? Sorry, Mum. I know it's a bit awkward for you, but if it means Oliver and I can be together…"

There were tears of elation in her eyes. As she kissed her, Deborah wiped them away.

"If you are his daughter, have you thought what else it could mean? He might want to meet you, get to know you. God, even introduce you to his family."

"No thanks," Savannah said firmly. "I'm not interested in any of that stuff. Just so long as his blood matches mine, that'll do me."

—⁓—

Savannah was still in bed and Deborah was downstairs in the kitchen when the phone rang at ten the next morning.

The voice on the other end of the line was unmistakable. "Deborah? It's me. I got your message."

"Oh, right. Hang on a sec." Jerkily she reached for her purse on the dresser. "Dizzy, we need bread and…um, tea bags. Get some from the shop, would you?"

Dizzy frowned. What was going on? Yesterday his mother had slipped him twenty quid and told him to spend the day in Harleston. And now here she was, getting rid of him again.

"*Now*, darling, please."

When he had ambled out, glancing suspiciously over his shoulder, Deborah returned her attention to the phone. The blood was pounding through her body like a herd of marathon runners; she hadn't expected him to get back to her so soon.

"David, hello. Um…is this phone safe?" It was weird, speaking to him again

"Absolutely. Now, what's all this about?"

David Mansfield sat in his office and thought back to the last time he had slept with Deborah, all those years ago. His parliamentary career had begun to take off shortly afterward and he had never risked another affair since then. There was far too much at stake.

Deborah told him everything.

David listened in silence.

"I'm so sorry, David. I've done my best to talk her out of it, but she won't listen. You know how strong-willed teenage girls can be."

"I can't believe I'm hearing this." In his oak-paneled office, David experienced a vivid mental image of his career flashing before his eyes before disappearing down the nearest toilet. "Deborah, Deborah. This cannot happen."

"Oh, David, it's happening. I'm not thrilled about it either." Fumbling in the kitchen drawer, Deborah found an old packet of Rothmans and lit one up. "If Toby finds out, he's not going to forgive me. He'll want a divorce."

David thought about his own marriage. He loved his wife. He loved her almost as much as he loved being a government minister.

Jesus Christ, what had he ever done to deserve this?

"We need to stop her."

"We can't," Deborah sighed. "You'll have to go along with it. It's the only way."

"Oh yes, right. Terrific."

"Look, Savannah doesn't want publicity, just proof that you're her father. Nobody else needs to know."

"Deborah, my whole life is at stake here!" David Mansfield closed his eyes—those famous blue eyes—and willed himself to come up with some kind of solution.

"Okay, let me put it this way." The time had come, Deborah decided, to be blunt. "If you provide the blood sample, you can cross your fingers and pray the story doesn't leak out. If you don't"—she paused, making sure he understood—"Savannah will go to the press and the moving vans will be pulling up outside your office faster than you can blink."

―∽∾―

The film Toby was promoting in the States wasn't great, but until its target audience saw it for themselves, they wouldn't know that. The advance publicity had been expertly orchestrated, the advertising had had millions of dollars poured into it, and the stars were doing the rounds of the talk shows, hyping it like mad and making it sound like the best thing to hit the cinema screens since *The Godfather*.

Toby had just done Jimmy Kimmel—*big* honor—and thirteen magazine interviews. From tomorrow, he had another nine TV appearances lined up and twenty radio shows to do. You had to try not to repeat yourself, though this was all but impossible. You had to be endlessly enthusiastic. You had to remember the names of the people interviewing you and use them. You had to shuttle from one radio or TV station to the next and look as if you were actually enjoying yourself.

You even had to stay awake.

————

Jessie was dreaming she'd bought a house in Saint Austell Bay. Literally *in* the bay, so it could be reached only by boat. In her dream, she was gazing out of her bedroom window at Toby, standing on the beach with a megaphone. He was yelling across the water at her: "You won't get rid of me that easily, you know! *I can swim!*"

When the phone began to ring beside the bed, Jessie answered it without waking up properly first.

"Jess?"

"Toby?"

"It's a terrible line. Jess, is that you?"

"Use your megaphone," said Jessie. "No, never mind, just swim across."

A stunned silence greeted this suggestion. Jessie opened her eyes and got her bearings.

It was one o'clock in the morning, and she'd forgotten to close her curtains. Through the window, an almost-full moon hung above Compass Hill Wood, silhouetting the trees against the gray-black sky. In the distance a fox cried out. She was in her own bed, surrounded by real estate agents' leaflets that crackled when she moved. She didn't live in a cottage in the middle of Saint Austell Bay and Toby Gillespie wasn't standing barefoot on the beach, bawling at her through a megaphone.

That had been a dream.

Frowning, she looked at the receiver in her hand.

The only puzzle now was, who was this on the other end of the phone?

"Jess?"

Toby. It was still him.

"I was asleep. It's okay, I'm awake now."

"I'm sorry."

"I was dreaming about you."

Jessie knew it was a stupid thing to say but she hadn't had time to gather her wits.

Toby was absurdly pleased. He couldn't bear it that they'd parted on chilly terms. The reason he'd rung now was because he missed her so much.

"What was the dream about?" He pictured Jessie lying in bed. Maybe in the dream he'd been lying in it with her.

"You were chasing after me. I was trying to get away but you kept chasing me."

So much for romance.

"Oh." Despite the disappointment, Toby managed a brief smile. "I do apologize."

"Where are you anyway?" Jessie sat up, sending her map of Cornwall and a few sheets of house details slithering to the floor.

"New York. The Saint Regis Hotel. Shall I describe my room to you? The carpet is light blue, the curtains are dark blue, the wallpaper is a kind of stripy blue and—"

"Toby, why are you calling?"

A pause. "I just wanted to talk."

"Couldn't you have phoned Deborah?"

"You know what I mean."

"Toby—"

"I know, I know." His tone was rueful. "But I can't help how I feel, Jess."

Jessie picked up one of the leaflets on the bed. There was a photograph fixed to the front of a pink-washed cottage with an overgrown front yard. What it didn't show was the fish-and-chip shop next door and the tattoo parlor opposite.

"This isn't fair."

"I know that too. But some things—"

"I'm selling the cottage," said Jessie. "Moving away."

Toby clenched the receiver in alarm. The hairs stood up on the back of his neck. "Shit, no! Jess, you mustn't do that. You *can't*."

"I'm not sure I have a choice." *Oh hell*, Jessie thought. *Now I sound totally pathetic.* But he'd caught her at a vulnerable time and she had to make him understand. "It isn't easy for me either, you know."

"I'm sorry. God, I'm so sorry," said Toby. "But you don't have to move away. Jess, I love you. You already know that. But I don't want there to be any awkwardness between us. I know I screwed things up the other week, but I swear that won't happen again. You have my word on it. No more hassle," he went on urgently. "I promise. From now on we'll be just friends."

───※───

"Hello," Savannah said cheerfully, "is Doug in? I wondered if I could have a word with him."

Jamie, who had answered the door, gazed in wonder at Savannah's cropped white tank top and handkerchief-sized skirt. Bloody hell, Doug was a lucky sod.

"He's here, but he's…uh…upstairs. Asleep."

"Actually, it's quite urgent." Savannah beamed at Jamie. "Could you wake him up?"

Drew wandered out of the kitchen clutching a bowl of cornflakes and a fork. "Maybe it's something we could help you with," he offered. Doug had only finished his night shift two hours earlier.

"I don't think so. You see, I've got this massive splinter in my bottom."

"I'm great with splinters," Jamie volunteered enthusiastically.

Savannah gave him an apologetic look. "Well, I think I'd prefer a doctor to take it out."

Chapter 36

"I DON'T REALLY HAVE a splinter," Savannah explained as they made their way back to Sisley House. "I need to ask you a favor."

"I see."

Doug gave her a guarded look. Something was up. Surely she hadn't seen him legging it across her backyard yesterday morning.

"A big favor. Huge, actually."

"What?"

"The thing is," Savannah said, "you know how to keep secrets, don't you? I mean, you're a doctor and you take that oath thingy, so I can definitely trust you one hundred percent. Whatever it is, you won't breathe a word to another living soul."

Doug frowned. "Well no, of course I wouldn't. But if it's something serious, you really should be seeing—"

"It isn't that kind of serious," Savannah assured him gaily. "More...well, sensitive. Not open heart surgery on the kitchen table, if that's what's worrying you."

"Maybe you'd better tell me what this is about," Doug said, although he could hazard a guess. Either Savannah thought she might be pregnant or she was afraid she'd caught some form of sexually transmitted disease.

But as they rounded the corner, he was taken aback to see Deborah's car parked at the top of the drive.

"Um...does this involve your mother?"

"Oh yes."

Shit. He hoped Deborah didn't have some form of sexually transmitted disease. "Look," he said warily, "if someone's ill   "

"Nobody's ill. We're expecting a visitor." There was an air of excitement about Savannah; her eyes were almost feverishly bright. "And I want you to take a couple of blood samples, that's all."

Doug looked at her. "*Blood* samples?"

"You mustn't let them out of your sight until you send them off to the lab." Savannah had read enough Jeffrey Archer novels to know you couldn't trust politicians. "Then when the results come back," she concluded triumphantly, "you give them to me."

This was surreal.

Doug slid the hypodermic needle into the bulging vein and slowly drew back the plunger. Right first time, thank God—the blood flowed smoothly into the syringe.

David Mansfield watched him withdraw the needle and decant the sample into a thin plastic vial. He had driven down, alone, to Upper Sisley. Now he watched Doug Flynn write a fictitious name on the vial's label.

He rolled down his sleeve and looked across at Deborah Gillespie's daughter, perched on the edge of the kitchen table in a barely there skirt and a tank top that stopped short of her navel. If she were his daughter, he thought with an irrational flash of annoyance, he'd tell her to put some proper clothes on and stop dressing like a tart.

"Well, that's done," said Deborah with some relief. "Now, can I get anyone a drink?"

David Mansfield stood up. "I should be going."

Deborah poured herself a massive vodka and tonic anyway. She needed it, even if nobody else did.

"I'll show you out," Savannah said, jumping down from the

table. "It's all right," she added kindly as she saw David Mansfield to the front door. "I'm doing this for love, not money. You don't have to worry. I won't blab."

"Where's Dizzy?" Doug asked while he and Deborah were alone in the kitchen.

"Up in his room."

"Christ, isn't that a bit risky?"

"I drove into Harleston this morning and bought him a new game for his computer." Deborah managed a faint smile. "Thank goodness for *Command & Conquer*. He won't come downstairs for a week."

Doug shook his head. "I can't believe I just did that. I can't believe you had an affair with David Mansfield."

"I know. Weird, isn't it? I never even voted for him." Deborah rattled the ice in her tumbler. "Are you sure you wouldn't like a drink?"

"No thanks." A drink was the last thing he wanted.

"Anyway, we don't have to worry," said Deborah. "All you need to do now is swap his blood for some of your own. Then it'll come back negative."

Doug had just finished a grueling twenty-four-hour shift. He had been asleep for less than an hour when Savannah had gotten him out of bed. He wasn't normally so slow on the uptake.

"You mean switch the samples?"

"Of course switch the samples! Savannah's won't match yours, will it? And she'll never know—"

"I can't do that," said Doug. He began to sweat. This was too much; he was already far more involved than he wanted to be. But at least so far, he hadn't done anything unethical. "I'm sorry, there's no way I'm doing that," he told Deborah abruptly. "Tampering with blood samples is fraudulent. We're talking gross professional misconduct."

"Phuh, some father he is!" Savannah remarked cheerfully, coming back into the kitchen and helping herself to a can of Coke from the fridge. "What a grumpy drawers. He didn't even wave good-bye."

—ᴍᴍ—

"Well?" Jamie was avid for details. He'd been fantasizing about Savannah Gillespie's wondrous bottom for the last twenty minutes. Now Doug was back, he could hear about it from the horse's mouth...so to speak.

"Well what?"

"What was it *like*?"

Doug put his medical bag into the cupboard under the stairs. The medical bag containing a vial of David Mansfield's blood. He stood looking at it, deep in thought.

"He's in shock," Drew said with a grin. "It's all been too much for him."

Ever hopeful, Jamie said, "Was it like a little peach?"

"What?" Doug was still hovering by the cupboard, wondering if he should take the samples straight to the lab.

"Savannah's bottom, you idiot! Did she squeal when you took the splinter out?" Jamie's eyes lit up. "Did you keep it as a souvenir?"

"Oh, right... No."

It was useless. Doug simply wasn't going to tell him what he wanted to hear. He was selfishly keeping the details to himself. "Life is so unfair," Jamie grumbled. "If you'd been at work, she would've asked me to help. I'd've have done it. I'd've been over there like a shot."

Damn, I wish you had, thought Doug.

—ᴍᴍ—

When the phone rang on Wednesday afternoon, Deborah picked it up and held her breath.

"Well?"

"The results just came back. It's a match," said Doug.

"Oh shit." Fumbling for her lighter, Deborah lit a cigarette.

"I'm sorry."

"You know what this means, don't you? The end of my marriage. And it's going to kill Toby—"

"Look, I'm pretty busy. I have to get back to work."

"It still isn't too late." Deborah glanced sideways over her shoulder to make sure she wasn't being overheard. But Dizzy was still upstairs, closeted in his room with *Command & Conquer*, and she hadn't seen Savannah all day. "You can alter the report, Doug. Just Wite-Out out the crucial bits, write negative instead of positive, then photocopy it! Savannah will never know."

"Er…actually," said Doug, "she already does."

"But how—"

"Hi, Mum!" Savannah's voice, in the background, sang down the phone before Doug could speak again.

"She's been sitting here in reception since nine o'clock this morning," he said drily, "waiting for the results to come back."

———

Jessie was sitting in the backyard painting her toenails, drinking soda and half listening to an advice phone-in show on the radio. She was making short work of a packet of licorice allsorts and thinking about Toby's phone call the other night, when the familiar sound of Oliver's car pulling up outside reminded her that it was high time she told him about Cornwall.

Poor Oliver. At this rate, he was going to come back one day from a lunchtime shift at the Bells and find somebody else living in his house.

"There you are," Jessie said when he appeared clutching two chilled cans of Fosters. Heavens, this was quite nerve-wracking; she wasn't sure where to start. "Sit down, Olly. I've got something to tell you." There, she'd done it; she'd started. "The thing is, I saw this brilliant cottage when Jonathan and I were down in Cornwall and I'd really like to buy it. I want to sell this place and move to Saint Austell. Now, how do you feel about that? Is it okay with you?" As she ran out of breath, Jessie wondered why Oliver wasn't reacting. He seemed to be paying more attention to the kleptomaniac on the radio than to her own big news.

"Uh…fine."

"I mean, I know it must come as a bit of a shock, but this won't really affect you that much, will it? You're twenty-one, off to Europe…and when you get back, you'll be going wherever your career takes you, sharing apartments, living your own life—"

"Mum, it's okay. I don't *mind*," said Oliver, wondering when he might get a word in edgewise.

"The thing is, you'd be able to come and stay whenever you liked," Jessie rattled on frantically, "and if you wanted to come here, I'm sure Toby would be glad to have you at his house. So really it means you'll have more choices than before, which is *great*—"

"Mum, I've got something to tell you too."

"Oh." Jessie ground to a halt, surprised by the abruptness of Oliver's tone. Still, at least that was that out of the way now. She'd done it, told him she was going, and he hadn't asked her why.

No awkward questions about Toby—phew.

Rummaging in the licorice allsorts bag, Jessie found one left—only a boring pink coconut one, but better than nothing. Then she took a swig of Fosters.

Ugh, it didn't go.

Oliver closed his eyes for a second. He had to say it; he had to. No backing out now.

"It's about Savannah. She isn't my sister."

"Oliver, of course she is! What a thing to say!" Jessie protested. "Why else would I have told you about Toby and me? It's hardly the kind of thing I'd make up."

"We aren't talking about me. I know Toby's my father," said Oliver. "The thing is, he isn't Savannah's."

"Oh, now this is too—"

"Mum, it's true. Deborah had an affair."

Briefly, without naming names, he ran through the facts.

Jessie was horrified.

"Poor Toby. Poor Savannah! She must be devastated. This Phoebe person has to be crazy. Whatever possessed her to suddenly blurt everything out like that?"

"I don't know. She just did." Oliver had finished his lager. He could do with another one. Considering that none of this was his fault, he was feeling strangely racked with guilt.

On the radio, a worried-sounding woman from Gwent was saying, "You see, Anna, I don't know how to break it to him. He worked so hard for that money and I spent it all on lotto scratchers. He's going to be so upset when he finds out."

Jessie found herself listening without meaning to.

Anna, who had a firm, authoritative voice laced with compassion, heaved a sigh and said, "Oh dear, oh dear, you've got yourself into a right pickle, haven't you?"

"I have, Anna. I know I have."

"Well, my advice to you is: *don't* tell him." Anna paused for dramatic effect, then went on, "Take a part-time job, earn back all the money you lost, pay it into that joint bank account of yours, and"—in a voice like a kindly rumble of thunder—"DO NOT SPEND IT ON LOTTO SCRATCHERS."

What this country needs, Jessie thought, *is someone like Anna running it. She'd soon have us all sorted.*

"Hang on." She sat up abruptly as the significance of Anna's wise words sank in. "There's no need for Toby to know about this! Savannah doesn't have to tell him."

"She does."

Oliver was fiddling with his empty lager can, denting and undenting it.

"But *why?*"

As he hesitated, Jessie saw his neck begin to redden. This had to be the first blush she had seen on her handsome, twenty-one-year-old son since he was about fourteen.

Oliver simply wasn't the going-red type. "Because me and... and Savannah..."

Jessie continued to watch, mystified. Heavens, even his grammar was going to pot.

"Yes?" she prompted helpfully. "You and Savannah *what?*"

"Um...er...well, we're in love."

Chapter 37

DEBORAH HAD THREE CIGARETTES in a row before ringing the private number David Mansfield had given her. Remembering how violently opposed he was to smoking, she pinched one of Dizzy's sticks of Juicy Fruit before picking up the phone. Just in time—since he'd never been mad about the sound of gum being chewed either—she took it out of her mouth.

"Oh, hello." David didn't sound enchanted to hear from her. "Well?"

Deborah tried to drop the bit of gum into the ashtray, but it was stuck to her finger. She shook her hand and the chewed wad flew across the kitchen.

"It was a positive match."

"Shit."

"Sorry."

"Bit late for sorry."

Deborah wished she'd hung on to the chewing gum now. Wasn't this just typical of bloody men?

"Well"—she bristled—"what else do you want me to say?"

"Not a lot you can say." David sounded resigned rather than angry. "Apart from, 'Wake up, David, you've been having a bad dream.'"

"Don't tell me you never suspected," Deborah sighed. "You aren't stupid. One minute we were fine. The next I was telling you I couldn't see you again. And eight months later—hey, presto—Savannah was born. David, it must have occurred to you that she could be...well, yours."

She had been about to say *government issue* but sensed that David wasn't in the mood for humor.

"You didn't say anything. I took that to mean she wasn't. Shit. *Shit!*" he raged down the phone. "This is my *career!*"

God, he was so selfish.

"Savannah won't go to the papers," Deborah said consolingly.

David Mansfield's laughter was hollow. "Come on, she's eighteen years old. She dresses like a trollop and all she cares about is getting her own way. Of course she'll go to the papers."

When Deborah had hung up, she rang Doug's cell phone.

"Where are you?"

"At home."

"I need cheering up," said Deborah. "Can I come over?"

"Drew's here."

Next door at Keeper's Cottage, Drew was putting on his jacket. "I'm just off," he said, in case Doug hadn't noticed.

But Doug shook his head. "No, he'll be in all evening. And I'm on duty tomorrow. No, no, that would be difficult… Yes, I'll ring you."

Drew was grinning by the time Doug switched off the phone.

"Who was that?"

"New physiotherapist at the hospital."

"New married physiotherapist if the only place she can meet you is here." Drew, who had been called out to a heifer in labor, said briskly, "Could be trouble."

Tell me about it, thought Doug. He couldn't cope with Deborah Gillespie right now; he needed breathing space.

"I know." He yawned, feigning boredom. "That's why I turned her down."

The Sindy Silverman Show went out live at nine in the evening. Afterward, in the green room, Sindy chatted briefly with her two other guests—a blind snake charmer and a raddled rock star fresh out of rehab—before homing in on Toby.

"Hey, you were good tonight."

"Not really." Toby thought he'd been okay, but good was pushing it.

"At least you were on this planet." She nodded briefly in the direction of the leather-clad rock star. "That guy is coked to the eyeballs. He kept calling me Barbie. One more trip to the bathroom and he won't even know his own name."

Never mind drugs. Toby was beginning to know how he felt. This publicity tour felt as if it had been going on for months. Stifling a yawn, he put down his empty glass.

"We could go out to dinner." Sindy lowered her voice and moved nearer. Up close, her heavy makeup was showing signs of wear. It made her look like a drag queen.

Without it, thought Toby, *she'd be fine.* Beneath all that glistening foundation and troweled-on crimson lipstick, she had a sweet smile and a pretty face.

"Thanks, but I had something earlier. And I'm pretty tired."

"Maybe you're just tired of being alone." Sindy gave his arm a sympathetic pat. "Look, we don't have to eat. I could show you my apartment," she offered with a playful lift of her eyebrows. "It's only five blocks from here."

Toby looked at her. How old was she? Thirty-five? Her nose had been fixed, so had the cheekbones, and the lips were collagen-enhanced. Was she on her second face-lift or third?

"Thank you," he said again, "but I'm married."

"Well, I know that." The collagen mouth twitched with amusement. "I do read my researchers' notes, you know. But she's in England, right? And you're over here…"

"It's not that kind of marriage," said Toby.

The plucked eyebrows shot up even higher. "You're not serious! You mean you're actually *faithful*?"

"The dreaded f-word." Toby smiled briefly and nodded. "I'm afraid so."

"Amazing. Nice for her, shame for me." Sindy Silverman gave a good-natured shrug. "She's a lucky lady."

"Thanks."

For the first time all evening, she seemed genuinely curious. "Is it…you know, *easy?*"

Toby watched the rock star reel toward the door, almost crashing into the snake charmer's basket of cobras en route. He thought of all the times in the last few days when he had looked at a telephone and longed—Christ, *ached*—to ring Jessie. "Not always easy," he admitted.

Sometimes it wasn't easy at all.

—⁓—

Oliver could smell Savannah's perfume as they made their way across the village green together by moonlight. An old Simon and Garfunkel song was playing over and over again in his head. It wasn't until Savannah slipped her fingers into his that he figured out why.

God, it was the music from *The Graduate*, and he was as twitchy as Dustin Hoffman, faced with the terrifying, predatory advances of Mrs. Robinson.

"Olly, come on. Don't do that."

"Don't do what?"

"Take your hand away." Savannah reached for it again and held it more firmly this time. "It's okay now. It's allowed."

Oh Christ.

"Someone could see us," said Oliver.

"So?"

"So, *they* don't know it's allowed. Please, just let go."

"I don't care what other people think. It's none of their business." She stopped walking and turned to face him. "Olly, I love you. We aren't related. That means we can do anything we like!" In the darkness, the whites of her eyes gleamed like opals. "It's been three whole days now and you still won't even *kiss* me."

Oliver carried on walking. "It doesn't feel right."

"But it *is* right. It's what you wanted." Savannah sounded as if she were about to explode with frustration. "It's what we *both* wanted."

Oliver couldn't speak. He just wanted to go home. Okay, he had fancied Savannah; he'd fancied her quite a lot. And seeing her being chatted up by other blokes had been awful. But on a scale of one to ten, his lust for her had rated... What? A seven?

Maybe an eight.

The trouble was, Savannah had gone overboard. Her feelings for him rated 290.

"Your dad doesn't even know yet." This was Oliver's excuse, but he could only use it for another forty-eight hours. And what would happen when Toby found out was anybody's guess. He couldn't bring himself even to think that far ahead.

"We don't have to go home yet," Savannah urged. "We could go for a walk in the woods. Nobody would see us there."

Oliver, who had no intention of taking her anywhere, said, "Compass Hill Wood is full of bats."

―⁓―

It was almost midnight when Savannah let herself into the house, but Dizzy was downstairs in the kitchen foraging for food.

"That looks so gross." She pried the lid off the cookie tin, took out a handful of chocolate cookies, and pushed past him on the way to the fridge.

Dizzy was painstakingly—and messily—putting together a massive sandwich of ham, peanut butter, Marmite, and mayonnaise. He watched Savannah crumble the cookies into a bowl and pour heavy cream on top.

The words *pot*, *kettle*, and *black* sprang to mind.

"What d'you want to be when you grow up?" he countered. "An elephant seal?"

A thump on the arm would have been par for the course, but Savannah couldn't be bothered. She found a teaspoon and began to eat, ignoring Dizzy and brooding fretfully over Oliver.

It isn't going well, she thought, suffused with misery. *Everything should be great and it isn't. Oh shit, I love him, I love him, I love him* so much—

"Look, am I missing something here?" Dizzy was frowning. Now he came to think about it, his mother had been pretty quiet for the past few days as well. Okay, he hadn't spent much time downstairs, but was it his imagination, or was there a bit of a strained atmosphere in this house?

And why hadn't Savannah thumped him just now? She always gave him a thump when he called her fat.

Savannah, leaning against the fridge, ignored him and carried on eating.

"Is something going on that I don't know about?" Dizzy persisted.

"No."

"There is." He shot her an accusing look. "You're acting weird. Mum's acting weird too. And when I saw Jessie coming out of the shop this afternoon, she asked me if I was okay."

Toby had to be told before Dizzy. Her mother had been adamant on that score.

Savannah mashed the last dregs of the chocolate cookies into the cream and piled it onto her spoon. She flicked Dizzy a you-don't-need-to-know look and a dismissive shrug. "Nobody's acting weird."

"Don't give me that." He hated it when she acted all condescending and superior, deliberately treating him like a kid. "Something *is* going on," he whined. "Tell me what it is."

"Oh, shut up, Dizzy! Don't pester me, okay? Give it a rest." Losing patience, Savannah clattered her bowl into the sink and stalked toward the door. "Just get back to your precious computer," she snapped over her shoulder. "Zap a few aliens and leave me alone."

Chapter 38

JESSIE GOT HOME FROM work at six o'clock. Toby was due back at around eight. Unable to relax, she had a shower, sorted out her underwear drawer, and finally—heavens, she must be desperate—lugged a great armful of ironing downstairs.

Twenty minutes later, she saw Deborah coming up the front path.

"Hi. I've got the jitters." Deborah held out a bottle of wine, her smile rueful. "Can I come in?"

"I've got the jitters too," said Jessie. She fetched two glasses and followed Deborah into the laundry-strewn living room. "Ironing's supposed to be soothing."

"And is it?"

"Can't say it's doing much for me." Gloomily, Jessie held up a white silk shirt complete with shriveled scorch mark down the front, the shape of South America. "I didn't feel very soothed when I did this."

"That's your favorite shirt," Deborah protested.

"Well, it was."

"I've got one I don't wear anymore. It's a Jasper Conran. You can have it." Deftly Deborah uncorked the wine and filled the glasses.

"Why?"

"Because I've got four white silk shirts and you've just wrecked your only one." She shrugged and rolled her dark eyes. "If only all our problems could be so easily solved. Oh well. Cheers!"

They made short work of the first two glasses. When Jessie went to unplug the iron, Deborah stopped her.

"No, leave it on. If it's soothing, I'll give it a go." She picked up one of Oliver's Nike sweatshirts and began ironing the sleeves.

"Are you hungry?" Jessie asked. "I could stick a pizza in the oven."

Deborah shook her head. "I couldn't eat a thing. My stomach feels like a washing machine stuck on spin. Anyway, reeking of garlic may not be such a great move. Toby might regard it as the ultimate insult."

Jessie privately felt that the ultimate insult as far as Toby was concerned was the fact that his wife had had an affair—and a child—with a supersmooth, if not downright slimy, politician.

Still, this was Deborah's problem, not hers.

"Are you scared?"

"Witless. Oh God, everyone makes mistakes, don't they? I made mine eighteen years ago." Deborah heaved a mammoth sigh. "And now I'm about to get my comeuppance."

She couldn't stop looking at her watch, and every few seconds, she put the iron down and took another swig of Frascati. Jessie didn't hold out much hope for Oliver's beloved pink sweatshirt; any minute now, the lettering on the front was going to end up melted like toffee and superglued to the iron.

"Have you tried reasoning with Savannah? I mean, does she understand just how much chaos she's going to cause?"

Deborah gave her a wry look. "I've reasoned with her until I'm navy blue in the face. I'd have more joy persuading Dizzy to clean his room. You know what teenagers are like, endlessly self-centered." She flipped back her dark hair with a weary gesture and the lettering on the sweatshirt, trapped beneath the iron, went *sssssss.* "The trouble is, I can't even be angry with her. It's all my own fault. Oh *shit.*" She gazed in dismay at the frazzled letters on the bottom of the iron. "I'm sorry. Now Oliver's going to want to kill me too, and he'll be so pissed off when he finds out he can't because Toby's done it alr—"

"Here, sit down." Jessie took the iron and guided her over to the sofa. "Maybe it won't be as bad as you think." *Hmm, long shot.* "Toby might be okay about it, once he gets over the…um, shock."

"Oh, please!" Deborah interrupted, half laughing. "We both know that won't happen. I don't want us to split up—God knows, my marriage is more important to me than anything—but I'm really going to have my work cut out, persuading Toby not to divorce me."

Jessie watched her twirl the broad silver bracelet on her wrist. Sitting there, so elegant in a topaz-yellow tank top, narrow white trousers, and yellow-and-silver strappy sandals, it was hard to imagine anyone wanting to divorce her.

"Do you know what I think he'll do?" Deborah said suddenly. "I think he'll throw me out of the house like the cheap, shameless hussy I am and get back together with you."

What?

Jessie took another hasty slurp of wine, praying that the glass at least partly shielded her face from Deborah's disconcertingly piercing gaze. "Me! Heavens, why me? What on earth makes you say that?"

"Come on, I'm not daft." Deborah's dark-brown eyes lit up with genuine amusement. Affectionately, she reached over and patted Jessie's wrist. "And you aren't either. You know Toby still likes you."

Oh, good grief.

"Er…well, we get on okay, I suppose."

"Trust me, Jess, it's more than that. If Toby and I were to split up, I'm telling you, he'd be here like a shot. It's the old hurt-pride thing, that male need to retaliate. And he wouldn't have to go out and *find* someone else," she explained brightly. "Well, because you're already here!"

"I don't think so," Jessie lied. She picked up the Frascati bottle, but it was empty.

"I'm sorry. I'm really not trying to embarrass you," said Deborah.

"I just know I'm right. It's what men are like. Why go to all the trouble of introducing yourself to somebody new when you can just leap into bed with an old flame?" She shrugged. "They always do that, given the choice. They're so predictable."

This had a certain ring of truth to it. The dear, old, better-the-devil-you-know syndrome was something Jessie had, in the past, been on nodding acquaintance with herself. It wasn't very flattering, that was the trouble. Being called up out of the blue by some ex-lover who's just broken up with his girlfriend always felt, somehow, like being awarded fourth prize in a talent competition when only four people have bothered to turn up.

"So what are you saying?" Jessie peered into the depths of her glass. Empty as well. At this rate, she'd soon be making arrangements with Lorna Blake for fresh bottles of wine to be delivered from the pub to her doorstep each day, like milk.

"Oh Lord, I'm not trying to warn you off!" Deborah cried, appalled. "That isn't what I mean at all. If you want to sleep with Toby, feel free," she urged. "Please, just go ahead! It's what I deserve, and I wouldn't dream of asking you not to."

"I might not want to," said Jessie, by this time thoroughly confused.

"Well, as I say, it's up to you." Deborah checked her watch again and rose to her feet with reluctance. "All I'm asking is for you to put in a good word for me."

Jessie's mind was a blank. Her brain felt as if it had been Etch A Sketched and shaken clean.

"A good word?"

"We're friends, aren't we?" Deborah gave her a pleading look. "Oh God, I really have to go now. It's just scary—this is my whole life at stake here. Well, wish me tons of luck, Jess." Deborah's dark eyes swam with tears for a second, then she smiled a bracing smile and brushed them away. "And stick up for me every now and again." She gave Jessie a quick Chanel-scented hug. "I know I did a bad thing, but it all happened so long ago, and I love Toby so much. If anyone can save my marriage, you can."

Jessie felt sick. "But…but…"

"Oh please, Jess. He'll listen to you. *Please* say you'll be on my side."

———

Falling asleep clearly wasn't going to happen. It wasn't on the night's agenda. At half past two, after three hours of frenzied tossing, turning, and pillow punching, Jessie gave up and climbed out of bed.

Opening the back door, she stepped outside. The yard was in darkness, but that didn't matter. She could find her way around it with her eyes shut.

The smooth Cotswold stone paving slabs beneath her bare feet were slightly chilly in the dark of the night. Jessie reached the wooden seat at the far end of the yard and sat down, hugging her knees and wrapping her long, white nightie around her ankles.

A moth whirred past her head, and in the distance, an owl hooted, but Jessie was oblivious to these distractions. Less than three hundred yards separated her cottage from Sisley House, and she couldn't stop her mind running feverishly through all the likely scenarios of what might be going on there.

And quite a few unlikely ones too.

It was horrible, not knowing and not being able to do anything. Jessie hated feeling so helpless. She didn't know how Oliver could just sleep as if nothing had happened.

Suddenly it occurred to her that Toby, fresh off the plane from New York, could well be sleeping too. Deborah had told him what she had to tell him and he had been shocked, appalled, furious, etc., but in the end, jet lag had knocked him for a loop.

Outraged, Jessie sat bolt upright on the wooden bench. She didn't want to be the only person awake and worrying herself sick at three o'clock in the morning. Bloody hell, that simply wasn't *fair*.

She ran up the path, in through the back door, out through the front door, and across Compass Lane. The village was silent no sounds of anguished screaming or plate smashing, at least.

Jessie was on the green now. She slowed to a walk and felt the dry grass tickle her ankles and the soles of her feet. As she approached the duck pond, the first rushes brushed against her knees. From this angle, she couldn't quite see Sisley House, but if she moved a little to the left, she would just be able to glimpse it through the trees—

"Oh shit," she squeaked as one foot hit an unexpected slope and the other—cartoon style—stepped into fresh air.

Chapter 39

NOT VERY GRACEFULLY, JESSIE half slithered, half tumbled into the water. Luckily, she didn't make much noise, landing with a muted plop rather than a splash.

"Quaaack," murmured a mallard duck, registering his irritation at being woken up.

"Bugger, bugger," Jessie muttered, hauling herself upright and wading toward the bank. Bits of weed clung to her arms and legs; the bottom of the pond was squishy, and she was going to have her work cut out scrambling back up onto dry land.

At least the water was warm.

"Here, grab hold of me," said a familiar voice, and a hand appeared through the rushes.

Jessie, astonished but grateful, gripped the strong hand and was efficiently hauled out.

"Phew. Thanks."

"No problem." Moll Harper was grinning at her. "Do I ask what you were doing in the pond or shall we gloss over that one?"

"Um…I just couldn't sleep." *Feeble, feeble.*

"Don't worry. I'm discreet." Moll's teeth gleamed white in the darkness.

"Why are you here, anyway?" Jess countered, genuinely puzzled.

Moll jerked her head in the direction of Keeper's Cottage, next to Sisley House.

"Went back with Doug after the pub closed this evening. But

Jamie's snoring like a train in the next bedroom"—she pulled a face—"and Doug has to be up at six. I decided I'd rather spend the rest of the night in my own bed."

"Lucky for me you did," said Jessie, wringing out her sopping wet nightie. "Well, I'd better get inside and dry off. Thanks for winching me out."

"No problem." Moll shook back her hair and gazed around her, listening to the rhythmic rasp of a nearby grasshopper. "Quiet, isn't it? Peaceful. Feels like we're the only ones awake."

"It's three o'clock in the morning," said Jessie. "I should think we are."

"Hmm. There are lights on over at the Gillespies' place." Moll smiled slightly, watching Jessie's face. "Bye."

Jessie watched her make her way across the village green. When she had disappeared, Jessie turned and headed slowly back toward the cottage. Only when she reached the front gate was she able to make out the dark silhouette of a figure, half-obscured by the branches of an overhanging ash tree, farther up Compass Lane.

Jessie stopped in her tracks and the figure moved toward her. When he stepped out of the shadows, she saw that it was Toby.

It was dark, but she recognized the outline of his body. When he drew closer, she saw how pale he was, with shock and grief.

"I knew you'd be awake." His voice was low. "I had to see you."

Jessie reached for his hand. "Come in."

"What happened?" Toby said when they were in the living room. "And who was that with you by the pond?"

"Moll. I fell in. She appeared from nowhere and pulled me out."

Although it wasn't cold, Jessie began to shiver. Puddles of pond water were dripping onto the carpet and there were bits of weed stuck to her feet. But changing out of a sodden nightie didn't seem important right now.

"How did you fall into the pond?"

"Not looking where I was going. Trying to see if there were any lights on in your house."

He looked exhausted; there were charcoal-gray shadows under his eyes and the muscles around his jaw were clenched. Jessie wished she had more to offer him than tea, but she'd finished the wine.

"I'll put the kettle on. I'm sorry there's nothing stronger. I should have—"

"I don't want anything to drink." Shaking his head, Toby moved one step closer and took both her hands in his. "I came to see *you*, Jess. To say I told you so."

She blinked. "Told me so what?"

"You didn't believe me when I tried to tell you my marriage wasn't that perfect. You thought it was a line and you despised me for it. Well," he said evenly, "maybe now you'll believe me."

"I'm sorry."

"I've never lied to you in my life, Jess." He shook his head. "And I never will."

"I'm so sorry about everything." Jessie's knees were trembling. She sank onto the sofa. "You must be feeling... Oh, I can't imagine how horrible it must have been, finding out about...well, you know."

"You mean finding out that my daughter is in love with my son—except it doesn't matter; it's not illegal or anything, because my daughter isn't actually my daughter anyway," Toby said grimly. "But my unfaithful wife never told me about this because she was never absolutely sure herself. That's the great thing about having an affair with a man whose coloring roughly matches that of your husband... and besides, she wasn't terribly keen on me finding out she had been unfaithful, what with us being such a *happily* married couple."

He had to talk; he had to get it out of his system. Bottling it up, Jessie knew, would be the worst thing he could do.

She said gently, "Did you never suspect anything?"

Another shake of the head. "Not then." Toby sounded bitter. "Last year, maybe. And two years ago, almost definitely. Deborah's good, but she's not that good at covering her tracks." He closed his eyes for a second. "But eighteen years ago? No, I had no idea she was screwing someone behind my back. Jesus!" he exclaimed furiously. "We'd only been married a year or so ourselves. Why would she even *want* to?"

There was no answer to this, Jessie thought miserably. Some people just did.

"So that's it," Toby declared. "Marriage over."

"But—"

"Not because my wife slept with someone else. Not just because of that," he amended, rubbing his hand hard against his forehead. "It's the deceit I can't handle. How dare she pass off some other bloke's child as mine?"

He was shaking with fury. Jessie felt the clammy wetness of her nightie around her bottom. She stood up again before it seeped into the sofa and made her look incontinent.

"So what are you saying—that you don't love Savannah anymore?" Under the circumstances, maybe blunt was best. "She isn't genetically yours, so from now on, she's on her own? You no longer *have* a daughter?"

"Of course I'm not saying that. Don't be ridiculous," Toby almost shouted back. "I'm not angry with Savannah. This isn't her fault, is it? It's Deborah's fault. She's the one I don't love anymore."

"The main thing is not to rush into anything. You don't have to make any decisions straightaway." Jessie knew this was good, honest advice columnist material. It might not be the kind of thing she'd ever do herself, but it sounded excellent.

"Oh, shut up," Toby drawled, not taken in for a minute. "I know exactly what I'm going to do."

Jessie tried shaking her head at him. "You might regret it."

"I'll get a divorce."

"Toby, you've had a terrible shock. You *think* you want a divorce—"

"Then I'll marry you."

"Oh, good grief!"

"But first things first." Toby moved toward her. "Can I stay here tonight?"

He didn't want to go home. It was perfectly understandable. It was, Jessie told herself, a reasonable enough request.

"Well, yes, of course." She patted the back of the sofa in a vague this-is-*really*-comfortable manner, but Toby was shaking his head.

"I meant with you, Jess. I want to sleep with you."

It felt almost as if Deborah were in the room with them, Jessie could hear her words so clearly: "Trust me, Jess... If Toby and I were to split up, I'm telling you, he'd be round here like a shot. It's the old hurt pride thing, that male need to retaliate... He wouldn't have to go out and find someone else...because you're already here."

Worst of all, Deborah hadn't even said it bitchily. It wasn't meant as a put-down, Jessie realized. It was just...well, true.

"You want to sleep with me as a way of getting back at Deborah," she said to make him understand.

"I don't."

"You do. It's a revenge thing. You want to hurt her as much as she's hurt you."

"I wanted to sleep with you before," Toby reminded her. "And she hadn't hurt me then."

"Look, this wouldn't be the right thing to do."

It was hard, saying no when you didn't want to. Bloody hard.

"Anyway." Toby ignored Jessie's feeble protest and slid the strap of her nightie off her shoulder. "It's not as if we're talking about a quick screw here, a meaningless one-off. I meant it about the divorce, you know. And I want to marry you, Jess. Christ, I should have married you *twenty years ago*."

Jessie watched the other strap go. The clammy, wet nightie slid off her and plopped—not very romantically—to the ground.

Chapter 40

GLAD TO BE OUT of it at least, Jessie reached into the laundry basket of things that hadn't gotten around to being ironed earlier, pulled out a crumpled blue shirt, and put that on instead.

"Toby, you can have the sofa. I'm going up to bed. I'll throw down a couple of blankets, but I'm sure you won't be—"

"Jess, I want to sleep with you."

"Toby, you can't."

"Why not?" His eyes darkened. "If this has something to do with that chap with the sports car…"

"Actually, it's more to do with contraception," Jessie sighed. Oh well, sometimes honesty was the best policy. Especially when you'd run out of plausible lies. When in doubt, be blunt.

Who said romance was dead?

"I don't care about that."

Hmm, certainly not Toby.

"Oh, thanks," Jessie exclaimed.

"I want to make you pregnant. I want us to have another baby."

"Well, I don't!"

"Jess, I love you." He held her shoulders and gazed down at her, his eyes serious but his mouth beginning to twitch. "Even if you are as bloody stubborn as you ever were."

She kissed his cheek and moved toward the stairs. "I just don't fancy climbing ladders and painting ceilings with a baby slung over my shoulder, that's all."

Condoms, condoms, thought Jessie. *How about Keeper's Cottage?* Three healthy, rugby-playing, lager-swilling lads like that must have whole cupboards full of the things. For heaven's sake, there was probably a vending machine by the front door.

She tried to imagine knocking on their front door at half past three in the morning and asking if they had any to spare.

"You wouldn't have to paint ceilings," said Toby. "Not if you were my wife."

He had just seen her stark naked, but Jessie still found herself clutching the crumpled shirttails around her thighs as she climbed the stairs. It wasn't even a gorgeous shirt, just one of Oliver's ancient castoffs that she used when she was painting. *Lord*, thought Jessie, *talk about glamorous.*

And then another thought occurred to her—*ding*—like a light bulb going on in her head.

"All right, I give in," Toby said. "You can relax. I'll sleep down here."

"Right."

"I can tell when you aren't going to change your mind."

"Good," said Jessie.

"You're a cruel, heartless woman. You know that, don't you?"

"Oh yes."

"I shouldn't think I'll be able to sleep at all." He looked mournful.

Jessie smiled. "Toby, you'll sleep like a log."

Oliver had only half drawn his bedroom curtains. Pale moonlight filtered through the gap, enabling Jessie to find her way across the room without breaking her toes on bits of furniture.

She eased the top right-hand drawer of the old chest of drawers open, terrified it might squeak. Next to her, sprawled diagonally across his bed, Oliver breathed in and out, undisturbed.

There were car magazines, old key rings, Oliver's passport, a battered copy of *The Traveler's Guide to Europe*, a broken watch, and a penknife.

She found what she was looking for in the left-hand drawer.

Twenty minutes later, Jessie heard the creak of footsteps on the stairs.

Her bedroom door swung open.

Toby, his voice low, said, "Are you still awake?"

"Yes."

"You didn't throw a blanket down."

"You're cold?"

He nodded. "And there's a bloody damp patch on the sofa from your nightdress."

Jessie bit her lip, trying not to smile. "I'm sorry."

"What are those?"

"Well, if you don't know…"

"Okay. Where did you get them?"

Jessie watched him pick up the unopened packet of condoms from the bedside table. Now why hadn't she hidden them? Why hadn't she stuffed them under her pillow when she heard him coming up the stairs?

Silly question.

"I found them in Oliver's room."

Even sillier answer.

"And?" Toby sat down on the bed next to her. "What was the plan?"

"I don't know."

"Were you going to blow them up and twist them into animal shapes, maybe? Here's a giraffe. Here's a rabbit."

Jessie trembled. He was so close to her. Half of her wanted desperately to undress him and pull him into bed, but the other half—the one bearing an alarming resemblance to Lili's mother-in-law—was tapping a disapproving foot and reminding her tartly that these kinds of shenanigans weren't going to solve anything at all.

The worst bit, the most humiliating part of all this, was having practically been given permission to sleep with Toby by his wife.

I want to, Jessie thought helplessly, *and Toby wants to. The trouble is, the really off-putting thing is, Deborah wants us to as well.*

"Okay, I get the message." Toby stood up again. "It's cold down there, but never mind. I'll ignore the damp patch and the fact that you have the most uncomfortable sofa in England. If not sleeping with me means that much to you, then fine. I understand. I may even still respect you in the mor—What are you doing?"

"What does it look like?"

Toby watched, dry-mouthed, as Jessie peeled the cellophane off the pack of condoms. The muted gold glow from the bedside lamp lit up her tumbling ringlets. She was frowning with concentration, her mouth slightly open. The crumpled shirt was sliding off one brown shoulder.

She looked so, so beautiful...

"Come on." She reached for his hand. Her expression might have been casual, but she didn't fool Toby. "Wouldn't want you to get cold."

As she pulled him into bed, he felt the manic hammering of her heart against his chest.

"Jess, are you sure?" *Christ,* thought Toby, *I must be mad. What am I trying to do now—put her off?*

But it wasn't that. He just didn't want her to hate herself in the morning. Not that he could see why she should, but Jess had never been one for doing things by the book. She was willful and stubborn and fiercely proud.

A real one-off.

Jessie smiled up at him, one warm arm curling around his neck. "I changed my mind. And I'm really, really sure. Well, on one condition."

Anything, anything. Dress up in a rubber diving suit? Do it in the village pond, singing "Yellow Submarine" through a snorkel? No problem at all.

"What?" Toby murmured, kissing her neck and sliding one hand beneath the crumpled, fresh-from-the-laundry-basket shirt.

Jessie tapped him on the nose with the condom packet. "First thing in the morning, you get out of here without being seen. *By anyone.* Then you have to drive into Harleston and buy another packet exactly like this one."

"Good grief, what are you?" said Toby with a grin. "Sex mad?"

She tapped him again. "Look, I stole these from Oliver's drawer. Do you have any idea how embarrassing that is? They *have* to be replaced before he wakes up."

Oh, Jessie Roscoe, I love you.

"You mean, whatever happens, Oliver mustn't find out his mother's had sex with his father?" Toby's smile broadened.

"It's not that," Jessie fibbed, because it *was* partly that. "It's the sneaking into his bedroom in the middle of the night and stealing them." She went pink at the awful thought of Oliver finding out. "It sounds so teenagey, so…so desperate."

"I've waited twenty-one years for this." Toby helped her out of the faded blue shirt. "I *am* desperate."

"You still have to promise."

The shirt slid to the floor. Jessie might not go around flaunting it, he thought, but she had a terrific figure.

"All right, I promise. But I don't need to drive all the way into Harleston." Innocently Toby said, "I'll just pop across and pick some up from Myrtle Armitage's shop."

Chapter 41

"IMPOTENT! WHAT D'YOU MEAN, impotent? You can't be!"

"I can," said Oliver sadly. "I am." He hung his head. "I'm sorry."

It was Thursday morning. By the time he had staggered downstairs at ten o'clock, the cottage was empty. Jessie, who had left for work earlier, had been in a bit of a daze herself, by the look of things. In the kitchen, Oliver had discovered six slices of burned toast, an untouched cup of coffee, and the milk left out of the fridge. In the living room, on the floor by the sofa, there was a dripping-wet nightdress.

Frowning, Oliver had struggled to figure it out. Jessie must have jumped under the shower, forgetting to take off her nightie first. In a fit of tidiness, he'd bent down and picked it up. Mysteriously, a long strand of something resembling pondweed had been stuck to the hem.

Oliver had given up. Anyway, he had other things to think about. Savannah would be here soon—she had said tennish, which meant eleven—and he hadn't even figured out yet what he was going to say.

Crikey, that was more important than a bit of slimy, old pondweed!

"You're early," he had told Savannah when she arrived.

She'd looked taken aback.

"I'm not. It's ten to eleven."

"Well, earlier than I expected." Oliver had been nervous. He'd pushed his hands through his blond hair and wondered—not for the first time—how he had managed to get himself into this mess. "So, how did it go last night?"

He hadn't been in her way, but Savannah had squeezed past him and made sure her hips brushed suggestively against his as she made her way through to the kitchen.

"Pretty much as expected. Dad got back from Heathrow. Mum told Dad. Dad went berserk. Mum cried a bit. I came downstairs and cried a bit too. I hugged Dad. He hugged me. I told him I loved him and how happy I was with you. Then Dizzy wandered in like an idiot and said, 'What's going on?' so Mum had to explain everything all over again and Dizzy kept whining, 'Why didn't anybody tell me about this before?' As if *that* was all that mattered." Savannah had rolled her eyes as she dumped a shopping bag on the table and pulled out a box of frozen banana doughnuts. "Here, stick these in the microwave. We can have three each."

"What's going to happen now?" Oliver had asked. He didn't know if he could face one banana doughnut, let alone three.

"Nothing much." Savannah had shrugged. "It'll blow over."

Oliver was feeling horribly responsible for all this. He had to check. "They're not going to split up, then?"

"Nooo! Oh, Dad ranted on a bit about getting a divorce, but he'd never do it. That's just what people say when they're upset. Anyway, Mum'll get around him. She's great at that kind of stuff."

"But—"

Beep went the microwave. Greedily, Savannah had swung the door open and tried to pick up a steaming doughnut.

"Honestly, aren't microwaves brilliant? One minute everything's frozen, and the next—OUCH!" She'd fanned her mouth violently, hopping from one foot to the other.

"Everything's hot?" Oliver had suggested.

Savannah had come up to him, looking plaintive and pointing to her lower lip.

"Well, it's a bit red." Personally, Oliver thought anyone daft enough to eat doughnuts straight from the microwave deserved to be scalded with molten banana puree.

"You could kiss it better," Savannah had whispered.

Oh God, thought Oliver, flinching away. *Here we go again.*

"Ollie, what's the matter?".

"Nothing, nothing." There was something else in the shopping bag. Desperate to change the subject, he had begun to investigate. "God, what's this?" Delving farther, he'd pulled out a small paintbrush. He'd stared at it in utter bewilderment. "Sav?"

Savannah's eyes were bright. She'd pointed to the jar in his left hand. "It's chocolate body paint. You paint it on"—she had touched the brush in his other hand—"with this." Her voice had dropped to a whisper. "Then you lick it off."

Oliver had dropped the brush. "Jesus! *Why?*"

"It's fun. And it's sexy." Savannah had stood her ground; there was a feverish glitter in her eyes. Those things hadn't just accidentally toppled into the shopping bag, Oliver realized. They'd been put there for a purpose.

"Sounds messy to me," he'd prevaricated, wondering desperately how to change the subject.

God, this was crazy. Two weeks ago, he'd have given both arms for this to be happening…and now that it was, he was backing away like a startled sheep.

"It's *meant* to be messy. That's part of the fun," Savannah had insisted. She'd smiled and ran her pink tongue around her lips. To Oliver it was all horribly reminiscent of a cat about to pounce.

I'm not even a sheep anymore, he thought. *I'm a mouse.*

Just tell her. Just tell her you don't fancy her anymore, a voice in his head had howled, but Oliver knew he couldn't bring himself to do it.

Too much had happened, and it was all his fault. He had been attracted to Savannah and he hadn't been able to hide it. Now, thanks to him, a perfectly good marriage lay in tatters, Savannah's father was no longer her father,,,and, doubtless, somewhere in Westminster, a philandering cabinet minister was knocking back blood-pressure pills by the bucketful and rehearsing his resignation speech.

Oliver's mouth had gone dry at the thought of all the havoc his hormones had unwittingly caused.

There was no way, no way on earth, he could back out now.

"I know what it is," Savannah had announced. "I've figured it out. You're shy."

Shy was okay; shy was good. Shy would definitely buy him time.

Numbly, Oliver had nodded.

Savannah had looked triumphant. "See? I *knew* there had to be a reason for the way you've been acting lately. But you don't have to worry, because this is why I'm here today. To get you over it!"

"Um…I don't think you—"

"Of *course* I can!" Gaily Savannah had waved the brush and jar at him. "That's the brilliant thing about body paint. Once you're covered in this stuff, it's impossible to be shy. You just relax, go with the flow, and before you know it, all your inhibitions have—"

"I'm not shy. I'm impotent," Oliver had blurted out in desperation.

Stunned silence. At least he'd managed to shut her up.

Finally, she'd said, "What?"

"I'm impotent. That's why I've been a bit…well, offish. I just didn't know how to tell you."

"Impotent! What d'you mean, impotent?" Savannah wailed. "You can't be!"

"I can," said Oliver sadly. "I am." He hung his head. "I'm sorry."

"But I could cure that too. I know I could. There are all sorts of things you can do to—"

"Tried them," he cut in firmly.

"Not with me!"

"It's no good, Sav. Nothing works."

Horrified, Savannah clutched his arm. "But you can't just suffer in silence! You have to see a doctor, get it sorted out." Beseechingly, she added, "I could ask Doug Flynn to take a look at you."

Oh yes, terrific, thought Oliver. *That's all I need.*

"No." He shook his head, quite pleased with himself and wondering why he hadn't thought of this before. "I've already been seen by the specialists. It all started in the spring when I got kneed during a college rugby match. There's nothing they can do, but at least it isn't permanent. I just have to be patient," he explained with regret, "and wait for the…um…feeling to come back. But it's going to be out of action for at least a year."

Upstairs in his room, Dizzy was doing his best to destroy the enemy and conquer the universe, but things weren't going too well. It was hard to conquer the universe when you couldn't see the screen properly and everything was blurred.

Dizzy gave up and rubbed his eyes with the sleeve of his Harry Potter sweatshirt. He wasn't crying. Only sissies cried. His eyes were just watering a bit because he'd been staring at the screen for too long.

But it isn't fair. It bloody isn't, he thought, biting his lip. *Nobody tells me anything in this house. They don't care about me. I don't know why they bothered to bring me down here with them; they might as well have left me in London, chucked me into that Dumpster along with the rest of the unwanted rubbish that would only clutter up their smart, new house.*

What really got to him was how it hadn't seemed to occur to any of them that he might have wanted to be told what was going on.

Bloody hell, he thought miserably. *Is that so unreasonable?* It was pretty major stuff, after all. But no—all Savannah had snapped when he'd protested that nobody had said anything to him was, "Oh, stop whining, Dizzy. Why would anyone in their right mind *want* to?"

Bitch. At that moment, he had hated her so much, he could have pulled all her stupid blond hair out.

Dizzy sighed and switched off his computer. He would go over to the shop, buy a load of chocolate, and eat it all in one go. Maybe he'd bump into Moll, and she'd sense how pissed off he was and say in that slow, sexy voice of hers, "Hey, Dizzy, you look down in the dumps. Why don't we go somewhere quiet, just the two of us, and you can tell me all about it? Maybe I could help to cheer you up."

―――

"Two Crunchies." Dizzy dug into the pocket of his baggy jeans and pulled out a fiver. "A Kit Kat, a Lion bar, and one of those big packets of Maltesers. Oh, and ten Marlboro Lights," he added. "For my mother."

Myrtle Armitage gave him a who-are-you-trying-to-kid look. "I don't sell cigarettes to minors. Tell your mother she'll have to buy her own."

"She's ill," said Dizzy. "In bed. That's why she asked me to get them for her."

"If she's ill," Myrtle replied with an air of triumph, "she won't be needing cigarettes, will she?"

Look, I'm under a lot of stress, Dizzy wanted to yell—but it was no good. He knew he couldn't win. The whole world was against him, treating him like some stupid little kid.

Outside the shop, he collided with Harriet Ferguson and Blitz. Harriet was trying, without much success, to tie the dog's leash to the trash can.

"Oh, hi." She looked relieved to see Dizzy. "Dogs aren't allowed in the shop. Could you just hold him for a minute while I run inside?"

"Why should I?" said Dizzy. Too right. Nobody ever did him any sodding favors.

Taken aback, Harriet said, "I'd only be a second. I wanted to pick up my magazine."

"Wanted" was the understatement of the year. There was a full-size poster of Harry Styles free with this week's issue. She'd spent the last hour clearing a space for it on her bedroom wall.

"I can't hold him, okay?" Dizzy's tone was dismissive. "My hands are full."

Harriet looked at the half dozen or so bars of chocolate he was clutching. "Put them in your pockets."

He shot her a look of disgust. "Oh great, then they'd melt."

"Well, why don't you—"

"Woof!"

Recognizing the smell of chocolate, Blitz leaped up ecstatically on his back legs. Startled, Dizzy took a step backward and the Lion bar slipped from his grasp. Blitz caught it before it hit the ground and wolfed it down in three seconds flat, wrapper and all.

He eyed Dizzy eagerly, hopeful of a repeat.

"That was my Lion bar!" Dizzy howled. "You stupid, bloody dog! How dare you eat my Lion bar! It was *MINE*!"

"Sor-ry." Harriet privately felt he was making a big fuss over nothing. How many bars of chocolate could anyone eat in one go anyway? But to humor Dizzy she wagged a finger at Blitz and said, "Naughty boy."

Blitz wagged his tail back at her happily.

"Isn't he gorgeous?" Harriet grinned, forgetting all about Dizzy's mood.

Dizzy hadn't. "No he isn't," he sneered. "He's bloody ugly. And I don't know what you're looking so smug about, because you're buying me another Lion bar."

"I am not!" Harriet was outraged. "You shouldn't have dropped it in the first place. Anyway, I haven't got enough money." Her voice rose. "And our dog isn't ugly! How *dare* you call him that!"

Dizzy hated the world. He scowled mightily, kicked his shoe against the trash can—*claaang*—and muttered, "He is. He's as ugly as you are."

Blitz began to gag as a bit of chewed wrapper worked its way back into his throat. Harriet was delighted when he brought up the Lion bar over Dizzy's other shoe.

She fixed Dizzy with the disdainful glare she'd been practicing for ages in front of her bedroom mirror. It was a Simon-Cowell-meets-Sharon-Osbourne kind of glare, and rather effective if she did say so herself. Whenever she used it on her little brother it reduced him to tears.

Dizzy didn't cry. He said mockingly, "Oh, I'm *sooo* frightened."

Harriet bent down and gave Blitz a consoling ear rub. "Come on, darling. I'm taking you home. We might be ugly"—she smiled sweetly up at Dizzy—"but at least we don't dye our hair with toilet cleaning bleach."

Chapter 42

DIZZY HAD TO DO something about his vomit-stained shoe. He sat on the bank, dangled both feet in the village pond, and ate his way morosely through the family bag of Maltesers and one of the Crunchie bars.

He couldn't decide whom he hated most: Harriet, for taunting him about the toilet bleach; her mother, for telling her about it; or Jessie Roscoe, for dragging him over there in the first place and *promising* him that no one else would ever find out.

Ha, Dizzy thought bitterly. And now the whole village knew. *Bloody women. They were all the same.*

Well, nearly.

He didn't look up when he heard a door slam shut. It wasn't until he heard footsteps rustling across the dry grass that he bothered to raise his head.

And there she was, sauntering toward him. *Like the way you always wish it would happen*, thought Dizzy, *but it never does in real life.*

But wasn't that weird, when he'd just that moment been thinking about her?

It had to be fate.

Without thinking what he was doing, he put his hand up and waved.

Moll was wearing a tight-fitting black tank top, a long, flowing yellow-and-black skirt, and her usual armfuls of bangles. Her tawny hair was loose today, streaming down her back, and she was carrying an orange cardigan.

Dizzy watched her veer toward him. In his earlier fantasy, she had said, "You look down in the dumps, Dizzy," and offered to cheer him up. The trouble was, she could hardly say that now—not when he had a daft grin plastered all over his face.

"Hi," she said, glancing at Dizzy's thin legs with his jeans rolled up and his big sneakers bobbing like torpedoes beneath the surface of the water. "Bet that feels nice."

"Join me." Dizzy felt like a character in a film. Recklessly, he patted the grass next to him. "Got a cigarette?"

Moll grinned and stuck her hand into the side pocket of her skirt. She pulled out a packet of cigarettes and a heavy gold lighter.

"Help yourself." She sat down next to him on the grass.

Dizzy, who had seen it done in the films, lit two cigarettes and handed one to Moll.

"Ta."

"What were you doing over there?" He nodded casually in the direction of Keeper's Cottage, where Doug's dark-blue MG was parked outside.

"Popped back for a beer with the boys after closing last night. Left this behind." Moll patted the orange cardigan, then blew a lazy smoke ring. "Just called around to pick it up."

Dizzy couldn't help noticing the black, lacy bra strap poking out from between the folds of orange wool. The cardigan clearly wasn't the only thing she'd taken off and left behind last night.

He wondered if Moll had slept with Doug or Drew or Jamie.

Or all three.

Perspiration prickled behind his ears and down his neck.

"Watch that lighter," Moll said. "Don't drop it in the pond."

Dizzy stopped fiddling with the heavy lighter. "It's nice," he said lamely, holding it up and turning it this way and that. "Did someone give it to you?"

Moll winked. "Call it a present from a grateful customer."

What does that wink mean? Dizzy wondered in a frenzy of indecision. *Why's she winking at me—and what* kind *of grateful customer?*

"Enjoying summer vacation?"

"Boring," muttered Dizzy.

"And your family—how are they?"

"Huh, don't ask."

Sex, Dizzy thought. *That's what I need. I'm sixteen and I haven't done it yet. That's why I'm so miserable.*

He was sex-starved; it was bound to be having an effect. It couldn't be natural to have this many hormones and be celibate.

"Hello." Moll passed her hand in front of his face. "What's up? You're miles away."

Dizzy looked at her. He was having trouble breathing. "I've got seventy-three pounds in my post office savings account. If I gave it to you, would you have sex with me?"

Moll chucked her cigarette end into the pond, an act of vandalism guaranteed to send Eleanor Ferguson—if she was watching—into paroxysms of rage.

"Dizzy, I don't sleep with men for money."

Oh dear, she thought wryly, *is that the kind of reputation I have around here? Is that really what everyone thinks?*

"No?" In desperation, he said, "Well, how about for free?"

Moll almost smiled. She shook her head. "Sorry. I only sleep with men because I want to."

Dizzy could have cried. He wanted to sleep with Moll Harper more than anything in the world. It was *so unfair*.

"Who gave you this, then?" he said sulkily, nudging the gold lighter with his elbow.

"Ah, I get it." Moll looked entertained. "You thought I meant *that* kind of grateful customer."

Dizzy could feel his lower lip beginning to jut. He'd taken the risk and been rejected. Moll could have taken his god-awful, hideous life and made it better, but she hadn't. She'd chosen not to.

It was just another letdown to add to all the rest.

"I don't see why any bloke would give you a gold lighter just because you served him a drink at the bar." It came out as a challenge.

"Actually, I did more than that. Some guy came into the pub, and when I went outside, this lad was breaking into his Rolls-Royce." Moll smiled to herself, remembering the events of that afternoon. "I dragged him out by his earrings and sat on him until the police arrived." She shrugged. "The guy was grateful. He gave me his lighter, that's all."

Honestly, some blokes had all the luck. Dizzy wished he could be sat on by Moll.

"Anyway"—Moll stretched and yawned—"I'd better be off."

Dizzy watched her stand up and brush the grass from her skirt. It was only a cheap one, nothing like the kind of thing his mother would wear.

Seventy-three pounds and she still won't have sex with me, he thought morosely. *God, I'm a loser.*

"I hate this place." Dizzy chucked a stone into the pond.

"What you need is to get yourself a girlfriend. That'd buck you up." Poor lad, she felt quite sorry for him.

Oh yeah, thought Dizzy, *and there are so many thousands of girls to choose from.*

"Here, have another cigarette," Moll said kindly.

"Thanks. Uh…you won't tell anyone about what I…um…"

"Your business proposal, you mean?" She looked amused. "Don't worry. I'm discreet."

Dizzy watched her go. Outside the pub, Lorna Blake was putting out ashtrays. He saw her speak to Moll, and Moll say something in return. Then, half turning, Moll gestured toward the pond with the hand clutching the orange cardigan and said something else. Lorna burst out laughing and swiveled around to follow the direction of Moll's arm.

Dizzy wanted to die. So much for discretion. It was obvious what they were laughing about.

Him.

When he got home the house was empty. Not even a note on the kitchen table to let him know where everyone else had gone or when they might be back.

That's how much they care about me, Dizzy thought, squelching upstairs in his waterlogged shoes.

It didn't take him long to chuck a few T-shirts and a couple of pairs of jeans into a sports bag. He added his post office savings book, his CD player, half a dozen favorite CDs, and a baseball cap. Halfway down the stairs, he remembered bathroom stuff and went back for his toothbrush, shampoo, Clearasil, and a bottle of Savannah's expensive conditioner because his hair still felt like coconut matting after he washed it.

In the kitchen, he made himself a sandwich and emptied the milk money out of the teapot on the top shelf of the china cabinet. This netted him an extra twenty-three pounds, which would come in handy until he mastered the art of sitting outside a tube station on a grubby blanket looking suitably hungry and homeless.

A grubby blanket…

But they didn't have one. Dizzy had to make do with his mother's rather smart tartan picnic rug instead.

———

"Hop in if you want a lift," Jessie said, pulling up at the bus stop. "Blimey, what's in there?"

Dizzy thudded his Nike bag into the back of the van and climbed into the passenger seat. "Just stuff."

"Quite a lot of stuff." When Jessie had seen him with his sports bag, she had assumed he was going swimming. "What's up? Running away from home?"

"Nah. Staying with a mate in London for a few days. He phoned this morning." Dizzy wound the window down so he could rest his arm out of it. "Mum said it was a great idea."

Jessie could believe that. The goings-on in Sisley House must have unsettled Dizzy; it would do him good to be away from all the hassle for a few days.

Wary of saying the wrong thing, she waited for Dizzy to raise the subject. When he didn't, she turned on the radio and let him hum happily along to the music instead.

"Enjoy yourself." Jessie dropped Dizzy and his overloaded bag outside the train station. "Have fun."

"Oh, I will." Dizzy looked and sounded more cheerful than she'd ever seen him look before. "I'll have a great time. Don't worry about me."

Chapter 43

Jamie Lyall was a pig.

Drew, who could think of a hundred things he'd rather be doing than tackling the mountain of dirty dishes left by Jamie, plowed on with the grim business of scraping two-day-old Cheerios off bowls, dried-up curry off plates, and mold off the inside of half a dozen mugs. The kitchen trash bulged with empty lager cans. He had already discovered an ancient pizza welded to the wire rack in the oven. And wherever he walked, cornflakes crunched under his feet.

It took an hour, but Drew finally got the kitchen looking tidy and moderately hygienic once more. What irritated him most was knowing that when Jamie came home, he wouldn't stop and admire Drew's efforts because he simply wouldn't notice. He'd just make himself a coffee, a mountain of toast, and another bowl of cereal; wander through to the sitting room; and make yet more mess.

Because that, basically, was what he always did.

The coffee might taste a bit better than usual because it wasn't flavored with mold, but that was all. It wouldn't occur to Jamie that the mug had actually been washed.

I must be getting old, Drew mused. *Living in squalor never used to bother me like this.*

It wasn't as if he loved housework; it had just gradually crept up on him that doing some every now and again made day-to-day living that much more bearable. It was actually a reasonable thing to do.

Jesus, I'll be taking up knitting next, Drew thought in alarm. *Buying cushions and dried flowers and becoming really interested in discovering what all those mysterious attachments on the Hoover actually do.*

Still, that was enough domesticity for one day. Now he deserved a reward. Idly glancing out of the sitting-room window, Drew saw Blitz hurtling around the village green like a one-dog relay team, only instead of a baton, he had his leash between his teeth.

Lili and Harriet were trying to catch him, without much luck. Blitz, his tail going like a propeller, was enjoying himself far too much.

Grinning broadly, Drew watched as Harriet crept to the left and Lili to the right, attempting to corner him sheepdog style. Except the green had no corners and Blitz was quicker than both of them. Stopping dead, he crouched on the grass and let them get within a few feet of him. Then he leaped up again, zigzagging around Lili and haring past Harriet faster than a whippet.

Drew left the cottage, crossed the lane to the green, stuck his fingers in his mouth, and let out a piercing whistle. Blitz, recognizing him, spun around in delight and bounded over.

"You dimwit," Drew said affectionately, grabbing the dog by the collar and removing the end of the leash from his drooling mouth.

"My hero," puffed Lili, staggering up to them. "Thanks, Drew. From the bottom of my lungs."

"Good exercise," he remarked while she got her breath back. "Maybe Blitz should release a workout video. He could give Jillian Michaels a run for her money."

Harriet took the leash from him. "Poor Blitz, he thought you were on his side. Now he'll never trust you again."

"No more Mr. Nice Guy." Drew winked at her. "Story of my life."

"I'm supposed to be taking him up to Compass Hill Wood." Lili was still panting. "And I'm exhausted already."

On the spur of the moment—and encouraged by the fact that she had said "I" rather than "we"—Drew said, "I could do with some exercise myself. Would you mind if I came too?"

He directed the question at Harriet, who shrugged. "I'm not going. I only came out to help Mum catch Blitz. There's something I want to watch on TV."

"Oh well," said Drew. He looked at Lili. "Fancy some company then? Say no if you'd rather be—"

"Why not?" Just slightly pink, Lili smiled up at him. "I could do with some professional know-how. You can teach this useless animal to do as he's told."

———

They walked companionably together up Compass Hill with Blitz straining on his leash between them. By the time they reached the path leading into the woods, they had talked about Jamie's allergy to housework, Doug's complicated sex life—though neither of them knew quite *how* complicated—and how to crush garlic without getting the smell of it on your hands.

"We haven't talked about you yet." Lili bent to unclip Blitz's leash so he could run on ahead and chase squirrels. "What have you been up to lately?"

"Washing dishes, mainly." Looking soulful, Drew splayed his fingers in front of him. "What can I say? Dishpan hands."

"Very soft." Teasingly, Lili touched them. "Much nicer for the cows when you have to stick your arm up their bottoms."

He looked at her—she was bright-eyed from their uphill walk and had wisps of hair escaping from her ponytail. She was wearing a pale-green shirt over slightly crumpled, white trousers and her face was free of makeup. She looked comfortable rather than smart, which he liked. If Lili had been done up, he would have felt scruffy by comparison in his faded Guinness T-shirt and jogging pants.

"I've been working. Nothing much else." Drew was more interested in finding out more about Lili. "How's it going at home? Got used to having Michael back yet?"

"I suppose." Lili sighed without meaning to. Ahead of them Blitz spotted his first squirrel and let out a yelp of delight. "He goes out a lot. Sometimes I have a moan about it; other times I'm secretly relieved. He's out again this evening," she went on. "That's why he's looking after Will and Lottie now. I told him he could jolly well spend a bit of quality time with them while I took Blitz for a walk."

"Couldn't you all have come out together?"

Lili half smiled. "You mean like a storybook family? If I suggested that, he'd just look horrified and say, 'What's the point?'"

More yelps of frustration echoed through the woods as Blitz attempted to scramble up a vertical tree trunk. Forty feet above his head, a squirrel leaped from branch to branch with elaborate ease, taunting him.

"Is he faithful?"

"Who?" Lili thought for a moment he meant Blitz.

"Your husband."

"Oh. Well…maybe not all the time."

Drew saw the telltale flush creep up her neck. "Not *all* the time?" Incredulous, he stopped walking.

"I mean, he might have the odd fling when he's working abroad, but that's kind of…well, understandable, isn't it? When you're away from your wife and family for months on end, you're bound to get a bit fed up, a bit bored."

"Lili, you don't have to make excuses for him!"

"I'm not. It's called being realistic. I'm not naive; I know these things go on." Lili stuffed her hands into the front pockets of her trousers, avoiding Drew's gaze. "But it's only when he's away, when I'm not around. He wouldn't do it here." She shrugged. "Why would he need to?"

Because he's a prize shit, probably, thought Drew. He was furious. "If he loved you, he wouldn't do it at all," he said coldly.

"Oh, shut up. I wish I'd never told you now."

Lili felt her throat begin to tighten. She didn't even know why she *had* told Drew. Bleating on about her husband's suspected infidelities—okay, okay, *probable* infidelities—wasn't something she made a habit of.

"Woo-oof!" Blitz howled, losing his grip and sliding in an undignified fashion down the tree trunk. He landed in a heap at the bottom and glanced over his shoulder, embarrassed, to see if anyone had noticed.

"You're criticizing me. You think I'm stupid." Lili tried to swallow the lump in her throat. Dammit, now she *felt* stupid. She really, really wished she'd kept her mouth shut.

"I don't—it's not that. I just think you deserve so much better." Drew was struggling to explain. Michael Ferguson was a philanderer, and Drew wanted to punch his lights out. He wanted Lili to understand that she didn't have to settle for being cheated on, that she was worth more than that.

But mainly, he wanted to put his arms around her and kiss her and kiss her and kiss her...

"It isn't as simple as that." Lili was shaking her head, kicking her way through a pile of dead leaves. "When you have children, they come first. And they need their dad."

From the sound of it, Michael Ferguson wasn't likely to be shortlisted for Father of the Year. But Drew was more interested in hearing more from Lili than arguing with her.

He forced himself to say, "Of course they do."

"Then there's that other thing, the old devil-you-know business," Lili went on. She was doing it again, saying more than she meant to say. How did Drew *do* that?

"You mean, at least he's not a raving psychopath?"

"Look, a lot of women leave their husbands and regret it later. They think it'll be fun, being single again, but it doesn't turn out like that. They end up lonely and depressed instead. They search and search but they never find Mr. Right. And in the end, they realize the chap they were once married to was actually Mr. Almost Right, which is about as good as it gets."

Drew stared at Lili in amazement. "Finished?"

She nodded, embarrassed. "Finished."

"Well, that is the most depressing reason I've ever heard for staying married to a jerk."

"Trust me, it happens. I read the personal columns," said Lili. "The world is full of stunning divorcées who can't find a half-decent man. And if *they* can't manage it…" she added with a dismissive shake of her head. "Well, let's be honest, how much hope is there for someone like me?"

Enough was enough.

"Come here." Drew grabbed her hand and kissed her, very firmly indeed, until Lili began to make running-out-of-air noises.

"That's for being stupid," Drew told her, trembling with emotion but determined to sound cross. "And I don't ever want to hear you say anything so ridiculous again. Got it?"

"Got it," whispered Lili.

"What was all that gurgle-gurgle business, anyway?"

She hung her head, ashamed. The last time she'd been kissed with anything approaching passion must have been twenty years ago. "Sorry. Forgot to breathe."

"Well, just don't forget next time."

"Oh, Drew…"

"You know what your trouble is?" he said gruffly.

"What?"

"It doesn't seem to have occurred to you that splitting up doesn't have to mean being miserable for the rest of your life. You don't hear about all the thousands of happily remarried divorcées because they don't advertise in the personal columns."

"It's easy for you to say that. You've never been married, and you don't have…um, children."

Lili was having trouble concentrating. Drew's hands were on her shoulders, his thumbs gently massaging her collarbones. He looked as if he was about to kiss her again. She could smell his warm skin, and her knees were buckling. Up ahead, sunlight filtered through the canopy of trees, dappling the ground. Blitz crashed like a hooligan through a maze of young bracken. High above them—and sounding badly in need of throat lozenges—a rook cawed.

"I know I haven't, but I'll tell you something." Drew's mouth was moving closer. "If I had a wife and family, we'd all walk the dog together. And we'd have fun doing it."

Lili closed her eyes. Heavens, what a voice; it was like warm chocolate.

"I'm going to kiss you again now." Drew sounded serious. "Don't forget, okay?"

"Forget what?"

"To keep breathing this time."

Maybe I'm having an out-of-body experience, Lili thought. Her fingers had somehow managed to creep upward and start stroking his cheek completely of their own accord.

"Things like this just don't happen to me," she murmured.

"They do now."

"We really shouldn't be doing"—she gestured idiotically around her—"all this stuff."

Drew punctuated his reply with kisses. "Oh yes"—*kiss*—"we definitely"—*kiss*—"definitely"—*kiss*—"should."

"I'm still breathing," Lili murmured as his arms slid around her. Drew was such a fantastic kisser. And as for the sensations her poor, tired, old body was experiencing…

Oops, nearly forgot to breathe again.

In, out. In, out. In, out.

"Oh, Drew…" She pressed herself quite shamelessly against him.

"Oh shit," Drew groaned. The kiss stopped abruptly. Looking stricken, he half pulled away.

Oh no. Poor Drew, Lili thought, her heart going out to him. *How awful to suffer from premature ejaculation.*

And heavens, that *had* been premature!

"I'm so sorry about this," Drew muttered into her hair.

"It doesn't matter. Really, it doesn't." Rushing to reassure him, Lili buried her head against his broad chest and hugged him tighter still. "Golly, it happens to loads of men. If anything, I'm flattered—"

"Perhaps you should look behind you," Drew said, gently turning her around.

Chapter 44

FELICITY STOOD IN A sun-dappled clearing less than fifty yards away from Lili and Drew. Blitz was close by, snuffling in the undergrowth, undeterred by her arrival. Used to seeing Felicity every day when she dropped Freya off at the house, it clearly hadn't occurred to him to bark.

Lili couldn't move. All the old clichés seemed to be clamoring to get out of her brain. She wished a big hole would open up and swallow her; she wished it could be a terrible dream. She wished she could do what two-year-old Will did when he didn't want anyone to see him and cover her own eyes.

It took a second or two before Lili realized that Felicity was standing there, in her immaculate black-and-white shirtdress and black patent leather pumps, *crying*.

"Felicity?"

Lili's whole body was drenched in panicky sweat. She didn't have a clue what to say next, but she knew she had to try to say something. This was awful, her worse nightmare; she needed to come up with some kind of plausible excuse, fast.

But Felicity was shaking her head, signaling her not to speak. The tears were still pouring down her cheeks, and she was clearly without a handkerchief. She stood there, staring at them through red-rimmed eyes, sniffing and gulping like a child.

"Felicity, I'm sorry. I know what you must be th-thinking," Lili faltered, "but I swear to you, we—"

"Don't," Felicity sobbed, making no attempt to wipe her eyes. The expression in them was utterly desolate. "Just don't try to explain, okay? Because right now I can't bear to hear it."

She turned and ran back through the woods the way she had come, her thin legs gawky and stumbling on the uneven path in her rush to get away.

Blitz, his tail wagging and a politely bemused expression on his face, watched her go.

"Oh my God oh my God," groaned Lili. "This is *awful*."

Drew longed to put a comforting arm around her, but he didn't quite dare. All the blissful intimacy between them had vanished in a moment, evaporated into thin air.

"She won't say anything," he tried to reassure Lili, who was now trembling for a different reason. She was in deep shock.

"You don't know Felicity. She disapproves of me so much already."

"Okay, but it was only a kiss."

Drew wished he were better at spur-of-the-moment excuses. Unlike Doug, he simply hadn't had the practice.

"Drew." Despite her panic-stricken state, Lili gave him a pitying look. "There are kisses and there are *kisses*. What Felicity saw just now was pretty much a giveaway, I'd say. It hardly fell into the category of quick social peck on the cheek."

"I didn't mean it like that," said Drew. "Look, you're fairly convinced Michael's played away himself in the past. How much of a fuss can he kick up if he does hear about this?"

"I've no idea." Lili didn't hold out much hope for instant understanding and total forgiveness. "I'll give you a ring, shall I, and let you know when I find out?"

Drew hated feeling so useless. What a mess! *How many blokes*, he thought with a surge of self-disgust, *could wreck a meaningful relationship before it was even two minutes old?*

Lili had been thinking too.

"Was Felicity crying already? Was she walking through the woods having a good old cry when she happened to bump into us?"

She looked hopeful until Drew shook his head.

"Sorry, other way around. She saw us, *then* burst into tears."

Eleanor Ferguson, who had been on one of her periodic knitting benders, arrived at the Old Vicarage just as Michael was reversing the Volvo out of the drive.

"Snooker," he told his mother, dutifully admiring the three Aran cardigans she whisked out of a shopping bag to show him. "The kids'll love them. Mum, I've got a match at seven. Mustn't keep the others waiting."

"You go and enjoy yourself," Eleanor told him fondly. "You deserve an evening off."

Lili wished she had film in her camera, to capture the expressions on the faces of Will, Lottie, and Harriet as their grandmother lined them up, von Trapp fashion, in their matching porridge-toned cardigans.

"You all look very smart." Eleanor moved briskly from one to the next, tweaking leather buttons and turned-up sleeves into place. "And don't worry. There's plenty of room for growth."

Lili knew her children would have to be chloroformed before they would ever wear these cardigans of their own free will. She said, "Eleanor, they're wonderful. I don't know how you do it. You could win competitions with knitting as brilliant as that."

Unused to such fulsome flattery from her daughter-in-law, Eleanor was more than happy to babysit for an hour while Lili popped over to Duck Cottage.

As she raced across the green, Lili couldn't help wondering how Eleanor would react if she knew the real reason she was so eager to see Jess.

"We have to talk," Lili announced breathlessly, barging in without knocking and almost tripping over a suitcase in the hall. "Jess, I'm desperate. I've done something terrible and now Michael's going to find out." She hopped from foot to foot in anguish. "I need you to tell me what to do."

Jessie looked up from her packing. "You've been putting rat poison in his bacon sandwiches?"

"No." Lili cringed. "Worse."

"What then?"

"Oh, help. I'm going to blush. I kissed Drew Darcy."

Jessie watched her blush. "And who saw you?"

"Felicity."

"What did she do?"

"Burst into tears."

"Was it nice?"

Lili gazed at her in astonishment. Was Jessie trying not to smile? "What, watching Felicity burst into tears?"

"Don't be daft. Kissing Drew."

"It was heaven," Lili said miserably. "Oh God, I know it's hopeless but I really like him. And I think he really likes me. Except now everything's ruined. Felicity's going to take Freya away because I'm a bad moral influence, and she's bound to tell Michael, who'll go ballistic—"

"Right, let's get this sorted out." Jessie stood up and stepped over the open suitcase. "First, we go and see Felicity. Find out if she *is* going to tell Michael."

Horrified, Lili gasped. "Oh, we can't do that!"

"You need to know, don't you?" Jessie grabbed her by the arm, pulling her over the suitcase and through the front door. "Look, you can grovel if you want to. Shed a few tears yourself. Tell Felicity it was a one-off, a momentary lapse. God, you're only human, after all."

"Except Felicity *isn't* human, is she?" said Lili, petrified. "She's perfect."

———

Hugh's car, thankfully, wasn't in the driveway.

Jessie rang the doorbell three times before Felicity came to the door.

"Hi," said Jessie, "Lili would like to talk to you and I'm here as moral support."

More like immoral support, thought Lili.

"So," Jessie went on cheerfully, "can we come in?"

Felicity was pale, wet-haired, and wrapped in a pale-green satin robe. The makeup was gone, and her eyelids were swollen. She looked as if she'd been crying for hours.

As she nodded and led the way through to the sitting room, Lili wondered suddenly if Felicity was this distraught because she too had a crush on Drew Darcy. Mortified, blushing furiously, and hating every second, she gazed down at the flawless pistachio-green carpet and stumbled through her excuses and apologies. It was shameful and not terribly likely to work, but she begged anyway.

"So there it is. It's up to you. I know I shouldn't have done what I did, but I promise you I'm not having an affair with Drew Darcy." Dry-mouthed and still unable to drag her eyes above baseboard level—incredibly *clean* boards they were too—Lili reached the end of her grovel. "It's just one more mistake to add to all my other hundreds of mistakes," she concluded hopelessly. "I wish I could be perfect, like you and Hugh, but I'm not."

Felicity stood up, clutching her robe tightly around her narrow waist. "Wait there. I've got something to show you."

She was back less than a minute later with an ivory leather photograph album.

"Your wedding album?" Lili's heart sank at the sight of gold-edged pages. *Oh crikey, what now?* Was she really in for a stern lecture on the sanctity of marriage?

Chapter 45

FELICITY PLACED THE HEAVY album on the floor in front of them and knelt down next to it.

"This is what I was doing when you rang the doorbell."

She flipped over the first page and Lili's hand flew to her mouth. The photograph of Felicity arriving at the church had been neatly cut into quarters.

In silence, Felicity leafed steadily through the pages, showing them that she hadn't stopped until she'd reached the end. Every single photograph had been snipped to pieces.

"That's how perfect my marriage is." Felicity spoke at last, her voice wobbling with emotion. "See that wedding dress? Sonia Rykiel. See the limos and the bridesmaids' outfits and the hotel where we had the reception?" With her index finger she prodded chopped-up sections of different photographs, pointing them out. "Everything cost a fortune. All our guests kept telling us it was the most fabulous wedding they'd ever been to. And all the time they were saying it, I was thinking, *You have no idea.*" She stopped and glanced up, her eyes brimming with fresh tears. "Because do you know how much Hugh loved me? Well, he didn't. Not at all."

This was awful. Lili couldn't bear it. Impulsively she reached over and squeezed Felicity's arm. Heavens, it was thinner than one of Bambi's ankles. "You don't know that. Even if you've had a fight and he said it, I bet you anything he didn't mean it. Sometimes people yell terrible things when they don't—"

"It wasn't a fight. And Hugh didn't tell me." Felicity took a deep, shuddery breath. "I've just always known it."

"Where is he now?" Jessie asked. Felicity had used a sharp pair of scissors on those photos. She hoped they weren't dealing with a body-in-the-bedroom situation here.

"He's left me." Felicity propped her knees under her chin and wrapped her arms around her legs. "He promised he never would, but he has."

"How awful! You poor, poor thing," Lili said. "I'm so sorry."

"And I know what you're both thinking," Felicity blurted out. "But no, he didn't leave me for another woman. Hugh's gay, you see. He's left me for another man."

Lili gasped. "Oh, good grief!"

"You don't have to tell us this," said Jessie, but Felicity was shaking her blond head.

"If I don't tell someone, I'll explode."

"Maybe he'll change his mind and come back," Lili suggested. "He might just be...well, confused."

Felicity examined a fingernail with a jagged edge. Without even bothering to phone her manicurist for an emergency consultation, she bit off the end. "Hugh isn't bisexual. He's *gay*. One hundred percent."

Lili frowned. "He can't be. What about Freya?"

"We bought a plastic syringe at the pharmacy."

"So you've never had sex?" Lili was finding this hard to fathom; her perfect couple was disintegrating around her ears.

"Never had sex," Felicity agreed simply. "Not with Hugh." A pause. "Not with anyone else either."

"What, *no one*?"

Before Lili's astonishment went into orbit, Jessie intervened. "If you knew he was gay, why did you marry him?"

Felicity heaved a sigh. "I was naive and lonely, and he swept me off my feet. By the time he told me, it was too late. I was so in love with him, I said it didn't matter. After all," she said sadly, "what you've never had, you can't miss. And people are always saying sex isn't as important as friendship."

"I'm sorry if this is a rude question," said Jessie, "but could we open a bottle of wine?"

The wine was fetched from the fridge and poured into Waterford crystal glasses.

"Hugh had to marry. His boss was a complete bigot, obsessed with the image of the company," Felicity explained. "If you weren't a family man, basically, you didn't get promoted."

"He's brilliant with Freya," said Lili.

"Of course he is. He adores her. We both do."

"If this comes out, will he get the sack?" Jessie asked.

"I don't know. Maybe. But he doesn't care." Felicity shrugged. "It isn't a fling this time, you see. For the first time in his life, Hugh's fallen in love. And I can't begin to compete."

She paused and took a great swig of Chablis, shuddering as the iciness of it caught in her throat.

"Heavens," said Lili, feeling humble. "I don't know what to say. No wonder you were upset when we saw you this afternoon in the woods."

"Well, yes." For the first time a faint, wry smile lit up Felicity's pale features. "But the reason I burst into tears at the sight of the two of you was because I was so...so *jealous*."

Lili's eyebrows shot up. "Jealous?"

"No, not jealous. Envious. In the same way that you envied me my marriage, I suppose." Another smile, a bit broader this time. "You see, I envy *you*, Lili. As far as I'm concerned, you're the one with the perfect life."

"Another drink," Lili gasped, holding out her empty glass. "My God, you think *my* life is perfect!"

"I'm not a relaxed person. I love the way you treat Freya. And nothing ever fazes you, and you have three happy children and a husband who adores you—"

"I say, steady on there." Lili was half laughing, half embarrassed.

"Okay, but you have a husband who comes home and makes mad passionate love to you on the kitchen table. Or would have done if we hadn't turned up at the wrong moment. Thanks," Felicity said as Jess refilled her glass to the brim. "If that's empty, there's another one in the fridge. You see, nobody's ever done that to me," she went on sadly. "And when I realized what we'd interrupted, I was so *envious*."

"You must have thought I was a right trollop," said Lili, "when you caught me today, cheating on Michael."

Felicity shook her head. "But I didn't, not at all. I just thought how lucky you were, to have a husband *and* a lover. You see, I was envious of that too."

Jessie fetched the second bottle from the fridge. Through the baby alarm, they heard Freya upstairs, stirring then settling again in her crib.

"I feel better now I've said all that." Felicity combed her pale fingers through her hair. "It's such a relief to talk about it. Even if you do think I'm stupid."

"You aren't stupid," Lili protested.

"Gullible, then. A bit of a sad case." Felicity bit her lip. "God, wait until this gets out. I'll be the laughingstock of the village."

"You won't be. It won't get out. Nobody in the village needs to know," said Jessie. "We won't tell anyone."

Lili was shaking her head vigorously, but Felicity seemed unconvinced.

"Look," said Lili, "I'm not going to breathe a word, am I? Because I know if I did, you could run around the village blabbing about me and Drew."

Felicity nodded.

The silence in the room lengthened.

Felicity glanced up from under her eyelashes at Jessie.

"Okay, okay," Jessie caved in, "if it makes you happier, I'll throw my secret into the pot too."

"What secret?" Lili demanded.

"I slept with Toby last night."

"You did *what*?" Lili shrieked, almost bouncing off the sofa. "You didn't tell me about this!"

"There hasn't been time," Jessie protested mildly.

Enthralled, Felicity refilled their glasses. "Gosh."

Lili dismissed the thought of her mother-in-law sitting at home minding her children and casting disapproving glances at the clock. "Go on then," she declared. "Tell us everything. We've got time now."

"You've had your nose pressed against that window for the last two hours," said Jamie, chucking a pizza crust at Drew's head. "What's going on out there—Kim Kardashian taking her clothes off?"

Drew ignored him. Jamie was sprawled in his favorite armchair in front of the television, laughing himself sick at an ancient Benny Hill rerun. He clearly had big tits on the brain.

Anyway, nothing was going on outside now. Earlier, he had watched Lili scurrying over to Jessie's cottage. Within minutes, they had set off together up Compass Hill, making for Hugh and Felicity Seymour's house, presumably.

But that had been ages ago. There had been no sign of them since.

Not knowing what was going on was hideous; it was doing Drew's head in. He longed to rush after them and hammer on the Seymours' front door, yelling, "Don't blame Lili! It was all my fault. I *love* her!" Except he wouldn't, of course. Because though it might be true, it would also make him look a prize fool.

And it was hardly likely to help Lili.

"This is bloody funny," Jamie cackled as Benny Hill fell out of a plane and landed in a haystack with a parachute made of garter belts and bras. Jamie tossed a handful of peanuts into the air, tried to catch them in his mouth, and missed. "You should be watching this. It's brilliant."

Not half as brilliant as the way I feel about Lili Ferguson, thought Drew, wishing he could phone her.

Blimey, he must have it bad. Right now, the thought of Lili with all her clothes on was far more of a thrill than Kim Kardashian taking her clothes off.

Chapter 46

OLIVER WAS WORKING IN the pub, but his mind wasn't on the job. He had overcharged one customer tonight, undercharged several others, and given one chap fifteen pounds' change from a fiver.

Lorna, keeping a close eye on him, watched him fill a pint glass to the brim with Fosters. "The customer asked for shandy," she reminded him.

He shook his head apologetically, tipped half the lager away, and began filling the glass with tonic water instead.

"Olly, let me do that. One of the barrels needs changing in the cellar."

Lorna watched him thread his way through the pub. Savannah, she realized, was keeping an eye on him too, swiveling around on her barstool so her pink skirt rode all the way up her thighs. It hadn't escaped Lorna's notice that the atmosphere between them this evening had been strained.

"Haven't seen your mum and dad in here for a while." Lighting a cigarette, she offered one to Savannah.

"That's because they haven't been in for a while." Realizing this sounded ruder than she'd meant it to, Savannah took a cigarette even though she didn't want one. To make amends, she said, "They've been pretty busy…working, that kind of thing."

Lorna, who didn't believe in shilly-shallying around, propped her elbows on the bar and said bluntly, "Oliver's not himself tonight."

Savannah didn't reply to this; she simply shrugged and took a drag of her cigarette.

"Look, he's a good boy. I'm very fond of him," Lorna said, "and something's troubling him. Before he comes back, why don't you tell me what's up?"

Up. How apt.

Savannah wanted to cry. She was wearing her shortest skirt, and not once this evening had Oliver glanced at her legs. She'd even squashed herself into a too-tight Wonderbra— unbelievably uncomfortable, but the results were dramatic—and for all the attention he'd paid her cleavage, she might as well be wearing a sack.

Oliver wasn't just impotent, it seemed. He'd turned into a full-blown eunuch.

"Nothing's up," Savannah said bitterly, avoiding Lorna's gaze. "Nothing at all."

"It's ten o'clock," came the frosty accusation when Lili slipped into the sitting room, as if by doing so stealthily Eleanor somehow wouldn't notice the time.

"I know. I'm sorry."

Lili, breathless from running, tried to breathe through her nose so Eleanor wouldn't smell the alcohol fumes. Oh Lord, she sounded like a steam train.

"You're late."

Lili wondered rebelliously why she always had to get the dressing down. Michael was late too—later than she was—but Eleanor would never dream of implying that he was a thoughtless, neglectful father. Oh no, Michael was her precious son, Lili thought, swaying a bit. That made him perfect…

But she forced herself to look suitably penitent. "I really am sorry. It won't happen again. Did…um…anybody ring?"

"Like who?"

Like Drew, you nosy, old witch. "I don't know." Lili shrugged. "Anyone."

But Eleanor shook her head. "Only some chap selling double glazing. I told him you weren't interested."

Lili's heart did a back flip. Had it been Drew?

When she had groveled some more and Eleanor had left, she rang 1471.

Number withheld.

Oh bum.

———

Begging wasn't all it was cracked up to be. Dizzy had made seventy-two pence in five hours and been given a soggy corned-beef sandwich by some old dear who'd ranted on at him to confess his sins to the Good Lord and pray for entrance to the Kingdom of Heaven.

"She's barking mad, mate. Barking Beryl we call her," announced a skinny lad with dyed yellow hair, squatting down in the doorway next to him. "Don't touch that sandwich whatever you do. It ain't corned beef. It's Pedigree Chum. Hey, neat blanket."

"Nicked it," Dizzy mumbled. Privately, he blamed the picnic blanket for his low earnings. He'd muddied it up a bit, but it still didn't look authentic.

"Who'd you nick it from, the Queen?" The boy grinned. "I'm Skunk, by the way. Got anything on you?" He winked and patted the filthy pocket of his denim shirt.

"Um…no."

"Well if you want any, I'm your man. See ya 'round." The boy gave Dizzy a friendly nudge in the ribs and hauled himself to his feet.

"Yeah, great." Dizzy nodded and stifled a yawn. It had been an eventful day. "Anyway, I'm going to have a nap."

He woke up shivering an hour later, minus his mother's picnic rug. The sports bag was gone too.

This is more like it, thought Dizzy, relieved to feel his wallet still stuffed down the front of his jeans. *This is more authentic.*

He lay back down in the newsstand's doorway and imagined the chaos at home. His family would be frantic with worry; they'd have called the police by now. The news that he was missing would have spread around the village and Moll would be feeling terrible, blaming herself.

Happily, Dizzy closed his eyes, imagining his mother and sister in floods of tears and his father, distraught, telling the police he'd do anything, pay any amount of money, so long as his son was returned safe and sound.

Bugger, he thought as he drifted back to sleep. *Should have left a ransom note.*

April didn't need to study the evidence in her bathroom mirror to see if she looked different these days; she *knew* she looked different. She felt different too, as if her whole personality had been locked up for years in a box too small for it, and had now burst free.

Everyone at work had noticed the transformation—the nurses, the cleaners, some of the doctors. Even Doug Flynn had winked at her across the reception desk the other day and said, "Whatever you're on, sweetheart, I wouldn't mind some of it."

She had blushed, of course—that hadn't gone away—and Rosie, the resident, had joined in with a grin. "I think April's won the lottery and isn't telling us."

April had wanted to say, "Better than that," because winning a squillion pounds was nothing compared with falling in love with the most wonderful man in the world—particularly when you'd given up hope of ever finding happiness again.

There was a tap on the bathroom door before Michael pushed it open. "What are you doing in here? You've been ages." He came up behind her and slid his arms around her waist, growling, "Come back to bed this minute."

They smiled at each other in the mirror and Michael pretended to bite her neck.

"I was just thinking how lucky I am." April leaned back against him. Oh, how she loved that solid feeling, that sense of utter security.

"I was just thinking how lonely I was, all on my own in that big old bed."

Laughing, she let him carry her back into the bedroom and make love to her again. It was so easy to let herself go with Michael; his enthusiasm was infectious. To April, it felt as if she'd been on the strictest possible diet all her life, and now she was being introduced to the joys of real food by a gourmet.

"Next time we'll have to try out your bed," she told him afterward, her head nestling against his shoulder. "I haven't even seen your house yet."

"I told you, I've got the decorators in." Over the top of her head, Michael glanced at his watch: ten thirty already. "Cans of paint and dust sheets everywhere."

"I wouldn't mind. I'd still like to see where you live."

"It's a mess, and I'd mind." He gave her a hug. "God, I'm hot. Okay if I take a quick shower before I go?"

Go?

"Have a shower if you want. But don't go," April begged, stroking his collarbone. "Please."

"I must."

"Why? Will the cans of paint miss you?"

Michael sighed. It was no good; this was getting too complicated. He had to tell her.

"April, listen to me."

"Hmm?" She was busy trailing kisses across his chest.

"I told you I was separated from my wife…"

April's head jerked up in alarm.

"…and I am," Michael said hastily. "I mean, the marriage is over, I swear it is…"

"But…" April's eyes were as big as Bambi's. She looked terrified. "But what?"

"But the property market being as it is, I haven't been able to move out yet."

April felt her heart crashing painfully against her ribs. She whispered, "You still live with your wife?"

Michael nodded. "We live separate lives. I sleep in the spare room, of course. But you have to understand. I can't exactly take you home and introduce you to the family. That would be…well, cruel."

April was too shocked to cry. All she could hear was Bernadette's voice on the phone the other night, gently warning her not to get too carried away because Things Could Go Wrong.

"Why do you have to *do* this?" she had demanded at the time, irritated by Bernadette's prophecies of doom and gloom. "I'm happy. Nothing's going to go wrong. Stop trying to depress me."

Bernadette had tried to placate her. "I'm not. I just don't want you to get hurt."

"Oh, change the record," she had snapped back. "That one's stuck."

"April, nothing's changed." Michael climbed out of bed. "I still love you. But if you don't want to see me anymore, I'll understand."

He looked sad as he headed for the bathroom. April lay in bed listening to the muffled roar of the shower.

Oh God, I can't lose him, not now.

And he was right, she thought, chewing a thumbnail. Nothing *had* changed. They still shared the same feelings for each other, didn't they?

Okay, it was inconvenient, but that wasn't Michael's fault.

It wasn't the end of the world either.

Just a housing problem, really.

When Michael emerged from the shower with one of her pink towels slung around his hips, April held her arms out to him.

"I'm sorry. It was the shock, that's all." She clung to him. "I love you too."

Chapter 47

TOBY HAD BEEN RINGING and ringing Jessie's number, but there was still no answer.

"That's weird," said Deborah, coming into his study. "I thought Dizzy was in his room. But I've just been up there and it's empty."

It was a sign of the current dismal state of their marriage, Toby thought, that these were the first words she had spoken to him all day. They were like two strangers, he realized, in a hospital waiting room—deliberately avoiding eye contact, each lost in their own thoughts. The easygoing rapport between them had well and truly vanished.

What was more, he no longer even cared.

Still no reply. Wearily, Toby hung up the phone. "Where is he, then? I haven't seen him."

Deborah shrugged. "No idea."

When Toby came back downstairs, she was in the kitchen spreading Brie on crackers.

"His CD player is gone. And his CDs. And some stuff's missing from the bathroom," he announced grimly.

Deborah looked up. "What, you mean he's taken them with him? He's run away? What about clothes?"

"I can't tell. The wardrobe isn't bare, if that's what you mean." Toby pushed his fingers through his blond hair. "But some things may have gone."

"Toby! What do we do?"

"I'll try the pub. Ask Savannah. Maybe he said something to her."

Deborah licked gooey Brie from her fingers. "Will you go and see Jess too?"

"I might."

Was Jessie out, or had she simply not been answering the phone?

"You slept with her last night."

Toby's eyes didn't flicker. "Yes."

"It's okay," Deborah said with a faint smile. "I told her you would."

―――⁓―――

"Dizzy?" Jessie stood in the doorway of the cottage, frowning. "Yes, I saw him. I gave him a lift to the train station this afternoon."

Toby exhaled slowly. "The train station. Did he say where he was going?"

"Well, of course he did—to stay with a friend in London." She looked puzzled. "Didn't Deborah tell you?"

"Deborah's just been up to his room and discovered he's missing."

"But he said she thought it was a great idea... Oh well, he was obviously lying. Sorry," said Jessie, shaking her head. "I just saw him waiting at the bus stop with his bag, thought I was doing him a favor."

"Did he seem upset?"

"No. Quite cheerful actually."

Toby said, "Can I come in?"

"What will you do, phone the police?"

He hesitated. "No, not yet anyway. I've got a few of his friends' parents' numbers somewhere. I'll call tomorrow, see if I can track him down." He gazed steadily at Jessie. "But I'd still like to come in. I've spent the last two hours trying to ring you."

"Look, last night was a huge mistake." Jessie followed him into the dimly lit living room but didn't sit down. She fiddled with the sleeves of her gray sweatshirt, pulling them over her knuckles and folding her arms across her chest.

"It wasn't a mistake." Toby's voice was gentle. "You know how much I love you."

"Deborah was unfaithful to you, so you were unfaithful to her. It was a revenge thing." Jessie blinked and turned away. "And two wrongs don't make a right."

Toby thought they did. "Jess, you aren't—"

"I shouldn't have slept with you last night and I'm definitely not going to sleep with you again."

First Dizzy, now this. It was too much to cope with in one evening. With a sense of impending doom, Toby said, "Why not?"

"Because it's humiliating. Next time you want to get back at Deborah, you'll just have to find someone else to have sex with." Meaning it, Jessie said, "Let them find out how it feels to be the consolation prize."

Despite the gallons of wine she had swallowed, Lili woke up at once when the bedroom door creaked open. She watched through her eyelashes as Michael moved quietly around the room, taking off his clothes and dropping them on the floor for her to pick up in the morning. Everything except his trousers, anyway, which for some reason were exempt from this routine. The trousers were always meticulously folded and hung up.

In the dim and distant past, Lili remembered, she had found this foible quaint.

"I'm awake," she murmured when he climbed into bed next to her.

"Shh, go to sleep."

"Did you win?"

"Win what?"

"The snooker match."

"Knocked out in the semifinals."

"Bad luck. Okay, g'night."

Michael patted her thigh and leaned over to give her a brief kiss on the ear. For a worrying second, Lili wondered if this meant he wanted to have sex with her, but he turned back over and hauled the duvet up over his shoulders, sign language for *Good night, Irene*.

As she drifted back to sleep, Lili caught the faint whiff of magnolias. In the dim, subconscious recess of her mind, it occurred to her that, for a man who had just spent six hours in the smoky confines of a snooker club, Michael smelled astonishingly clean.

"Oy, you! Out of the way."

Dizzy blinked, screwed up his face, and winced as a none-too-gentle boot prodded him in the back.

"Ouch. What time is it?"

"Four thirty."

"*What?*"

The man above him cackled with unsympathetic laughter. "And you must be new to this lark, else you wouldn't sleep in my doorway. This is a newsstand, sunbeam. If it's sleeping in you're after, try the shoe shop next door. They don't open till nine."

But Dizzy was out of luck. The doorway of the shoe shop was already taken, as were most of the other doorways in the street. Now he knew why the other occupants had been smirking at him and nudging each other last night.

He'd even managed to get sleeping rough wrong.

By lunchtime, the novelty of being on the streets was beginning to wear off. Dizzy had been cornered by Barking Beryl again and forced to endure a Bible reading. Two teenage boys whizzing past on skateboards had spat at him with hideous accuracy. A middle-aged businessman had called him scum. And when a pretty girl had dropped something into his upturned baseball cap, Dizzy had called "thank you" after her before realizing it wasn't a coin but a wad of used chewing gum.

Being minus his CD player was no fun either. Time dragged horribly without music blasting holes in your eardrums.

Worst of all, with no feeling left in his bottom from sitting on the pavement, Dizzy had ventured into a small park and sunk thankfully onto the softer grass. It wasn't until an hour later when he was searching for more daisies for his daisy chain that he swiveled around and discovered a used syringe—complete with bloodstained needle—lying under a dandelion leaf just inches from his previously numb bum. Shaking, he imagined the possible consequences if he'd sat on it.

Dizzy ran out of the park, across the main road, and into the warm, welcoming, blissfully familiar arms of Burger King. But even the perky, little redhead serving behind the counter didn't seem to smile at him as brightly as she did the other customers. Sitting down at a table by the window, Dizzy surreptitiously sniffed his armpits. Without deodorant and a change of clothes, he was definitely beginning to stink.

Oh dear, there was such a thing as *too* authentic.

He found himself gazing longingly at the phone booth across the street. Could he phone Baz, his best friend from school, and ask him to put him up for a couple of days? Then he could have a bath, wash his hair, and sleep in a real bed.

Maybe even borrow a CD player.

No, that was no good. Dispiritedly, Dizzy picked a shred of lettuce out of his Whopper. Baz's mother would be suspicious; she'd only phone up his mother and give the game away. Tempting though the thought of a hot bath was—and Dizzy had never imagined he'd hear himself thinking *that*—it simply wasn't on. He wanted his parents—okay, and Moll and even stupid Harriet Ferguson—to worry themselves sick about him. And how could they be worried sick if they knew he was swanning around Baz's mother's bloody great five-story house—Christ, it was practically a *palace*—in Kensington?

Dizzy was gripped suddenly by a great wave of homesickness. He shredded his bun, rolled the bits of bread into pellets, and watched a girl in a baseball cap Rollerblade into the phone booth. She was wearing pink shorts and one of those tiny, stretchy top things, and when she took off her cap, he saw that she had long, silver-blond hair.

The effect was both attention getting and familiar. She looked, Dizzy realized, a lot like Sav.

Blimey, things had to be tough when you were reduced to missing your own grumpy pain-in-the-neck sister.

Savannah was painting her toenails white when the phone began to ring. Cursing with annoyance, she waddled like a goose across the room to answer it.

"Hello?"

Nothing.

"Hello?"

Still nothing.

"Look, is anybody there?" she said briskly. "Because this is getting boring."

No reply.

"Right." She hung up.

In London, deeply disappointed, Dizzy hung up too.

Well, so much for everyone being out of their minds with worry.

As he pushed his way out of the phone booth, which reeked of the Rollerblading girl's cheap perfume, Dizzy was struck by a terrible thought.

What if nobody had even noticed yet that he'd gone?

Chapter 48

"I'M AMAZED I MANAGED to make it through the door, my nose feels so long," said Lili. "I've never told so many lies before in my life."

"I'm glad you came."

Drew hadn't been able to stop thinking about her; he had hardly slept last night. He wanted to kiss Lili now, but there were three vet nurses in the next room, and the door could be flung open at any moment.

Instead, he lifted Blitz up onto the examination table and gave his ears an affectionate rub.

Blitz wagged his tail.

"He's fine, I take it?"

Lili blushed and nodded. "I told Michael he'd swallowed a tennis ball."

Blitz looked astonished.

"And then I thought if I tell your receptionist that, you'll have to do loads of X-rays, so I said he'd been sick a few times instead."

Blitz panted happily and licked Drew's hand.

"We'll just say he ate something that disagreed with him. And you can tell Michael that the tennis ball passed through... er...naturally."

A pained expression appeared in the dog's soulful, dark eyes.

"Ouch," said Lili.

Drew glanced across at her. "Anyway, I pity the next poor sod who tries to sell double glazing to your mother-in-law."

"So it was you." She grinned. "I wondered, but the number was withheld."

"Ah well, you don't share a house with Doug Flynn without picking up a few pointers." Then he grew serious. "I saw you and Jess setting out last night. How did it go?"

"Felicity's fine about it. She won't tell anyone. She and Hugh have broken up," Lili added briefly, without going into details. "She was crying because she envied me having a husband and a hunky lover too."

"Hunky!" It made him sound like Jean-Claude Van Damme. "I'm not hunky."

Lili, who thought he was, said, "You're not my lover either."

No, but I want to be, thought Drew.

The charged silence was broken by Fiona, one of the nurses, popping her head around the door.

"Drew, Mrs. Childerley's outside with her boa constrictor. Any chance of seeing them before it swallows Richie Bigelow's kitten?"

Relieved not to be playing third wheel anymore, Blitz leaped off the table and licked Fiona's hand.

"Right, well, we're just about finished here. I'll be out in a sec," said Drew, a bit too heartily.

"You're busy," said Lili when the door had closed behind them. "I shouldn't have come. I could've just phoned to let you know all this."

But she hadn't been able to stay away. A phone call wouldn't have been enough. Just the thought of seeing Drew again had made her go fizzy all over, like seltzer.

It was a full-blown addiction, and Lili couldn't say no.

"This is better than a phone call." Drew recognized the craving; he had it too. Quickly, taking her by surprise, he kissed Lili's half-open mouth. She tasted of Starbursts.

Out in the waiting room, someone screamed. A woman's voice scolded, "Bad boy, Percy! The lady doesn't want you on her lap."

"See if you can get away this afternoon. I'm off at three," Drew murmured, lovingly stroking Lili's hair. "Ring me."

I'm practically an adulteress, Lili marveled, nodding happily. *I should be ashamed of myself.*

Oh, but how could something so wicked feel so right?

—⁄⁄⁄—

Savannah was sunbathing on the terrace when she heard Toby and Deborah return home. They had driven into Harleston to report Dizzy's disappearance to the police. Shielding her eyes from the one o'clock sun, Savannah thought how desperately worried her father looked.

"Any news?" he said. "Any phone calls?"

"Nope. Well, one call," she amended, to be accurate, "but there was nobody there."

Toby frowned. "You mean it was a silent call?"

Savannah shrugged. "I guess."

"It could have been Dizzy."

Oh God, could it? She experienced a spasm of guilt. "But that's stupid. Why would he phone up and not say anything?"

Toby sighed. "Look, I have to take some photos of Dizzy over to the police station. If the phone rings again, let your mother answer it."

"Are they out looking for him?" Savannah said brightly. "Is it like that film with Harrison Ford? You know, *The Fugitive?*" She imagined helicopters circling noisily overhead, convoys of police cars closing in on Dizzy, officers with bullhorns ordering him to give himself up.

"They took down his details," said Toby, "that's all."

Savannah looked disappointed. "What's the point of that?"

Toby shook his head. The point of it was that a body plucked out of the Thames could be compared with the descriptions of all reported missing persons.

But he couldn't tell Savannah that.

"It's just the best they can do." As he ran his fingers through his hair, it occurred to him that he could dial 1471 and ring the number back. Maybe Dizzy—if it had been Dizzy—was still there.

But as he was heading back to the house, the phone shrilled again.

"Who was that?" he said as Deborah replaced the receiver.

"Baz's mother. She hasn't seen Dizzy. She just wondered if we'd heard anything yet."

"Great." Now it was pointless dialing 1471.

Toby flipped through the photograph album Deborah had brought into the kitchen and took out three of the most recent pictures of Dizzy.

"I'm off then. I'll be back in an hour."

Dizzy would be fine, Deborah reassured herself. He was a teenager going through a tricky phase, but he'd be back in no time at all. Toby might be in a complete state about his disappearance, but he was overreacting as usual. *Typical actor*, Deborah thought. *Having to make a drama out of the situation, automatically imagining the worst.*

As the front door slammed behind Toby, Savannah wandered into the kitchen, pulling a lime-green T-shirt over her bikini. "May as well go to the pub," she said. "Oliver's working over there."

"Good idea, sweetheart."

Fondly, Deborah watched her go. Then she dialed the number of Keeper's Cottage.

When Doug answered, she murmured, "I'm free."

―――⁓―――

Telling yourself you weren't going to get involved with someone as potentially risky as Deborah Gillespie was all very well, but when you picked up the phone and heard that silky voice breathing those words down your ear, saying "Well, actually, it's very kind of you to offer but I'm busy right now" wasn't the response that sprang most immediately to mind.

And Doug hadn't been busy.

And it was certainly a more entertaining way of spending forty minutes, rather than reading up on the latest pharmaceutical treatment for syphilis.

―᠁―

"Where the hell have you been?" demanded Jamie, who was in the kitchen making himself a fried egg sandwich. He stared at Doug, standing at the open back door. "I came home half an hour ago. Your car was here and the house was empty." He looked confused. "What were you doing out *there!*"

This was a fair question. The backyard of Keeper's Cottage was a waist-high jungle of grass and weeds. Nobody ventured out into it of their own free will.

Apart from Doug, of course, when he was hopping discreetly over the back wall.

"I saw something on TV about crop circles. Wondered how they were made, that's all."

Jamie's eggs were burning. He frowned and gave them a prod. "Crop circles? You mean you've been out there making a *weed* circle?"

Doug stretched his arms and yawned. "Thought about it, sat down to think about it, must have crashed out. Next thing I knew it was an hour later and I heard you banging around in here."

"You fell asleep in the yard?" Jamie still didn't sound convinced. "But there isn't anywhere to lie down, you must—"

Doug was saved by Kim clattering to the floor.

Jamie's Kim Kardashian calendar was his most treasured possession. He rushed over to rescue her. It was the third time in a week she'd done this.

"You need a nail in that wall," Doug observed. "Blu-Tack isn't strong enough."

The implausibility of him having fallen asleep in the yard was forgotten. All Jamie cared about was Kim's well-being.

Still, she seemed unharmed. Lovingly he stroked her astonishing cleavage.

"Poor darling. Must be the weight of her boobs."

———

Dizzy took a deep breath, fed the coins into the slot, and tried again.

This time, to his relief, his father answered.

"Hello?"

Dizzy said nothing.

"Dizzy, is that you?"

Yes, yes, it's me!

"Dizzy, if that's you, say something. We need to know you're safe."

So you've noticed I've gone, then.

"Listen, Dizzy, we want you to come home. We love you. We miss you. Please." Toby's voice, so urgent, began to crack with emotion. "Nothing else matters. I know things have been difficult lately, but we can sort that out. We just need you back with us."

Silence.

"And nobody's going to yell at you for running away, or for taking that money."

Ah, so the milkman had come around.

"Dizzy, speak to me. Your mother's frantic with worry. We all are."

What, even Savannah?

"Dizzy, *please…*"

Dizzy put the phone down and backed out of the phone booth, smiling to himself.

Yeah, result!

But he wouldn't go home just yet.

Chapter 49

LILI WATCHED FROM THE kitchen window as Michael, with Will hoisted onto his shoulders, chased Lottie around the backyard. She heard their screams of delight as Lottie raced across a flower bed and Michael, roaring like a dinosaur, charged after her. Giggling helplessly, Will yelled, "Again, Daddy, again!"

Michael couldn't be bothered, as a rule, to play rough-and-tumble with them, so they appreciated it all the more when he did.

Even more unexpectedly, upon returning from Harleston, she had found him in the kitchen doing the dishes.

Lili wished he hadn't chosen today of all days to be Mr. Wonderful Husband-and-Father.

"Can't catch me, can't catch me!" Lottie screamed, flashing her *Finding Dory* underwear as she dived into the playhouse.

Will shouted, "Huff and puff, Daddy, and blow the house down!"

As Michael began to huff and puff, Lili thought: *What am I doing? How can I even contemplate having an affair with Drew Darcy?*

It had seemed so much easier yesterday. When Drew had gently questioned her about the state of her marriage, she had almost managed to convince herself that sleeping with him wouldn't be that terrible a thing to do, because Michael had probably, in the past, been unfaithful to her.

And if he had, then it was only fair that she should have her turn.

But I don't have any proof, Lili thought guiltily. *Maybe I just want him to have slept around, to make it all right.*

And what if he never had? What if he'd been tempted but had always said no, because he was married—happily married?

Oh God.

"Lunch ready?" Michael said, coming into the kitchen with a child under each arm. "We're starving."

"As starving as dinosaurs." Lottie giggled.

"Poo," Will announced with pride. "Big poo."

"Ah well, that's your department." Deftly Michael handed his son over to Lili. "I'll go get my uniform together while you deal with him. Where are my cricket trousers, in the closet?"

"Your cricket trousers?"

"I got chatting to one of the guys at the snooker club last night. Told him I hadn't played for ages, but he offered me a place on his team. We're playing a match this afternoon."

"Who for?" said Lili, bemused.

"Just some pub thing. I didn't think you'd mind." Michael sounded peeved. "I've spent enough time entertaining the kids, haven't I? And cleaning all those dishes."

"I don't mind," Lili assured him, her smile bright. If he could be nice, so could she. Maybe this was all their marriage needed, a bit of extra effort. "It's a gorgeous afternoon. We could come and watch. Bring a picnic, cheer you on, give your team some support—"

"Trouble is, they're playing away. No idea where. I just know we're being picked up in a bus—er, minibus, at four."

"Oh. So you won't be back until…?"

"Your guess is as good as mine." Michael shrugged and tickled the back of Will's neck, making him squeal with delight. "Latish."

Lili nodded. It meant she wouldn't be able to see Drew.

Hmm, maybe this was just as well.

—∾∾—

It wasn't the most comfortable of situations, walking into the grocery store and bumping unexpectedly into the wife of someone you'd recently slept with.

It was even more awkward when you looked a wreck and she was exuding more glamour than Sophia Loren and Diana Ross put together.

Jessie, who had called in on her way home from work to pick up a pint of milk and a packet of toilet paper—*très chic*—was acutely aware of her shiny, unmade face, messy hair, and scruffy jeans. There were circles of sweat under the arms of her mauve T-shirt and splashes of bottle-green paint on her face and chest.

Oh, and she smelled of turpentine.

"Jess, hi!" Deborah finished paying for her copy of *Vogue* and waited while Jessie bought her milk.

The toilet paper would just have to wait. Jessie couldn't face buying it in front of Deborah.

"You look as if you've got green measles," Deborah cheerfully informed her when they were outside.

"I know. I've been rollering a ceiling." For something to do, Jessie rubbed at her speckled forearms. "So. How is, um, everything?"

Deborah shrugged and leaned against the dusty hood of Jessie's van. "No news yet about Dizzy. Toby's raced up to London to pound the streets looking for him, although I told him it was a waste of time. Still, fingers crossed." She fiddled with the arms of her sunglasses and glanced at Jessie. "As for me and Toby—you know as much as I do. We're just getting through it, taking things day by day."

"Well...good."

Jessie didn't know if she meant it. She couldn't think of anything else to say. All she could really think of was how much she wanted a bath.

"I'd better be getting back. Dizzy might ring." Deborah smiled and pulled herself upright, adding easily, "Pop over later for a drink if you'd like to."

"Maybe." This was definitely a lie.

"Oh, Jess, I forgot to ask." Turning back, Deborah gazed at her with concern. "What happened last night? Toby came home looking completely fed up. I wasn't even expecting him back," she added. "I thought he'd stay with you."

Parking the car as she returned from her monthly visit to the hairdresser in Harleston, Bernadette Thomas saw her next-door neighbor eagerly poking her head out of her open sitting-room window.

"Yoo-hoo," Eleanor Ferguson trilled, emerging from her front door clutching a parcel before Bernadette even had her key out of the ignition. "This arrived while you were out. From your publishers, by the look of it."

"Thank you." As she held out her hands, Bernadette was grateful her neighbor was basically uninterested in books; otherwise, she might have noticed that this parcel hadn't been sent by the firm that published Antonia Kay's dreary efforts.

"How exciting! Copies of the new novel, hot off the press?"

Eleanor might not be interested in books, but she still enjoyed telling all her friends she lived next door to a real author.

"Afraid not. Just proofs," Bernadette replied firmly, before the older woman could grab the parcel back from her and tear the wrapper off.

"Oh."

Eleanor didn't know what proofs were.

"For copyediting."

"Ah, I see." Eleanor was still gazing at it longingly.

"Very dull job," Bernadette assured her.

"Still, not long now before the next book comes out." Eleanor brightened. "You said August, didn't you?"

"That's right. August the tenth."

"What's it called again?"

Damn, what was it called?

"*A Strand of Honeysuckle*. No, a *Frond*," Bernadette corrected herself rapidly. "*A Frond of Honeysuckle*." She patted her newly done hair. "My editor was keen on *strand*, but I managed to convince her *frond* was better."

"Well, it sounds marvelous." Eleanor wondered if this one had any lesbians in it. She sincerely hoped not, although she probably wouldn't read it anyway. The last one had been about as much fun as darning a mesh tank top.

"You shall have a signed copy," Bernadette told her gravely.

"Lovely!" trilled Eleanor. "Can't wait!"

———

While she was waiting for Michael to arrive, April phoned Bernadette. Instead of defending herself against Bernadette's thinly veiled warnings, she had decided, from now on, she would take the initiative and tell her how wonderful Michael was.

First, she had to listen to the story of Bernadette's most recent encounter with Eleanor, her terrifyingly bossy next-door neighbor.

"Why aren't you at the hospital?" Bernadette said at last. "You told me you were working days this week."

"I swapped shifts with one of the other girls. Michael's coming over at four." April curled up on the sofa and hugged her knees to her chest. "He's taking me to this fantastic restaurant he knows in Cheltenham."

"At four o'clock in the afternoon?"

Ah, here we go. "He said he couldn't wait to see me. The table's booked for eight." Defiantly April added, "Don't worry. I'm sure we'll find something to occupy us until then."

A brief silence. "Has he told his wife about you?"

Be calm, be calm. "He doesn't have to report back to his wife.

They're almost divorced." Instead of snapping, April kept her tone pleasant and flexed her toes, admiring the neat, freshly painted nails. "The papers are due any day now." As she said the words, she could almost believe them to be true. The more she thought about Michael's unknown but clearly neurotic wife, the easier it became to imagine the divorce going through.

Not right away, perhaps, but *soon*.

"You haven't told me where he lives," Bernadette said.

April smiled to herself. "Oh, he's letting his wife keep the house. He's just bought a gorgeous new one on the outskirts of Harleston. Detached, of course. Four bedrooms, huge yard. At the moment, we're knee-deep in paint charts and wallpaper samples, trying to decide how it should look."

Another pause—lengthier this time. "Well, there's someone here in the village who's an excellent painter and decorator. I've heard very good reports of her work. If you'd like her number, I could get it for you," Bernadette offered. "Her name's Jessie something-or-other."

"Perhaps." April checked her watch: twenty to four. She wondered how Jessie something-or-other would feel about being hired to hang imaginary wallpaper on walls in a house that didn't exist.

"So, will you be moving in with this, um…?"

"Michael," April prompted. She loved saying his name aloud.

"Yes. Michael."

"Oh, I'm sure I will. He's asked me to marry him, of course." April shivered with pleasure. "But there's no need to rush into things, is there? We'll probably just live together first."

In our invisible four-bedroom house…

"Well," Bernadette hesitated, still not sounding convinced, "you seem happy enough. But don't forget what I said the other—"

Rrriiing!

Phew, saved by the bell and not a moment too soon.

Relieved to be spared the lecture, April jumped up and ran her fingers through her short, newly highlighted hair. "Bernie, he's here! I have to go. I'll speak to you soon, okay?"

"Remember, any problems at all and you know where I am—" Bernadette began, but April had already hung up.

When she flung open the front door, Michael was frowning.

"I haven't asked you to marry me."

"What? Oh!" *Whoosh.* April felt herself go bright red. "How long have you been here?"

He smiled slightly. "Couple of minutes."

"On the—um, on the doorstep."

"Less than six feet away from where you were sitting." Michael nodded in the direction of the living-room window, flung open to coax some air into the stuffy apartment. "A word of advice, sweetheart. If you'd prefer not to be overheard, keep your windows shut. I don't know..." He tutted. "At this rate, you're never going to get that job with MI5."

April was awash with embarrassment. She hung her head. "No—sorry. I know you didn't ask me to marry you."

"Haven't bought a house either." Michael raised a quizzical eyebrow. "So who were you talking to? What's going on?"

"It was just a friend being all disapproving about you," April admitted. "I don't think she wants me to be happy, basically. She's all on her own and probably jealous."

"Sure she's a friend?" Michael observed drily.

"Well, we were close once. S-sometimes it's hard," she stammered, "to break away."

"Maybe you should try it. After all"—his arms slipped around her waist—"you've got me now. I'm your new friend."

Relieved, April clung to him. "I didn't mean to say all those things. I just wanted her to know how happy I am."

"So you thought you'd wind her up, make her a bit more jealous?"

Michael idly stroked her clean hair. "Who is she? D'you see much of her?"

April shook her head. "Not for ages. We just talk on the phone every now and again. She's no one special."

Grinning, Michael lifted her into his arms, kicked the front door shut, and carried her through the apartment to the bedroom. "Glad to hear it. Now, we've got a few hours to kill before dinner." Skillfully, through the thin cotton of her shirt, he unfastened April's bra. "Don't want to waste them, do we?"

———

It didn't take Toby long to concede that Deborah had been right. Coming up to London was something he'd felt compelled to do, simply because the alternative—sitting at home, *waiting*—was unbearable.

But six hours traipsing around the West End, searching frantically for Dizzy, had only served to emphasize the hopelessness of the situation. Thousands upon thousands of people were milling around. *And this is just Piccadilly Circus*, Toby thought, close to despair as he scanned the sea of bobbing heads around him.

Worse still, he didn't even know if Dizzy was in London. Dialing 1471 after this morning's call had been no help. The number had been withheld. Dizzy could be anywhere in the country.

Toby's shoulders sagged. He was, as Deborah had pointed out so dismissively, never going to get anywhere. *Time to go home*, he thought, feeling useless.

Oh well, at least he'd tried.

Chapter 50

WHEN DIZZY HAD BOOKED a hotel just off Piccadilly Circus, the plan had been to have a bath and spend the rest of the evening quietly in the bar. This meant he would have just enough money left for a train ticket back to Harleston the next morning. He much preferred traveling by rail than in a stupid bus.

In the event, however, the hotel bar had been deserted and the bartender had, humiliatingly, demanded to see some ID before he'd serve Dizzy anything stronger than a Coke.

Determined by this stage, at least, to have a proper drink while he was in London, Dizzy had wandered out onto the streets, finally managing to buy four bottles of beer in a liquor store. When he had guzzled them down one after the other, he made his way unsteadily toward Soho, where a friendly bloke invited him into a club where the girls—he assured Dizzy—had to be seen to be believed.

So had the prices of the drinks they served, but by this time Dizzy no longer cared. One of the girls, who looked a bit like Moll if you half closed your eyes and squinted, invited him in a friendly fashion to press a ten pound note down the front of her G-string. Half closing his eyes and squinting for all he was worth, Dizzy happily did as he was told and almost fell backward off his chair when she gyrated her pelvis just inches from his face. Her fake tan was blotchy and she was on the flabby side, but Dizzy didn't mind. What was a bit of cellulite between friends?

Waking up in his hotel room the next morning, he was irritated to find himself on the floor next to his bed, which seemed an awful waste of forty-six pounds.

Struggling to his feet—ouch, his head hurt—Dizzy then made the even more annoying discovery that his wallet was empty.

This was seriously bad news. Now he didn't even have enough money for a bus, let alone a train ticket.

Downstairs in the dining room, determined to get his money's worth—breakfast was inclusive—he drank four cups of coffee and ate seven hot croissants with butter and black cherry jam.

He only just made it to the loo before throwing up.

There were four black cabs lined up outside the hotel with their for hire signs up. After two "On-yer-bike's" and a "You must be bleedin' jokin', mate," Dizzy realized he was going to have to pull out all the stops.

He was the son of an actor, wasn't he?

Right, he'd see if he could act.

"'Ere comes Mr. Popular," the fourth cab driver declared as Dizzy approached his window. He watched him over the top of yesterday's *Evening Standard*. "If that lot sent you packing, what makes you think I'm gonna do any different?" Dizzy summoned up his worst-ever, most humiliating fantasy, where a beautiful woman—okay, let's call her Moll—announced in a loud voice in front of a huge crowd of people: "My God, Dizzy Gillespie, that is the smallest willy I have ever seen in my life!"

"Well?" the cab driver demanded with an impatient flick of the sports section. "Are ya gonna say somethin' or aren't ya?"

Everyone in the crowd was turning to look and laugh at Dizzy. He wanted to run away and hide, but there was no escape. And now people were beginning to tug enthusiastically at his jeans, all wanting to see the world's smallest willy for themselves...

Dizzy promptly burst into tears. "You'll think I'm lying, but

I'm not," he told the startled cabbie between sobs. "I ran away from home and now I want to go back, but someone stole my wallet. If you take me, my parents'll pay the fare, honest they will. They'll probably give you a reward too."

The driver hesitated. "Where d'you live?"

"Um, Harleston."

"What, in Gloucestershire? Christ, you must be joking!"

Crying was a piece of cake. For the first time, Dizzy experienced the thrill of real acting. He might not be on a stage, but this was a challenge he couldn't resist. He was going to make this bloke take him to Upper Sisley if it killed him.

"Please, please," he wept. "I just want to go home. I want my m-m-mum!"

The tears streaming down his face would have done Kenneth Branagh proud. They were Oscar-winning tears.

"Look, why don't I take you to the nearest police station and—"

"Nooo!" wailed Dizzy, clutching the side of the cab. Wow, talk about street theater. Thrillingly, people were stopping to watch him. This was like starring in *Hamlet*.

"Or you could phone them?" the cab driver suggested helplessly.

"Nooo! I want my mum!"

"Will they definitely pay the fare?"

"Yeees!"

The boy was clearly distraught. But he was also well-spoken.

The story rang true.

The cab driver, who had read enough newspaper articles in his time about runaway teenagers and the anguish they caused their parents, heaved a sigh and put aside his crumpled *Evening Standard*. "Okay, hop in. Too softhearted for my own good, that's what I am." He shook his head, touched by the woebegone look on the lad's tear-streaked face. "They'd just bleedin' better pay up, that's all."

It was one of the best moments of Dizzy's life.

When the cab pulled up on the graveled drive, nothing happened for a second. Then a bedroom window was flung open and Savannah's blond head poked out. All the anxiety she had worked so hard to conceal from her parents crumbled in an instant.

"It's Dizzy! Mum, it's Dizzy! He's *here*!" she yelled, and the next minute, his mother was racing down the front steps crying, "Oh, Dizzy, I can't believe you're back!"

Dizzy found himself crying real tears this time, which was a bit embarrassing, but most of them got soaked into his mother's white shirt, so it probably didn't notice too much. And when his dad came out and hugged him too, saying, "Was that you on the phone, Dizzy? Was it?" his joy was complete.

He was the center of attention, the prodigal son come home at last.

It felt great.

The cab driver, dazed to discover who Dizzy's parents were, longed to be invited into the house so he could tell them the heroic part he had played in their son's return.

"You didn't tell me your old man was Toby Gillespie," he said to Dizzy, thinking a cup of tea wouldn't go amiss either.

'*Course not*, Dizzy thought. *Then it wouldn't have been a challenge, would it?*

"All the others turned 'im away," the cabbie told Toby modestly. "But I couldn't do it, could I? Got an 'eart of gold, me. If someone needs an 'elping 'and, I can't turn 'em away, it just ain't in my nature, see—"

"How much do I owe you?" Toby said, picturing the story on the front of next week's *News of the World*.

"Call it a 'undred and forty, guv. Course, I've met some stars in my time. I've 'ad Su Pollard in this cab. Almost 'ad James Corden once—"

"Here's two hundred." Toby counted the notes into the man's hand. "We're very grateful, but I'm sure you understand that this is a private matter. Any publicity is the last thing my son needs."

"I get your drift, guv. Don't worry about it. Soul of discretion, me. 'Ad Mick Jagger in the back of me cab once—shoulda seen the fings 'e was gettin' up to wiv this blond bird—"

"Right," said Toby. "Well, thanks again. Have a safe journey home."

Embellishing wildly, Dizzy regaled his family with stories of drug dealers, rent boys, and muggers with knives.

"But I really liked that picnic blanket," said Deborah, dismayed. "It was cashmere."

"Didn't have much choice," Dizzy told her sorrowfully. "This bloke was desperate. It was a case of my picnic blanket or my life."

"Never mind. We'll get another one." His mother hugged him. "You're back, that's all that matters."

"Why did you do it, Dizzy?" Toby was frowning. "What made you run away?"

"I didn't think you cared about me. I was miserable." Dizzy reveled unashamedly in their attention; this would make a great film, especially if he starred in it. "Ever since we moved here, it's been all Sav this and Sav that." His chin began to wobble. "I felt like she was the only one you cared about."

"Oh great." Savannah rolled her eyes. "I might have known I'd get the blame."

"You called me a beastly little shit."

"You *are* a beastly little shit."

"Sav, Dizzy, stop it!" Deborah protested. "We love *both* of you."

"And then there was the Oliver thing." Suppressing a qualm of guilt, because he really liked Oliver, Dizzy looked miserable. "He's cleverer than I am, and better looking, and everyone thinks he's great. I just thought you liked him better than me."

Savannah made sick noises. "That's it, blame Oliver as well."

"Savannah, that's enough!" Toby said sharply.

"Now listen to me, Dizzy." Deborah's arm tightened around his shoulders. "We love you and don't you ever forget it. I know the last couple of months haven't been easy, but that's all in the past. From now on, things will be better. We just want you to be happy, because that's all that matters." She kissed him on the forehead. "Promise."

"Thanks, Mum."

Blimey, thought Dizzy, it was like waking up and finding yourself in *The Waltons*. Maybe he should change his name to Jim-Bob.

"Are you hungry?" Toby asked.

Dizzy nodded. He was, actually.

"Of course he's hungry!" Deborah jumped up from the sofa. "Tell me what you'd like, Dizzy. Your favorite meal—anything at all. I'll make it!"

Savannah stared at her mother in astonishment.

This is more like it, Dizzy thought happily. *I could get used to this.*

"Uh…how about a takeout pizza?"

A letter addressed to Toby in familiar writing arrived in the post the next morning.

Wondering why he even bothered to open it, Toby tore apart the envelope.

"A second-class stamp for a second-rate actor," the note informed him. "What did Upper Sisley ever do to deserve you? When are you going to leave?"

Charming, thought Toby.

The note was the usual, wobbly-lettered affair, and as a bonus, the sender had included an old newspaper review of a West End play Toby had appeared in months earlier. The famously acerbic theater critic had lain into all aspects of the production and had called Toby's performance "singularly underwhelming."

Everyone suffered the occasional bad review, but nobody enjoyed getting them. Toby was as hurt reading this one again as he had been the first time he'd seen it.

He wished he had the address of whoever had posted it to him. Then he could send copies of some of his brilliant reviews back.

He phoned Jessie. "Dizzy's home."

"I know. Savannah told Oliver. I'm so glad."

"Jess, we need to talk."

"Why?"

"I want to see you."

"Well, you can't," said Jessie, and hung up.

Toby knew why.

Dizzy had run away from home because he was unhappy. Seeing his parents split up wasn't going to make him happier.

Jessie was letting him know he owed it to his children to sort out his troubled marriage.

———∽∼∼∽———

When Toby made his way back to the kitchen, he found Dizzy plowing through a bowl of cereal. Rice Krispies littered the table and the milk jug was sitting in a puddle of milk.

"Hi, Dad." Dizzy spoke through a mouthful of cereal.

"You're up early."

"Going into Harleston, aren't I? Dad, can I have some money?"

Toby poured himself a ferociously strong black coffee. "What d'you want money for?"

When he looked up, Dizzy was rolling his eyes in amazement. It was clearly a dumb question. "I got mugged, didn't I? I need a new CD player, new CDs...new *everything*."

Loving your children, Toby discovered, didn't mean you weren't tempted, sometimes, to shake them until their teeth rattled.

"It's not long till your birthday. We could buy you a CD player then." He spoke evenly. "And you could have the CDs at Christmas."

"Daaad!"

"What?"

"I can't wait till then," said Dizzy, outraged. "I need them *now*."

Toby lost his temper. "You spoiled brat! If you want the money, you'll bloody well earn it."

"I can't." Horrified, Dizzy stopped eating. "Where can I get a job? There isn't anything around here that—"

"As soon as you've finished your breakfast, you can clean the cars. When they're done, you can mow the lawn. And when that's finished," said Toby, his expression ominously grim, "I'll give you twenty-five pounds."

Mow the lawn? What, all *of it?* "Is this a joke?"

"No joke."

"But we've got that gardening bloke," Dizzy protested. "He mows the lawn. It's *his* job."

"Dizzy, I am not doling out money like a crazed lottery winner."

Take it from me, Dizzy thought sulkily. *You're nothing like any kind of lottery winner.*

"If mowing lawns isn't your thing, Paddy Birley's looking for a lad to work on his farm." Untrue, but a pretty safe fib, Toby felt. "If you'd rather clean out cowsheds for five pounds an hour, that's fine by me."

Chapter 51

HARRIET WAS SITTING ON the garden wall, drumming her heels against the stonework, when she saw Dizzy meandering across the green toward her. His hands were in his pockets and he was kicking a stone along, pretending not to have noticed her.

"You're back then," said Harriet. *Wow, I'm so original.*

"No, this is just a hologram." Dizzy smirked and poked himself in the chest. "Looks real though, doesn't it?"

Harriet immediately hated him for making her feel stupid. "You weren't gone for long. Chicken out, did you?"

"Living rough doesn't scare me," Dizzy sneered. "I just knew everyone was worried about me, so I came home."

"I wasn't worried about you. Didn't bother me."

This wasn't going to plan at all. Dizzy had wanted to be welcomed home like a hero. He'd wanted Harriet Ferguson to be pleased to see him and apologetic for the toilet bleach slur; then he could have forgiven her and told her all about his adventures on the streets of London—the exciting version, of course. Not the real one.

But Harriet didn't appear to be interested. All she was doing was swinging her skinny legs and smirking down at him in a really stupid and immature way.

Now he definitely couldn't ask her if she had a spare CD player he could borrow.

So much for the honeymoon period, thought Dizzy, filled with resentment. Less than twenty-four hours and it was over. Everything was back to boring normality. And his arms ached like nobody's business from all that bloody car washing.

God, life was *so* unfair.

"Out of interest," Harriet said eagerly, "why *did* you run away? Was it anything to do with my joke about the toilet bleach?"

There was an avid gleam in her eye. Dizzy itched to shove her off the wall. So much for thinking Harriet might have been sobbing into her pillow, blaming herself. Huh, all she wanted to do was take the credit.

"Funny," he mused. "I always thought your dog was the one with the bad breath. Now that Blitz isn't here, I realize it was you all along."

———

Mowing the lawn was even worse than washing the cars, but Dizzy grimly carried on until the job was done. Since his father had warned his mother not to give in and slip him a check, he didn't have a lot of choice.

Slave labor, that's what it was. At this rate, by the time he had enough money to buy one, CD players would be obsolete.

Two hours later and twenty-five measly quid better off, Dizzy was bored again. He was stuck here in this crappy village with nothing to do, no friends, nothing to look forward to, and no money.

Moping around, trailing grass cuttings into the hall, he pulled open the drawer where bills were generally slung, in case by some miracle any post had arrived for him while he was away.

None had. All that was in there was a bunch of fan mail, a red electricity bill, last week's *Stage*, and a couple of requests for Toby to donate something to charity or show up at some function in aid of orphaned earwigs.

To amuse himself, Dizzy skimmed through a few of the fan letters. It was a pretty weird experience, reading stuff from women drooling over your own father, but they kept on writing and sending photos, and sometimes they were good for a laugh, especially the really gross ones who sent in pictures of themselves all dressed up in corsets with stockings and garters.

There weren't any of those today, just half a dozen pretty normal letters. Toby made an effort to sit down each week and reply to them; otherwise, they mounted up.

Dizzy turned over the last letter and realized it wasn't from a fan.

As Toby had done earlier, he read the anonymous note. Brief and to the point, as usual. And this time a newspaper cutting too.

Nice touch.

Dizzy thought idly that whoever was sending this stuff must get a real kick out of it; otherwise, why would they bother?

It must be quite exciting, going as far as you dared and making sure you didn't get caught. Thinking up new things to do, hugging the secret to yourself, experiencing that buzz...

This is right up my street, thought Dizzy, his mind working overtime. *This is my chance to get back at all of them.*

This could be a real laugh.

———

"Dizzy, are you okay?"

Deborah knocked and waited before popping her head around the door. Dizzy was in bed with only his head visible. He nodded and raised a feeble smile.

"Yeah. Just tired. And I ache all over." He moved a bit and winced. "Still, never mind. Thought I'd have an early night. Dad says I can clean the windows tomorrow."

It was only eight thirty.

"Darling, don't worry about the money," Deborah whispered. "Your father's in a bad mood, that's all. We'll sort something out."

As soon as his mother had gone, Dizzy sat up, snapped the

bedroom light back on, gleefully flexed his rubber-gloved fingers, and pulled the box of work in progress out from under the bed.

By eleven o'clock, he was almost finished. The adverts in the paper had been great; within days, that bossy old cow Eleanor Ferguson would be receiving a free brochure telling her what to do about Embarrassing Facial Hair. Doug Flynn was getting Transform Your Sex Life with a Penile Extension. He had answered a lonely-hearts ad in Harriet Ferguson's name—to a seventy-three-year-old pig farmer, ha! And Paddy Birley, who lived in a bungalow, could look forward to a visit from someone keen to sell him a stair lift.

Dizzy sniggered to himself and shuffled through the rest of the letters, which looked just like the ones downstairs. He had written them with his left hand and kept the style much the same, only this time, Toby Gillespie wouldn't be the only recipient.

Dear Moll,
      Silicone is bad *for you. Get those implants taken out at once!*

Dear Myrtle Armitage,
      You couldn't run an egg and spoon race, let alone a shop.

Dear Mr. Gillespie,
      You are a useless actor. Why don't you and your family move back to London?

This was what Dizzy wanted more than anything.

He put the letters back into the box, carefully peeled off his rubber gloves—ugh, his hands were really sweaty—and settled happily down to sleep.

—〰—

A week later, the villagers were up in arms.

Dizzy loved every minute.

"A bloody stair lift, I ask you!" spluttered Paddy Birley when he went into the shop. "Couldn't get rid of the bloke! I said to him, I said, look at this place. It ain't *got* no bleeding stairs, but did that put him off? Did it heck as like. He spent two hours trying to persuade me to put in an upstairs extension."

"Everybody's got something," Myrtle Armitage muttered.

"Old Cecil got one of them brochure things about hair transplants," Paddy Birley told her as the door clanged open and Dizzy came in. "And yesterday they phoned him up. He told them he'd managed all right without hair for the last fifty years and he wasn't about to start buying shampoo now."

"That Lorna from the pub got sent a load of papers on how to get your teeth white." Myrtle narrowed her eyes in Dizzy's direction. "What d'you want? And before you ask, I'm not selling you no cigarettes."

"Just a packet of chewing gum," said Dizzy politely. "Please." He looked at the envelope in Myrtle's heavily veined hand. "You got one as well, did you? What did yours say?"

Myrtle bristled. "Told me I didn't know how to run a shop."

Dizzy kept a straight face. This was brilliant.

"Dad's been getting them for ages, ever since we moved in. Saying he's a crap actor and why doesn't he go back to London. Poor old Dad. It really upsets him." He frowned. "Who do you think's sending all this stuff?"

The devil makes work for idle hands, and Dizzy was certainly idle. It was, Myrtle had decided, just the sort of trick a bored schoolboy would play.

Now, though, her private suspicion that Dizzy could have been behind the campaign began to crumble. If his own father was receiving letters, it couldn't be him. Surely.

Promptly reverting to second choice, she said, "One of them lads from Keeper's Cottage, I reckon. Not Doug. He's a doctor. But I wouldn't put it past that Jamie," she went on, her tone brisk. "He's always up to mischief. It's the kind of prank he'd think was funny."

Dizzy paid for his chewing gum. "Well, I don't think it's funny. It's cruel. I mean, you're hurting people's feelings, aren't you? I think you run a brilliant shop."

Myrtle, whose feelings had definitely been hurt, softened toward the boy at once. Of course it wasn't Dizzy. He was a kind lad, nicely brought up. And he'd been to a posh school. "My money's on that young vet," she pronounced. "And he won't get away with it, I'm telling you now. Next time I see him, I'll give him a piece of my mind."

———

Harriet was mystified to receive a letter from someone called Frank Huntingdon. Written on musty-smelling heavy stationery in an old-fashioned hand, it went:

> *Dear Harriet,*
>
> *Many thanks for your nice letter and yes, I would very much like to meet you. I was also extremely pleased to learn that you share my passion for pigs. Maybe in due course I could show you over my farm.*
>
> *As requested, I am enclosing a snapshot of myself, which I hope won't scare you off. Country dancing and hard work has kept me in pretty good health over the years. Not bad for seventy-three, all in all, and I still have my own teeth.*
>
> *Please do ring me, so we can arrange a meeting. As*

you say, loneliness is a terrible thing and so unnecessary.
Who knows, maybe we can find happiness together?

Yours most respectfully,
Frank Huntingdon

Harriet turned over the snap, which had been taken in one of those passport photo booths. Frank had white hair, a ruddy, outdoorsy complexion, a big grin, and an even bigger hole in his ancient hand-knitted sweater.

Poor old bugger, all alone and desperate for company. Glancing at the address at the top of the letter, she saw that he lived less than twelve miles away. He had advertised for a partner in the local paper and somebody—one of her daft friends from school, no doubt—had written back pretending to be Harriet.

I should ring and tell him it was a prank, thought Harriet, but the prospect was too toe-curling. Frank was seventy-three and she was fourteen. He would be embarrassed and so would she.

Anyway, he was bound to have had dozens of other women writing to him, she decided with some relief, real women who were every bit as ancient as they said they were. Frank, bless his lonely heart, would be busy with all of them. He wouldn't even notice her name missing from the list.

Glad that she was on her own in the kitchen, Harriet tore up the letter and the photo and shoved the pieces deep into the trash.

Chapter 52

"IT's OKAY. I KNOW he isn't there," said Drew. "I just saw him leave."

Oh, how she loved the sound of his voice: low-pitched, intimate, and sexy.

"Where are you?"

"Living room."

Lili felt her insides do a lightning squirm, like a shoal of tiny fish darting around within her stomach. She stretched the phone cord as far as it would go and walked across to the bedroom window.

There he was, on the other side of the green.

"I can see you, just." It was so heavenly to hear from him. "What are you doing?"

"Grinning like an idiot. What's that white thing you're wearing, a strapless dress?"

"Strapless bath towel." Lili giggled. "I've just had a shower."

"You mean…" Drew let out a low whistle. "So what's under the bath towel?"

"Stretch marks, mainly. I wouldn't bother getting out your binoculars. Some things are better viewed from a distance."

"I'd rather see you close up." Drew marveled at her lack of self-esteem. If Lili would only let him, he'd happily kiss each and every stretch mark. "Go on. I dare you. Accidentally drop the towel."

"Unfair." Lili blushed with pleasure. "Would you take your clothes off in full view of the village?"

"Love to. Except if I did it, I'd be arrested. Whereas you'd get a round of applause."

"I'm still not going to," said Lili.

"Chicken."

"But not exactly a spring one."

She was always putting herself down. Drew wished he could restore some of that shattered self-confidence.

"Lili, you're gorgeous. If you were twenty-two with a figure like a wire coat hanger, I wouldn't be on this phone with you now." Before she could come up with some new derogatory remark about herself he went on. "I've got to see you again. It's killing me, only being able to talk on the phone."

It was killing her too, but she didn't know what else they could do. Before, she had been able to visit Keeper's Cottage without a qualm. Waving to Myrtle Armitage from Drew's bedroom window had been funny. But that was when they'd had nothing to hide. Now that they did, waltzing over to the cottage was out of the question. The idea that anyone might suspect them of being up to no good wasn't funny at all.

"How about tonight?" Drew persisted. "Say you've taken up evening classes in Harleston. Tell Michael he's watching the kids because you'll be weaving baskets between seven and ten."

As he spoke, Jessie's run-down van roared into view down Compass Hill and along the main street.

"Michael's got another cricket match on." Lili peered out of the window as the van drew to a halt outside the front of the house. "Anyway, here's Jess. I must go."

"I don't want you to go," Drew said. He watched Jessie jump out of the driver's seat, pause to retie the yellow scarf in her hair, and wave up at Lili.

"Back door's open," Lili bellowed out of the window. To Drew she added, "I have to hang up now."

Where there's a will there's a way, thought Drew.

"No you don't." He spoke quickly. "Let me talk to Jess."

———⁓———

Lili was so nervous she missed the turn and drove straight past the entrance to the hotel. Two miles down the road, doing a clumsy, sweaty-palmed U-turn, she almost ended up in a ditch. By the time she pulled up at the top of the drive, it was twenty past eight and the butterflies in her stomach had reached fever pitch.

Drew was standing on the hotel steps waiting for her. He looked smarter than she'd ever seen him look before, in a dark suit, freshly ironed white shirt, and an actual, honest-to-goodness tie.

"Wow!" Lili kissed him, touched that he should have made such an effort. Even the wayward hair had been combed into submission.

Up close, she saw that the tie was patterned with golden retrievers. Drew gave her a stern look. "You're late."

"Sorry, got lost."

In the stone doorway, he stroked her flushed cheek. "I thought you weren't coming."

"I'm here," Lili whispered, "but I have to be home by eleven."

Two and a half hours. Not ideal, but better than nothing at all.

"Right," said Drew, "this place has three bars, two restaurants, and eighty-four rooms." He gazed steadily into Lili's wide hazel eyes. "Up to you."

"Oh, Drew, we can't book a room."

We can, we can. "Okay, fine."

Over drinks in a secluded corner of the first bar they came to, Lili struggled to explain. "It's not that I don't want to—"

Me neither, thought Drew, filled with longing.

"—but I'm married." Lili shook her head. She had spent the last few days wrestling with her conscience.

"What if Michael's been unfaithful to you hundreds of times?"

"What if he hasn't?"

She looked so miserable. Drew couldn't bear it. For the first time in his life, he now realized, he was in love.

And as if the fact that she was married wasn't bad enough, he'd had to go and fall for someone with—oh God, could you credit it?—*scruples*.

—⁓—

"Well?" Jessie demanded, twisting around on the sofa when the sitting-room door opened and closed behind her. Blitz, curled up on her lap, opened an equally inquiring eye and—like a conductor calling his orchestra to attention—thumped his tail three times against the arm of the sofa.

"We had a great time." Lili threw herself into the scruffy but comfortable chair opposite.

Jess raised an eyebrow. "Doesn't look as if you did."

Lili's eyes filled with tears. "It was the best two hours of my life. I didn't want to leave."

"Oh!" Agog, Jessie bounced into a sitting position. "And did you...you know?"

Lili fumbled up her sleeve for a tissue. She blew her nose and shook her head, praying that Michael wouldn't choose this moment to come home.

"I couldn't. I just couldn't. I'm in hot enough water as it is. I told him we had to stop it while we still could. Oh, Jess, it's all over. I said I wasn't going to see him again. What we're doing is *wrong*."

Silently, Jessie reached for the half-empty bottle of rough-and-ready Spanish wine she had brought with her on babysitting duty. She poured, handed the glass to Lili, and made her drink.

"What did Drew say?"

"That he loved me." More hot tears trickled down Lili's cheeks. "But if it was what I wanted, he wouldn't try to change my mind."

Jessie put her arms around her.

"God, I hope Michael knows how lucky he is," she told Lili. "Not only an angel for a wife, but a considerate rival for her affections too."

———

"You look a mess," said Michael the next morning. "What happened to your eyes?"

Lili flinched. She had pretended to be asleep when he had crept in shortly after midnight, but when Michael's snores had begun to shake the bed, she had given up trying to hold back the tears. They had slid into her ears, down her neck, and into the pillow. Knowing that she had done the honorable thing didn't make it any easier to bear.

She had managed an hour's sleep at the very most, and now her brain felt full of grit.

"Lili?" When she didn't say anything, Michael stopped spreading marmalade on his toast and looked up. What was going on? Had she somehow found out about April? Christ, had someone seen them together last night?

He put down the knife. *Deny everything. Deny, deny.*

"Sweetheart, what's wrong?"

Oh, how could I ever have thought of cheating on him? thought Lili, awash with shame. *Look, he's worried about me! He can see I'm upset and he cares—*

"Mum, when can Aunt Jess look after us again?" Lottie raced into the kitchen and grabbed two bananas from the fruit bowl. "She told us a story about monsters with underwear on their heads and hats on their bottoms. It was loads better than Postman-boring-Pat."

"I'd forgotten about Jess babysitting last night," said Michael when Lottie had left them to it. Outside in the garden, she was shooting Will with both bananas. "Doing someone's hair, weren't you? Where was that?" He floundered, wondering if Lili had followed him, had actually watched him disappear inside April's apartment. "In Harleston?"

Guilt was gnawing away at Lili's stomach like battery acid. She'd always been a useless liar.

She nodded.

"But you've been crying." Michael couldn't give up now; he had to know. "Lili, tell me what's wrong."

"It's nothing. One of Felicity's friends wanted a perm, that's all. And when I'd finished, she didn't like it. Said I'd made her l-look like a sheep." Haltingly, Lili stammered out the excuse Jess had had the foresight to concoct. "She called me a useless amateur. That's why I was upset."

It was a toss-up who was more relieved: Lili, because he believed her story, or Michael, because he hadn't, after all, been found out.

He gave her an awkward hug. "There there. You're a terrific hairdresser. Come on. Sit down and I'll make you a cup of tea."

I'm sorry. I'm so sorry I was almost unfaithful to you, Lili thought, biting her lip and trying desperately hard not to compare the hug with one of Drew's.

"Can I make a catapult out of a pair of underwear like Aunt Jess taught me last night?" Lottie, hurtling back into the kitchen, skidded to a halt. "Then I can shoot grapes at Will's head— Oh yuck, don't hug each other; that's how babies get born. And you don't want any more children," she informed them scornfully. "Three's *quite* enough."

Chapter 53

DIZZY WAS KEEN TO branch out. The letters had been great, but now it was time to diversify. Come nightfall, he decided, he would sneak out of the house and see what he could do. He'd already set his heart on scrawling something obscene, with weed killer, across the middle of the village green.

Now, as he dawdled along with his hands stuffed into his pockets, he saw Bernadette Thomas heading toward him in her car.

Dizzy nodded and waved as she drove past, and Bernadette acknowledged him with a brief smile in return. Odd woman—never said much, kept herself to herself. Dizzy, turning to watch her go, realized that Bernadette Thomas was heading for Harleston.

Which meant her cottage was empty.

When a frog landed with a plop on the front of his left shoe less than a minute later, Dizzy decided it must be fate.

Yeah!

All women were scared stupid of frogs.

Bending down, he swiftly scooped up the creature and dropped it into his jeans pocket. Then he sauntered casually back past the pond, across the road, and along Waters Lane.

Eleanor Ferguson's was the first house he came to, but a quick glance up at the windows revealed no sign of her.

Quick as a flash, while no one else was in sight, Dizzy raced up the path to Bernadette Thomas's front door, held open the letter box, and posted the frog into the hall.

Then, unable to resist the temptation, he crouched and peered through the slit to follow its progress.

Brilliant!

Boinggg, boinggg, the frog sprang through the hallway into the sitting room. That would make Bernadette scream, thought Dizzy, trampling a flower bed and pressing his nose against the sitting room window just in time to see the frog leap up onto the mantelpiece and send a china candlestick flying.

"What on earth do you think you're doing?" barked a terrifying voice behind him.

Dizzy, leaning precariously sideways, lost his footing and fell into a rosebush.

Shit, bugger, ouch.

"Well?" demanded Eleanor Ferguson, who had been in the back garden tending her tomato plants.

"I-I was just p-passing," Dizzy stammered. "I thought I heard s-somebody shout for help."

He was an actor, wasn't he? He could act his way out of this.

But Eleanor Ferguson was giving him a forbidding look. "There's no one in there. And when you were peering through the window just now you were laughing to yourself."

"I wasn't," Dizzy protested, wide-eyed, but it was no good. Eleanor marched around to join him. When she glanced through her neighbor's window, it didn't take her long to spot the frog, by this time leaping happily on and off the sofa like Gene Kelly in *Singin' in the Rain.*

"It was only meant to be a joke," Dizzy mumbled.

"A joke? What, like the anonymous letters everyone's been getting in the post?" Eleanor's sidelong glance was shrewd. "That was you as well, I imagine."

Dizzy's acting abilities promptly deserted him. He shook his head and muttered, "No." *Hopeless,* hopeless.

"Oh, I think it was."

Eleanor watched him trying to avoid her gaze. She wondered why she wasn't shouting at him. Then it came to her. With that truculent expression and those drooping, defeated shoulders, Dizzy reminded her of her own son at fifteen. She had caught Michael letting down the tires on the bikes of a group of lads who hadn't wanted him to join their group.

"Dizzy." Her voice softened. "Why are you doing it?"

And this time, when he desperately didn't want to cry, Dizzy found himself with tears dripping down his cheeks.

"Everyone ignores me." He hiccupped and wiped his eyes on his sleeve. "It was so great when I came back from London, being made a fuss of and stuff, but it didn't last two minutes. Now it's just as awful as it was before."

Eleanor remembered Michael, all those years ago, wailing, "Why haven't I got any *friends*?"

A lump came to her throat. "Look, I won't tell Bernadette this was your doing." She indicated the frog through the window. "And I won't say anything about the letters either. But you must stop now, Dizzy. Don't send any more. There's talk of the police being called in, and if you're caught, you'll only be in more trouble."

Dizzy could hardly believe what he was hearing. Eleanor Ferguson was an old witch, everyone knew that. He sniffed loudly. Why would a bossy, interfering old witch be on his side?

"I know what you're thinking," Eleanor said without rancor. She rummaged up her sleeve and passed him a clean tissue. "But this shall be our secret, you have my word. As long as it stops." Firmly she added, "No more letters, no more frogs. And nobody but you and me will be any the wiser, all right?"

⁓

Back at the house, Savannah was forty minutes into a phone call to her best friend from school and seriously beginning to regret ever picking up the phone in the first place. There was nothing more nauseating than being forced to listen to someone else spout on and on about the fantastic new love of their life. But having to hear every last tedious detail of what they were getting up to when you yourself weren't getting up to *anything at all*—well, that was deeply depressing stuff.

"...and the next night we did it in the sea," Mandy giggled. "Sav, you *have* to try it. I can't describe how it feels!"

But you'll give it a damn good try, thought Savannah, gloomily picking at a hole in the knee of her jeans. What was she going to do about Oliver? What was she going to *do*?

"God, listen to me rabbiting away and not letting you get a word in edgewise," Mandy trilled twenty minutes later. "Tell me how things are going with you and your chap!"

"Oh, you know, same as you." Savannah forced herself to sound jaunty. "Brilliant sex, every position you can think of—"

"I know, I know, aren't men just insatiable? Honestly, I don't know where Harry gets his energy from. We're just doing it morning, noon, and night!"

"Yeah, we are too."

Savannah wanted to cry. How could she ever confide in anyone, admit to them that Oliver was impotent?

Oh, the shame, the terrible humiliation.

She would never live it down.

Lili was on the phone to Felicity two days later when she saw Lottie, in the front yard, struggling to climb one of the walnut trees.

"Lottie, get down!" she shouted through the window.

Puffing and struggling to get a better foothold, Lottie yelled back, "I can *do* it!"

"I won't keep you," Felicity said. "I just rang to let you know I'm taking a few more days off work, so I won't need you to look after Freya this week." Apologetically she added, "If that's okay with you."

"No problem." Lili, who would get paid anyway, was grateful for the reprieve. As the long summer vacation wore on, she had enough on her plate coping with her own boisterous brood. "Felicity, thanks for ringing, but I'm going to have to go. Lottie's halfway up a tree."

As she was running out of the front door, Lottie lost her precarious grip on a branch. With an earsplitting scream, she tumbled out of the tree, ricocheted off the stone wall beneath it, and landed on the narrow pavement with a thud.

"Oh my God, Lottie!"

"MUMMEEEE!"

Lili, her heart pounding, knelt beside her gray-faced daughter. Lottie's eyes rolled and flickered momentarily with the shock. Then she opened her mouth and let out a howl like a wild animal.

"Ow…ow…it hurts. Don't touch me! Don't touch my arm. It *hurts*!"

"All right, darling, you're all right. Don't try to move. Michael!" Lili shouted, but she knew he was in the shower—he wouldn't be able to hear her.

"I'm not all right!" Lottie roared between screams. "Ow, Mummy, ow. Make it *go away*!"

Lili heard the sound of running footsteps. When she looked up and saw Drew, she almost wept with relief.

"I was just leaving the pub." He crouched down and took Lottie's pulse. "Heard the screams. It's okay, sweetheart. I'm not going to hurt you. Looks like you've broken that arm."

"Is Doug at home?" Lili asked, but Drew shook his head.

"On duty."

"Oh God, shall I phone for an ambulance?"

"It'll be twenty minutes before it gets here. Was she knocked out?"

"No. Did you bang your head, sweetheart?"

"No!" Lottie howled, struggling to sit up. "Not my head, my *arm*!"

"Quicker if we take her ourselves," Drew said, rolling up his sleeves. "There don't seem to be any other injuries, but she needs to be checked over." He glanced at the open front door. "Where's Michael?"

"In the shower. And Will's asleep upstairs, and Harriet's taken Blitz for a walk."

"Okay, I'll bring my car over and we'll put Lottie across the backseat. Michael can bring Will and Harriet along to the hospital in his own time."

He knew just what to do. Speechless with gratitude, Lili nodded.

"Pull my dress down!" Lottie bellowed, tugging frantically at the hem with her good arm. "I don't want everyone to see my underwear!"

<hr/>

Doug came through to see Lottie as soon as they arrived in the ER. Lili guiltily avoided the glares of outrage from the other patients who had been sitting there for hours without so much as a sniff of a doctor. The female patients in particular, when they saw how good-looking Doug was, were clearly wondering what Lili had that they didn't.

"This is like nepotism," she whispered to Drew.

"I know. Good, isn't it?" he replied cheerfully. "Unless of course you'd rather sit here for the rest of the afternoon listening to Lottie yelling her head off."

Doug finished his brief preliminary examination and straightened up. "Right, we'll take her through to a cubicle. When I've had a proper look at her, we'll get the X-rays organized. Lili, you'll need to give the receptionist some details."

Lili stroked her daughter's clammy forehead. "Shouldn't I stay with Lottie?"

But Lottie's good arm tightened possessively around Drew's neck. "Drew can come with me. I like Drew."

Doug's mouth twitched. "Come on then. He can carry you to the cubicle. Your mum'll be through in a minute. Over there," he told Lili, nodding in the direction of the reception desk.

"Why?" Lottie demanded.

Doug was surprisingly good with children. Keeping a straight face, he leaned closer to her. "Because that's April, our receptionist behind the desk." His whisper was conspiratorial. "And she needs to know everything there is to know about you."

Lottie looked outraged. "What, even the color of my underwear?"

Chapter 54

BITING HER LIP, LILI watched Drew lift her daughter effortlessly into his arms and carry her off down the corridor. Then she made her way over to the desk.

The receptionist's neat hair and freshly applied lipstick made Lili acutely conscious of how disheveled she must look by comparison. She had been polishing windows before Felicity had rung, and her old, yellow shirt was smudged with Windex. Worse still, she couldn't remember brushing her hair this morning—a look that only the Sandra Bullocks of this world could carry off—and yesterday's mascara had welded her eyelashes into clumps.

There are two kinds of women in this world, Lili thought. *The ones like me and the receptionist types who always take their mascara off at night.*

She wondered with a pang what Drew must have thought when he saw her like this.

No, no, mustn't even think about Drew. Definitely not allowed.

"Sorry." Hastily Lili tried to comb Windex-impregnated fingers through her embarrassing hair. "I just realized what a fright I must look."

"Not at all." The receptionist's smile was reassuring. "You're a friend of Doug's, I take it?"

"Well, kind of. We live in the same village."

Manicured fingernails hovered above the computer keyboard.

"Could you tell me your daughter's name?"

"Lottie Ferguson. Charlotte Ferguson," Lili corrected herself.

The receptionist keyed in the details. "Address?"

"The Old Vicarage, Upper Sisley."

The *tap-tapping* faltered for a second. April gazed at the screen, saw that she had typed *Siz* instead of *Sis*, and hurriedly deleted the *z*. How extraordinary—she hadn't realized that Doug Flynn lived in the same village as Bernadette...

It didn't matter. Of course it didn't. Just a coincidence, that was all.

She composed herself and glanced up at the woman in front of her. The woman must also know Bernadette.

"Any previous admissions?"

Lili shook her head. "No."

"Name and address of GP?"

"Dr. Mather. Um... Oh Lord, I can't remember her address."

"Would your husband know?" The receptionist glanced briefly behind her, in the direction of the corridor, and Lili realized what she meant.

"Oh no. Gosh, that isn't my husband. Drew shares a house with Doug; he just gave us a lift here." Flushing at the implication, Lili hurried to explain. "My husband's at home with the baby. He'll come in as soon as our elder daughter gets home. In fact, I need to ring him, tell him what to bring in case Lottie has to stay here overnight." She scrabbled in the pocket of her jeans for the emergency fiver she had grabbed on the way out of the house. "You wouldn't have change for the phone, would you? I want to catch him before he leaves."

It was against the rules, but April didn't have any change on her, so she pushed her phone across the desk and lowered her voice. "Here, use this one."

"Thanks. I'll be quick, I promise." Grinning with relief, Lili punched out the number. It was answered on the second ring.

"Darling? Yes, it's me. Doug's seeing to Lottie now." Pause.

"No, they're doing X-rays, but he doesn't think there's anything to worry about, just the arm. Yes, definitely broken." Long pause. "No, Michael, it can't wait. If his diaper's dirty you have to change it *now*." Lili rolled her eyes in disbelief. "Why? Because if you leave it, he'll get raging diaper rash. Now listen, I have to get off this phone. Throw a few things together before you leave, in case they keep Lottie in—a couple of clean nighties, toothbrush, that kind of thing. No, I washed and dried them this morning. They're in a big pile on our bed…"

April dropped the file she had been putting together and slid off her stool to retrieve it from under her desk. Her hands were shaking, her heart was pounding, and she didn't know if she was going to be able to get up again.

Ferguson.

Michael Ferguson.

Surely not. Oh please, it couldn't be…

Her mind raced. All the separate details were battering around inside her head.

Not her Michael

He and Doug knew each other, but Michael had only described him as a passing acquaintance; he hadn't said they lived in the same village.

But Michael had never told her exactly where he *did* live. Not in a deliberate I-don't-want-you-to-know way, of course; he had simply veered away from the question, describing it vaguely as a quiet, little place and turning the conversation to something else.

And she, not wanting to irritate him, had let it pass. He had his family to consider, after all. April understood that. He might be living separately from his wife, but there were still her feelings to consider. If she'd pressed for details, he might start to panic that he had a *Fatal Attraction*–type scenario on his hands.

Except…

Still crouched on the floor, April experienced a tidal wave of nausea.

Except…if they were talking about the same Michael Ferguson here, he wasn't sounding too separated from his wife.

This woman had just called him "darling." And not in that polite, teeth-gritted-together way some couples do when they clearly can't stand each other.

She'd said "our bed" too.

Our bed, meaning the one *they* slept in.

Together.

April was feeling sicker by the minute. She might actually have to throw up in her wastepaper basket.

"Okay, darling, come as soon as Harriet gets back. See you soon."

Above her, Lili hung up. Seconds later, she was peering over the edge of the desk.

"Hello. Are you okay down there?"

April forced herself to nod. "Just dropped the file."

"Oh. Well, thanks for letting me use your phone. Have you got all the details you need?"

Another nod.

"I'll go through then, see how Lottie is. Will you be able to let me know when the troops arrive?"

"Troops?"

"Husband, teenage daughter, small, noisy son, even noisier dog." Lili grinned down at her. "Well, maybe not the dog."

April's hands were still trembling uncontrollably as she gathered together the sheets from the file. She forced herself to take a deep breath. "Right, yes, I'll tell you."

"Brilliant." With a cheery wave, Lili disappeared from view. "Thanks!"

—⁓—

The next thirty minutes were the longest of April's life as she waited for Lottie Ferguson's father to appear through the sliding doors. When he did, she knew at once that the desperate excuses she had spent the last half hour manufacturing on his behalf had been a waste of time.

The expression on Michael's face when he saw her behind the desk said it all. A combination of shifty-eyed guilt and bravado—because as far as he was concerned, there was still a chance he could get away with this.

He does, he really does, April thought incredulously as he and the children approached the desk. *He thinks he can pull this off.*

"Hello, my name's Michael Ferguson." He winked at her with the eye farthest from his teenage daughter. "I'm Lottie Ferguson's father. She's here with my...er, wife."

The "er" bit, April realized, was significant too. He was implying that Lili might be his wife, but it was a marriage in name only.

Feeling numb, she nodded. "If you take a seat, I'll tell her you're here."

April heard herself saying the words, but only just. There was a rushing noise, like an approaching typhoon, in her ears. She wanted to scream at Michael but she couldn't, not with the children at his side. Wondering how she was going to make it along the corridor, she turned. But luck was on her side and Doug's friend was coming toward her.

"Um...Mr. Ferguson's arrived."

Drew glanced across at Harriet and Michael and smiled briefly at Will, who was sitting on the floor playing with his beloved headless Barbie. That was it; he wasn't needed anymore. Michael was here now. "I'll tell Lili," he offered. "Then it's time I was gone."

"Oh, help," April murmured, realizing she could no longer see properly. Everything was spinning, going gray, and the typhoon noise in her ears was getting louder.

"Oh, help what? Is something wrong?" Drew frowned, then saw the color drain from her face.

He managed to catch her just as she crumpled to the floor.

Eleanor Ferguson loved to boast that she was far too busy to watch TV. It was such rubbish, and there always seemed to be so many more worthwhile things to do.

But every now and again, in the privacy of your own sitting room, it was nice to be able to make yourself a cup of tea, throw a couple of homemade cookies onto a plate, put your feet up, and let a bit of mindless afternoon television wash over you.

As long as nobody else knew you were doing it.

Eleanor almost choked on her cookie when she heard the broadcaster talking about *The Jack Astley Show*, due to air at five thirty.

"…and Jack's guest today is little-known novelist Antonia Kay, whose latest book is about to be turned into a Hollywood blockbuster."

This time there was no "almost" about it. Eleanor did choke on her cookie. Spluttering and banging her bony chest, she sat bolt upright and stared at the screen. Her very own next-door neighbor? Good grief, this was unbelievable! A film company in Hollywood was actually making a film of Bernadette's novel.

And she hadn't told anyone, Eleanor realized with a jolt of betrayal. *Not even me.*

She leaped up, tea and cookie forgotten, and ran to the window. Bernadette's car wasn't parked in its usual place and the windows next door were all shut. There was no one at home.

Of course, she would be at the television studios, Eleanor reminded herself. *The Jack Astley Show* went out live.

It would be a huge ordeal for someone as private and publicity shy as Bernadette. Eleanor wondered why she had agreed to appear, then dismissed the question from her mind. That was irrelevant now. The show was set to start in an hour and it was up to her—it was her *duty*, no less—to spread the word to as many of the villagers as possible.

After all, if Bernadette was going to flaunt herself on national television, her identity was hardly going to be a secret anymore.

———

Fifty minutes later and still bristling with importance, Eleanor swept into the shop.

"Well well," marveled Myrtle Armitage when she heard the news. "Who'd've thought it? Quiet as a mouse, looks like she wouldn't say boo to a bowl of custard, and all this time she's been doing deals with them Hollywood types." She cast a regretful glance at her watch. "Looks like I'm going to have to miss it. I can't close the shop yet."

Eleanor couldn't bear anyone to miss this. Bernadette was her next-door neighbor, and she felt as if she'd discovered her single-handedly.

"Set your TV up out here. It's a portable, isn't it?" She pushed the carefully arranged rows of magazines to one side, clearing a space on the counter. "You wait there. I'll bring it through myself."

As Eleanor disappeared through the door leading into Myrtle's living room, Myrtle called after her, "But it's half past five now. You won't be home in time."

Eleanor returned, holding the portable television aloft. Dust free, she was pleased to note.

"No problem. I'll watch it here with you."

Chapter 55

AS SHE HAD BEEN recovering from her faint, April had heard Lili greeting Michael over by the coffee machine.

"Hello, sweetheart! I was wondering when you'd get here!"

If April had looked up at that moment, she would have seen that Lili was kissing Harriet, not Michael. But all she heard was the sound of the kiss, then Lili's voice again, pitched lower this time.

"What's going on over there?"

"One of the receptionists fainted." Michael had sounded vague, uninterested.

"Oh, that poor girl! She didn't seem well when I was talking to her earlier. I wondered then if she felt a bit—"

"Anyway," Michael had interrupted brusquely, "how's Lottie?"

"Oh, fine. Come and see her. She's dying to show off her plaster cast."

That had been over an hour ago. Shortly afterward, one of the nurses who was going off duty had given April a lift home.

"Take it easy," she had advised. "You still look dreadful. I'd go to bed if I were you."

April had managed a nod and a brief frozen smile of thanks, but bed was out of the question. She was seized with rage and grief and helplessness. Michael Ferguson had lied to her, made an utter fool of her, destroyed her chance of happiness.

April couldn't believe it was happening to her all over again.

"We're here, love." The taxi driver pulled up outside the cottage and twisted around, checking that his fare hadn't thrown up all over the backseat. "That'll be eight quid."

At least Bernie's car was outside. When April had called for a cab, it hadn't occurred to her to phone and check first. But then it hadn't occurred to her either to wonder if what she was doing was right. Coming here had been instinctive, simply the only thing *to* do.

Because, despite everything that had happened in the past, she knew Bernie loved her.

And what April needed now, more than ever before, was someone who would understand and sympathize.

Someone who would be on her side.

Bernadette, just back from a trip to the garden center, heard the sound of an unfamiliar car outside. When she went to the window and saw who was climbing out of the idling taxi, she had to step back and catch her breath.

April.

What in heaven's name was she doing here?

Bernadette didn't have to wait long to find out. When she opened the door, April was stumbling up the front path, tears streaming from her eyes. Instinctively Bernadette held out her arms. The last time she had seen April was less than two months ago, when she had hidden in a shop doorway in Harleston in order to glimpse her across the street.

But it had been over two years since April had set eyes on her.

"Oh, Bernie, I had to come. Please don't be angry with me." She buried her head against Bernadette's shoulder, the stiff, lace-edged frill of Bernadette's blouse scratching her wet cheek. "I'm so sorry. I just didn't know what else to do."

"Shhh, it's okay. I'm glad you came," Bernadette murmured in soothing tones. "Now, tell me what's wrong." As she led her into the sitting room, Bernadette stroked April's soft, blond hair. She had never stopped loving her. If there was anything, *anything* she could do to make the pain go away, she would do it.

———

Over at the grocery store, Eleanor Ferguson was quivering like a rat's whiskers. Outrage vied with bitter humiliation, and she could scarcely bear to meet Myrtle Armitage's beady gaze.

Because Antonia Kay was on the television exchanging flirtatious banter with Jack Astley. What was more, Jack Astley was visibly enjoying himself, because Antonia Kay was blond and pretty and wore a miniskirt that showed off her long, shapely legs.

There had been no mistake, because they were talking about *A Frond of Honeysuckle*, and Jack was holding a copy of the book up to the camera.

Eleanor flushed an ever-deepening shade of red. This was more than outrageous; it was intolerable. Bernadette Thomas had lied to her, not just once but over and over again.

She's made me look a complete fool, Eleanor thought, jowls aquiver as she remembered how she had raced around the village boasting about Bernadette's appearance on TV and exhorting everyone to watch.

She's the one pretending—God alone knows why—to be someone she isn't, Eleanor fumed, *and* I'm *the one left with egg on my face.*

Myrtle Armitage, secretly delighted to be witnessing bossy Eleanor Ferguson's long-awaited comeuppance, spoke with feigned innocence.

"Maybe you misunderstood her. She could've said she *knew* a novelist and you thought she said she *was* one."

"It wasn't a misunderstanding." Grimly Eleanor stood up. She'd had enough. "That woman deliberately lied to me, and I'm going to give her a piece of my mind!"

———

"What are you doing?" April stammered, clutching fearfully at Bernadette's sleeve.

But Bernadette had already wrenched open the front door. Michael Ferguson had done this to April and, one way or another, he would pay for it.

So angry she could barely see straight, Bernadette marched straight into Eleanor Ferguson storming through the front gate.

"You"—Eleanor pointed a rigid, accusing finger at Bernadette— "have some explaining to do, madam."

"If anyone has any explaining to do, it's your son. Where is he?"

Openmouthed, Eleanor took a step backward. Who was supposed to be the accuser here?

The next second, she recognized the slender, distraught-looking blond clinging to Bernadette's arm. This was the girl whose photograph stood in a silver frame on the table in Bernadette's hall. Eleanor's nostrils twitched with disgust. *Ugh! Filthy lesbians, the pair of them.*

"Bernie, no, leave it," the girl pleaded. "He's probably still at the hospital anyway."

"Hospital? *Hospital?*" Eleanor barked. "My son, Michael—is that who you're talking about? How ridiculous! I saw him myself less than two minutes ago, walking across to the pub." To her eternal shame, she remembered how she had poked her head around the door of the Seven Bells and said archly to Lorna Blake: "Tune in to *The Jack Astley Show* at five thirty and you could be in for a big surprise."

With grim satisfaction, Bernadette said, "Right, the pub it is!"

"Bernie, you mustn't!" April begged, but her protesting hand was shaken off. And April, who knew she didn't mean it anyway, experienced a furtive thrill deep down in the pit of her stomach.

Was this why I came here? she wondered as they set off at speed down the lane. *Was this why I had to see Bernie again—for comfort and some kind of revenge?*

"I don't know what you think you're playing at." Eleanor spoke through gritted teeth, racing to keep up as they approached the village green. "But I've just been watching the *real* Antonia Kay on television. Now you'd better tell me what this is all about."

"You'll find out soon enough."

"Heaven knows I tried to be a good neighbor to you, and this is how you repay me. You're nothing but a liar and a cheat!"

Bernadette strode on ahead without speaking, leading the mini convoy of three. She didn't even glance at Eleanor as she reached the far side of the green, marched across the road to the Seven Bells, and pushed open the heavy oak door.

Despite never having actually set foot in the pub before, Bernadette recognized quite a few of the people in there. For six o'clock in the evening, it was busier than she had expected too—another bonus. Maybe forty or fifty customers in all, among them Toby and Savannah Gillespie and the two young vets from Keeper's Cottage.

As people turned their attention from the TV set up on the wall, Bernadette's level gaze swung the length of the pub. Tall, good-looking Oliver Roscoe was working behind the bar, one hand on a beer pump as he filled a pint mug to the brim. Next to him, unloading a tray of glasses, Moll the trollop, whose reputation even Bernadette was aware of. And farther along, smoking a cigarette and chatting to a customer perched on one of the leather-topped barstools, gravel-voiced Lorna Blake.

Bernadette heard April behind her, still gasping for breath.

She looked directly at Michael Ferguson, the customer perched on the stool engaged in desultory conversation with Lorna.

Bernadette coughed and announced in a clear voice, "Mr. Ferguson."

Michael turned, a questioning tilt to his eyebrows. "Yes?"

Then he saw April, standing two feet behind Bernadette, her eyes desolate and swollen with tears.

"What's this about?" The sudden pallor of Michael's face matched the frothy just-poured beer.

"Oh, I think you know," said Bernadette.

Michael's jaw stuck out at a belligerent angle. "Should I?"

"You recognize this lady, I take it?"

He hesitated, then shrugged. "I saw her at the hospital earlier, if that's what you mean."

In the doorway, Eleanor protested furiously, "This is ridiculous! You can't—"

But Bernadette was off. In less than a second, she had crossed the flagstone floor, pulled back her arm, and delivered a right hook like a hammer blow to Michael Ferguson's jutting chin.

He fell off his stool, crashed heavily to the ground, and lay there, dazed, as Bernadette picked up his pint glass and poured the frothy contents over his head.

"And you think *I'm* a liar and a cheat," she told Eleanor, her tone almost conversational as she flicked the last dregs of beer dismissively in his face.

The rest of the pub stared, agog, at the surreal sight of Bernadette standing over Michael Ferguson. It had been a punch like no other they had ever witnessed, a punch that would have done credit to Evander Holyfield.

"Wh-what's going on?" Michael was spluttering and wiping the beer from his stinging eyes. "What's this got to do with you, for Christ's sake?"

"Let's just say I care about what happens to April," Bernadette told him icily. It might have been twenty years ago now, but once a boxer always a boxer. "You see, she's my ex-wife."

Chapter 56

"I STILL CAN'T BELIEVE it," Lili exclaimed the next morning, shaking her head as she tipped a packet of chocolate cookies into the cookie tin. "Bernadette Thomas used to be a *man*."

"I wish I could have been there." Jessie winced and shot her a semi-apologetic glance across the kitchen table. "Sorry, I know Michael's your husband and all that, but Oliver did say it was the most amazing sight."

Lili was busy cramming a cookie into her mouth. "Don't look so guilty. I wish I'd been there too. I just thought you could always tell when men had had a sex change. You know, five-o'clock shadow breaking through their foundation."

"Gruff voices."

"Thick, black hairs poking out through their tights."

"And leather-studded miniskirts." Jessie helped herself to another cookie.

If it hadn't been such a hot day, the kitchen door wouldn't have been left wide open and Bernadette Thomas, about to tap on it, would not have overheard this conversation.

But since it was, and she had, she cleared her throat instead and said from the doorway, "Electrolysis works wonders these days. And the hormone replacements, they help too. As for the clothes…well, we don't all want to wear leather-studded miniskirts."

Across the table, Lili gasped and went pink. Jessie coughed, struggling to swallow her mouthful of cookie.

"Hi!" said Lili. "Come in. God, sorry, what must you think of us? We were just—"

"Saying what everyone else in the village has been saying since word got out?" Bernadette suggested drily. "Don't worry. I understand. Transsexuals are an object of fascination. It's only natural to be curious."

"Which is why you kept quiet about it for so long." Jessie could sympathize; she knew how it felt to be gossiped about. "But now everybody knows. So what made you decide to blow your cover?"

Bernadette, who was as carefully made-up as ever, smiled briefly. She brushed a stray thread from the front of her high-necked, cream blouse. "Well, yes, of course I could have rushed in there and scratched his eyes out," she admitted, "or tried stabbing him with a crochet hook. That would have been more ladylike. But I wasn't thinking that clearly. Or maybe I didn't care anymore. When you work yourself up into that much of a state, the old instincts take over. You see, I was in the army for many years, did a lot of boxing. All I wanted to do was hurt him as much as he'd hurt April." Bernadette paused, gazing down at her clenched knuckles. "And possibly to assuage my own guilt, because of course I hurt April too. I should never have married her, I know that, but at the time, I thought it might make the other feelings go away. And I loved her," Bernadette concluded sadly. "Very much indeed. I still do."

There were so many questions. Jessie pushed the sugar bowl across the table as Lili poured Bernadette a mug of tea.

"Why did you tell Eleanor you were Antonia Kay?"

"A journalist came around. Somebody from the support group I used to attend gave him my name and address. When Eleanor started asking questions, I had to come up with a plausible answer."

"But a writer!"

"Ah, but I *am* a writer." Bernadette looked amused as she sipped her tea. "I'm just not Antonia Kay."

Bewildered, Lili said, "Who are you, then?"

"Bernard Thomas."

"You write spy thrillers!" Jessie recognized the name at once. "Oliver's got all your books. He tried to make me read one once, but it was so tough, so hard-hitting… Gosh, sorry, that sounds rude—"

"They're men's books." Bernadette waved aside the apology. "It's okay. I'm not offended. Men love them; women hate them."

Lili was fascinated. "Do your publishers know about…?"

"Oh yes, I told them. They almost fainted," Bernadette said good-naturedly. "Made me promise not to let the cat out of the bag. If word got out, they knew sales would plummet. It's a question of image, you see. As my editor pointed out, it would be rather like asking the public to accept James Bond in stockings and a corset."

"Have some more tea." Lili picked up the teapot. "I have to say, I'm not sure my mother-in-law will ever speak to you again. But then again, that could be a blessing."

Bernadette took the teapot from Lili's trembling hands and set it back down on the table. "Look, we've talked enough about me. That's not why I came here. I wanted to apologize to you."

"Oh Lord, no need for that," said Lili, embarrassed.

"Of course there is. Your husband was carrying on with April and now, thanks to me, the whole village knows. You must be devastated." Bernadette frowned. "Unless…you already knew?"

Lili's hands had stopped trembling. Really, she didn't feel too bad at all.

"No, I didn't know." She shook her fringe out of her eyes. "But…well, put it this way: it was a relief to find out."

Having made himself scarce for most of the day, Michael felt he had given Lili time to get over the shock.

"Look, okay, I accept that I shouldn't have done it," he said generously, facing Lili across their double bed while she threw shirt after crumpled shirt into an open case. "But don't you think you're overreacting here? It was a fling, that's all. She didn't *mean* anything. It's no reason to break up a perfectly good marriage."

As he finished speaking, something registered that hadn't registered before. *Unironed* shirts.

What a slob, Michael thought, outraged. His mother had always told him he deserved better, and she'd been right.

"This isn't a perfectly good marriage," Lili said with unnerving calm. "It's a completely crappy one."

"But we've got three children!"

"Which is why I stuck it out for so long. Otherwise, believe me, I'd have been out of here years ago." She pulled open Michael's underwear drawer and began hurling socks and pants higgledy-piggledy on top of the mountain of shirts. "Still, never mind. This time you can be the one to go."

Michael glared at her. Lili never ironed underwear either. Unlike his mother, who had always lovingly pressed and folded them in serried ranks in his drawer.

"You're being ridiculous!" he snapped. "Thousands of women accept their husbands' harmless little affairs. Why can't you? Why do *you* have to be the one who kicks up an almighty fuss?"

"Maybe because this is the last straw." Lili knew the way she was flinging stuff into the suitcase was irritating him, which only made doing it more enjoyable. "Maybe they figured out the pros and cons and decided their marriages were worth saving." She held up an orange-and-pink Argyle sock and raised an eyebrow. "Whereas I've just had enough."

"But—"

"No, let me say it. I've put up with all sorts of stuff from you, because I always told myself that at least you were faithful. Then, when I began to think that maybe you were playing away in Dubai,

I told myself that at least you weren't doing it here, right under my nose." Lili chucked a can of shaving foam on top of the underwear and watched the lid roll onto the floor. "So you see, we've pretty much hit rock bottom now, haven't we? I can't think of a single reason why I should stay married to you anymore."

Michael began to sweat; he felt himself go hot and cold all over. He'd never seen Lili like this before. God, what with child-support payments and alimony, she could totally wipe him out.

"The children…*our* children," he blustered, "need a father."

Lili had had enough. This was hypocrisy on a grand scale. "I know they do," she said flatly. "Still, they've managed without one for this long—"

"Lili, I love you!"

But even begging, it seemed, wasn't going to work. She snapped the case shut and pushed it across the bed.

"Don't lie, Michael. And don't try to make me feel guilty, because I just won't. All this is your fault, not mine."

"You can't do this to me!" he retaliated furiously. "Where the hell am I supposed to go?"

Lili shrugged. "I don't know and I don't care. Ask Bernadette's ex-wife—what's her name? April. Maybe she'll put you up."

Chapter 57

Two hours later, Michael dragged his cases—properly packed this time—down the stairs. A hurried phone call to his office followed by another to Heathrow had completed the arrangements to return to Dubai sooner than planned. If Lili needed a while to cool off, he would give it to her. By the time of his next leave, Michael had confidently decided, she would be more than happy to welcome him back.

"Dad, look at my arm." Lottie waved the plaster cast under his nose, her expression gleeful. "I wrote my name on it, and then I wrote *bum*!" Spotting the cases in the hall, she said, "Where are you going?"

Lili was in the kitchen. Making sure she could overhear, Michael crouched down and gave Lottie an emotional hug.

"Away, sweetheart. Back to Dubai, I'm afraid. I'll be gone for a long time."

But Lottie, disappointingly, planted only a dutiful peck on his cheek before wriggling out of his grasp. "Okay. And see what Harriet drew? A picture of Blitz. It's meant to look like a tattoo."

"I'll bring back lots of presents," Michael promised in desperation.

"You always tell us that but you never do. You always say you forgot."

Harriet seemed equally unimpressed when, wandering out into the hall, she found herself on the receiving end of a suffocating embrace and the promise of regular postcards.

She frowned. "But you always said you were too busy to buy them."

"Not this time," Michael told her humbly. How had this happened? When had his own children turned against him?

It was galling to realize that the most enthusiastic good-bye came from Blitz. He didn't even like the wretched dog, but at least he licked Michael's hand. All Will could manage, when roused from his afternoon nap, was an indignant wail and a raspberry-yogurt-flavored burp.

Rubbing his chin, still sore from yesterday and sorer now from finding itself on the receiving end of one of Will's flailing rabbit punches, Michael made his way through to the kitchen.

"Right, I'm off."

Lili was at the sink, draining pasta. She turned, half-enveloped in clouds of steam. "Okay."

He gave her one last chance.

"It was a one-off; you have to believe that. It's never happened before, *ever*."

Lili looked at him for several seconds. "Yes it has."

He shook his head. "You're wrong."

"Michael, she rang me. From Dubai."

Jesus Christ, that bitch!

"When?" Reddening, Michael silently cursed Sandra; whatever had possessed her to do something so stupid? "She had no right to do that! When did she ring? And what did she tell you?"

Lili exhaled slowly. "Nothing. Nobody rang. I just said it to see how you'd react."

She wondered if she should be bursting into tears—surely she should be more upset than this?—but all she felt was an overwhelming sense of release.

"You mean you were *bluffing*?" Michael was incredulous.

"I just wanted to make sure I was right." Lili gave the colander one last shake, then carefully began tipping pasta on to plates. "And now I know I am."

Toby tore open the familiarly addressed envelope, wondering why he was even bothering to do so. He should have been throwing these letters, unopened, straight into the trash.

Or handing them over to the police, he thought wearily. Maybe the time had come to take that step.

"Toby Gillespie, useless actor. Isn't it time you moved on?"

That was all it said. Hardly a death threat.

He glanced up as Dizzy ambled into the sitting room.

"What's that?"

"Another of those letters, if you can call it that."

Frowning, Dizzy took it and read the wobbly words. He hadn't written this one, but if Eleanor Ferguson got to hear about it, she would think he had. *And let's face it*, he thought morosely, *everyone in this bloody village gets to hear about everything.*

Still, he couldn't help experiencing a brief pang of envy. Somebody else was still getting a kick out of doing what he was no longer allowed to do.

It was so unfair.

He handed the letter back to his father. "What are you going to do?"

"I don't know." Toby sighed. "Pass it on to the police."

Startled, Dizzy said, "They might get fed up and stop doing it. Then you wouldn't need to."

"I've been thinking that for months, but it hasn't happened yet. And now other people are getting them as well."

"I was in the shop this morning. Nobody's had anything for the last three days."

Grimly Toby held up the letter. "I have."

"I'd still leave it for a week or so." Dizzy was beginning to sweat. "You never know—this could be the last one."

—⁓—

Twenty minutes later, Toby heard footsteps on the stairs. When he glanced up, he saw Deborah rubbing perfume into her neck and wrists. She had changed her clothes and put on fresh makeup, he noticed.

Am I meant to ask where she's going?

Appalled, Toby realized he simply didn't care. The atmosphere in the house remained at subzero, and he had no urge to remedy it.

For all her surface charm, Deborah had always done exactly what she wanted.

Well, she could carry on doing it now, Toby thought, unmoved. It no longer bothered him.

Living separate lives suited him just fine.

—⁂—

Doug Flynn didn't look thrilled when he answered the door and found Deborah on the front step. He glanced across the green, wondering who else had spotted her there.

"This isn't a good idea."

"I didn't have much choice." Deborah was as elegant as ever in a black silk sweater, black trousers, and a cloud of Rive Gauche. "You've been avoiding me, Doug. And you aren't returning my calls."

These days, when Doug's cell phone began to ring, he habitually checked the caller's number as it flashed up. If he recognized it as Deborah's, he let voice mail pick up.

It had recorded quite a few lately.

"I told you, it's all too much of a risk. I don't want to be involved anymore."

"And I told you, I don't care about that." Deborah's dark eyes were bright with impatience. She wasn't the type to stamp her foot, but she looked as if she wanted to. Pushing the door farther open, she moved toward him. "Doug, let me in. I have to talk to you. I'm going mad next door. Toby's being a *pig*—"

"Jamie's upstairs."

"So? We'll talk quietly."

He sighed and let Deborah into the cottage. A scene on the doorstep was the last thing either of them needed. "Five minutes then. I'm on duty at six."

"But you aren't working this weekend, are you?"

Taken aback, Doug said, "How do you know?"

"Well, I hardly needed to hire a private investigator." Deborah gently mocked his astonishment. "I rang the emergency department, asked if you'd be there on Saturday afternoon. They said you had the whole weekend off."

"So?"

"So I thought we could go away together. I'll tell Toby I'm going up to London to stay with friends. You can—"

"I'm already going away."

"Great, I'll come with you."

"I've made other arrangements."

"Unmake them." Smiling, Deborah trailed her fingers down his cheek. "I mean, be honest. She wouldn't compare to me anyway, would she?"

Upstairs, they heard Jamie crashing around in his bedroom, hunting in his wardrobe for something clean to wear.

"At least she isn't married," said Doug. He wasn't taking anyone with him—he had an interview for a job in Manchester—but he was buggered if he was going to let Deborah know that.

"I may not be married for much longer," she said calmly. "I did my best, but Toby's never going to forgive me. I'm telling you, it's hell in that house. But you and I...we'd be brilliant together." Deborah's tone grew more urgent. "I've been thinking about it—you could jack in that lousy NHS job and go into private practice. Imagine, your own office in Harley Street! With your looks and my connections, how could it fail? You'd make a fortune as doctor to the stars. We could get you a stint on TV—"

"I don't want to be on television," Doug said coldly. "And I certainly don't want to spend my days doling out diet pills and telling neurotic thirty-year-old actresses they need a face-lift. Now, I have to get to work."

"Phone in. Tell them you're sick," Deborah pleaded, pressing herself against him. "You can't do this to me. Toby's such a bastard, he won't even sleep with me. I haven't had sex for weeks!"

Her desperation repulsed him. Doug managed to push her away moments before Jamie clattered downstairs in jeans and one of Drew's best shirts.

"It's just a minor eye infection," he told Deborah. "Keep using the drops and it'll clear up in a couple of days."

When he had shown her out and closed the front door, Jamie gave him an odd look.

"What was she doing here?"

"Nothing." Doug picked up his jacket and car keys. "Getting hysterical over a bit of conjunctivitis."

"But I thought I heard her say…" Jamie's courage failed him. "Um, I couldn't see any sign of conjunctivitis."

"Exactly." Doug's tone was curt as he made his way out. "She was just making a big fuss."

⁓

Drew and Jamie were the last to leave the Seven Bells that night. As they made their way across the green, Jamie was still harping on about Deborah Gillespie.

"I do, I reckon there's something going on between those two. It's that perfume she wears. I smelled it once before, that time Doug said he'd fallen asleep in the backyard. It was on his shirt. I swear it was."

"You've already told me this. About fifty times this evening." Drew was less enthralled. All he could think about was Lili, whom he hadn't dared to phone.

"I'm allowed to repeat myself; I'm drunk. And I swear I heard her say she hadn't had sex for weeks."

Drew muttered, "I know the feeling."

"Lucky bastard. What's he got that we haven't?"

"Good looks," said Drew.

"Huh."

"Sports car."

"Oh well."

"The letters MD after his name."

"Psh."

"And he treats women like dirt."

"I tried treating a bird like dirt once," Jamie said gloomily. "I really fancied her."

"What happened?"

"Bloody bitch dumped me."

"Who's that over there?"

"Eh?"

Drew squinted across the green. Ahead of them, fifty yards to the right of Keeper's Cottage, where Compass Lane joined Waters Lane, something was glinting in the darkness.

"Someone's trying to hide behind those bushes."

Jamie sounded hopeful. "Could be Deborah Gillespie and Doug having a shag."

Drew didn't think this was likely, but whoever it was, they were acting in a pretty furtive manner. "Come on. Let's see what they're up to."

When they reached the bushes, it didn't take a genius to work it out. The glinting had come from a can of spray paint. The sign saying WATERS LANE—the road on which Bernadette Thomas and Eleanor Ferguson lived—had been altered to read SEX-CHANGE LANE.

And the person crouching in the undergrowth clutching the spray can was Toby Gillespie's son, Dizzy.

Afterward, Drew realized that if the boy had looked a bit sheepish, given them an apologetic grin and maybe made a bit of a joke of it, they would more than likely have let him go. Compared with the drunken pranks they had played at college, defacing a road sign was pretty tame. But Dizzy hadn't tried to laugh it off. He had gazed at them, wide-eyed with horror, and made a frantic bid for freedom.

This had been his big mistake; years of rugby training had induced an almost Pavlovian reaction in Jamie.

If it moves, tackle it.

Jamie promptly hurled himself after Dizzy, grabbing him by the knees and bringing him to the ground with a thud.

Two white envelopes flew out of the back pocket of Dizzy's jeans, and the can of paint skidded across the grass.

"Let go of me! Just leave me alone!" Dizzy begged.

"Yes, let go of him," said Drew, embarrassed by Jamie's overreaction. Before the wind could catch Dizzy's envelopes and carry them off, he bent down and picked them up himself.

"What?" Deeply disappointed, Jamie said, "Can't I make a citizen's arrest?"

This was what nine pints of Guinness did to you—made you all of a sudden astonishingly law-abiding.

"No you can't."

Idly Drew turned the envelopes over. The next second his pulse began to quicken. Even in almost total blackness he could make out the writing on the front of them.

They were both stamped, and one was addressed to Toby Gillespie. The other was for Moll.

"Hang on to him," Drew instructed Jamie as he began to tear open the second envelope.

"Don't," Dizzy bleated, white-faced with terror. "You can't read that," he added in desperation. "It's private—it's not addressed to you!"

Chapter 58

"WHAT'S GOING ON?" TOBY Gillespie looked concerned when he opened the front door at midnight and found Drew Darcy on his doorstep.

"Sorry about this," said Drew, "but it's about your son."

"Dizzy? He's in bed."

Jamie dragged Dizzy across the gravel and into view.

"Here." Drew handed the two letters over to Toby. "I'll leave these with you. They fell out of Dizzy's pocket earlier."

Toby skimmed the contents in less than five seconds:

> *Moll,*
>
> *It's no fun sleeping with you anymore. All that silicone sloshing about sounds like two hot-water bottles strapped to your chest.*

The second one, addressed to him, said:

> *You're a lousy actor. Nobody wants you here. Sell your house and move back to London.*

Oh Christ, thought Toby. *I do not believe this.*

"Thanks," he told Drew evenly, wondering if life could possibly get more disastrous. "I'll take over now."

⁓

"It's not fair!" Dizzy wailed. "I get the blame for everything! I didn't *start* it!"

Toby rubbed his hands over his face. "You mean there are two people in this village sending anonymous letters?"

"Yes, yes!"

"Oh, Dizzy." He shook his head. Discovering that the person who had been sending you hate mail was your own son...now that *was* a kick in the teeth.

"Honest!" Dizzy was desperate. Not being believed was awful. "Somebody else started it and I just kind of...joined in. I made them look the same, that's all."

Still skeptical, Toby said, "Why?"

"Dunno. For a laugh."

"A *laugh?*"

Dizzy shifted uncomfortably on the sofa and pulled the frayed sleeves of his sweater up over his knuckles. "I hate it here. I wanted you to sell the house, move back to London."

"And how long did you think you'd be able to get away with this?"

Dizzy nodded miserably at the two letters lying on the coffee table between them. "These were the last ones. Then I was going to stop." He tried to be as honest as he could. "I stopped three days ago. Then this morning you got one of the other ones. I didn't send that one." He glanced up to see if his father believed him. "But you were talking about going to the police, so I thought I'd just have one last go."

"Go at what?"

"Making you sell the house."

Toby sighed. Then he tapped the other letter. "And this one? Have you really slept with Moll?"

Dizzy looked as if he might cry. His bottom lip wobbled.

"No, but everybody else has."

———

Felicity Seymour, never having been much of a pub person, was astounded to find herself enjoying her visits to the Seven Bells more and more.

At first, when Hugh had made his twice-weekly visits to the house to see Freya, she had shut herself upstairs in her room and sobbed. After a couple of weeks, however, when the sobbing had subsided, she'd taken to going for a drive or calling in on Lili for coffee and a chat.

One evening when she had dropped by with three long hours to kill, Lili had been strapping Will into his stroller and attempting to drag a brush through Lottie's tangled curls.

"It's such a gorgeous evening, I thought we'd go to the pub," Lili had explained. "The kids love playing in the yard, and Lorna doesn't mind as long as they stay outside."

Hesitating, not wanting to be a third wheel, Felicity had asked, "Will Drew be there?"

Lili had finished brushing Play-Doh out of Lottie's hair and straightened up. "I don't know."

"Have you spoken to him yet?"

Vigorously, Lili shook her head. "God no! Poor chap. He's probably scared witless. One minute he's having a bit of a harmless flirt with an old married woman, then…*whooomph!* The next thing he knows, she's kicked out her husband."

"Maybe it's what he wanted to happen."

"I don't think so." Lili had spent hours perfecting her careless smile. "I mean, let's be honest. If you were Drew, would you want to be saddled with someone else's three kids?"

"I still think you should phone him," said Felicity.

"Better if I don't." Lili, who had her pride, had spoken as if it couldn't matter less. But inside her brain, the same words kept churning around and around like a washing machine: if he wanted to, he could always phone me.

From that first sunny evening at the Seven Bells, Felicity had been struck by the friendliness of the bar staff. When Lili had prepared to leave with her children, Lorna Blake had cornered Felicity and said in her husky, do-as-I-tell-you voice, "You can stay for one more, can't you? Go on, I could do with the company." And whisking her empty glass from her, not even giving her a chance to refuse, she had filled it to the brim with Frascati.

The pair of them had clicked immediately. Felicity had no idea why—they could hardly be more different, after all—but somehow their differences were irrelevant. Lorna was simply easy to talk to. Beneath the brusque exterior, the cynical smile, and the troweled-on makeup, Felicity suspected, lay an altogether gentler character than Lorna liked to make out.

Tonight she had come to the pub on her own and found it practically deserted.

"The darts team are playing an away match," Lorna drawled. "And they're such useless buggers they needed the rest of my regulars to cheer them on."

The lack of customers meant they could talk uninterrupted.

"How's it going with Hugh?" Lorna asked, lighting up her umpteenth cigarette and leaning her elbows companionably on the bar.

Felicity shrugged. "It's easier being out of the house while he's there."

"Seeing anyone else, is he?"

Only Lorna could ask such a blunt question and make her laugh. *I'm getting better*, Felicity thought with gratitude. *Only a couple of weeks ago I'd have burst into floods of tears.*

Instead, she said mischievously, "Why? Interested?"

Lorna almost choked on her Scotch. "Not my type!"

"No, well, you aren't his type either." Felicity took a deep breath; until now she hadn't told anyone other than Lili and Jess. "Hugh's gay."

"Is he?" Raising one painted eyebrow, Lorna looked amused. "So am I."

"Oh, good Lord!" It simply hadn't occurred to Felicity before. She had vaguely assumed Lorna Blake to be a divorcée, childless by choice. "Am I the only person in the village who didn't know?"

The corner of Lorna's mouth twitched. "No, you're the only one who does."

An hour later, while they were discussing the hopelessness of the darts team with Moll, one of Lorna's cats appeared behind the bar, snaking itself around Moll's shapely legs. Moll looked as if she'd quite like to give it a kick.

Lorna, cooing like a mother hen, scooped the purring creature up into her arms. "Who's my beautiful boy, then? You shouldn't be down here. Oh no you shouldn't."

Moll made sick noises and rolled her eyes.

"Just ignore her," Lorna whispered consolingly in the cat's ear. "She's horrible."

Felicity put out a hand and stroked the soft fur. "I love cats. I'm thinking of getting one when I move into the new house."

Beneath the heftily applied layers of mascara, Lorna's eyes lit up. "I haven't introduced you to the rest of the family yet! Why don't you come up and meet them properly?"

"Um…" Felicity hesitated and checked her watch.

"Of course," Lorna went on hurriedly, "if you'd rather not—"

"I'd love to," said Felicity before Lorna could think she was afraid to venture upstairs alone with her. She slid off her barstool.

"Think you can manage down here?" Lorna winked at Moll.

At that moment, the door swung open and Drew Darcy came in, closely followed by Doug Flynn. Moll, glad she'd worn the emerald-green bra and low-cut red velvet top, felt Doug's dark gaze flicker over her and registered his approval.

Running her tongue briefly over her lips to make them glisten, she breathed in to let Lorna past. "Don't worry about me." Moll's grin was confident. "You know I always give the customers what they want."

Chapter 59

UPSTAIRS, FELICITY WAS FORMALLY introduced to the other two cats. Then Lorna pulled a photograph album out of a drawer and lovingly went through every page, pointing out each of them as kittens.

"We'd only cramp Moll's style if we went back down," she told Felicity. "Shall I put the kettle on? I fancy a cup of tea."

This made Felicity smile. "You don't seem the tea type. I thought you drank gin for breakfast, gin for lunch, and gin for tea."

"People aren't always the way they seem." Back from the tiny kitchen, Lorna leaned against the doorframe. "As you've discovered tonight." She pulled a face. "As we all discovered the other week when Bernadette Thomas came hurtling in here and punched Michael Ferguson off his stool."

"I don't know…" Felicity sighed, fondling the youngest cat's ears. "One way or another, husbands always manage to be embarrassing." *Embarrassing*—that was an understatement. Hers had wrecked her life.

"Do you want to talk about Hugh?"

Felicity glanced nervously again at her watch. "I said I'd be home by ten. He's meant to be meeting up with…um, someone, later."

"You mean his new chap?" Calmly Lorna picked up the phone and passed it across. "Give him a ring. Say you'll be late."

Feeling terribly daring, Felicity did as she was told. It gave her a thrill to hear the note of irritation in his voice. Now Hugh would have to cancel his night out, and he so hated letting people down. Other people, that was. Wives didn't count.

"But who are you with?" he demanded.

Lorna, eavesdropping next to her, shook her head.

"Just a friend," said Felicity.

"Are you at Lili's house?"

"No."

Irritation was replaced by curiosity. "So where then? Is this a male friend?"

Vigorously, Lorna nodded.

"Hugh, you aren't the only one allowed to have male friends, okay? I'll be back by midnight."

Pleased with herself, Felicity put the phone down. "I don't know why that makes me feel better, but it does."

Lorna grinned and lit yet another cigarette. "Make yourself comfortable. I'll go and make that tea."

Felicity had told her everything, and Lorna listened without interrupting her once. Downstairs as the clock struck eleven, they heard Moll call time at the bar.

Twenty minutes later, she poked her head around the door. "All cleared up. See you in the morning."

When the door had closed behind her, Lorna glanced with amusement at Felicity, who was clearly confused.

"Must be Doug's lucky night."

The next moment amusement turned to dismay as Felicity burst into tears.

Feeling helpless, Lorna watched her sob. She so wanted to put a comforting arm around her but didn't quite dare in case Felicity thought it was a come-on.

Instead, she made another pot of tea, opened a fresh box of

tissues because Felicity had gone through the last lot, and waited for the torrent of tears to end.

It did, finally.

"Sorry…sorry. It was just saying it was Doug's lucky night." Miserably, Felicity blinked her red-rimmed eyes. "I mean, it's not that I want to be Moll—"

"I should think not," Lorna interjected brusquely. "Girl's a slut. She's slept with more men than I've had double Scotches."

"But I've never slept with any." A fresh tear the size of a pea rolled down the side of Felicity's nose. "It's never been any man's lucky night with me. I'm so useless and stupid and…and a-a-ashamed of myself… Oh God!" She buried her face in her hands. "I wish I'd never told you now. You must think I'm a pathetic case."

"I don't, I don't. We've all done things we're ashamed of." As Lorna said it, the hairs at the back of her neck began to prickle and she knew the time had come. She couldn't bottle it up any longer; she needed to confide in someone as badly as Felicity had needed to confide in her.

Without even thinking, she reached out and touched Felicity's thin hand. "You've told me your embarrassing thing. Now I'll tell you mine. Hang on, I need a drink before I do this."

When she had splashed an inch of gin into a tumbler, Lorna crossed to the mantelpiece and took down a photograph in a frame.

"I saw it earlier when you were in the kitchen," Felicity said. She looked again at the picture of a younger Lorna, sitting on a wall with her arm around the shoulder of another girl in a wheelchair. "Who is she?"

"My twin sister, Paula. She was mentally handicapped." One of the cats jumped onto Lorna's lap and lay there purring, lazily kneading its paws. Lorna closed her eyes. "She died ten years ago. I loved her so much."

Felicity didn't say anything. Lorna gulped down her gin and

went on. "Paula was besotted with Toby Gillespie. Her room was plastered with pictures of him, she watched videos of his films endlessly. She even called her cat Toby."

"I called my goldfish Adam," said Felicity, "after Adam Ant."

Lorna smiled briefly. "Anyway, Paula wrote to him asking for a signed photo. After six weeks, when nothing had arrived, I sent her a letter myself, pretending it was from him." The smile had gone now; her expression was grim. "Paula didn't know the difference, of course. She was thrilled."

"Oh no," said Felicity, "don't tell me. She found out."

"No. She developed pneumonia. And I, stupidly giving Toby Gillespie the benefit of the doubt, wrote to him myself." Lorna took another slug of gin. Her hands shook as she lit a cigarette. "I told him all about Paula and how ill she was and begged him to come and see her." A longer pause. "I even offered to pay."

Felicity's eyes were wide. "And did he get in touch?"

Lorna shook her head. "No. He ignored my letter too. We lived in Devon then, and a week later there were pictures in all the papers of the Gillespies on vacation in Devon. They were staying less than five miles away," she went on bitterly, "and he couldn't even be bothered to spare an hour to visit my sister." She took a shuddering breath. "Three days later, Paula died."

"But that wasn't your fault!" Felicity exclaimed. "You didn't do anything to be ashamed of!"

Lorna shook her head. "Haven't you figured it out yet? It was me, sending the anonymous letters."

"You! But how could it have been you? It was Dizzy Gillespie," said Felicity, bewildered. "They caught him red-handed."

A crooked smile, wreathed in cigarette smoke. "Dizzy got the idea from me. He wanted Toby to sell the house almost as much as I did. I couldn't help it," said Lorna in a low voice. "Toby Gillespie had let my sister down. I hated him with a vengeance. I couldn't bear the thought of him living here…and everyone thinking he was so great. I just wanted to hurt him as much as he'd hurt our family."

Felicity sat back, struggling to take it all in. She shook her head. "Well, I can understand that. It seems odd though," she said diffidently. "I mean, I don't know Toby Gillespie, but I do know he does a lot of work for charity. From what I've heard, he doesn't seem the kind of person who'd ignore a cry for help."

"That's what I thought." Lorna pressed her lips together. "But he'd ignored mine, so I carried on sending the letters." *And the pizzas and the endless taxis*, she thought with a pang of guilt. "Then, last week, I overheard Savannah in the bar, complaining that her father was too busy to play tennis with her. She said, 'Ten hours he's been sitting there, working through a drawerful of fan mail. He even had the nerve to tell me if I was bored, I could stamp the envelopes.' And when Oliver asked her why Toby didn't employ a secretary to deal with them, Savannah said, 'He doesn't trust anyone else to do it. He had a useless PA years ago.' Apparently," Lorna said drily, "it wasn't until after he'd sacked her that he discovered she'd been chucking all the fan letters in the trash unopened because she couldn't be bothered to read them."

Chapter 60

HONESTLY, SAVANNAH THOUGHT, LIFTING her sunglasses to get a better view. She liked Moll, but there was no getting away from it—the girl was a complete tart.

As she approached the pub and took a closer look at the person Moll was flinging her arms around, Savannah changed that to a tart with taste. This guy, whoever he might be, was gorgeous.

Savannah wondered idly what it was about lean, rangy men on motorbikes, with leather trousers and dark hair curling over their collars, that made them so irresistible.

Moll was still hugging him when Savannah reached them. Turning at the sound of footsteps, Moll grinned at Savannah.

"What d'you think then? Not bad?"

God, how embarrassing! Aware that the boy on the motorbike was lazily surveying her, Savannah shrugged and went pink.

"Aren't you jealous?" teased Moll.

Argh, this was awful. Never mind pink; now she was aubergine. Worse still, she had the most terrifying urge to yell "*Yes yes yes!*"

"Ignore her," said the boy on the bike, addressing Savannah and pinching Moll's ample waist. "She's far too fat for me. I go for girls who can ride pillion without bursting my tires."

Savannah gazed at him, lost for words.

"God, you're rude!" In retaliation, Moll gave him a good-natured punch on the arm. But she'd forgiven him already. Never mind bursting tires; she wanted to burst with pride. Not that he deserved it, of course, thought Moll. She just couldn't help it. She loved him so much. "Sav, meet Stevie," she announced joyfully, "my completely vile little brother."

I love Oliver, I love Oliver, Savannah repeated over and over in her mind. Perched on her stool next to the bar, she tapped her fingers on her thighs in time with the words in an effort to keep the mantra going.

Oh, but it was hard, when your gaze kept sliding—practically of its own accord—to the other end of the bar.

Especially when every time you glimpsed those strong, suntanned arms, that dark, curly hair, and that heavenly smile, something low down in the very pit of your stomach went *piiing…*

Not that Oliver didn't have a heavenly smile too, of course. And a gorgeous body. But there was no getting away from the fact that the *piiing* factor had been sadly lacking in recent weeks.

Savannah, forgetting to tap and picking at the edges of a coaster instead, couldn't help reflecting that things in that department weren't what they used to be. Maintaining eternal optimism in the face of impotence wasn't easy. She'd done her level best to be patient and understanding, but where was it getting her?

Not laid, that was for sure.

Oliver, who was wiping down the bar, had noticed the way Savannah kept glancing down the bar and quickly back again. He lowered his voice. "Do you like him?"

Startled, Savannah said, "What?"

"Moll's brother. I mean, he's good-looking, isn't he?"

"So?"

She was definitely on the defensive. *This could be it*, thought Oliver with a surge of hope. *This could be the answer to everything.*

"Look," he murmured, "I'd understand. I know it hasn't been easy for you, what with…well, the way things are. I wouldn't mind if you…well, you know."

Savannah stared at him. Was he *serious*? What did he expect her to say? *Oh, okay then. We'll carry on being secretly in love with each other but on Tuesday and Friday evenings I'll slope off with some tall, dark total stranger and have mindless sex?*

God, it was like a husband whose idea of hell was trailing around the shops saying, "You know I don't care much for that kind of thing, dear. Why don't you go with one of your friends instead?"

"Are you *mad*?" Savannah declared furiously. "What do you think I am, a complete sex maniac?"

"No, no. I just—"

"Shut up then," she hissed, "because I don't even fancy him, okay?" She shot a look of disdain in Stevie Harper's direction to prove her point. "He couldn't be less my type."

Ten minutes later, on her way back from the loo, Savannah bumped into Stevie in the corridor.

"You gave me a terrible look just now. I saw you," he admonished. "What did I do to deserve that?"

There was no getting away from it—he was outrageously attractive. Her stomach pinging for all it was worth, Savannah flicked back her hair and said, "Nothing."

Talk about original. But Stevie didn't seem to mind.

"I asked Moll about you. I thought the blond guy behind the bar might be your boyfriend, but she tells me he's your brother."

"That's right."

"So how about you and me going for a drink tomorrow night?"

He was smiling at her. She could smell soap and leather and that sexy, oily, motorbike smell. He also had the longest eyelashes she'd ever seen.

She squirmed with desire. "I thought that's what we were doing now."

"Come on, you know what I mean—without your big brother and my big sister looking on."

"I don't know anything about you." It was a feeble protest.

"Ah well, now's your chance to find out. I'll pick you up at eight. We'll go into Harleston."

Savannah thought, *I haven't even said yes.*

But then, was it ever likely that she'd say no?

She nodded quickly. "Okay, but don't pick me up." She was buggered if Oliver was going to find out about this. "I'll meet you at the Iguana Bar in Brunswick Square."

———

"Haven't seen you here for a while," said Lorna.

Toby's smile was brief. "I've been trying to spend more time with Dizzy. Not that he's too impressed."

"Scotch?"

Lorna wished her hands would stop shaking. Felicity had said, "You should tell him, explain everything. Just admit it was you and let him know how sorry you are." Calmly she'd added, "I'm sure he'd understand."

Maybe he would, but Lorna cringed at the thought of admitting the letters had come from her. She wasn't the apologizing type.

"A large one," Toby said as she poured some Johnny Walker. "I need it."

He looked tired. There were dark shadows beneath his eyes, and his jaw was set. *Hardly surprising*, Lorna thought with a rush of guilt. *He's been the victim of a hate campaign and he hasn't even done anything to deserve it.*

"On the house," she said brusquely as Toby held out a tenner.

"Oh, thanks." He looked taken aback, as well he might. She had never offered to buy him a drink before.

Say it, say it.

Don't go on, Lorna begged her nagging conscience. *I just can't.*

But Oliver, back from the cellar, had spotted Toby. He'd be over in a minute to say hello, and the opportunity would be lost.

"Actually, I'm glad you came in. There's something I need to tell you."

Aargh, what am I doing?

"Oh?" Toby looked wary. "About Savannah? What's she been up to now?"

"Nothing. Well, not that I know of," Lorna amended. It seemed unlikely that a pretty, blond teenager wouldn't be up to something, somewhere along the line. "The thing is, being a pub owner is a bit like being a priest. People have a few drinks and confide in you. And they trust you not to blab their secrets around the village."

"I see." Toby wondered just how bad this was going to be. His stomach lurched. Was it something to do with Jess?

"Dizzy didn't write all those anonymous letters. Some of them were sent by someone else in the village." Lorna lit a cigarette, forgetting the one already smoldering in the ashtray.

Toby looked at her. "Who?"

She shook her head. "I can't tell you that. I promised I wouldn't. But they're very sorry. It was never meant to be malicious. It was just a—well, a prank that got out of hand." She swallowed, forcing herself to meet Toby Gillespie's steady gaze. "And they want you to know it's over now. They'll never do it again."

———

Oliver was desperate for sex. It was seriously starting to get him down. What with fending off Savannah—who was so anxious to cure him she had recently started dropping dark hints about counseling and therapists—and not seeing anyone else because there simply wasn't the opportunity, he was beginning to feel like a heroin addict in need of a fix.

"You're working tonight, aren't you?" Savannah asked when she called into Duck Cottage at lunchtime.

"Mmm."

Oliver was eating his way through a packet of Jammy Dodgers and reading an article in the paper about touring Scandinavia by bus. Plenty of beautiful blonds with liberated attitudes in Scandinavia.

"It's just that I won't be coming to the pub. One of my friends is down from London, staying with her stepfather in Cheltenham. She rang and invited me over for the evening."

Oliver didn't dare look up. Reaching across the kitchen table, he helped himself to another cookie. "Fine."

"You don't mind, do you? It won't be that great, but she begged me to go. We'll just have a couple of drinks and a girlie gossip—"

"Of course I don't mind."

Go. Go!

As soon as Savannah had left, Oliver leaped to his feet and dialed the pub.

"Moll, is that you? Moll, you know I love you."

"What do you want?" said Moll.

"It's your evening off tonight, right?"

"You can't whisk me away to Paris, Oliver. You're working."

He grinned; she knew exactly what he wanted.

"Swap?"

She kept him dangling for a second. "What's in it for me?"

"My share of next week's tips."

"Ha! That just gives you an excuse to spend the next seven days being vile to everybody."

"Please?"

"Okay."

"Moll, you're brilliant." Exultantly, Oliver reached for the phone book.

"Yeah, I know."

―――

He picked Mel up from her apartment at seven o'clock on the dot.

"So, what's brought this on?" Mel's Lycra skirt slithered up her thighs as she climbed into the passenger seat. "Three months of deafening silence, then a phone call out of the blue. I thought you'd emigrated or died or something."

It was good to see Mel again. Oliver leaned over and kissed her. "No, still alive. There's just been a lot going on recently. Working and family stuff…you know."

"I read about it in the papers. Imagine, Toby Gillespie turning out to be your dad. What's he like?"

"Great."

"And the rest of them?" Mel was incurably nosy. "Are they okay?"

Oliver nodded, still smiling. If it was good to see Mel again, it was even better knowing that four drinks and she was anybody's.

"I saw the photos of you and the daughter. Savannah, that's her name isn't it? She's really pretty."

Oliver didn't want to talk about Savannah. He'd come out tonight to get away from all that.

He said, "So are you."

The engine was still idling; they hadn't pulled away from the curb yet.

Mel looked at him. "I wouldn't want you to think I was cheap…"

"I'd never do that," Oliver assured her. "Have you seen the price of those things you drink lately?"

Mel burst out laughing. They'd always got on so well together. And the sex had never been less than brilliant. "I was just going to say, the apartment's empty. We don't have to go out yet."

"You might think I'm cheap," Oliver protested.

"I won't. I promise."

"You're a terrible influence on an innocent, young country boy," Oliver sighed, flicking off the ignition. "Go on then. You've twisted my arm."

Chapter 61

LESS THAN A MILE away, in the Iguana Bar, Savannah was having a weak-at-the-knees experience. Watching heads swivel in admiration as Stevie Harper made his way toward her, she wondered why Oliver no longer had this kind of effect on her.

Except, deep down, she knew the answer. It was because Oliver might give the impression of being sexy, but it was all a facade. It was like trying to have a meaningful relationship with a poster of your favorite pop star.

"Hi." Stevie looked as if he was about to kiss her, then stopped at the last second. Talk about being in control. God, he was so gorgeous, so *cool*.

And that was the difference between him and Oliver, Savannah thought with a shudder of pleasure as she watched him stride easily up to the bar. When you looked at Stevie Harper you knew—you just knew for sure—that he delivered what he promised.

He simply wasn't the impotent type.

--~~~--

Oliver was happy. This was more like it: terrific sex and no complications.

Thank heavens for Mel.

Beneath the duvet, warm fingers began to dance their way up the inside of his thigh.

"We don't have to get up. We could just stay here," she suggested.

Oliver was tempted, but that wouldn't be fair to her. "No, we'll go out. You said you wanted to see that friend of yours before she leaves for the States."

"She'll be in the Iguana Bar," Mel said happily.

"What's going on?" Oliver breathed out slowly as the warm hand traveled farther up his thigh.

Mel, her eyes bright and her hair tousled, murmured, "We don't have to be there before nine."

—∿∿—

Savannah hoped she didn't look as idiotically besotted as she felt. She was trying so hard to play it cool, but it wasn't easy when your body all of a sudden appeared to be swarming with too much electricity.

Stevie Harper might be only twenty-three, but he had been everywhere and done everything.

Toured the United States on his motorbike.

Worked out there briefly as a stunt double.

Tried—even more briefly—a spot of modeling.

"It was a nightmare. They kept nagging at me to wear moisturizer," Stevie told her with disgust, "and panicking that I'd fly off my bike and wreck my face."

Savannah was mesmerized. "What did you do next?"

"Worked as a croupier in Las Vegas, washed dishes in a few hotels, had a bash at male prostitution. Anything really"—he shrugged—"to earn a bit of cash."

Savannah's mouth dropped open.

"Joke," said Stevie. "Just wanted to make sure you were paying attention."

He's teasing me, Savannah thought joyfully. *I love it, love it, love it.*

"So how long have you been back in this country?"

"Three months. I headed down to the south coast, took a job with a traveling fair."

"A fair! Which ride?"

She knew at once it had to be one of the rides. Stevie wasn't the three-darts-for-a-pound, win-a-goldfish type.

"Tilt-A-Whirl." His dark eyes glittered with remembered amusement. "Spinning the chairs, making all the girls scream for more."

"This is making me feel *so* much better about failing my exams." Savannah sighed.

"Why?"

"Well, look at you!" Crikey, she couldn't *stop* looking at him; he was the long-haired, leather-trousered, rebellious bad boy of her dreams. "You didn't need them, did you? You just went out there and did stuff." She flung her arms wide. "*Exciting stuff—*"

"I've got a certificate in music," Stevie offered.

"Exactly!"

"And eleven in academic subjects. And four A levels. Oh," he added, "and a degree in physics."

"Wow!" Savannah was dumbfounded.

But impressed.

"I'm sorry." Stevie raised an inquiring eyebrow. "Have I blown it? Do you prefer your men thick?"

"No, *no!*"

Heavens, he was perfect. Now even her parents would love him too. *Except… Oh God—*

"What?" said Stevie.

"How long are you going to be here?" The words tumbled out in a panic. If he was only visiting Moll for a few days before disappearing again, how could she bear it?

Stevie looked at her. "No plans. If there's a good reason to stay, I'll stay."

"Oh."

"So which would you prefer?"

"What?"

"Shall I stick around?" He put his drink down and rose to his feet. "Or go?"

"Don't!" Savannah shrieked without thinking.

People at nearby tables turned and stared. She bit her lip, trying to ignore them.

"Oh dear." Stevie started to laugh. "Now everyone thinks I put my hand up your skirt."

"Sit down," Savannah pleaded, but instead of sitting, he was pulling her upright.

"In a minute. I'm afraid I have to kiss you first."

By this time, they were the center of attention, but Savannah no longer cared. Stevie Harper was a heavenly kisser, and the way his hands were sliding over her bare shoulders made all the little hairs on her arms stand on end.

Keeping her eyes closed, Savannah willed the kiss to go on forever and let her own trembling fingers begin to roam over the back pockets of his leather jeans.

She didn't know how she was going to break the news to Oliver; he'd be devastated when he found out.

Still, never mind about that now. This was meant to happen, Savannah thought ecstatically. *This is fate.*

When the kiss finally ended, she opened her eyes and gazed up at Stevie. God, he was divine…

"Somebody's watching us," he told her.

"Blimey, I should think everyone is."

"I'm talking about your brother."

It was like someone saying, "Don't look now, but there's a spider the size of a *dinner* plate behind you." You still had to look.

Cringing, because this was worse than any spider, Savannah peeled herself away from Stevie and turned slowly around.

There was Oliver with a strange expression on his face.

And a pretty, dark-haired girl clinging lovingly to his arm.

—◦◦◦—

"Well," Oliver said when everyone had been introduced. Mel had dashed to the loo and Stevie was over at the bar ordering more drinks. "This is…interesting."

Since they only had a couple of minutes, Savannah thought she may as well come right out and say it.

"I really like him."

Oliver nodded. "So I noticed."

"Do you really like her?" She jerked her head in the direction of the loos.

"Mel's an ex of mine. She's good fun."

Baffled, recalling the way Mel had acted while Oliver was introducing her, Savannah said, "Does she know she's an ex? Have you *told* her you're impotent?"

Oliver's dark eyes flickered.

"Oh, oh, I *see*." All of a sudden Savannah understood; it was like finally figuring out a magic trick. "You aren't, are you? You're not impotent."

"Sorry."

Savannah knew she should be outraged. Instead, she felt like a caged bird unexpectedly set free. All these weeks she had done her best to convince herself she still loved Oliver.

But she hadn't—not really. He had been a crush, that was all, a fixation that had escalated because it was forbidden. And by the time that hurdle had been overcome, the crush had run its course.

As teenage crushes do.

"Well, I'm glad," said Savannah with a faint smile. "For your sake, I mean."

"It wouldn't have felt right." Oliver sounded relieved too. "I think we get on better as brother and sister."

Back from the loo, Mel bounced up to them.

"What's this about getting on better? God, that's abnormal—me and my brother fight like cat and dog!"

Savannah and Oliver grinned at each other.

"We're pretty new to it," said Oliver, as Stevie returned with the drinks. "Give us time. We will too."

—᠁—

"What have you got that the rest of us haven't?" Jamie protested. "Lorna never says 'on the house' when I'm buying a drink."

"It's Felicity's last night in the village," said Lorna. "She's moving to Cheltenham tomorrow."

"I'll buy you a drink," Felicity told him.

"Will you?" Jamie looked surprised and ridiculously pleased.

"There." Lorna filled his pint glass with best bitter and slid it in front of him. "Now perhaps you'll cheer up."

"I can't cheer up." Jamie sounded mournful. "I'm depressed."

Lorna snorted with laughter and winked at Felicity. "You! A strapping young lad with a good job. What have you got to be depressed about?"

"I'm a strapping young lad with a good job and no girlfriend," Jamie announced gloomily. "And no bloody sex life."

This was his seventh pint.

"Oh well, that's tragic." Lorna lifted his elbow out of a puddle of beer and briskly wiped the bar dry.

"It is. It's *bloody* tragic. Especially when you're sharing a house with Dr. Kil-bloody-dare. It's sickening, I tell you." Jamie shook his head. "And it's not *fair*. He gets sex sex sex all the time, and I don't get any of it."

Well, thought Felicity, *I know how that feels.*

Lorna was doing her best to be philosophical. "Ah, but is he happy?"

Jamie gazed at her in incredulous, slightly cross-eyed fashion. "Wouldn't you be?"

"Look," said Felicity, feeling unaccountably brave, "sex isn't the be-all and end-all. There are other things in life, you know."

"Huh," said Jamie. "Name five."

"Rugby, cricket, lager." Lorna was still trying to help. "Um, getting drunk…"

"That doesn't count." Jamie was scornful. "It's the same as lager."

Lorna's patience ran out. "Oh well, maybe Mother Nature's trying to tell you something. You could just be useless in bed."

Felicity winced. The expression on Jamie's face was so despondent she wanted to give him a big hug.

"But the thing is, I'm not. I'm pretty good," he said sorrowfully, "when I get the chance."

An hour later Lorna called time, and the few remaining regulars made their way out. Felicity, by now sitting at a corner table with Jamie, watched Lorna busy herself with the clearing up.

"I should be getting home," she told Jamie.

Five gin and tonics were more than she was used to, but Felicity didn't feel fuzzy-headed. And why shouldn't she have a few drinks, anyway? The house had been sold. It was her last night in the village, and Hugh had taken Freya over to his place to allow her to get the packing finished without interruption. That was all done now. Everything was in boxes ready to go into the moving van. By this time tomorrow, she'd be back with her parents. Just temporarily, of course, until she found a place of her own—but she knew only too well what the next few weeks would be like.

Back in my old bedroom, thought Felicity, not much looking forward to the prospect, *with my mother fussing over me, telling me I'm too thin and forcing me to eat steak and kidney pie.*

She knew, too, exactly what her mother would be like with Freya. Trying so hard not to take over but unable to resist saying, "Darling, why don't we try doing it *this* way?"

I've been married, I've given birth, and I'm an intelligent, successful businesswoman…and it isn't going to make a blind bit of difference to my mother, Felicity thought with rising frustration. *As far as she's concerned, I'm still her shy, gawky, virginal teenager.*

Well, the virginal bit was still true.

"One more drink," said Jamie, his hand brushing against hers as he reached for her empty glass.

"The pub's closed."

"Ah, Lorna won't mind." He gave her a conspiratorial wink before raising his voice. "Lorna? One for the road?"

"No. Go home."

Jamie looked crestfallen. "You're no fun."

Lorna was behind the bar, cashing out the till. She looked at the two of them, sitting so close together their knees were practically touching. "If you want to carry on yakking, why don't you ask Felicity back to your place for a drink?"

Jamie brightened, then his shoulders sagged again. "Doug's there with some nurse."

Lorna shrugged and raised an eyebrow fractionally in Felicity's direction.

"What are you doing?" said Felicity, when Jamie had ambled off to the loo.

"Oh, come on. I've been watching the pair of you for the last hour. Don't tell me it hasn't occurred to you."

"Are you serious? You think I should take him home, throw him on to my bed, and *ravish* him?"

Lorna shrugged. "It's your last night. You have a virginity you want to be rid of. And you do *like* him."

"I hardly know him!" wailed Felicity.

"You knew Hugh and look where that got you."

"Lorna, I couldn't possibly. It would be too…too…sordid for words."

"Okay, just a suggestion. Forget I mentioned it."

Felicity hesitated, biting her lip. "Anyway, he's drunk."

"Not that drunk," said Lorna, who had been quietly serving Jamie alcohol-free beer for the last hour and a half. "I'm sure he'd manage." She smiled slightly before adding, "And he did say he was good in bed."

Chapter 62

LILI WAS DOING A bit of frenzied dusting in the living room when she heard footsteps on the gravel outside.

Quickly hiding the can of spray polish in case it was Eleanor (*Oh, Lili, you should use Mansion Wax; how can you expect something out of an aerosol to nourish the wood?*), she raced through to the kitchen and swept all the cornflake-encrusted cereal bowls off the table and into the sink.

Opening the door, Lili heaved a sigh of relief.

"Thank goodness it's you! I thought you were my mother-in-law carrying out one of her dawn raids. Oh my word, are those for me?"

It wasn't dawn, it was nine thirty in the morning, but Felicity looked as if she'd been up for hours. In a crisp, pink shirt and extremely clean jeans, she looked as glossy and bright-eyed as a squirrel.

"Just to say thank you for looking after Freya. Well, and for everything else." She beamed at Lili, thrust the massive bunch of white lilies into her arms, and plonked two bottles of champagne on the kitchen table.

"Heavens, moving house must really suit you." Lili was full of admiration. "Most people look totally frazzled, but you're...well, you're *glowing*."

She was. It was extraordinary. Eleanor would certainly approve, Lili decided. Felicity looked as if she'd been given a thorough going over with a tin of Mansion Wax.

"It's a new start. I'm going to make the most of it," Felicity agreed happily.

Impulsively, Lili ripped the foil off one of the bottles and unfastened the wire. "Then we definitely have to celebrate. Just one glass each," she said as the cork flew out, "to toast your brilliant new life. There. If my mother-in-law turns up now, she'll really know I've gone to the dogs."

The moving men were arriving at ten o'clock. Lottie, Will, and Blitz sat in the other room glued to a Teletubbies video, and Lili wondered why Felicity looked as if she were bursting to tell her a secret but was unable to find the words.

Instead, they talked about Freya and the smart day care she would be attending in Cheltenham while Felicity was at work, then about Will and the decidedly un-smart new habit he had of weeing in his potty, then trying to wash his hands in it.

"I was fast asleep this morning," said Lili, "when Lottie came into the bedroom, tapped me on the shoulder, and said, 'Mummy, can you and me sing "If you're happy and you know it clap your hands"?'"

Felicity grinned. She was happy and she certainly knew it. She was also dying to tell Lili about last night... Oh, but what if Lili thought she was a slut?

Instead, she said, "Any news of Drew?"

Lili shook her head. She hadn't seen him for weeks now. Impossible though it seemed in a village this size, Drew had managed to turn himself into the invisible man.

He clearly wasn't interested. Then again, why should he be? She was no Jennifer Garner.

Dammit, she wasn't even a James Garner...

Oh well, she thought with the resigned sigh of one who has been over it a thousand times. *I suppose I'll live.*

Two minutes later, they both jumped a mile as the doorbell rang.

"Shit, it's my mother-in-law! Hide the bottles, give me the glasses, run a dish towel under the cold water—"

"Why?" Felicity looked startled.

"If Eleanor smells alcohol on my breath, she's going to snort fire out of her nostrils."

But Blitz was barking and Lottie, in the front room, had climbed onto a chair in order to peer out of the bay window. With a shriek of delight, she yelled, "Mum, open the door! It's Drew!"

Even if he hadn't been in love with her already, Drew's heart would have melted at the sight of Lili's tentative, struggling-to-be-normal smile. It was hopeless; keeping his distance for the past few weeks had half killed him, and what good had it done?

None at all.

Not one bloody iota.

"What's in there?" Lili pointed at the cardboard box he was holding.

"Oh God, I feel like a vacuum cleaner salesman. Look, I've got something to show you, but there's no need to be polite. If you aren't interested, just say so."

"We don't really need another vacuum cleaner. We've got Blitz." *Oh, help*, Lili thought. *Talk about feeble.* "Sorry. Do come in."

Felicity, looking more cheerful than Drew had ever seen her look before, greeted him with a broad smile. "Hi! We're celebrating my moving day. That's your glass there." She gestured to a full one. "I've got to go in a minute. Lottie, mind that bottle."

"Open the box!" barked Lottie, and Lili almost said, "Take the money!" Realizing that she was probably the only person in the room ancient enough to remember the TV catchphrase, she stopped herself just in time.

"Oh wow!" Lottie squealed as Drew peeled back the lid and showed her the kittens.

"Paddy Birley dumped them on me an hour ago," he explained. "Asked me to get rid of them. Old bugger must be going soft in his old age," he added in an undertone to Lili. "He usually drowns them in a bucket. Sorry, this isn't meant to be emotional blackmail. I just wondered if you'd want one."

This wasn't true. He had been desperate for an excuse to call in on Lili, and Paddy Birley, the world's most unlikely fairy godmother, had provided it.

"Oh, Mum, can we have a kitten? Can we, can we, can we?"

There were five in the box. Lili picked up a mewling black-and-white bundle of warm fur and wondered if Blitz would eat it. Until five minutes ago, she hadn't wanted a cat, but if Drew was offering her one...well, that was different.

"I'll have two," Felicity cried, eagerly scooping them out of the box. "Hugh would never let me have a cat. And Lorna was saying the other day that she'd love a couple more."

Blitz, nosing his way between Lili and Drew, sniffed the kitten on Lili's lap. Cautiously, he wagged his tail.

Relieved that he wasn't actually salivating, Lili said, "We'll take this one."

"Done." Drew began to relax. He grinned at her. "Sold to the lady in the pink slippers with the champagne glass in her hand. Maybe I should become a door-to-door vacuum cleaner salesman after all."

Lili wished she weren't wearing her pink slippers; they were hardly chic.

"I can't take them now." Felicity checked her watch. "Damn, and it's ten o'clock."

"Don't worry. I'll take them into the clinic and give them the once-over. Ring me this afternoon," Drew said easily, "and we'll sort something out."

"Cup of tea?" Lili said when they were alone in the kitchen.

"No thanks. How have you been?"

Polite, polite.

"Oh, well, okay." Lili busied herself with the kettle.

"Is it really all over between you and Michael?"

She nodded and dropped two tea bags into the milk jug.

"I wanted to phone you," said Drew.

"Doesn't matter. I understand."

"Understand what?"

"Well, that you didn't want to be involved."

The kettle clicked off. Lili, trembling violently, poured boiling water into the milk jug.

"Not quite right. I *do* want to be involved." Drew, who wanted it more than anything, chose his words with care. "But not until you know for certain that it's what you want too."

She turned to look at him. "Truly?"

He nodded. "You'd be on the rebound. And rebound relationships never work out."

Despite herself, Lili started to laugh. "What?"

"Look, all the nurses at our practice are female. So is the cleaner, so are the receptionists. You don't work with eight gossiping women," Drew said gravely, "without learning all there is to know about relationships doomed to disaster. I don't think you want to drink that," he added, fishing the tea bags out of the milk jug and tipping the murky liquid down the sink.

Lili wondered if it still counted as "on the rebound" when the marriage you'd just escaped from was as lousy as hers had been. She'd actually experienced a few twinges of guilt, thinking that she should be feeling a lot more miserable than this.

But she knew what Drew meant. "So what do we do?"

Drew shrugged. He knew exactly what he'd like to do. "Take it slowly, I suppose. Give you time to get over…well, all the stuff you need to get over."

Right. Lili nodded. That was sensible. Boring but definitely sensible. "Okay. How long d'you think that'll take?"

Drew reached for the glass of champagne he hadn't yet had a chance to drink. "Five or six years."

"Five or six *years*?" Lili wailed. "Oh my God, we could be dead by then! That is *so* unfair—"

"Five or six months then?"

Lili stared at him. It was certainly better, but five or six months still felt like an awfully long way away.

She proceeded with caution. "Before what?"

"Before we get involved," said Drew.

"Oh. And what happens in the meantime?"

His mouth twitched. Lili really was adorable. "Well, I could get to know your children properly. We could see each other maybe a couple of times a week."

"Or more," Lili suggested. Hastily she added, "So long as we made sure we weren't getting involved."

Drew looked thoughtful. He nodded his head. "I could go along with that."

"Only if you want to."

"Oh no, I think that'd be fine."

He was teasing her, Lili realized. Everything was going to be all right. She felt as if she could explode with joy.

"What about kissing and stuff?" she ventured bravely.

"Stuff?"

"Bed-type stuff."

"Oh well, I'm all in favor of that," said Drew. "All that… bed-type stuff."

"And kissing," Lili reminded him.

"Kissing too."

"So you think it would be all right to do that," she double-checked, light-headed with anticipation.

"Oh, definitely." Unable to help himself, Drew took her in his arms. As his mouth brushed hers, he murmured, "Just so long as we don't get involved."

Chapter 63

FELICITY, BALANCING FREYA ON her hip in order to open the front door, was astonished to find Jamie on the doorstep.

"Oh! When I rang Drew he said one of the veterinary clinic's nurses would drop them off on her way home."

"I was passing," Jamie fibbed. "I offered to bring them instead." Gauche but desperate, he went on, "I haven't been able to stop thinking about you all day."

Felicity was lost for words. Last night had been amazing and she hadn't been able to stop thinking about it either. But her thoughts had all been of the sex, not of Jamie.

Since he was so obviously not her type, she hadn't imagined their encounter ever being more than a miraculous one-night stand.

"I did them myself." Jamie held up the cat basket. "They've had their worming tablets and inoculations." Hopefully he said, "Shall I bring them in?"

"My mother's here." Felicity glanced nervously over her shoulder. "I don't really think…"

"Okay, I understand, but can I see you again? How about tomorrow night?"

Caught off guard, Felicity found herself prevaricating helplessly. "Look, how much do I owe you for this?" She was edging toward the hall table, actually reaching for her handbag as she spoke.

"Nothing!"

"But the injections—"

"Let me take you out tomorrow night." Jamie was close to despair. "And we'll call it quits." *Bloody hell, this never happened to Doug.* "Please," he begged.

"I wasn't expecting this."

"So? All you have to do is say yes."

He willed her to say it, but Felicity was shaking her head, unable to speak.

"You don't want to see me." Jamie was filled with dismay. God, this was so humiliating! "You used me, and now you don't want to see me ever again."

Felicity, who had used him precisely *because* she'd thought she wouldn't see him again, said in a low voice, "I thought you just wanted sex with someone, you didn't care who."

"Okay, okay, maybe I did, but that was last night," Jamie blurted out in an anguished whisper. "And now I *do* care—"

"Who is it, dear? The girl with the kittens?" The voice of Felicity's mother drifted down the hall toward them.

"Please," Jamie tried again frantically. "Take a few days to think about it, if you like. But just let me ring you."

"Look, I've got the number of the clinic." Flustered, Felicity grabbed the cat basket from him as her mother's footsteps echoed along the parquet floor. "If I decide to see you again, I'll ring you."

———

"What are you doing?" said Toby.

Jess, on her knees in front of a lichen-covered tombstone, was trimming the grass around the grave with a pair of nail scissors.

"I broke my garden shears."

"Whose grave is this?"

Jessie leaned back on her heels and pushed her hair out of her eyes. She waited for Toby to scan the simple wording on the stone:

In Loving Memory of Susan Wilder, Died aged Fifty-Eight. Devoted Wife and Mother.

"She was old Cecil's wife."

Old Cecil, with his smelly dog and smellier pipe, was a more-or-less permanent fixture in the corner of the Seven Bells, where he spent his days playing either dominoes or cribbage.

"Died twenty-five years ago." Toby raised an eyebrow.

"He adored her. Look how beautifully he's kept the grave." Jessie ran her fingers over the velvety, weed-free grass. "His rheumatism's bad this week; that's why he asked me to come and give it a tidy up."

Toby watched her unwrap the flowers she had brought with her from old Cecil's garden and arrange them in the weighted-down vase.

"I didn't realize old Cecil had been married."

"Forty-two years. He was seventeen; she was sixteen." Jessie tweaked a nodding foxglove into place. "He still misses her dreadfully."

"What happened to the children?"

"Two boys. Moved away, lost contact." Jessie shrugged. "It could happen to any of us. Just because they're our kids, we can't force them to keep in touch." She glanced up at Toby. "How's Dizzy?"

"Grumpy, belligerent, sulky, rude. All the normal teenage stuff."

"And what are you doing here?"

Shielding her eyes from the afternoon sun, Jessie glanced around the churchyard, with its unregimented hotchpotch of tombs and headstones, some centuries old and tilting at jaunty angles, others gleaming and new.

"Learning lines." Toby took a folded script from his inside jacket pocket. "Graveyards are great places to learn lines." With a wry smile he added, "Unless you bump into someone you know."

"Don't let me stop you."

Toby watched her rearrange the flowers. Was this how it was always going to be? Talking about trivia and taking care to avoid anything remotely important?

"You haven't mentioned it," he said, "but you must know about Oliver and Savannah."

Jessie nodded. "It was bound to happen, sooner or later. Not very nice for you though."

"Why not?"

"Well, all that trouble for nothing. You needn't have found out about Deborah's affair or you not being Savannah's father. Dizzy wouldn't have run away."

"Jess, I told you months ago that my marriage wasn't all it was cracked up to be. You were the one who made me realize just—"

"Oh no, don't start that again," Jessie warned. "That's not fair. Anyway, you and Deborah have to stay together now. For Dizzy's sake."

"Even if he doesn't appreciate it?"

"Yes!"

"But—"

"Look, if you two split up and Dizzy runs away again and begs on the streets and becomes a crack addict and *dies*, it'll be on your conscience for the rest of your life." Jessie took a deep breath before adding slowly, "And if I were in any way involved with you, it would be on my conscience too."

—⁓—

Savannah and Stevie were in the yard talking so intently to each other that they wouldn't have noticed if the SAS had swung out of the trees and smoke-bombed the gazebo.

Deborah, watching them together, experienced a pang of envy. *No danger of anything like that happening to me just now*, she thought with simmering frustration. Toby was being *so* unreasonable. And Doug, damn him, was still refusing to take her calls.

She sighed, drumming her fingers against the window frame, on edge because she wasn't used to being treated like this.

Oh, what the hell.

She picked up the phone, rang Doug's cell, and waited for the electronic voice to inform her—as it always did nowadays—that the person she was calling wasn't available right now, but if she wished to leave a—

"Yes?"

"Doug! Don't hang up."

"I'm with a patient."

"Can I see you later?"

"Sorry, busy."

"If you don't say yes, I'm telling Toby everything."

God, listen *to me,* Deborah thought, appalled. *I sound completely* desperate. *And I'm not. I'm not. I'm Deborah Gillespie; I can have any man I want.*

"You do that." Doug sounded bored. "Although what good you think it'll do, I can't imagine."

"Please…"

Deborah felt the hot tears welling up. Outside, Stevie Harper was kissing her daughter. Toby had disappeared, heaven only knew where. This wasn't how her life was supposed to turn out.

"Have to go now," Doug said briskly. "Bye."

―⁓―

"Nobody in the world has ever been as happy as meee," sang Savannah, reeling into the sitting room twenty minutes later. "Mum, we're going over to Bath. Are my Levi's clean?"

"Don't know. Try the closet."

But Savannah was frowning at the television. "Have you lost the remote again? *Countdown's* on Channel 4."

"It's quite interesting, actually. All about…um…tax and stuff."

Deborah had turned on the television intending to watch *Countdown*—she had a soft spot for game shows—but had gotten waylaid by BBC2 instead. *Parliament Today* was on, and there was David, addressing a packed House of Commons, effortlessly commanding their attention.

And hers too.

"God, there he is. Look at him!" Savannah jeered and made sick noises. "Mr. Smooth. Whatever did you see in him, Mum?"

"He's very good-looking." Deborah was filled with indignation. "Anyway, that's no way to speak about your father."

"Don't call him that. Dad's my proper father. And I've already looked in the closet."

Savannah might have been more concerned with locating her jeans, but Deborah was finding it increasingly hard to tear her eyes away from the figure currently occupying center stage on the television screen. They had both been so on edge when he had driven down to Sisley House, it had hardly been an ideal reunion.

But that had been two months ago.

And now…well, things were quite different.

"Mum, you're not listening to me. Where are my *jeans*?"

There was no getting away from it—David Mansfield was an awfully attractive man.

Having stomped out, Savannah stomped back in again. "I looked in the dryer. It's empty."

Then again, involvement with politics was known to have a remarkable effect on the ugliest of men. It was the power thing; it gave them a kind of glittery aura.

Deborah smiled to herself, relishing the challenge of getting intimate with David's own extra-glittery aura.

Imagine, not just an MP but a member of the Cabinet!

Handsome!

Married!

Terrified by the prospect of scandal but at the same time irresistibly drawn to the idea—because, after all, the greater the risk, the bigger the adrenaline rush. And they didn't come much bigger than this…

Gazing at the screen, Deborah wondered what it would be like, actually making love to David on the floor of the House of Commons, with Members of Parliament on both sides cheering them on and the speaker barking, "Order, order" in an attempt to—

"Mum, *where are my jeans?*"

Some fantasies were too enthralling to abandon. Impatiently, Deborah waved her away. "You can borrow mine."

Savannah shot her a look of undiluted disgust.

"Yours have got creases ironed down the front."

Chapter 64

DOUG PULLED OPEN THE front door of Keeper's Cottage, hauled his cases out to the car, and loaded them into the trunk.

It was six thirty in the morning, and the sky was a clear, duck-egg blue tinged with pink. The village green was silvered with dew.

Doug paused to take one last look around. This was where he had spent the last year. Now it was time to move on. His contract with Harleston General was up. Although the Manchester interview hadn't come to anything, he had struck lucky with his second, at a children's hospital in Kent. *Good-bye, ER. Hello, pediatrics*, he thought, watching a pair of undulating squirrels race along the garden wall.

Good-bye, Harleston; hello, Maidstone.

Good-bye, girls; hello, more girls.

He left his front-door key on the kitchen table, along with a check for the rent he owed. He hadn't expected Drew and Jamie to get up at this hour and see him off; this wasn't *Friends*, after all. Just three blokes sharing a house.

Apart from the two squirrels now romping across the green, the village was still and silent. Doug started up the MG's engine and revved it once, wondering if Deborah would hear the noise.

He drove past the entrance to Sisley House. The bedroom curtains were drawn—no signs of life.

Doug shook his head and headed slowly along Compass Lane. That was a lesson he had learned the hard way: some women simply weren't worth getting involved with.

Then again, some were.

Moll was sitting on the front step of the Seven Bells, playing with one of Lorna's new kittens. She looked up and grinned as Doug turned left onto the main street and pulled up alongside the pub.

"Ready?"

"Ready."

Moll disentangled the kitten's needle-sharp claws from her long, red skirt, hauled herself upright, and threw her case into the space behind the driver's seat.

"Is that all?"

"I travel light."

"Are you sure about this?"

Moll looked amused. "Time to move on."

Doug leaned across and opened the passenger door for her. He had only told her last night that he was off, but Moll had taken the news in her usual easy stride. When he had half-jokingly said, "Come with me," she hadn't hesitated for a moment before replying, "Okay."

Now, as she climbed into the MG and shook back her tortoise-shell hair, Doug felt his spirits lift.

They understood each other, he and Moll. They were two of a kind.

"Lorna isn't going to be pleased, losing her star barmaid."

"She'll be fine. Stevie needs a job to tide him over."

"I thought your brother was only here for a few days, visiting you."

"Ah well, that was before he clapped eyes on Savannah Gillespie."

Doug slid the car into gear. "That won't last."

"So? They're enjoying themselves," Moll said comfortably. "That's what counts."

"There's enjoying yourself and there's *enjoying yourself*," Doug murmured. "And if you want to get there in one piece, you'd better take your hand out of my trousers."

Moll burst out laughing. "Spoilsport! Myrtle Armitage is

watching us from her bedroom window. I wanted to give the old bag one last shock."

~~~

It was the last week of summer vacation, and Harriet was looking forward to getting back to school. She had a new bra to show off in the locker room, a new graffiti-free satchel—soon remedy that—and more gossip than usual to relate.

She sat on the front garden wall, kicking her heels against the stonework and dangling a yo-yo inches above the pavement. Every time the kitten launched itself at the yo-yo, she twitched it out of reach.

So:

New bra, which was great, with yellow daisies on it, and padded bits that slotted in and out depending on how bouncy you wanted to look—which was basically very pneumatic indeed.

New kitten.

Newish dog.

Parents separated.

Father had affair with the ex-wife of a man who became a woman. Hmm, maybe she wouldn't mention that bit.

Mother *possibly* having affair with hunky younger vet. Ah, big improvement. Far less shameful too. Since a vet was currently a seriously cool thing to be, this was something you could definitely boast about.

Particularly when his name was Mr. Darcy.

Then there's me, thought Harriet, dipping and twitching the yo-yo like a metronome. *What have I done with myself during break?*

Nothing.

Nothing at all.

She closed her eyes for a second, imagining just how left out she was going to feel when all the other girls in her class babbled on and on about their boyfriends. During the course of the last couple of terms, it had turned into something of an epidemic.

And I still haven't got one, thought Harriet.

New bra, new cat, new dog   no boyfriend.

Talk about a failure.

Realistically, though, how much choice was there when you lived in a stupid village, ten miles from the nearest town?

The only teenage boy in Upper Sisley was Dizzy Gillespie.

And famous parents or no famous parents, Harriet thought with grim satisfaction, she wasn't that desperate.

She knew why she was thinking about boys. Fifty yards away, sitting on the green with his bike lying on its side next to him, was one she hadn't seen before. And every time she glanced casually in his direction—hell's bells, it was happening *again*—he seemed to be casually glancing back.

Harriet hadn't been paying attention. With a high-pitched meow of triumph, the kitten launched itself at the dangling yo-yo and promptly cannoned into the wall.

"You daft animal." Jumping down, Harriet cradled the kitten in her hands. "You'll give yourself brain damage."

The kitten, predictably, peed all over her jeans.

When she looked across, Harriet could have sworn the boy with the bicycle was laughing to himself.

She longed to see his face more clearly. A pair of binoculars would come in useful. You'd have to be discreet about it, of course.

Harriet wished she could stay outside, but there was no arguing with the smell of cat pee. She went into the house, changed her jeans, slapped on a bit of dark mascara, checked through the sitting-room window that the boy was still there—yes!—added a dash of lip gloss—oops, not all over her chin—pinched twenty pence from Lottie's piggy bank, and dashed back outside.

She felt the boy's eyes on her as she sauntered casually but sexily past him on her way to the grocery store. It really was astonishing the difference a new bra could make, even if it was only a 34AA. Okay, so maybe the results weren't as eye popping as a pair of hockey socks shoved in there, but this way was a lot more secure.

Having bought her packet of chewing gum, Harriet headed—casually and sexily—back to the house. But by this time, her curiosity was well and truly aroused.

Who was this boy, and what was he doing here?

Most weird of all, when she was walking down the road, why on earth did he still keep glancing over at her house?

"Excuse me," said Harriet, pausing at the edge of the green, "but you are waiting for someone?"

Now that she was standing less than twenty feet away from him, she could see his face properly.

Hmm, not bad.

No acne, at least.

"Great timing." The boy grinned up at her. "I was just about to ask you for help. Although you have to understand, this is an undercover mission."

There was a conspiratorial twinkle in his eye. Harriet decided she liked him already.

No acne and a sense of humor. Almost too good to be true.

"What, you mean you're a secret agent?"

"Got it in one."

Harriet giggled. "Like James Bond?"

"What d'you mean, *like* James Bond?" The boy raised one eyebrow. "I *am* James Bond. Press the hidden lever," he went on, patting his bicycle, "and this turns into an Aston Martin."

Beaming with delight, Harriet flopped down onto the grass next to him.

"Who are you looking for?"

"Soviet agent." He lowered his voice to a passable Sean Connery–type growl. "Known as the Russian Widow, eats men for breakfast. Very beautiful. Extremely dangerous."

Entranced, Harriet whispered back, "What's her real name?"

"Harriet Ferguson,"

Hang on a second... "That's my name."

"Is it? Well, not you, obviously. The other one."

"Why not me, *obviously*?" Harriet sat up, nettled. "And *what* other one?"

The boy frowned. "You're supposed to tell me. Grandmother was my guess. The Harriet Ferguson I'm looking for is in her late sixties."

"Well, I'm the only one there is."

He looked across at the house. "The Old Vicarage, right?"

"Right."

"Are you sure you aren't in your late sixties?" Eyes narrowing, he peered more closely at her face. "You could be a master of disguise."

"You aren't James Bond. James Bond doesn't make mistakes like this," said Harriet. "Come on, what's your real name?"

"Alfie Huntingdon."

"*Alfie?*"

"I know." He pulled a face. "Bad news, isn't it? Alfie and Harriet. We sound like a right pair of geriatrics."

"Huntingdon!" Harriet exclaimed suddenly.

"Oh, great, you're going to criticize that too. Actually, I'm quite fond of—"

"The letter. You must be related to Frank."

"He's my grandfather. So you *did* write to him." Alfie's eyebrows went up at angles. "Now I'm definitely confused."

"I didn't write to him. Somebody else did. It was their idea of a joke." Briefly, Harriet explained. "When I got your grandfather's letter, I meant to write back and tell him. But I thought he'd have hundreds of other replies," she said apologetically, "so in the end I didn't bother."

"He had two, but the other woman wasn't keen on pigs. He liked the sound of you best," Alfie explained, "but you didn't write back. He was disappointed, but he didn't want to pester you."

Harriet loved the way Alfie's eyebrows moved when he talked, as if they had a life of their own.

"So what are you doing here?"

"I volunteered to come over and check the situation out, see what Harriet Ferguson looked like, find out if she was Grandad's type. If I thought she was, I'd have persuaded him to write again, give her another chance."

"God, I'm sorry." Harriet felt mortified, as if it were all her fault. "I wish I were seventy. I really do."

Alfie leaned back on his elbows and surveyed her without a trace of embarrassment. "You aren't to blame. Anyway, every cloud…" He broke into a grin. "I'm glad you're not seventy."

Harriet was glad too.

"Is your grandad really nice?"

"Yeah, he's great. Just lonely." Alfie looked unperturbed. "Don't panic. We'll find someone else for him."

Harriet wondered how Frank had worded his original ad.

"Maybe it was the pig thing that put them off," she said helpfully. "Some women are funny about pigs."

"Good thinking, Moneypenny." Alfie wiggled his eyebrows at her. "Either that or we put the next ad in *Farmer's Weekly*."

Chapter 65

"I'm telling you, the atmosphere in that house is terrible," said Oliver. "You should go up there. Then you'd know what I mean." He was putting together a spaghetti Bolognese, practically the only thing he could make. Every work surface in the kitchen was awash with piles of chopped-up mushrooms, tomatoes, onions, and garlic.

"That's like saying 'This milk is off. Go on, try it,'" Jessie pointed out. "Why do people always say that?"

But Oliver wasn't going to be sidetracked. "It's awful. You can't imagine how bad. Have you talked to Toby lately?"

Jessie pinched a mushroom while he wasn't looking. "What good would that do?"

Oliver shrugged. "I don't know. It might help."

Hardly likely, thought Jessie, *if just the mention of his name makes my stomach do a double somersault*. Toby's remarks in the graveyard last week hadn't been encouraging either. As far as she was concerned, the most helpful thing she could do was keep out of his way.

Well out of his way.

Her hand sidled across to the half-empty bottle of red wine on the kitchen table.

"Don't," Oliver warned without turning around. "I need that for the Bolognese."

Oh well, Jessie thought, *just have to do it sober*. "I'm putting the cottage on the market," she said.

He stopped chopping and swung around to look at her, frowning.

"I thought you'd given up on that idea."

"No."

"But why?"

"I want to move." *Oh, Olly, don't you see? I have to move,* she pleaded silently.

"Move where?" He shot her a look of disbelief. "Not still Cornwall."

"Yes."

"But that's miles away!"

That, thought Jessie, *is the general idea.*

"Look, you're going to Europe." She tapped the pile of guidebooks Oliver had brought home from the bookstore that afternoon. "You'll be gone for the best part of a year. When you get back, you'll find a job and move away. Well, you *will*," she insisted. "Don't tell me you were planning on living with your old mother for the rest of your life."

"Is this something to do with Jonathan?" Oliver sounded suspicious. "Are you two moving in together?"

"No!"

Poor Jonathan—he had given up on her weeks ago. Going out platonically with someone you so badly wanted to sleep with, he had explained with rueful candor to Jess, was hell on wheels. Like gazing for hours at a classic car and not being allowed to lay a finger on it.

Apologizing profusely, Jessie had thanked him for being such a good friend, wished him well, and kissed him good-bye.

Within a fortnight, Jonathan had found himself another woman, one with a chassis he *could* touch.

"I just don't understand why," Oliver protested. For something to do, he was chopping the mushrooms into smaller and smaller pieces.

She couldn't bring herself to tell him the real reason. "I like Cornwall."

"I thought you liked living here."

Jessie gazed with longing at the bottle of Valpolicella. When she'd wanted to move before, Toby had persuaded her not to. He had managed to convince her that staying put was the best thing she could do, that running away wasn't the answer. According to Toby, there was no reason why the two of them couldn't coexist happily together in the same village.

Well, that was where he was wrong.

I gave it my best shot, Jessie reminded herself, *and it didn't work out.* A great wave of sadness swept over her.

"I do like living here," she told Oliver, semitruthfully. "I just think I'll like Cornwall more."

—⁂—

I'm looking old and tired, thought Eleanor Ferguson as she checked her appearance in the hall mirror before leaving the house. There were deep frown lines between her gray eyebrows, and her mouth was turned down at the corners as if gripped with disapproval.

This was hardly surprising, as Eleanor currently had a lot to disapprove of.

What Lili thought she was doing, she had no idea, but these days Eleanor could barely bring herself to speak to her shameless daughter-in-law. Quite clearly, the affair with Drew Darcy had been going on for months—oh, she could see that now—and this had been the reason for the breakup of her son's marriage; it hadn't been Michael's fault at all.

And those poor, innocent children—what they must be going through didn't bear thinking about.

Eleanor opened the front door a couple of inches and peered outside, checking that the coast was clear. She was taking immense pains to avoid Bernadette Thomas. How the rest of the village could allow such a creature to carry on living in their midst was beyond Eleanor, but nobody else seemed to care. Eleanor shuddered with revulsion every time she remembered she was living next door to a freak, a man who had undergone a sex change.

Furthermore, she would never forgive him for that nightmarish scene with Michael in the pub.

Eleanor double locked the front door and headed for her car. What with Myrtle Armitage's barbed remarks and never knowing who you might bump into without warning, it was easier to avoid the grocery store nowadays and drive to the grocery store in Harleston instead.

The car key was slotted into the driver's door when she heard the crackle of wheels on fallen leaves. Looking up, Eleanor saw two teenage boys on mountain bikes swerving along Waters Lane toward her. She didn't recognize them; they certainly weren't from Upper Sisley.

Spotting Eleanor, they glanced at each other and began to giggle. "It's her. It *is* her," she heard one of them say to the other. "You can tell just by looking—that's the bloke who had the sex change."

Eleanor froze. She stared at them as they whizzed past, sniggering openly.

When they were safely out of reach, the second boy swiveled around on his seat and yelled, "Oy, mate, what's it feel like to have your John Thomas chopped off?"

Tears of humiliation burned the back of Eleanor's eyes like acid. She couldn't go shopping now.

Heading back up the garden path, she saw to her further horror that Bernadette was standing in her front room, gazing out through the open window. Clearly, she had heard everything.

She addressed Eleanor with sympathy. "I'm so sorry about that. They're just boys. I try to ignore them."

Blinking back tears, Eleanor shot her a look of disdain. Without uttering a word, she stalked into the house.

Dizzy was consumed with a jealousy he hadn't known he possessed. Well, not where Harriet Ferguson was concerned at least. Mysteriously, all of a sudden, he fancied her like mad.

It was, he acknowledged with reluctance, more than likely something to do with the fact that Moll wasn't around to lust after anymore.

He made sure he happened to be sauntering past the grocery store when Harriet emerged from it clutching one of her precious magazines. This one, he observed, sported a glossy fluorescent-pink cover. It was called *Hey Girlz!!* and had a photo on the front of the hottest new teenage soap star currently being swooned over by every young girl in the country.

"Met him at a party up in London the other week," Dizzy lied, casually nodding at the picture. Well, it wasn't a complete lie; he'd met someone who'd stood next to him in a queue at McDonald's. "I could get you his autograph if you wanted."

"I'm not bothered." Harriet shrugged, unimpressed. "I don't like him much."

"How's your new kitten? What's its name?"

"Banana."

Struggling slightly, Dizzy said, "Banana—that's a good name."

Harriet shot him a suspicious look. *Dizzy? Being complimentary? Surely not.*

"It was Lottie's idea. I didn't choose it. Lottie's mad about bananas."

"I'm not doing anything right now," Dizzy offered. "If I came over, you could show me your kitten. I haven't seen it yet."

Harriet frowned. This was definitely weird. "It looks like a kitten, that's all. Anyway, I've got a friend coming over"—she checked her watch—"any minute now."

Dizzy took a deep breath. He had been practicing this bit all morning. "Look, I was wondering if you'd like to go to the cinema with me. They're showing the new James Bond in Harleston. We could catch the bus into town, get a burger—I'd pay, don't worry about that—then—"

"Seen it."

Instant deflation. "Oh. Oh, right."

Harriet's expression cleared. So that was why Dizzy was being nice! How completely *amazing*.

"Dizzy, were you asking me out on a date then?"

His ears went beetroot red. "Well, you know, um…not exactly a date…"

But Harriet was victorious. After all the jibes and put-downs of the past few months, she was going to really enjoy this.

In fact, the next couple of minutes could rank among the best of her life.

"You were. You were asking me out on a date," she announced triumphantly. "And do you know why I'm turning you down? Two reasons, actually. Because (a) you're a slime ball and I don't fancy you anyway. And (b) I've already got a boyfriend."

Stung, Dizzy hit back. "You have not!"

"Oh yes I have."

"In your dreams."

"No, he's real. Thanks to you."

He glared at her, not understanding. "What are you talking about?"

"You and all those pathetic letters you wrote." She smirked. "Surely you remember. You answered an ad in the local paper, pretending to be me."

Outraged, Dizzy said, "That was to some old guy! He was *ancient*."

"But his grandson isn't—he's fifteen." Harriet's joy was complete as, over Dizzy's shoulder, she spotted Alfie on his bike, pedaling down the main street toward her. "So there you go—it all turned out rather well. You should try it, Dizzy. It might even work for you."

"Hi!" puffed Alfie, screeching to a halt in a cloud of dust and grinning at Harriet.

Wondering if it was possible to actually explode with pride, she grinned back. He was better looking than Dizzy Gillespie. Taller too. And he thought nothing of cycling twelve miles to see her.

Harriet took immense delight in not introducing him to Dizzy. Tucking her arm through Alfie's, she said joyfully, "Come on. Let's go back to my place."

"Moneypenny, you always know exactly the right thing to say."

"Oh, that reminds me." As they began to move away, Harriet glanced over her shoulder at Dizzy. "Do go and see the Bond film. We thought it was great."

Chapter 66

IT WAS MID-SEPTEMBER, THE leaves were turning, and the woody scent of autumn hung in the air. Deborah Gillespie, walking slowly around her yard, saw glossy, brown chestnuts nestling in the long grass beneath the trees.

Nature's way of telling you your children are growing up, she thought drily. The days of avid collecting and hoarding were over. If she rushed inside now and told Dizzy there were chestnuts outside, he would roll his eyes and mutter, "Saaad."

Deborah bent and picked up a couple herself, holding them in the palm of her hand and rubbing her fingers over their waxy smoothness. Then she slid them into her jacket pocket alongside her cell phone.

The one that never rang nowadays.

She had called David Mansfield five days ago. He sounded horrified to hear from her.

"Nothing to panic about," she had announced cheerfully.

"Is this about Savannah?"

"Why would it be? Don't be so paranoid!"

Evidently thinking about the party conference and the potential scope for scandal, David had let out a groan of relief. She heard him relax. "So, how can I help?"

"I'm not asking for a favor, David." *Oh, that voice!* "You've been on my mind a lot lately, that's all. I wondered if you'd like to meet up."

"Ah…"

"I'll leave it with you," Deborah had said lightly. No pressure, no pressure. He knew what she was talking about and he knew he could trust her.

And philandering MPs don't easily change their spots.

"Look, Deborah—"

"You've got my number." Effortlessly, she deflected the protest. "Have a think about it. Ring me if you're interested."

Which all sounded great, in theory. Except he hadn't.

First Toby, then Doug Flynn, Deborah thought. *Now David too.*

Was this how the fat girls at school felt when they were last to be picked for the hockey team?

Was it how the really ugly ones felt at the end-of-term dance when nobody asked them to dance?

Bloody *men*!

Chestnuts in one pocket, terminally non-ringing phone in the other, she made her way back up the yard.

Toby came out onto the terrace as she approached the house.

"We need to talk."

"Toby, when are you going to stop looking so *grim*?" The last few weeks had been appalling; it was like being in endless detention. "I've said I'm sorry a hundred times. Why can't we just put it behind us and get back to how we were?"

He shook his head. "It's not going to work. I want a divorce."

Deborah felt a dull ache in her stomach.

"You mean you want Jessie. Okay, fine." She shrugged. "I owe you that much. Carry on seeing her. I won't say a word."

Toby only wished he could.

"She won't have anything to do with me," he said evenly. "She thinks you and I should stay together for the sake of the children."

He felt this was particularly bizarre advice, coming as it did from someone who had raised her own child single-handedly.

Deborah began to feel slightly desperate. "I think she's right."

But Toby's dark-blue eyes were fixed on the swaying poplars behind her. "I don't care what either of you think. I just know I can't carry on with this sham of a marriage. Either you move out," he said slowly, "or I do."

It was on the tip of Deborah's tongue to retort "Fine, you go" when it occurred to her that the alternative might not be as dire as she imagined. Okay, this was a big house, but would staying in it be a case of cutting off her nose to spite her face?

There's money in the bank, she thought, *and Toby's just signed the deal for the Spielberg film. I could find myself a nice little semidetached house in Putney or Hampstead. Okay, it might not compare pricewise, but at least I'd be back in London.*

Because Upper Sisley might be a picturesque village in the Cotswolds, but there was no denying the choice of men was limited.

And in all fairness, how many were really that attractive?

Basically, Deborah decided, the only ones worth having, she'd already had.

"You're splitting up?" Dizzy stared at his parents. "When?"

It tore at Toby's heart to think that this was what they had to do to gain their son's undivided attention.

"Your father's staying here," Deborah told him gently, "and I'm moving back to London."

"Oh wow, fan-*tas*-tic! Can I come with you?" Dizzy begged. "Pleeease?"

Deborah was taken aback. "Darling, that would be lovely, but you've just settled into your new school."

"I hate it. I'll go back to my old one," Dizzy promptly announced.

"You've spent the last five years hating that place."

"Huh, better than that bloody dump in Harleston."

The fees for the bloody dump amounted to several thousand pounds a year. "Dizzy, you don't—"

"But what I *really* want to do is go to stage school," he blurted out.

Savannah snorted with laughter. "You!"

Dizzy punched her on the shoulder. "I'm good at acting."

"Prove it!"

"Oh, Savannah, you're so beautiful. I'm so *lucky* to have a sister as wonderful as you…" He smirked and aimed another punch at her arm. "There, see? If I can say that with a straight face, I can say anything."

"Dizzy, are you serious about this?" Toby was frowning.

This wasn't the reaction he'd expected. "What, about Savannah being wonderful? Dad, pay attention, I was being an ac-tor!"

But Toby didn't smile.

Dizzy realized he had to press his case. "Deadly serious," he pleaded. God, more so than ever since yesterday's humiliating run-in with Harriet Ferguson. As she and that oh-so-witty boyfriend of hers had been making their way back to the Old Vicarage, Dizzy had heard him say: "Is that the one who sent all the letters?" And Harriet, not even bothering to lower her voice, had replied dismissively, "Yeah, he's just a nerd."

Startled, Toby looked across at his daughter. "How about you?"

Savannah didn't hesitate. "Oh, I'll stay here, thanks. With you."

"Can't bear to be away from sexy Stevie, you mean," Dizzy mocked. "Ouch, that *hurt!*"

"Unlike you, I care about my education."

Savannah was so blinded by love that she actually believed this lofty pronouncement. In fact, Stevie had persuaded her that retaking her dismally failed exams was a must. She was also thoroughly enjoying herself at Harleston Tech.

———

Deborah was lying in the bath when her phone rang. She was so comfortable she almost left it until voice mail picked up.

Almost.

"It's me."

She closed her eyes in triumph. "Who's me?"

"You know."

"Oh, hi."

Deborah wondered if the news that she and Toby were separating would scare him off. Married women were a far safer bet than the unattached kind.

Maybe she wouldn't tell him just yet.

"Ahem. Well. About this meeting you…er…suggested."

Deborah shivered pleasurably. This—*this* was what she most loved. The excitement, the subterfuge, the wicked, intoxicating thrill of it all. Imagine—someone, somewhere right now could be tapping into this very conversation, taping it, ready to do a Camillagate on them…

"Thank you for returning my call. I know how busy you must be." Deborah sank back into the water, still clutching the phone. "Now," she said happily, aware that David could hear the sound of splashing, would know she was in the bath, "you tell me when's good for you, and I'll see if I can fit you in."

———

Thanks to a mammoth blackberry-picking session, Lottie was stained purple from head to foot. By the time Lili had finished scrubbing her clean in the bath, the smell of cheese on toast was drifting up the stairs.

When she pushed open the sitting-room door, she had to swallow a great lump in her throat.

The fire had been lit. Harriet was sprawled in front of it, reading aloud something incomprehensible from a physics textbook. Drew, in the armchair, had Will balanced on one knee and Blitz draped adoringly over the other. He was listening to Harriet, answering her questions, and playing This Little Piggy with Will's toes. On the rug next to Harriet, Banana lay watching *Tom and Jerry* on the turned-down TV, her skinny tail swishing from side to side.

It was like one of those Victorian Christmas card scenes, thought Lili, feeling ridiculously emotional.

Well—apart from the television.

And Disco Barbie, legs splayed, poking out from behind one of the sofa cushions.

And Harriet's mud-encrusted Nike tennis shoes.

Drew looked up and winked at Lili. He mouthed *Marry me* at her.

Lottie, shoving past Lili in her Pocahontas pajamas and fighting for a place on Drew's knee, howled, "Get off, Will. It's my turn."

"Leave Drew alone," Harriet said. "He's helping me with my homework." She glanced up through her fringe. "So, what's the size of the contingent negative variation? Ten microvolts?"

Lili smiled. Her children adored him. He adored them. It was so perfect it was scary—and even scarier because it was all happening so quickly.

Drew, it seemed, could do no wrong.

Next moment, Blitz began to bark.

Then the smoke alarm went off in the hall, almost sending Banana into orbit.

Lili reflected that if love was blind, it must also have an effect on your sense of smell, because she'd been the one standing in the doorway and she hadn't even noticed the clouds of smoke billowing from the kitchen.

Drew, having tipped assorted children and animals off his lap, raced past her, silenced the alarm, and switched off the grill.

Four slices of cheese on toast, charred beyond recognition, went into the trash.

"Did I ever tell you I was a lousy cook?" said Drew.

Lili pinched his bottom; she felt a lot happier now.

"Just when I was beginning to think you were perfect."

———

Much later that evening, with the children in bed, Drew pulled Lili down on the sofa next to him. "I meant what I said earlier."

"Sorry about burning the cheese on toast? I should hope so. That was the last of the cheese."

"The marrying bit."

Lili looked at him, unable to speak.

"Oh bugger! *Bugger* it! I know I'm not supposed to be saying this." Drew heaved a sigh. "It's too soon. We're meant to wait until we're in our nineties at least, but I don't bloody *want* to wait until I'm ninety," he protested. "All this stuff about being just good friends and not getting emotionally involved… It isn't working. I want us to be a proper couple, a proper *family*."

Lili ran her hand over the bobbly, much-washed wool of his sweater, knitted for him by the grateful elderly owner of a Pekingese with asthma. "You know what we agreed, that rebound relationships are doomed to failure."

Gosh, it was hard to be sensible when every atom in your body was willing you to wave your underwear in the air and bellow, "Yes, yes!"

"I'm bored with that rebound stuff." The beginnings of a smile appeared around Drew's mouth. He slid his fingers beneath Lili's pink sweatshirt and began to tickle her waist. "I think somebody made it up. They got dumped and used it as an excuse."

Lili squirmed as he affectionately explored what he called her love handles.

She called them her fat bits.

"You could meet someone else," she protested. "Someone young and firm, with no kids, no stretch marks."

"Blond, with huge boobs," Drew agreed. "Out to here."

Lili smacked his hand. "All right, no need to get carried away. I'm just saying, you might go off me."

"Not going to happen," Drew said simply. Bending over, no longer teasing, he kissed her on the mouth. "You see, you're everything I never knew I wanted. I can't imagine life without you or your children."

The sitting-room door burst open. Drew just had time to whisk his hand out from under Lili's sweatshirt.

"Mum, I had a dream I was swimming." Lottie's Pocahontas pajamas were sodden, and a puddle was forming on the parquet floor. "And when I woke up, I'd wet the bed."

Chapter 67

CARLA, ONE OF THE vet nurses, was reading out the horoscopes in her new *Take a Break* magazine.

"What are you, Jamie?"

"Depressed."

"I mean what *sign*."

"Dunno. Taurus."

"Right, let's see." Carla scanned the lines optimistically, her head going from side to side.

"Don't tell me: I'm useless, my life is miserable, and I need to sort myself out."

"Um…basically, yes."

"Didn't need a stupid horoscope to tell me that."

Brenda, the receptionist, popped her head around the door. "Jamie? Mrs. Samson's here with Bailey."

Jamie raised a despairing eyebrow. "You mean Mrs. Bailey's here with Samson."

"Sorry, yes." When she giggled, Brenda sounded like Tickle Me Elmo. "For neutering."

But Jamie was unamused. "Pay attention, Brenda. Imagine if I neutered Mrs. Bailey by mistake."

Brenda's smile faltered.

"Ignore him," Carla declared breezily. "He's in a pissy mood, that's all."

Brenda, who had been away for a few days, gave Jamie a look of sympathy. "You weren't very cheerful last week either."

"It's the same pissy mood. It just goes on and on." Carla rolled her eyes. "Like chewing gum without any taste left."

Jamie wondered how anyone so kind to animals could be so heartless when it came to humans. "Carla, are you sure you want to be a counselor when you grow up?"

"Come on, don't be so gloomy. Look on the bright side!" She gave Jamie a reassuring punch on the arm. "At least *you* aren't the one being neutered."

Jamie took a mouthful of the coffee she had made him. They'd worked together for almost a year and Carla still couldn't remember that he took sugar.

All in all, he felt, it summed up his situation pretty neatly.

I don't matter *to anyone*, thought Jamie. *Nobody cares about me. Not bossy Carla.*

Not Brenda with her Dr. Scholl's sandals and her stupid giggle.

Not Moll Harper, who had up and left without so much as a good-bye, in Doug's dark-blue MG.

And not Felicity.

Oh no, certainly not Felicity.

Jamie knew he had to be realistic about this; he had to face facts. It had been over a fortnight since he'd seen her. Pretty obviously, she wasn't going to contact him now.

If you liked someone and wanted to see them again, you might leave it a day or two, just to be cool.

But you didn't leave it for fourteen.

Jamie spooned three sugars into his lukewarm coffee and, for the sake of appearances, flicked through Samson's notes. When were things going to get better? He'd lost all interest in his work. The only reason he bothered to come in was because being at home was worse.

In fact, home was *worse* than worse—it was bordering on

unbearable, what with Drew hardly able to scrape that smug grin off his face and every sentence uttered beginning with "Lili thinks" this and "Lili says" that.

If Drew wasn't talking about Lili, he was over at the Old Vicarage with her. These days he couldn't stop laughing, whistling, and making jokes.

Most irritating of all, as far as Jamie was concerned, he refused point-blank to discuss what was clearly a stupendous sex life.

Keeper's Cottage wasn't the same anymore, with Drew in his current state and Doug gone. Doug's replacement hadn't improved matters either.

When Stevie Harper had offered to move in, Jamie had been all for it. Stevie was Moll's brother, he was a good bloke, and he was single; they'd have a great laugh.

Except it hadn't worked out like that, because what he hadn't known at the time was that Stevie was seeing Savannah Gillespie. And he liked to have sex with her even more often than Drew had sex with Lili. But at least Drew had the decency to do it over at Lili's house, so Jamie didn't have to listen to every sigh, every shriek of ecstasy, every creak of the bed.

Three blokes sharing a house, Jamie thought sadly. *Two of them getting more sex than they know what to do with.*

And me, Norris No-Life, sitting up in bed with my copy of Wisden's Almanack *and cotton wool stuffed in my ears.*

Jamie gulped down his tepid coffee. He could hear agitated barking coming from the waiting room. Then again, he'd be agitated if he were in Samson's situation.

Time to get gowned and scrubbed up before Samson, poor sod, got cold feet.

Twenty minutes later, Brenda buzzed through to the operating room.

"Jamie, call for you."

Jamie's heart did its usual jerky flip-flop. He knew it was too late, Felicity would never phone now, but it still happened every time.

Jesus, what am I, some kind of girl?

He frowned, concentrating on tying off vessels. It wouldn't be her; it just wouldn't. He wasn't even going to ask.

"Who is it?"

"Walter Clutterbuck. He's worried about his tortoise. Her name's Lady Penelope—"

"What is she, a slow eater? For crying out loud!" Jamie exploded, glaring at the intercom. "We aren't playing strip poker in here. I'm in the middle of surgery. If Walter Clutterbuck wants an appointment, he can fucking make one. You do your job and I'll do mine, okay?"

Brenda sounded crushed. "Sorry, Jamie."

"And make sure you don't bother me again!"

"You should push that bed of yours up against the wall." Eyeing him above her mask, Carla slapped the scalpel into Jamie's hand with unnecessary force. "Then you wouldn't keep getting out the wrong side."

———

Morning surgery stretched on through lunch, thanks to an extra hysterectomy mistakenly booked in by last week's useless temporary receptionist. By the time Jamie finished the last procedure, it was past two o'clock. His stomach was rumbling with hunger, his hair was plastered to his head, and there was an unflattering mark across the bridge of his nose where the plastic clip from his mask had pinched into the skin.

Food. Got to have food.

"Brenda." Poking his head around the waiting-room door, he forced a smile by way of apology for yelling at her earlier. "I'm desperate for a shower. Any chance of you popping out and grabbing me a couple of cheese-and-pickle rolls?"

Brenda leaped to her feet, as wide-eyed and nervous as a rabbit. "Of course I will! Um—"

"And a Mars bar." Jamie felt guilty; she tried so hard to please. He dug in his pocket for change.

"Er, sorry, there's someone here to see you," Brenda blurted out. "I know it's your lunch break, but…"

Looking up, Jamie saw Felicity sitting on one of the orange plastic chairs at the far end of the waiting room.

"She hasn't got an appointment." Brenda was clearly petrified.

Flip-flop went Jamie's heart.

Felicity stood up and came over to the desk. "Hello, Jamie. I know you're busy…"

"It's his lunch break," said Brenda possessively.

"I phoned three times this morning."

"I told her you were busy."

"That's okay, Brenda. Thanks."

"I didn't know if it was just me you didn't want to speak to"—Felicity's smile was uncertain—"or people in general. Especially when you didn't return my calls last week."

"Last week?"

Flip-flop, flip-flop.

"I left a couple of messages. Not with you." Felicity turned to Brenda. "A woman with a Scottish accent."

The useless temp receptionist.

Relieved that this was something she couldn't be blamed for, Brenda shook her head. "That definitely wasn't me."

"Fine, Brenda." Jamie pressed a fiver into her palm. "Two ham-and-tomato rolls and a Lion bar. Please."

"But I thought you wanted cheese and—"

"Anything, anything." The coffee room would be empty. Jamie ran his fingers through his flattened hair and looked at Felicity. "Please, come on through."

In the messy, magazine-strewn coffee room, he set about filling the kettle and searching through cupboards for Carla's hidden tin of Earl Gray tea bags.

"I could be making a prize idiot of myself." Felicity sounded nervous. "You might have changed your mind about wanting to see me."

Jamie wasn't like Doug; he couldn't impress girls by knowing the name of their perfume. All he knew was that Felicity smelled gorgeous, and if perfume was supposed to make you want to get closer to someone, it was certainly doing its job.

"Why would I change my mind?"

Blast, where *had* Carla hidden those tea bags? How was he meant to impress someone like Felicity with Lipton?

"You might have done. You could have met someone else or decided you just weren't interested anymore."

Jamie couldn't play games like Doug either. "Well I haven't, okay?"

"Oh. I have."

"You have what?"

"Changed my mind. About you," Felicity explained with a shy smile. "I'd like us to go out—if that's okay with you. I mean, when you have a free evening…we could just try it, see how it goes… Sorry, this isn't coming out very well. I'm horribly out of p-practice." Her voice began to wobble. "Well, more than out of practice really, seeing as I've never asked anyone out before."

"This evening." It came out as a croak. Hastily Jamie cleared his throat and tried again. "This evening. I'm free." He wasn't, he was on call, but he had done enough favors for Drew in the last few weeks. "And I think you made a damn good job of it."

"Of course, we might not get on. We might decide we don't—"

"One step at a time," Jamie said, unable to resist giving her a quick kiss on the cheek.

Then, when Felicity didn't flinch away, another one an inch closer to her mouth.

She closed her eyes. He took aim for the third time.

Through the closed door, a female voice bellowed, "Where is he? Jamie Lyall, you're a lying bastard and you don't deserve to have people being nice to you!"

Felicity looked stunned.

"There you are!" Carla flung open the door to the coffee room, brandishing a glossy hardback edition of Usain Bolt's autobiography. "I felt sorry for you because your horoscope was so lousy. I thought maybe if I bought you a present, you'd cheer up."

Jamie, who was a huge fan of Usain Bolt, said, "Carla, that's really kind of—"

"Shut up!" Carla yelled, looking as if she'd like to hurl the book at his head. "And don't worry. I've learned my lesson. I'm never going to feel sorry for *you* again."

Jamie could feel Felicity shrinking away from him.

"Why?" Worried, she looked across at Carla. "What's he done wrong?"

"I've just looked at the calendar. His birthday's in December," Carla told an uncomprehending Felicity. "The lying toad isn't even a Taurus!"

Chapter 68

"DAD'S NOT TAKING IT well."

Savannah was sitting cross-legged on Jessie's sofa, drinking mineral water and absently picking at a hole in the sleeve of her black sweater. It was actually one of Stevie's sweaters, and she was drinking mineral water because Stevie had told her it was better for her than endless cans of Coke.

"No?"

Jessie thought she probably didn't want to hear this. She carried on buttering crumpets.

"I think he's missing Mum terribly."

Jessie definitely didn't want to hear this. "Crumpet?"

"Please. I mean, he says he isn't, but that's Dad. Men always bottle up their feelings, don't they? It's stupid."

"How is your mum?"

"Oh, having a whale of a time. Guess who she's having a fling with now?"

God, who?

Jessie shook her head, unable to guess. "Who?"

Savannah, busy cramming half a crumpet into her mouth, wiped melted butter from her chin with the sleeve of Stevie's sweater. "Yum, these are fab… The sperm donor."

"What?"

"My biological father. That pompous prat! She told me when I was up there last weekend. Top secret, of course." Savannah rolled her eyes. "Yuck, can you imagine?"

"I don't think I want to. MI5 might be listening." *Phew*, Jessie thought as she crammed another crumpet onto the toasting fork. "How long's this been going on?"

"Few weeks. Seeing Mum again when he came down here to give the blood sample sparked it off again, apparently." Marveling at the sequence of events, Savannah said, "And now they're mad about each other."

"Risky."

"Too right. If they get caught, according to Mum, it could practically bring down the government. And all because I had a bit of a crush on my brother," Savannah marveled, polishing off her second crumpet. Innocently she added, "If that happened, would it be all my fault?"

It seemed safer to steer the conversation away from Deborah. "Is Dizzy okay?"

"Happier than a pig in a trough. He's starting at the Serena Fox stage school next week. Amazingly, he did a brilliant audition and they snapped him up on the spot. When they found out afterward he was Toby Gillespie's son, they practically wet themselves with joy. Have you two had some kind of argument?" Savannah said suddenly.

Jessie looked astonished. "Who, me and Dizzy?"

"Come on. You and Dad."

"No." Fumbling slightly, Jessie stuck yet another crumpet onto the prongs of the fork. She shuffled on her knees closer to the fire.

"Sure?"

"Sure I'm sure." The heat from the flames—it was definitely the heat from the flames—had brought a rush of color to Jessie's cheeks. "What would we argue about?"

Savannah shrugged. "I don't know. You haven't been over to the house for ages, that's all."

"I've been busy." Jessie floundered for an excuse. "Selling the cottage, helping Oliver to get his trip organized—"

"Why don't you go and see Dad?"

"Well..."

"Please, Jess. He'd appreciate it. It's been a rough few weeks." Savannah pulled a face. "And it's going to get rougher when the press finds out about him and Mum splitting up. He needs someone to talk to, a real friend."

Hmm, thought Jessie, *or does he just need someone to sleep with?*

"I thought he was off to the States. Oliver said something about a Spielberg film."

"That's not until next week."

"Oh. Well, maybe I'll give him a ring."

Much as she hated fibbing, sometimes you just had to.

"Great. If anyone can cheer Dad up, it's you." Savannah beamed at Jessie, oblivious to her reluctance. "Now, any chance of another crumpet? Are you just going to let that one burn to a frazzle, or can I eat it?"

It was a miracle the press hadn't caught on to the story earlier.

"Just to warn you," Deborah said on the phone from London, "I got doorstepped by a couple of hacks from the *Mirror* yesterday. They knew something was up, so I told them we'd separated. All very amicable, nobody else involved, blah blah."

"Right." Toby spoke without emotion. "I'll tell my agent to release a statement. How's Dizzy?"

"You mean Kenneth Branagh?" Deborah sounded amused. "Up in his bedroom rehearsing a speech from *Hamlet*. Do you know, he hasn't switched on his computer once since we moved in?"

The phone didn't stop ringing the next day. Tantalized by the blandness of the press release, journalists and photographers descended on Upper Sisley in droves.

Toby, in no mood to speak to them, disconnected the doorbell and drew the curtains. It was a damp, cold day, not great for hanging around. Maybe, with nothing to report back to their editors, they would get bored and drift away.

When Jessie pulled up outside Duck Cottage at six o'clock, covered in cobalt-blue paint and desperate for a bath, there were three journalists in her overgrown front yard and a photographer snapping away at the back of the house.

"I know it's an easy mistake to make," said Jessie, "but this isn't a stately home and these grounds aren't actually open to the public."

"Jess, over here!" The photographer waved an arm to attract her attention. "No, no, stay by the van! *Great* van."

"Jessie, what do you have to say about the breakup of Toby and Deborah Gillespie's marriage?"

"Are you having an affair with Toby Gillespie?"

"How long have you two been seeing each other?" the third journalist piped up. "Was Deborah devastated when she found out?"

"Jessie, are you expecting Toby Gillespie's baby?"

Another car roared up the lane. Two more photographers jumped out, flashes going off like fireworks.

Jessie clapped her hand to the front of her baggy overalls. Honestly, the one day she didn't wear a belt...

"Jessie, is this the fairy-tale ending you always dreamed of?"

"Jess, Jess! When's the baby due?"

Hastily dragging two turpentine-soaked cloths and an unopened bag of marshmallows out of her front pockets, Jessie sucked herself in and patted her now much flatter stomach.

There again, a few sit-ups wouldn't go amiss.

God, journalists were cruel. But a snapped-out *No comment* would only convince them she had something to hide.

"I am not pregnant. Nor am I having an affair with Toby Gillespie." Jessie spoke slowly and clearly, like a teacher addressing a bunch of unruly five-year-olds. "The breakup of Toby and Deborah's marriage has nothing to do with me."

The difference was, a bunch of five-year-olds might have taken a bit of notice.

"Jessie, how does Deborah feel about you being pregnant?"

"How do you and Toby see your future together?"

"So, Jess, in your opinion, is Toby Gillespie a better lover now than when he was a lad?"

"You aren't listening," Jessie said. "I've just told you, there *is* no affair. I haven't seen Toby Gillespie for weeks... What are you *doing*?" One of the photographers was hauling cans of paint out of the back of the van and arranging them at her feet.

"Props, love. Don't worry. I won't spill 'em. Now, you just hold the paintbrush, rest one foot on this can, and give us a saucy smile. Confessions of a painter and decorator, that kind of thing..."

"You can't be serious!" Jessie was tempted to grab one of the cans and do a bit of spilling herself, but she needed the paint to finish a job. "Look, see that For Sale sign? I'm moving to Cornwall. If I were having an affair with Toby Gillespie," she pleaded, "I'd hardly go and live one hundred and fifty miles away, would I?"

"Turn to the left a bit, Jess! That your craving, is it—marshmallows? Hold the bag up. Are you two hoping for a girl or a boy?"

Jessie lost her temper. She picked up the cans of paint and began slinging them into the back of the van. "Look, I'm not interested in Toby Gillespie. He matters about as much to me as, as this"—she gestured with derision at a huge yellow slug, squirming in the wet grass at her feet—"this *slug*!" She marched into the house, hideously aware that the overalls were still bagging around her stomach. Before she could slam the front door shut behind her, one of the journalists called out, "Jess, are you and Toby planning to marry before the birth?"

———·····———

The next morning, like an answer to a prayer, a nice man in his early fifties came to take a look at Duck Cottage.

His name was Bob Keogh and he was a chemical engineer. Jessie, who didn't have a clue what that meant—something to do with designing chemical toilets?—also discovered that he was a widower with a nineteen-year-old daughter and enough money in the bank, thanks to his wife's life insurance policy, to buy the place outright. She wondered if he'd bumped his wife off in order to get his hands on the cash.

Bob Keogh seemed charming, but then those wife-murdering types generally did.

Anyway, Jessie didn't care. He liked Duck Cottage and that was far more important.

"You aren't wild about the colors, are you?" She watched his gaze flicker doubtfully across the bottle-green hall ceiling and ruby-red walls.

Bob Keogh blinked, ashamed. "I'm sorry, I know it looks good, but it just isn't my cup of tea. Plain white walls, that's what I go for."

Jessie was busy, but she was also desperate. "If you decide to buy this cottage, I'll paint every inch of it white. Whatever you want, I'll do." Well, paint-wise, anyway.

Bob Keogh was looking thoughtful. "Could I take another peep at the yard?"

"I'll paint that white too," Jessie offered. "Now, how about a cup of tea? A cookie?"

Chapter 69

TWENTY-FOUR HOURS LATER, TWO things happened almost simultaneously: one good, one bad.

The knock at the door came first. When Jessie went to answer it, she found Toby on the doorstep, grim-faced and clutching a newspaper.

Well, hardly the surprise of the century.

"Look, I'm sorry. I told them and told them I wasn't pregnant, but they just kept *on* about it, and I'm not trying to fob you off, but I really am late for work—"

"Jessie, stop babbling. Have you seen this?"

In the kitchen, the phone began to ring. "No, I've only just got out of—oh, hang on."

Jessie listened in a daze to Harry Norton, the real estate agent in Harleston, burble smoothly on about offers and asking prices, searches and surveyors' fees.

It was a while before she could get a word in. "You mean Bob Keogh wants to buy the cottage?"

"If you decide to accept his offer of one two five." Harry tapped his pen against the receiver as he spoke. "We're talking twelve grand off the asking price, Jess. Bit of a drop. You could certainly hold out for more, but that's Bob Keogh's final offer." Sounding intensely disapproving, Harry added, "He seems to think you'll take it too. Told me you sounded pretty desperate."

Twelve thousand less than I was hoping for, thought Jessie. *It's a hell of a drop. Then again, I* am *desperate.*

She looked down at the newspaper Toby had opened and spread out on the kitchen table in front of her. *Hmm, even more desperate than I thought.*

"So I suggest you take a few days to think about it…"

A huge picture of a yellow slug occupied the top half of page five. Below was a smaller one of Toby. On the facing page, a headline proclaimed, I KNOW WHICH ONE I'D RATHER SLEEP WITH, SAYS PAINT-JOB JESS.

Beneath it, they had used one of the overalls-cum-blimp pictures in which she not only looked six months' pregnant, but was also sporting a double chin.

Filled with indignation, Jessie thought, *But I don't have a double chin. Do I?*

"You never know, play hard to get and he might up it a couple of grand…"

Next to her, still hatchet-faced and not showing the least sign of being sympathetic, Toby waited for the phone call to end.

All of a sudden, Jessie was tempted to stay chatting to Smooth Harry for the next hour at least—about his new car, his last vacation, his favorite music, maybe even his whole life.

"Then again, he could find somewhere else…"

Jessie could feel Toby's breath on the back of her neck and it wasn't a comfortable sensation.

Oh Lord, he really was livid with her.

"One two five, that's fine," she blurted into the phone. "Tell Bob Keogh I accept. How soon can we complete?"

When the receiver had gone down, Toby stood in silence—for all the world like an exam proctor—while she read every word of the piece in the paper. When she had finished, he said slowly, "I've thought you were a lot of things, Jess, but I never thought of you as a coward."

"A coward!" She jabbed at the newspaper, outraged. "What's so cowardly about this? God, what did you *expect* me to tell them?"

"I'm talking about selling the cottage."

"Selling the cottage? Good grief!" Jessie wailed. "Can you blame me? I can't wait to get out of here!" She gave the newspaper another jab for emphasis. "Do you know what this makes me look like? A sad substitute…second best…a devoted groupie rushing to fill Deborah's shoes—even if they are two sizes smaller than mine!" She was shaking now, with anger and humiliation. "Because that's what everyone's expecting to happen, isn't it? You, the village, the newspapers—"

"I want it to happen," said Toby. "You know I do. And no, it doesn't make you look like a substitute—"

"Oh, get real!" Jessie snapped back. "It's like having your top-of-the-range Mercedes stolen. You might have to make do for a while with some old rust bucket—and at the time you're glad of it, because anything is better than no car at all—but sooner or later, you know you'll dump it. Either your stolen car turns up again or the insurance company pays out and you buy yourself a brand-new one. And that's it—bye-bye, old banger. It was fun while it lasted. Well, I don't need that kind of fun. And I'm moving down to Cornwall *because I want to!*"

Heavens, where had all that come from? From some dark, guilty corner of her subconscious, obviously.

Never mind, it was good.

"But you don't want to," said Toby. "You *can't*—"

"Look, anything that gets me away from this kind of hassle sounds great to me." Prodding was no longer enough; grabbing the paper, Jessie ripped it to shreds. "Because I don't need it, Toby! I don't need people sniggering about me behind my back—"

"Jess, it's okay. Calm down. It's just journalists, desperate to make something out of nothing."

"Hah!"

Toby heaved a sigh. This wasn't why he'd come here. They were on the same side, for God's sake. It was the press he was furious with, not Jess. She'd done her best. She simply didn't have the experience to deal with them.

"You should have said 'no comment.'"

How bloody patronizing could you get?

"Oh yes! That would have done the world of good," Jessie yelled, still shredding bits of newspaper and flinging them to the floor. "They ask me if I'm pregnant with your child and I say 'no comment'!" Seething with indignation she cried, "Even *I* know that people only say 'no comment' when the answer is yes. Jesus, I'm amazed *you* haven't asked me if I'm pregnant!"

Toby looked at her.

For a second he forgot to breathe.

"Are you?"

"*No!*"

With an effort, Toby recovered himself. "Look, it's a tabloid newspaper." He gestured at the shreds of newsprint whirling around the kitchen like confetti. "I know you didn't say any of this stuff."

He was off to Los Angeles tomorrow, and Jessie was glad. She could sell the cottage and be out of Upper Sisley before he got back.

"Ah well, that's where you're wrong," she said bitterly, "because the quote about the slug was true."

———⁓———

Brrrrr-brrrrrugh-brrruggh.

Eleanor Ferguson exhaled slowly, removed her hand-knitted gloves, and sat up a little straighter in the driver's seat of her highly polished Mini Cooper. She turned the key in the ignition once more and willed the car to start.

Brrrrr-brrrrrugh-brrruggh.

For heaven's sake—today of all days! Why did cars always have to let you down when you had to be somewhere and couldn't afford to be late?

Grimly determined, Eleanor let off the hand brake and allowed the car to roll forward down the sloping drive. The moment she reached the lane she would slam it into gear and hopefully it would bump start.

Cluuunk.

Eleanor's mouth narrowed with annoyance. This was ridiculous. Now she was stuck out in the middle of the road in pouring rain. Furthermore, it was only eight fifteen in the morning, which meant that there was no point even trying to phone the garage in Lower Sisley because it didn't open until nine o'clock.

Relief at hearing the sound of an approaching car turned to irritation when Eleanor saw who was driving it.

Drew Darcy, her daughter-in-law's fancy man. Well, that was just typical. Having made a particular point of not speaking to Drew since that sordid, little liaison had come to light, she certainly wasn't about to ask him for help now.

The car slowed to a halt. Eleanor kept her gaze pointedly averted.

But moments later, Drew was grinning at her through the driver's window, motioning her to open it.

"Problems?"

"Nothing I can't handle." Eleanor spoke through stiff lips.

"Well, you're blocking the lane. Shall I give you a hand moving it?"

This was intolerable. Eleanor managed a curt nod and gripped the steering wheel.

Several seconds later Drew reappeared at the window. "Actually, it helps if you free the hand brake."

Oh.

And it got worse, far worse.

"There you go," Drew announced when the Metro had been maneuvered to the side of the road, and it wasn't until Eleanor turned around that she realized he hadn't been the only one pushing the car.

"I heard you trying to start it." Bernadette Thomas sounded

almost apologetic. She was wearing a dark-blue raincoat and her face was wet with rain. "If you put the hood up, I'll take a look. Could be the carburetor or damp plugs."

Eleanor, who had spent the last few weeks pointedly ignoring her next-door neighbor too, was tempted to say, "No thank you. I would prefer to call the garage." But this was her morning running the Women's Royal Volunteer Service cafeteria at Harleston General, and she had to be there by nine o'clock to open up. Nobody else could do it; she had the keys.

Unable to speak, she released the hood catch and climbed jerkily out of the car.

"I'm not great at this," Drew was saying, his green Barbour jacket already drenched and his unruly hair dripping into his eyes. But Bernadette was already busy checking leads with capable fingers.

"It's probably something straightforward. I spent a year on vehicle maintenance during my army days. Hmm, spark plug cable seems okay. Right, let's have a look at these points…"

They were still trying to get the car started twenty minutes later. The rain was coming down in sheets now, whipped to an angle by the ferocious October wind.

Eleanor was in an agony of indecision. Every time she tried to say "Look, it doesn't matter; I'll phone the mechanic," Bernadette and Drew dismissed her awkward protest and carried on working together, plunging their hands into the depths of the engine like surgeons in search of a lost swab.

"Can't get any wetter than this," Drew told her cheerfully. "May as well see the job through."

The sense of obligation was crushing. Finally, unable to bear it a second longer, Eleanor blurted out, "Let me ring for a taxi. I need to be at work by nine."

Drew lifted his head above hood level.

"Why didn't you say? I'll give you a lift."

"Really, there's no need—"

"Don't be daft, I'm not the chief mechanic here anyway." He winked—ugh, actually winked—at Bernadette. "I'm just the useless apprentice. Where d'you need to go?"

Only the thought of staff and patients waiting impatiently for the cafeteria to open forced Eleanor to reply. She couldn't, she just *couldn't* let them down. "Harleston General. I run the WRVS shop two days a week."

Drew nodded, wiping his oily hands on one of her pristine tea towels. "The General. Where Doug used to work."

"Where April works," Bernadette added mildly.

"Who's April?" asked Drew.

"My ex-wife."

Eleanor stiffened.

Glancing up at her, Bernadette said, "She uses the WRVS shop from time to time."

"I know."

April was someone else Eleanor pointedly ignored.

"Right, it's a quarter to." Shaking the rain out of his hair, Drew opened the passenger door of his own car and ushered Eleanor inside. "Let's get you to work. Bernadette, okay if I leave you to it?"

"No problem."

As Drew pulled away, Eleanor looked back at Bernadette, working diligently away beneath the hood of the Metro.

"Don't worry. She'll soon have your car fixed," Drew told her with a grin. "Bernadette's a good bloke."

—⁓—

Four hours later, Eleanor was heaping doughnuts and cookies onto plates when she saw April Thomas come into the canteen.

"Hello," April said shyly, and because Eleanor was the only person behind the counter, she was forced to mutter "hello" back.

Nervously, April pushed her short hair behind her ears. "I'm April Thomas, Bernie's—"

"Yes, yes, I know," Eleanor blurted out before she could say the words aloud.

"Um…Bernie's just rung. He asked me to come over and let you know he's—sorry, *she's* managed to fix the car."

"Oh. Right."

"It was something to do with the carburetor, apparently, but I couldn't tell you what." April blushed and smiled. "I'm useless with cars."

Eleanor wondered guiltily if it had taken all this time—over four hours—to get her Metro going again. It was still raining down buckets outside.

"Well, it was very good of…er, Bernadette. I'm most grateful." Oh dear, she so hated to be the beholden one; she much preferred being the beholder. "And…er, thank you for coming to let me know."

"Actually, I'll have a doughnut now I'm here," said April. "You shut at four o'clock, don't you?"

"That's right."

"I thought so. Bernie wanted to know." April chose an apple doughnut and gave Eleanor thirty pence. "She said she'll pick you up at five past four."

⁓

"This is most kind of you. I could have caught the bus."

"No problem," Bernadette replied easily. "Anyway, it's still raining."

It was indeed; it was a filthy, gray afternoon. As the temperature outside plummeted, the rain intermittently turned to sleet.

A nice, warming lamb casserole, thought Eleanor as they lapsed into silence. *That's what I'll make when I get home. And steamed syrup pudding with custard.*

"Would you mind stopping at the next liquor store?" she asked Bernadette.

Emerging from the store with a half bottle of whisky—she didn't buy a whole one, it wouldn't do to encourage alcoholism—Eleanor said with a touch of asperity, "It isn't for me. It's for Drew Darcy."

Bernadette nodded. "He seems charming."

"Mmm."

"Your grandchildren adore him. I'm sorry." Bernadette hesitated. "I know your loyalties must lie with your son. It can't be easy for you."

"It's hardly an ideal situation," Eleanor admitted with reluctance. "But at least the children are happy." She sighed. "I suppose it could be worse."

They drove the rest of the way in silence. When Bernadette pulled up outside the cottages, Eleanor reached for her purse. "I must give you something too. For the lift and for mending my car."

"Absolutely not." Bernadette was firm. "That's what neighbors are for."

Even, it seemed, if your neighbor was a man in a dress and an ex-army boxer to boot.

Oh dear, how times have changed, thought Eleanor. *Things like this simply didn't happen in my day.* Although—irony of ironies—until she had made this bizarre discovery, she had actually liked Bernadette.

"In that case," she said awkwardly, "you must come over for supper tonight. I'm making a lamb casserole and steamed syrup pudding."

Heavens, an olive branch. From Eleanor Ferguson. In fact, never mind an olive branch—practically a whole tree.

Supper with Eleanor was hardly her idea of a relaxing evening. *But under the circumstances*, thought Bernadette, *how can I refuse?*

She hesitated. "Really? Are you sure?"

Relief flooded through Eleanor. No longer beholden, she was back in charge.

So people in the village thought she was narrow-minded, did they? Well she'd soon show them.

Grandly she announced, "I insist."

Chapter 70

JESSIE STOOD IN THE middle of the empty living room and gazed around her ex-home.

The papers were completed and Duck Cottage was no longer hers. It belonged to Bob Keogh, and he had the newly painted walls and ceilings to prove it.

Which helped, in a way, because three coats of white vinyl silk emulsion throughout meant it no longer even faintly resembled Duck Cottage.

Instead of a bright-purple cotton sweater, ripped orange jeans, and a can of lukewarm soda, Jessie felt she should be wearing something white and elegant and sipping a glass of milk.

A resounding crash upstairs made her jump. The next moment Oliver clattered downstairs with a tea chest in his arms.

"Are you going to just stand there all day?" he panted, lugging the heavy chest into the hall. "Or do you think you might be able to give me a hand?"

Jessie mustered a smile. "Me? Your poor, frail old mother?"

"I just dropped a bookcase on my foot up there," Oliver grumbled.

"Have some soda. It's okay. The moving van won't be here for another hour. Actually, I thought I'd pop over to Lili's, say my good-byes."

"You've already been over to Lili's." Oliver checked his watch. "You said good-bye to her at ten o'clock."

"I know, but Will was asleep then. He'll be awake now."

But when she closed the front door behind her, Jessie didn't head across the village green toward the Old Vicarage. Instead, she found herself turning right along Compass Lane. As she passed Keeper's Cottage, she heard a squeal of laughter coming from one of the open bedroom windows. Recognizing the squeal as one of Savannah's—so she and Stevie were still at it like rabbits—Jessie walked on. With Toby still away filming in the States, that meant Sisley House was currently unoccupied.

When she reached the stone-pillared entrance to the house, she turned into it without even knowing why.

Walked slowly up to the leaf-strewn driveway without knowing why.

Stood at the top of the drive and gazed at the front of the house without kn—

Oh, come on, who am I trying to kid? thought Jessie despairingly. *Talk about pathetic delusions.*

Dammit, of course I know why!

Anyway, what did it matter how pathetic she was being? There was no one to see her; the house was empty.

No more Deborah.

No more Dizzy.

No Savannah, who was far too busy next door having rip-roaring sex with gorgeous Stevie Harper.

And no Toby.

Who was also gorgeous…

And in America.

Her body ached with misery.

The house was empty.

Oh dear, thought Jessie as she blinked back tears. *Like my heart.*

It was ridiculous, but she couldn't help it. Knowing that you couldn't have someone—or that you could have them but it would be a relationship doomed to end in failure—didn't stop you loving them so much it hurt.

Nobody else had ever come close. No other man had meant a millionth as much to her as Toby Gillespie. She'd tried her hardest to find one, but it simply hadn't happened.

And I was tempted, Jessie finally admitted to herself, her scalp prickling with yearning and shame. *I was so tempted to make a complete fool of myself and just go for it.*

Knowing it wouldn't last.

Knowing that after a few months Toby would say, "Look, it's been great, *but...*"

Knowing that he would move onward and upward, and find himself someone more famous and glamorous, someone infinitely more fitting for a film star of his stature.

Knowing that she would be left feeling a hundred times worse than she did now and that behind her back people would be smirking and sniggering to each other, "Well, what did she expect?"

Oh shit, this was no good. The tears were coming thick and fast now, and the last thing she needed was to be spotted emerging from Toby's driveway with blotchy cheeks and piggy eyes.

A sycamore seed, helicoptering down from an overhanging tree, landed on Jessie's head. Trying to disentangle it, she managed to pull out the old, green, knee-high stocking she had used as a makeshift ribbon to tie back her unbrushed hair.

A bloody knee-high, for heaven's sake!

If I were Deborah Gillespie, Jessie thought as she wiped her eyes with it, *it would be a seven denier, Christian Dior, sheer black stocking.*

"The solicitor just phoned," Oliver announced when she arrived back at the cottage. "He wants you to get over there as soon as you can to sign the completion papers."

"He said three o'clock."

"Change of plan. He's got a will reading in Cheltenham at two."

Jessie sighed. Oh well, get it over and done with.

"Can you manage here on your own?"

His look told her that he had spent most of the morning managing on his own. "I'll do my best."

"Don't forget to label the crates."

Oliver frowned. "Have you been crying?"

"Me? Don't be daft." Jessie reached hurriedly past him for the keys to the van. "One of those sycamore things flew into my eye."

—⁓—

Since she had to follow the moving truck down to Cornwall, Jessie stopped at the garage on the outskirts of Harleston to give the van a once-over. It was boring, but not as boring as breaking down on the M5.

She filled up with gas, squished air into the tires, topped up the water, and checked the oil. An uncharacteristic fit of conscience prompted her to put the van through the car wash. Well, it was indescribably filthy, and someone—probably Oliver—had written something rude to that effect across the back.

Anyway, that was why she was going, wasn't it? To make a clean start.

Sitting inside the van with soapy water streaming over it and the massive rollers thundering down the windshield, Jessie didn't see Oliver's car race past the garage on its way into Harleston.

—⁓—

The moving truck had arrived. Orders had been placed for tea. Oliver was heaping sugar into mugs when there was a knock on the kitchen door behind him. Expecting an overweight moving man with plumber's crack and a swallow tattooed on his neck, he said, "Coming up," and was taken aback when he realized he was talking instead to a fragile girl with short, black hair and slanting, green eyes.

"Sorry." She grinned at Oliver. "The front door was open and a chap with a tattoo told me to come on through. I'm Sammy Keogh, by the way. Bob's daughter." The unrepentant grin broadened. "And I drink mine black with no sugar."

She was gorgeous. A mischievous, emerald-eyed vision.

Oliver was instantly smitten.

"Right. I'm Oliver Roscoe. And you're…um, early."

The green eyes sparkled. "I drove down from Manchester. It didn't take as long as I expected. This is the first chance I've had to see my new home."

"Hang on." Hastily Oliver grabbed the mugs of tea. "Back in a sec."

When he returned, Sammy Keogh had refilled the kettle and was tapping her fingers restlessly on the worktop, waiting for it to boil. She was wearing a pale-gray Henley and red Levi's, with a Manchester University sweatshirt tied around her narrow hips.

She studied him in turn, her head tilted appraisingly to one side. "So, don't tell me. You're the only decent-looking guy in the village."

"What?" Oliver tried not to laugh.

"Story of my life." Sammy heaved a sigh of resignation. "Just as I move down here, you're moving away. We'll never see each other again."

"You probably will, actually. My dad still lives here, so I'll be coming back."

"Great!" Her smile lit up her heart-shaped face. "When, for Christmas?"

Oliver explained about his year off, backpacking around Europe. Happily, the fridge hadn't yet been loaded into the van and there were still a couple of bottles of beer languishing at the back, waiting to be drunk. He talked about the countries he'd be visiting and showed Sammy through the cottage, determinedly ignoring the winks and nudges and leering grins of the moving men as they carted wardrobes noisily down the stairs.

"You're so lucky. It sounds brilliant."

Sammy pushed her fingers through her dark hair, ruffling it into spikes as they wandered out into the front yard. The look of restlessness had returned to her eyes; something was clearly bothering her.

She smelled wonderful, like a bowl of freesias. Oliver, fighting the urge to kiss her neck, said, "What's wrong?"

"Oh God, I'm just not used to being somewhere so *quiet*. I've never lived in a village before." Her outstretched arm swept in an arc, encompassing the green and the collection of Cotswold stone houses surrounding it. She turned and gazed frustratedly at Oliver. "I mean, how have you managed not to die of boredom? Does anything interesting ever *happen* around here?"

Chapter 71

THERE WERE NEVER ANY spaces in the lawyer's minuscule parking lot, so Jessie left the van around the corner.

Well, this was it. Yesterday she had signed one set of completion papers for Duck Cottage. Now she was here to sign the second lot. Once that was done, the house in Cornwall would be hers.

Wishing she could feel a bit more enthusiastic about the move, Jessie rounded the corner.

The first thing she saw was Oliver's battered black VW Beetle crammed into the already full parking lot, blocking in a couple of sleek BMWs with personalized plates.

God, what was Oliver doing here? Something awful must have happened—

The second thing she saw was Toby in the driver's seat.

Jessie froze. This couldn't be happening; it definitely couldn't be happening.

Toby was in America.

Except he wasn't. He was here. Looking at her and stepping out of Oliver's ancient car.

"You're late."

Jessie's legs were shaking. She didn't have knees anymore; she had castanets.

"What?"

"You left home forty minutes ago." He checked his watch.

"Oliver said you were coming straight here. I left fifteen minutes after you and I still got here first."

Is this a hallucination? Jessie wondered. *Am I finally cracking up?*

But hallucination or otherwise, Toby clearly expected an answer. "Um...car wash."

As they gazed at each other, somebody inside the solicitor's offices tapped on a window, furiously indicating to Toby that he couldn't leave that heap of rust there.

Toby calmly ignored them. "Car wash. Of course."

Jessie's mouth was as dry as a sandbox. She tried to lick her lips. "You're supposed to be in Los Angeles."

"Flew back this morning."

"Why? Did you get sacked?"

He almost—*almost*—smiled. "O ye of little faith... Actually, I told them it was an emergency and I had to get back."

"You told Steven Spielberg it was an emergency? How did he take it?"

Jessie was joking. Toby wasn't.

He shrugged. "Pretty well. He said they could shoot around me for a couple of days. That's all he could give me, forty-eight hours. Still, long enough for me to find out one way or another what I need to know."

The sash window behind him thudded open. A cross-looking secretary stuck her head out.

"Excuse me, you *have* to move that vehicle."

"In a minute," said Toby. "I'm busy."

The woman bristled. "I'm warning you, if you don't move your car, our security guard will do it for you."

Toby turned and smiled at her. "He will? That's really kind. Thanks."

The secretary's jaw dropped open. Jessie heard her whisper frantically, "My God, it's Toby *Gillespie*."

The next moment the window slammed shut.

"Look, I still don't know what you're doing here." Jessie's legs felt really peculiar, but if she tried to lean against one of the gleaming cars, she was bound to set off some kind of screeching alarm.

"I've changed my mind about you. I don't think running off to Cornwall is a cowardly thing to do," said Toby. "I think it's brave. Misguided," he added, "but still brave."

"It's n-neither," Jessie stammered. "I just want to, that's all."

Toby ignored this. "You love me, but you don't trust me. You see, that's the difference between us, Jess. I love you *and* I trust you. I've always loved you—more than you'll ever know. If anyone was the substitute, if anyone was ever second best," he went on slowly, "it was Deborah."

Oh, this was too much. This wasn't fair. It was too *late*...

"The lawyer's waiting for me." Jessie, her feet like jelly, tried to move toward the building's glass-fronted entrance. "I've got to sign the completion papers."

"Don't do it."

"I have to! Duck Cottage is already sold. The moving men will be there by now!"

"I flew into Heathrow this morning." Toby shook his head. "I caught a cab home. I didn't know how I was going to persuade you to change your mind about leaving, but I knew I had to try. And then I saw you standing outside my house and I didn't know what that meant either—"

"You were *there*?" Jessie gasped, dumbstruck. "You mean you were there all the time, *watching* me?"

"Not all the time. I glanced out of the window and saw you, and I thought you might be crying but I wasn't sure."

"I wasn't crying!" Jessie blurted out defensively. "And if you saw me, why didn't you do anything? Why didn't you come out?"

"I had no idea why you were there." Again, Toby nearly smiled. "I half expected you to hurl eggs at the windows. But I didn't have a chance to react; the next thing I knew, you'd disappeared. And by the time I reached the cottage, you were on your way here."

Jessie couldn't take it in. Wearily, she shook her head. "It's still too late. I have to sign the papers."

A muscle was twitching in Toby's jaw. "This house in Cornwall. Does it overlook the sea?"

Wondering how this could be relevant, Jessie nodded.

"Okay. In that case, we'll sign. I've always fancied a vacation home in Cornwall anyway."

"*You've* always fancied a vacation home?" Jessie was struggling to keep up. What was he saying now—that he wanted to buy the house off her? Thoroughly confused, she stammered, "B-but then where would *I* live?"

Dimly aware that they were being watched—a sea of faces had, by this time, appeared at the window behind them—Jessie stayed where she was and let Toby come to her.

He took her hands and looked into her stricken eyes.

"With me, of course. Sod the press. Sod what you think everyone else is thinking. I love you, Jess, and I'm pretty sure you love me too. What's more, when you've felt this way about someone for over twenty years, it's no flash in the pan. I want to spend the rest of my life with you. And if it helps at all," he added drily, "Steven Spielberg wants me to spend the rest of my life with you too."

Jessie broke into something halfway between laughter and a sob. "Truly?"

"Truly. I had to tell him all about you."

"Name dropper."

"I'll stop at nothing." Toby's hands were in her hair. "Now, is that a yes?"

How could it not be?

Jessie nodded and breathed out slowly and at last, at long last, her knees relaxed and stopped doing their castanet impression. It felt blissfully, idyllically, like coming home—not to Cornwall, but to Upper Sisley.

Well, sometimes to Cornwall. For long weekends...and whenever they could get away.

Reading her mind, Toby said, "We'd better go inside, sign those papers."

Jessie nodded, loving the idea already. A vacation home would be great.

"And give Oliver a ring. Tell him to send the moving van around to my place," Toby went on. "Until we sort ourselves out."

Oh, to be a fly on the wall in Myrtle Armitage's shop, thought Jessie, *when word gets out that I've moved into Sisley House.*

"I can't believe this is happening."

She clung to him, pressing herself against him, wanting to feel every inch of his body touching hers. *Hmm...* She wiggled her hips—was that a gun in his pocket or was he just pleased to see her?

Although, if it was a gun, wasn't it a bit...um, small?

Once again, miraculously, Toby appeared to guess what she was thinking.

"Ah yes," he murmured, putting his hand in his pocket and taking out the rolled-up green knee sock he had found lying in his driveway earlier. "I believe this belongs to you."

About the Author

Jill Mansell lives with her family in Bristol. She used to work in the field of clinical neurophysiology but now writes full time. She watches far too much TV and would love to be one of those super-sporty types but basically can't be bothered. Nor can she cook—having once attempted to bake a cake for the hospital's Christmas fair, she was forced to watch while her coworkers played Frisbee with it. But she's good at Twitter!